EPHYRA RISING

Gears of War novels from Titan Books:

Gears of War: Ascendance by Jason M. Hough
Gears of War: Bloodlines by Jason M. Hough
Gears of War: Ephyra Rising by Michael A. Stackpole

GEARS OF WAR.

EPHYRA RISING

MICHAEL A. STACKPOLE

TITAN BOOKS

GEARS OF WAR: EPHYRA RISING
Print edition ISBN: 9781789095807
E-book edition ISBN: 9781789095814

Published by Titan Books
A division of Titan Publishing Group Ltd
144 Southwark St, London, SE1 0UP
www.titanbooks.com

First edition: November 2021
10 9 8 7 6 5 4 3 2

Editorial Consultants:
Bonnie Jean Mah, Matt Searcy

A CIP catalogue record for this title is available from the British Library.

Printed and bound by CPI Group (UK) Ltd, Croydon CR0 4YY

To the memory of Paul Garabedian, a wise man and a great friend. Gone much too soon.

ACT 1

1: ROAD TO THE STROUD ESTATE

NEAR EPHYRA, SERA

11 HARVEST 18 A.E. (AFTER EMERGENCE)

"Why, Marcus Fenix, I do believe you are smiling."

Marcus wasn't sure what was more unsettling: the note of surprise in Anya's voice, or the fact that he actually *was* smiling. He shifted his rucksack, giving himself a couple of seconds to consider her words, then he nodded. "I guess I am at that. Kind of scary, huh?"

Anya Stroud, walking beside him on a thin strip of paved road, reached out and caressed his cheek. "I like it, and will get used to seeing that smile. You've definitely earned it."

"A lot of us did. Earned the right to it." Marcus fought to keep the smile alive. *But so many will never smile again. So many. Too many. Dom. My father...* He sought to push aside the darker feelings, and tried to distract himself by looking around, but that did not help overly much. The roadway west from Ephyra had ditches slashed through it as if something giant had raked it with claws. And while some grasses had turned golden with the coming

— 9 —

of autumn, black swaths of burned vegetation twisted up and down hillsides. There wasn't a single spot where his gaze could rest without seeing signs of the war.

No. I am not ruining today. Marcus reached up and took Anya's hand in his. "Smiling is easier when I'm with you."

"I've missed you, too, Marcus." Anya returned his smile, her eyes bright. "I can't tell you how happy I was when you radioed to say you'd reach Ephyra this morning."

"I was actually in the suburbs when I radioed. There just wasn't enough left for me to recognize where I was." In the six months since the Imulsion Countermeasure had wiped out the Locust and the Lambent, the world had tried to heal itself. Grass and weeds grew again. A few trees actually blossomed and some had borne fruit. It wasn't much of a harvest and never would have been considered bountiful, save that so many people had died that humanity didn't have the hands necessary to harvest all that had grown wild.

While the natural world could heal, what man had wrought simply could not. The damage meted out to the works of humanity had dealt a near mortal wound to civilization. Marcus had traveled throughout the countryside. In some places, with isolated little farming communities, life that would have seemed normal for his grandparents still existed. In other places refugees clawed out a Stone-Age existence. And then perhaps twenty-five miles on, a single building might stand untouched in a town, complete with electricity and the other amenities that had once been normal.

Back when I was a kid. Even just back before Emergence Day.

He glanced at her. "How bad has it been in Ephyra? I know you've been helping Colonel Hoffman get us all squared away, but that can't have been as easy as you made it sound on the radio."

She shrugged. "Took a bit of getting used to, becoming an XO again instead of a Gear."

"Once a Gear, always a Gear, Anya." Marcus shook his head. "You were a Gear even before you stepped into the field. That's why I always trusted you. I could always count on you. We all did."

"And you always did the heavy lifting." She gave his hand a squeeze. "Well, in the three months since I headed back to Ephyra, Colonel Hoffman and I shifted from trying to help what was left of the COG army to just generally helping people. So many people feel abandoned and want to get back home—just to see if they have a home. We surveyed some blocks in the city, marked off the unsafe buildings, but people are alone and afraid of each other. Some of them seem…"

"Feral?"

"Yeah."

"I know." Marcus had been traveling widely in the last six months, helping Gears return home. Some communities welcomed their returning soldiers and began organizing local militias around them. In other places the people feared the Gears, afraid they'd summon the Hammer of Dawn and burn their settlements out of existence. Some people resented the Gears for having survived while their kith and kin had not.

And some people seemed to be ghosts, their spirits slain by the war, and their bodies just waiting to catch up.

"Colonel Hoffman was lucky to have you. Can't tell you all the times I wished you were still with me."

"I'm here now, Marcus. We're here."

His smile returned. "You sure about this?"

"Us? Completely." She glanced off toward the west. "Laying claim to my family's estate, mixed feelings. I never truly felt welcome there before. But with so much destroyed, it's as if the Locust took a meat cleaver and severed us from our past. I'm hoping that by reestablishing a link to my past, we can remember who we were, and who we ought to be."

"I get you. I like the thinking." Marcus *had* lost so much. So many friends. Men he considered brothers. *And my father. Twice.*

"Are you okay with it? Coming to my family's home?"

"For me, it's *your* home. My home is any place you are. And you know, after so much tearing down, I like the idea of building something back up."

They rounded a corner on the road and descended into a ravine through which a small stream ran sluggishly. The bridge over it had lost a chunk of pavement between spans, but local residents had laid planking down so pedestrians and vehicles could still pass. A small group of people were gathered at the bridge's far end, huddling together and looking off toward a small house further across a field.

The eldest adult—an older woman wearing an apron over a patched and worn dress—eyed the two of them suspiciously. "We didn't send word for you."

Anya offered the woman a smile. "We were just walking down the road. My family owns a place a bit further west."

The older woman looked her up and down. "Lived here all my life and I've never seen the likes of you before."

"I'm Anya Stroud."

The woman gave her the once-over again. "You Helena's girl?"

"Yes."

"I never much liked your mother." The older woman frowned. "The estate's still there. No one living in it. We respect the way it was, no matter the changes and trouble."

Marcus cleared his throat. "What's the trouble here?"

Another woman, who Marcus took to be the angry woman's daughter or granddaughter, lifted a hand from a girl's shoulder and pointed at the distant farmhouse. "We told our Daisy here to stay away from that place, but she didn't listen. Said she got a fright there, and it's Locust. I know it is." The woman began to shake and the little girl started to cry.

The older woman smacked her daughter across the arm with a backhanded slap. "Hush. You don't know nothing."

"Ma'am, the fact that Daisy was able to tell you about it means it's not Locust." Anya's voice came calmly and gently. "The Locust are all dead. They're not a threat anymore."

The old woman's eyes narrowed. "Know that for a fact, do you, Anya Stroud? You put a bullet in every one of their skulls?"

Marcus dropped his duffle bag, opened it, and pulled out his armor. "We'll take a look."

The younger woman stared at him wide-eyed. "You can't. It'll kill you."

Anya opened her duffle and pulled out a couple of spare clips for the Snub pistol riding high on her right hip. "We'll look. The Strouds understand their duties."

They closed up their duffels, shouldered them and started down a narrow footpath that paralleled the stream. Marcus waited until he was pretty sure they were out of earshot of the bridge before he looked back at her. "So what exactly *are* the duties of being a Stroud?"

Anya laughed lightly. "The estate employed a lot of people and while my grandfather could be an unfeeling tyrant with his own family, he liked to bestow favors on the surrounding folks, when they needed something. Ego-based philanthropy is what my mother used to call it. Kid gets lost, we beat the bushes. A barn burns down, we supply wood and manpower. I guess now that includes hunting down Locust."

"People afraid of their own shadows."

"Can't blame them, can we? Six months of peace doesn't erase sixteen years of terror."

"True." Marcus followed the path as it cut upslope toward the small house. "I see no signs of Locust."

"No, and the house appears to be in good shape." They both dropped to a crouch and shed their gear amid the long, golden grasses. "Make a circuit."

"It's a plan." Keeping his head low, Marcus advanced, heading toward the left of the house, between it and the ravine. The grasses showed no obvious signs of anyone passing, including Daisy. Aside from weathering, peeling paint and some dry rot, the house appeared intact. *So far, so good.*

As they came around the side to the back of the house, Marcus paused. A pair of external doors covered a stairway into the basement. Someone had bent one door back at the corner, but braces appeared to have been set in place from below, holding everything shut up tight. The would-be thieves had given up and he didn't see any indication that Locust had done the damage.

They approached the stairway and listened. He thought he heard something, but couldn't make out what it was. Marcus kept his pistol on the opening and signaled for Anya to pass behind him. She got to the furthest corner, glanced around it, then signaled him forward.

The far side of the house had a door that someone had pried open, splintering the doorjamb in the process. The door opened into the kitchen, where lots of the floor tiles had come up because of the rain and snow that had obviously poured in. Marcus saw signs of where modern appliances might once have stood, but they'd all been ripped out for salvage. A few pieces of furniture remained and the living room and area around the fireplace suggested that, at least for a short while, people had squatted there.

Anya found the door to the basement and opened it. She held a fist up for Marcus, then listened at the top of the stairs. She tapped her ear, then pointed down below. Marcus advanced quietly and listened.

He definitely heard something. Something *was* down in the basement, moving around, jostling things. And a steady, low thrum vibrated below the other sounds, akin to a tiny engine that was somehow muffled. *I don't know what that is, but it isn't a Locust.*

Marcus slid down on his belly and flicked on the light at the shoulder of his armor. He pulled himself to the head of the stairs, his own Snub pistol in his right hand. His mouth went dry and his pulse pounded in his ears. *Just because all the Locust are dead doesn't mean that what's down there can't hurt you.*

He started down the stairs head-first, descending cautiously one step at a time. The rickety wooden staircase creaked, which increased the sound from below and added a couple of whip cracks and hisses. Marcus looked down between the treads and his light flashed back at him from nearly a dozen golden dots. As he stared, some of the dots winked out, then others glowed to life a couple of feet away.

"What do you see, Marcus?"

He eased himself down about five inches and shifted slightly to redirect the light.

"Not Locust." Marcus pulled his knees in and twisted around so he sat about a third of the way down the stairs. He looked back at her and laughed. "It's a family of raccoons. They're not happy about our invading their homestead."

Anya slid her pistol back into its holster. "Think they're going to believe it when we tell them it's not Locust?"

Marcus tromped back up the stairs to a cacophony of growls and hisses. "The relief on our faces ought to be enough to convince them." He holstered his pistol, shut off the light, then pulled her into a hug. "I have missed you so much."

"Oh, Marcus, me, too." She clung to him and he relished the scent of her, the way her hair brushed against his cheek. "It felt good to be back in the field, even if it was only raccoons."

He pulled back. "They're pretty fierce raccoons. They probably killed any Locust that got in there."

"That was actually a joke. I could come to like this peacetime Marcus Fenix."

"I sure as hell hope so." He took her hand in his and led her from the building. He took a deep breath as the pulsing in his ears subsided, and they recovered their gear on the way back to the bridge.

The old woman glared. "Didn't hear no shooting."

Anya shook her head. "No Locust."

The little girl clung to her mother's leg. "But I heard it."

"What Daisy heard was a family of raccoons in the basement." Anya opened her hands. "As I mentioned before, there are no more Locust."

The older woman's eyes became slits. "Raccoons, you say."

Marcus nodded. "Eight to a dozen."

"Good." The old woman looked toward the house. "Make good eating if you brine 'em long enough. Winter's coming, maybe get a cap or two out of the skins."

"Good hunting, then." Anya gave them a warm smile. "I enjoyed meeting you."

The old woman nodded. "I guess you are a Stroud after all, and you do know the old ways. Welcome home, Anya Stroud."

Anya and Marcus walked away from the bridge in silence, each lost in their thoughts. Marcus couldn't recall when he'd last met anyone with that sort of hard-bitten attitude and determination. *Aaron Griffin, maybe?* Most of the people he'd dealt with were terrified or shell-shocked or Gears who understood more about the war than anyone else. Most of the civilians wanted to survive, but that woman had had a plan. *That's how she made it through the last fifteen years.*

A couple of miles further on they crested a hill and looked down toward the Stroud Estate. "There it is, Marcus, the family pile."

He scratched at the back of his head. "It has seen better days, but at least some of it is still standing."

"Yeah. The wings are gone, but the core building, the heart, it's still there." She reached out and took his hand in hers. "Lots to rebuild."

"Yep, but that's okay." Marcus raised her hand to his mouth and kissed it. "This is where our tomorrow is. We'll build it brick by brick, so we can make it exactly what we want it to be."

2: STROUD ESTATE

NEAR EPHYRA, SERA

11 HARVEST 18 A.E.

Marcus leaned on the shovel and used his left forearm to wipe sweat from his brow. Anya had departed early for Ephyra to tie up a few loose ends of the work she'd been doing with Colonel Hoffman. They'd been poring through lists of equipment caches that the COG military had hidden over the last fifty years, hoping to organize an effort to track them down and salvage any they could find. Anya didn't expect finalizing the list to take that long and planned to be back by nightfall.

He'd spent the morning making a quick survey of the immediate grounds, happy to have his heavy Gear boots to crunch through rubble. Destruction on the estate appeared more random than systematic, and he didn't see any signs of squatters or looters in what was left of the main building or the carriage house. *I guess the old woman wasn't lying.*

He paid special attention to the greenhouse at the far end of the garden. Slightly more than half of the glass panes had escaped destruction, which struck him as remarkable. In his experience, glass seemed to have a magnetic quality as far as bullets were concerned. He didn't see any signs of a fight around it, suggesting that a Locust had blundered in and then bashed its way back out again.

The scattered gardening books and little brass plaques on planter beds suggested that the greenhouse had once housed a variety of orchids, which seemed completely in keeping with the people the Strouds had been. Anya hadn't said much about her mother's family, other than the fact that they became distant when Helena joined the armed forces, and had not warmed up to Anya when her mother died in the service.

Marcus had seen people like that his entire career. They had no idea what it took to be in the trenches, fighting to keep them safe. They thought soldiers were all dumb grunts or murder-minded individuals who got off on watching others die. Such people had little connection to the practical world.

For them, growing a flower that is only ornamental is an art, while growing something practical, like tomatoes, is beneath them. They don't understand why we fight, or that they're just like their orchids.

He'd checked the carriage house to see if the storeroom there had any extra glass panes lying around. It didn't, but the windows on the ground floor had panes the same size as those in the greenhouse. He also found a dogcart, and a larger one meant to be drawn by a horse. At first glance he thought they were quaint antiques, but they appeared to be sturdy and, if he could find such animals, likely the best way to get around.

That prompted him to check the other outbuildings. To the north lay the stable and barn, at the base of a terraced hillside. The Strouds had raised grapes and made their own wine. Marcus walked straight across fields tangled with waist-high grasses, broken up by gray slashes where Locust had gouged scars through the earth. He saw no animals in the corral as he approached, but the fencing had gone down in a couple of places, so any livestock would have been able to roam free. As he drew closer, everything became preternaturally quiet.

He dropped to a knee about two hundred yards out.

Idiot, are you trying to get yourself killed? In his fatigues he'd made himself a big, beautiful target as he walked down. *You don't have a gun, you don't have a knife. You're losing it. Sharpen up, Fenix.*

In an instant the bucolic scene of grasses dancing in a light breeze became a battlescape, with enemies lurking in the shadows. He advanced, staying low, moving to put an old tree between him and the stables. Remaining in a crouch, he dashed to the tree, then squatted at its base. He peeked out around the side, but saw nothing. Slowing his breathing, he stood with his back to the trunk, then glanced out from the other side.

Nothing. Twenty-five yards to the stable. Relatively flat terrain. *I can cross that distance in no time.* Another glance. *Is the grass hiding a mine?*

Something thumped inside the stable. *Someone jumping down from the loft?* He strained his ears, but heard no repeat. His blood pounded in his skull, so he took a moment to slow his breathing, then nodded to himself. *To the corner, then the door. Go!*

He cut around the tree, head down, arms and legs pumping. Two steps left, then hard right for three, left again, then bursting forward. Boots crunched gravel on a stretch of track the grasses had hidden, then he was into the stable yard. Marcus reached the corner of the stable, glanced down the building's long side, then cut left and ducked in through the open doors.

The stench hit him immediately. Someone had died in there,

and not too long ago. He looked around, then snatched a pitchfork from a wall rack. Holding it out and wishing it was a Lancer, he advanced deeper into the building's cool interior. He inspected each stall as he worked his way forward and there, on the left side, third one down, he found the bodies.

The child had died first. Couldn't have been more than six months old. His mom had wrapped him up in a blanket and placed a knitted cap on his head. She'd laid the child in a nest of hay. Then she'd taken a pair of overalls, fashioned a noose, and hanged herself right there beside her child.

Marcus slid to the ground on the other side of the stall, staring at them. He'd seen death a million times in his life. He'd dealt death. It had always seen tragic, but this case… The child, given his age, had to have been born so very close to when Delta put an end to the Lambent Pandemic. The mother had gotten pregnant at a horrible time. She had carried the child to term, and given birth, in what could have been the last days of mankind. And then she had struggled on. She found the stables, and her child had died. Out of grief she killed herself. She had died all alone, her hope having perished with her child.

Anya and I had just returned to the main house. Had she looked out, had she looked up, she could have seen light, couldn't she? Why didn't she? Why did she surrender when we would have helped her? Marcus' hands balled into fists.

We could have saved her. Why didn't she keep on fighting?

He sat there with them for a while, then walked back up to the main house. Belting on his pistol, he tucked a knife in his boot. He grabbed a shovel from the greenhouse and returned to the stable. Finding a spot at the base of the hill, he began digging. It wasn't the first grave he'd dug, but seemed to take a lot longer than any of the others.

Returning to the stable he looked for canvas or something he could use to wrap the bodies. His search took him into the loft, and there he found a space where someone had been living. A loose shutter on a loft window had been what made the original thumping sound that attracted him. The half-open window provided enough breeze to rid the loft of the stench of death.

Marcus gathered up a worn blanket, then searched through the other stuff, hoping there might be a photo or letter or something to tell him who they were. He found nothing that would let him pin a name on them, but he got the impression the mother and child had not been alone. The space that had been cleared out was larger than the two of them needed, and the window had been pried open, but Marcus couldn't find the pry bar that had done the job.

The scenario unfolded in his mind easily enough.

They'd been traveling together as a small family. The baby got sick, but they didn't know what to do. They didn't have any medicine. Then the child's mother, maybe she got sick, too. Their traveling companion said he was going to go find help or medicine. He'd be back real soon. And then he just disappeared.

Her hope turns into despair. Then her child, her reason for living, dies.

He cut the woman down, laid the child in her arms, then dragged them to the grave. He eased them down into it, pulling the blanket up and around them both. He started filling the grave at her feet, working his way up, the whole time hoping she'd make a sound. She'd push the dirt away. She'd find hope again and fight against death.

He dropped the last shovelful of earth on top of the mound and tamped it down with the flat of the shovel. *A good winter rain and that will settle. Next spring no one will know it's here. Green grasses will grow up and the memory of them will evaporate.*

Marcus shook the sweat off his forearms. He knew he should say some words, something comforting, but he had nothing. Words like that had gone, same as Dom. His grief, his ability to be of comfort, he'd lost them somewhere out there. These people he'd buried, they'd loved each other. Someone had to love them, would miss them. And Marcus had fought for them. He'd sacrificed for them, sacrificed so they could live and, despite that, they hadn't.

Marcus bent forward, forearms leaning on the shovel's handle. His chest tightened and his heart began to pound again.

Is that the joke? We fought so hard, Dom died, my father died, so people could live—and it turns out that they don't have the will for it? That whoever abandoned her and the child could just walk away and leave them to die. What is wrong *with people?*

Something crunched behind him. Marcus spun, shovel raised, ready to see some wretch of a man crawling back to where he'd abandoned his wife and child. In a heartbeat Marcus would have happily crushed his skull.

At the sight of a large, angry man, the ground squirrel turned and dashed away through the grasses.

Marcus exhaled, his breath ragged, and sank to his knees. He leaned forward and wanted to howl and scream and rage, but choked all of those things down. *No! You will hold it together. You've been through the worst of it. No more. You didn't fall apart when the pressure was on, you're not doing it now.*

He slowed his breathing down and closed his eyes. He concentrated on the rustling of the grasses. He felt the breeze drying his sweat and heard the clumsy return of the ground squirrel, the flicking flutter of dragonfly wings as the insect whizzed past and then disappeared as another breeze teased the grasses.

He stayed there—for how long he wasn't certain—then he levered himself to his feet with the shovel. Marcus stared down at the grave, and exhaled slowly. "I'm sorry I didn't know you in life. I would have helped."

He shouldered the shovel and began the long walk back up to the main house.

That evening Marcus smiled as Anya alighted from a long, low-slung limousine. She emerged from the back compartment hauling two black garment bags. She spoke with the driver, who tossed her a quick salute. Marcus remained in the doorway while Anya waited for the vehicle to turn around, and she waved as it headed down the long drive to the main road.

Her long legs ate up the distance between them.

Marcus smiled. "I see Colonel Hoffman has some priorities straightened out. New uniforms?"

"Not exactly. It's been a weird day."

"You, too, huh?" He enfolded her in his arms and hugged her tightly. "I am so glad you're here."

"Oh, Marcus, me, too. I'm sorry I'm so late. We actually finished compiling the list early, then people arrived from the Shin Museum of Modern Culture."

"Is there actually any Modern Culture left on Sera?"

Anya laughed. "A little, maybe. I have two scraps here."

"I can't wait to hear, but first, I've actually *cooked*."

"Oh my."

He took her hand in his. "Come on." He led her inside to the kitchen, where he'd cleared out a small area and set up a table made of a door and legs he'd fashioned out of debris, then nailed on. He'd found mismatched plates and silverware, and two identical wine glasses. "I couldn't find a corkscrew, so I had to take the neck off the bottle."

She hung the garment bags on a nail in the wall. "Oh, Marcus. You even found flowers."

"Nasturtiums. They were growing wild, but I found a book in the greenhouse that identified them." He crossed to the oven and pulled out two bowls filled with steaming food, then sprinkled some orange nasturtium petals over them. "They're also edible."

Anya arched an eyebrow. "But the food looks like you found some old ration packets."

"Yeah, and these date from the Pendulum Wars. Your grandfather, or his father, stashed a bunch down in the wine cellar."

"There's a wine cellar?"

"Two." Marcus set the bowls on the table. "Over in the west wing, in what was a big dining room, there was access down to one wine cellar. People have gotten in there and pretty much cleaned it out. What's left is mostly vinegar. But over in the east wing, in what was his study, there was a panel behind bookcases. Someone had found it, but didn't have the tools to open it. I got curious. It was where your grandfather put the very best wine."

Anya picked the bottle up and studied the label. "That would be, what, five B.E.?"

"A good year for your vineyard. As for the food, well, when we can grow our own, things will be better. There's some game out there, too."

Anya poured wine into the glasses. "Seems as if you had a most productive day."

"It had its ups and downs." Marcus stared at the dark wine. "There was a body... two bodies. They died in the stable."

"Are you hurt?" She reached over and squeezed his hand.

He shook his head. "They weren't... I didn't have to kill them. Just folks who had built a home in the loft. Probably just passing through, but they just didn't make it. I buried them."

"Do you know who they were?"

"No, no sign. I think they might have been traveling with someone, but he's long gone." Marcus forced a smile and looked at her. "But you have to tell me about your day. Remember, today I was the house husband here. I live vicariously through you and your adventures."

"Believe me, your day was far more exciting than mine." Anya sighed. "As I said, we were doing accounting work, finished it up, then the museum folks arrived. They hauled me off to the museum and had me going through fashion archives."

Marcus blinked. "Civilization has pancaked, and you're being tasked with inventorying fashion archives?"

"Worse, Marcus, not *inventory*. They had me there for a *fitting!*"

"Anya, that's really not making a lot more sense than inventory."

"I know, and, you'll love this: one bag is for me, and the other is a uniform for *you!*"

"I'm going to kill Hoffman."

"I don't think this is his doing, Marcus." Anya quickly drained her glass of wine and reached for the bottle. "In the midst of all this, someone has decided to throw a reception in Ephyra. And, worse yet, they've decided that you and I have to attend."

3: SHIN MUSEUM OF MODERN CULTURE

EPHYRA, SERA
15 HARVEST 18 A.E.

Marcus Fenix checked his six. The stone wall behind him looked solid enough for cover. The vast chamber had four exits—one at each of the cardinal points on the compass. He'd come in from the west and had a clear line of sight east and south. North would be the issue—people packed that quadrant.

"Do you read me, Marcus?"

The warm tones of Anya Stroud's voice, the teasing trace of humor in her words, brought him back to reality. *A reality.*

"Uh, yeah. Sorry."

She smiled easily and stroked his left arm. "I know, you were drifting."

"No, no, I'll get better. I'll focus." He frowned, feeling one hundred percent naked without his body armor and the weight of a Mark 2 Lancer assault rifle slung over his back. He felt off-balance, and not *only* physically. He'd lost the weight of his combat kit, but the gravity of warfare still clung to him.

"Seriously. Mission and objective, that's me."

"You didn't toss in an 'affirmative' or 'Roger,' so we'll take that as progress." Anya shook her head, tucking a lock of blonde hair back behind her ear. "No one here is going to be shooting at you, Marcus."

"You've had a little more time to get used to life without your shell." Marcus rolled his shoulders to ease the tension. In the six months that had passed since they'd deployed his father's invention to destroy the Lambent and Locust, Anya's work had acquainted her more completely with the needs of the post-war world. Her communication, organizational and logistics skills, which had been vital during the fighting, counted for far more in the post-invasion world. *Worth more than the ability to shoot straight. Which is fine. She's done enough fighting. Saved my ass more times than I want to count. She's earned her peace.*

Marcus' wind-down had focused more on getting his people to their homes and helping out where he could. Locating and disarming booby-traps, locating and recovering ordnance, helping the other Gears search for their families and setting up secure communities had filled his days. In some ways that work exhausted him more than the gory grind of blowing through a Locust E-hole.

At least, with the Locust and Lambent, we knew there would be an end, he thought. *We had a goal. But now?*

Now I guess this is the new *world.*

As he'd promised Anya, he focused. He looked around the vast room—*not a chamber*—at the assembled people. A couple hundred, he estimated, all wearing the finest clothes they could find. The kind they'd have worn to weddings or graduations, benefits or balls. Bright colors showed here and there, but more often somber, with many of the outfits ill-fitting, since few still had their wardrobes from a decade and a half previous. Much of the clothing had been salvaged and altered as best as possible.

The room had survived the wars better than Marcus could have imagined. The Shin Museum of Modern Culture had once been a gem of the modern world. They gathered in the main gallery, beneath a high-domed ceiling and checkerboard marble floor, with centuries-old paintings hung on the walls. The gallery had survived, but the museum's wings had not. In preparation for arrivals that evening, crews had cleared narrow paths through the rubble for the guests.

That was one aspect of the fighting that always astounded Marcus. Whole neighborhoods could have been reduced to smoking rubble, with barely one brick left stacked atop another, yet a random building would stand there, pristine, as if anchoring the past so that men would be forced to acknowledge all the destruction they'd created. Marcus could sense no rhyme or reason for what got spared and what got obliterated.

I did a fair amount of the obliteration myself. That capriciousness of fate had scarred all of Sera, and all those who survived.

When they'd been invited to attend the reception, Jamila Shin—the most senior member of the family that had established the museum—had invited Anya to visit the museum ahead of time, where staff helped pick out a dress she could borrow for the evening. The building's storage vaults, located deep beneath their feet, had contained the paintings on the walls and other cultural artifacts, including the clothes worn by some of the attendees.

Anya had chosen a green dress from the Pendulum Wars era, before she was born, and appeared radiant in it, despite the big taffeta bow at the small of her back.

Marcus, for his part, wore most of a dress uniform supplied by the museum. He'd added bits he obtained by trading with rag-pickers for the best they had. An older couple recognized his name and gave him a jacket more appropriately sized for him—saying the uniform had belonged to their son, who hadn't made it back. They told him the son had spoken highly of Marcus, and his heart ached that he couldn't even remember the young man's name. The boots and belt—anything leather—required hard bargaining, but in the end he'd outfitted himself respectably, but without ostentation. He wore no medals or ribbons, and since the COG had collapsed, he wasn't sure if such things still got manufactured, or even existed.

"That's a new look for you, Fenix. The uniform, not the grim expression."

Marcus recognized the gruff voice immediately and straightened up. "Yes, sir, Colonel. You, likewise."

Colonel Hoffman gave his head a tiny shake. "It's a miracle that any of us are here." He turned and ushered forward a slender woman who wore her black hair long, with white locks at her temples. "Sergeant, let me introduce Jamila Shin. She organized this reception and talked me into helping host it. Dr. Shin, this is Lieutenant Anya Stroud and Sergeant Marcus Fenix."

Jamila, who wore a white jacket over a white cocktail dress, air-kissed Anya on both cheeks, then shook Marcus' hand. Though her hand all but disappeared into his, he found her grip surprisingly firm and strong.

"It is a pleasure to meet you two. I have looked forward to it." Jamila's eyes glittered. "Colonel Hoffman, when I can tease more than a sentence at a time from him, speaks very highly of you both. He leaves no doubt that if not for your efforts, no one would have survived the Locust."

Anya chuckled politely. "Forgive me, Colonel, but I think you have been exaggerating what we did, to hide what *you* did."

"No. I didn't spend as much time in the trenches as you did. That's where you got the work done. The praise goes where it is deserved." Colonel Hoffman looked Marcus straight in the eye. "I've never been easy on Fenix, but he did the job. You both have earned the praise."

Marcus gave the older man a nod. "Thank you, Colonel."

Jamila smiled. "I believe those of us who have survived have not thanked *any* of you well enough. We shall have to rectify that. But for the moment, gentlemen, would you mind if I borrowed dear Anya here? There are a few people I think she should meet."

Marcus gave Anya a wink. "Shoot a flare if you need extraction."

"I'll be fine." Anya gave his hand a squeeze. "Colonel, it's good to see you again."

"And you, Lieutenant." Colonel Hoffman shifted around to Marcus' side. "Feels good to have a wall at my back."

"I'm still missing my armor."

"And the rest of Delta?"

Marcus glanced over at the older man. "All of them."

"Me, too." Hoffman rested a hand on Marcus' shoulder. "We didn't see eye to eye, Sergeant, but that doesn't mean I was blind to what you were doing. I was hard on you because you could do things others couldn't. Things that would get others killed."

So many did get killed. Marcus nodded slowly. "Message received, Colonel."

"There's a first for everything, yeah?"

Both men fell silent and the music from the six-piece band gave them an excuse not to speak. A disparate assemblage of horns, strings, and a saxophone managed to make something beautiful out of a song that had been popular before the Pendulum Wars. Marcus wasn't certain what amazed him more: that the museum had somehow found six musicians to play, or that the musicians could bend museum-piece instruments to their will. He couldn't remember the last time he'd heard a live performance, and the crispness of the notes surprised him. As the music continued, Hoffman's expression softened in a way Marcus had never seen before.

The music has him remembering something. "I don't think I know the song, Colonel."

"Traditional folk song, goes by dozens of titles." The colonel's eyes focused distantly. "First time I ever danced with my wife, it was to this. Always reminds me of how I felt the day I laid eyes on her."

"I don't remember ever having met her, Colonel."

"Likely not, Sergeant. She's been gone over a decade." Hoffman brought his chin up. "In some ways it's a blessing. She loved Ephyra, the atmosphere, the architecture. And she grew up in Jacinto. The world she remembered didn't survive her."

"I'm sorry, Colonel."

"Thank you, Sergeant. Not a person here got out of the war unscathed. We all have losses. We all have scars." He looked Marcus up and down. "Luckily, some of us have a chance to get past that. That's what the fighting was all about, to give us that chance."

"The fighting was about getting one step closer to ending the fighting. One more effort to keep my people alive."

"From your perspective, that was true." The older man sighed. "I thought like you. Hated the hell out of leaving the line. I think I made the jump at the right time. Gave me some perspective. A bit of clarity, maybe. I hope you get that chance, Sergeant."

"I'm going to have to get a job first." Marcus grunted out a brief laugh. "First time in my life I don't have employment security."

"Is that a complaint?"

"No, Colonel."

"Never thought I'd live to see the day when you didn't complain, Sergeant." A wry grin curled Hoffman's lips. "Maybe I'm not dreaming, and the war truly is over."

"Why are we here, Colonel?" Marcus scanned the crowd with narrowed eyes. "Jamila Shin asking you to co-host. The few people I recognize, well, they and most of the rest look like they're traveling in the same circles. *High* circles. We don't fit."

Before Colonel Hoffman could answer, however, a dark-haired man intervened. He was about Marcus' height but with an average build and a goatee shot through with white. "Please don't underestimate yourself, Marcus Fenix, nor your friend, Anya Stroud. You *do* fit. We all do, now, more out of necessity and circumstance than by choice."

Marcus just gave the interloper a stare.

The man smiled slowly, neither intimidated by the stare nor apparently daunted by Marcus' silence. "It was rude of me to eavesdrop and interrupt. I am Raul Hasterwith. Colonel Hoffman, we've met before. At the proving grounds."

"I recall, yes." Hoffman turned toward Marcus. "Mr. Hasterwith is on the board of Seradyne Industries."

"I believe, Sergeant, you made good use of our products in your operations." The man's smile grew.

Marcus frowned. "I don't know what…"

"Of course you do, Sergeant. The Mark 2 Lancer, that's ours. Manufactured under a license, but we improved the chainsaw bayonet." The man pressed his hands together fingertip to fingertip. "I've seen some battle footage that suggests you came to rely upon that aspect of the weapon."

"Sure. I just never saw any brand names."

"Nor would you. Only the serial number would tell you, but you'd have to look for the prefix 'SI.'" Hasterwith turned. "And, Colonel, thank you for the last report you were able to send. It seems we had a higher percentage of functional Lancers as we approached the end of the conflict than any other manufacturer."

"That was just a field report." The older man shrugged. "Someday, if we ever recreate the armed forces, we'll put together something more definitive."

"I trust the final report will be just as satisfying." Hasterwith lowered his voice. "As for wondering why you are here, Sergeant Fenix, you are not alone in voicing that question. We will all learn, in time. I had actually hoped it was so some of us could show our appreciation for what you, Lieutenant Stroud, and Colonel Hoffman did for us all. While I am pleased Seradyne contributed to the effort against the Lambent and Locust threats, I have been the first to say that all we did would be for naught, save for the bravery and sacrifice of people like you. If no one else has said it, thank you, Sergeant."

"Just doing my duty, Mr. Hasterwith."

"A virtue in a time when so many others shirked that obligation." Hasterwith signaled for a passing server, who came over with a tray of wine glasses. He plucked one with white wine, then turned to his companions. "Gentlemen?"

Marcus shook his head.

Colonel Hoffman glanced at the server. "Thank you, no."

Hasterwith sipped then shook his head. "I seem to recall other vintages tasting better, but it may only be because I know I'll never enjoy the fruits of those wineries again. The cultivation of grapes, the fermentation of wine, may have pre-dated civilization, but we had refined such things, raised it to an art. And now, so much of it gone, gone with everything else."

"I don't remember shooting up a winery."

"If you had, Marcus, please—let me call you Marcus—you would have done it with my own guns, so the blame would fall to me." The man canted his head. "So, Marcus, a serious question: what will you do now?"

Marcus hesitated. Since the end of the Lambent threat, his entire life had been about tying off loose ends. Seeing to it that friends got home. Cleaning up problems. His life had been about endings, so much so that he hadn't devoted much time to beginnings.

"Haven't thought much about that."

"I can imagine, Marcus, that readjusting to civilian life will take time."

Yeah, like maybe the decades it's been since I've been a civilian.

Colonel Hoffman's eyes narrowed. "I thought Anya mentioned that the Stroud Estate needs some work."

"Yeah, the Locust did some damage. Fixing it up is as good a place to start as any."

"Yes, for a start, certainly," Hasterwith said. "You have earned some downtime, no doubt about it." He rolled the wine glass between his palms. "When you decide, Marcus, that you want to do more, Seradyne will have a place for you. Research and development, quality assurance, field testing—whatever you want to do. We will make a job to fit you, as a way of thanking you. And rest assured, as we recover and grow, your role will grow. Seradyne cares for its own. I have a vision, and you are part of it."

"That's very generous, Mr. Hasterwith, but I'm confused."

"About?"

"Does Seradyne have anything left?" Marcus studied the man's face, looking for any clue to what was going on behind the mildly pleased expression. "I've seen Seradyne facilities. Ruins. What do you still have?"

The man's face became a mask of sincerity. "It is true that the war devastated us. I am fairly certain you have a better idea than I do about the state of some of our facilities." Hasterwith peered into his wine glass. "However, fortune has smiled, and I have located a little archipelago of remaining sites. We are consolidating our operations. We are salvaging what we can and reorganizing. As we learn what we can repair, what we can make work and, quite frankly, what the world needs most, we will sharpen our focus. I daresay that is what everyone here plans to do.

"You see, Marcus, you saved our world." Hasterwith opened his arms wide. "It falls to the rest of us to determine what shape that world will take, and how swiftly we can make our vision come true."

4: SHIN MUSEUM OF MODERN CULTURE

EPHYRA, SERA
15 HARVEST 18 A.E.

Anya walked with Jamila Shin, the older woman clinging to her arm as if they were dear friends. Anya recognized the stroll for what it was. Others watched the two of them, the onlookers' faces registering curiosity, envy, anger and cunning. Jamila had pulled her aside to show her off, but Anya didn't understand the reason why.

"I was honored to get the invitation to attend," she said, "and I cannot thank you enough for the loan of this dress. It's been so very long…"

"For all of us, my dear." Jamila gave Anya a warm smile. "That dress has actually never been worn. My great-grandmother had it made in anticipation of a reception during the Pendulum Wars. Diplomats thought they'd arrived at an agreement to end the wars—my great-grandfather was our ambassador to the talks. Then it all fell through, and we had another quarter-century of fighting. I know it seems a silly thing, a foolish thing, to dress up, but the fact that we have survived is a reason to celebrate."

"Yes, it is, at least a little." Anya glanced back toward Marcus, hoping to find that his perpetual scowl was easing. A dark-haired man had joined him and Colonel Hoffman, and she could tell what Marcus was doing. Watching him, sizing him up as a potential foe.

That's so much a part of him, it will never go away. A tiny smile tugged at the corners of her mouth. *Then again, this could be more of a battle than a party.*

"Forgive me, Dr. Shin…"

"You must call me Jamila. All of my friends do, and I am determined that we become friends."

"Yes, Jamila," Anya said. "This is about more than a celebration, clearly."

Jamila laughed politely. "Everything is about more than one thing, when you think about it—but I also think you are aware of that, Anya."

"Then what else is this about?"

"Matter of fact. To the point. I like this about you." Jamila steered them to the right and stroked a man's shoulder with her free hand. "Aaron, are they taking care of you well?"

As the well-built black man turned, Anya recognized him immediately. Lights glowed off his shaved head, matching the glint from the heavy gold bracelet he wore around his right wrist. He had on a dark jacket and slacks, with leather trim on each. His smile, which had been growing as he turned, froze when he caught sight of Anya. He gave her a hard stare for a moment, then leaned down to kiss Jamila on the cheek.

"Aaron, have you met Anya Stroud? Anya, this is Aaron Griffin."

"Yes. Mr. Griffin and I have met."

"Lieutenant Stroud here and her band of Gears visited me in

my office in Char." Griffin's dark eyes tightened. "They made a... lasting impression."

"As did you, Mr. Griffin." Anya met his stare firmly. "If not for your help, we never would have stopped the Lambent."

"Yeah. Lot of good people died." Griffin gave his head a little shake. "Now we pick through the ashes and see what we can pull together. From the parts the COG left us."

Jamila pressed her right hand over Griffin's heart. "It will take people of industry to do that, people exactly like you, Aaron. We are very fortunate to have you join us here this evening. Please, enjoy yourself."

"Of course, Jamila." Griffin's eyes eased. "And you, Lieutenant. You survived. It says something."

Jamila turned Anya away from Aaron Griffin and toward the eastern doorway. "You did very well, my dear."

Anya pasted a simple smile on her face. "You knew we'd met, then. Did you know the circumstances?"

"I may have heard something." Jamila paused at a table lined with a phalanx of mismatched wine glasses. She handed one to Anya. "You prefer red, dry, hints of berry."

Anya accepted the glass. "If you know that, you know more about me than I do."

"I, on the other hand, prefer white, lighter and crisp." Jamila selected a glass for herself. "This isn't nearly cold enough, but working refrigeration is spotty. Come."

Anya followed her guide through the doors and onto a patio which had once been the exhibit floor of the museum's eastern wing. Debris had been cleared to the edges of rubble walls. The jagged ruins of buildings lurked at the periphery of the illumination that snuck through the doors. They moved off to the right, out of earshot of the people inside, and into shadows that cloaked them in anonymity.

"The fact is, Anya, that I know about things like the nuances of wines and the fine points of protocol when it comes to organizing a gathering like this. In a formal dining situation, I will always use the correct fork. I daresay that I intimately understand the rules for appearing well-bred and cultured in almost any situation. You may recall that my doctorate is in Fine Arts, and now it's quite likely that everything covered by my expertise is contained in this museum. Rather obviously, as this ragged cityscape suggests, all the knowledge for which I would have once been praised isn't worth a bucket of warm spit."

Anya's artificial smile turned genuine. "Marcus would just say that world's been shot to shit."

"Succinct and on point." Jamila gestured vaguely toward the reception. "I invited many of the people present this evening because I believe we all have a stake in the future. The Coalition of Ordered Governments is obviously gone, and we don't know what will rise in its place. People are out there remaking the world, and I think we all desire a return to the best of what we could be. A world where science and education make raising a family possible. A world where medicines free people from the tyranny of disease. But to build that we all have to be encouraged to think beyond our own desires, think beyond our individual conceptions of what we want for the world."

Anya sipped the wine. In it she tasted the berries Jamila had mentioned, and realized that this glass of wine was the last one in which she might taste them. *Not only might the grapes be lost, but the berries, as well. Even if someone cultivates them, how will I know? How would I find them?* That struck her as a petty concern, but the state of the world presented so many problems that the only way to begin to get a handle on it was to start with something small. *Like berries. Or dresses. Or a gathering of people who might be able to find solutions.*

"You want to rebuild the world, and you want everyone here to do it." Anya blinked. "That's a tall order."

"Oh yes, and one full of troubles." Jamila sighed. "In the last six months Aaron Griffin has organized whatever survivors he could find in Char. He is intent on recreating Griffin Imulsion Corporation, but he is aware that this requires infrastructure and personnel, as well, obviously, as a new core commodity. He's educating people. He's reminding them that they're not prey for the grubs, but human beings who have potential. He is recreating the world *his* way, and you know that with a man like him, once he has his power base secure, he will want to expand."

"I've seen him in action."

"There are others. Down in Hanover the commercial fishing fleet has become the organizational focus. They have a simple command structure and a functioning economy. They're almost at a point where they could begin exporting food to other locations. Other elements in Hanover are pitching in to bring the city back to life.

"Raul Hasterwith is intent on rebuilding Seradyne," she continued. "And then there are countless smaller settlements— encampments of Stranded—which have organized themselves. So much potential, both for good and for tragedy."

"Isn't this something you should be telling all of them, Jamila? Griffin and others ought to see the sense in people banding together."

"They *should*, but they don't see me as someone who has accomplished what they have. I've created no empires. In their eyes all I did in the past was spend the fortune that my forebears had amassed, and now that fortune is gone. Most of the institutions we endowed are dust. I am a curious relic of another age, an age that died a violent death. I am a creature that has no natural habitat in this world."

Anya's eyes narrowed. "And yet you organized this reception. You brought disparate people together, and they came even without knowing your agenda for the evening. That speaks to skills they don't know you have."

"And skills they will require for the future, yes." Jamila's dark eyes glinted. "But how they see me is of little consequence to my purpose."

"What is it you want of me, Jamila? What is the role you see for me here?"

"Isn't it obvious?" The older woman laughed lightly. "My dear, you, on the other hand, have actually done *something* in the world—and I don't just refer to your role in eliminating the Locust and Lambent. While an admirable accomplishment, and one well done, today it has less application to the future than my knowing the proper honorific to use when addressing a high court judge and her husband. Your communication skills, your facility for command and control, and your abilities in executing logistical tasks, provide you with the tools we will need in the *future*. Your crisis management skills are a resource we cannot afford to squander."

Anya frowned. "You want me to be your executive officer?"

"Goodness no, dear. If that were my goal, you'd not be here this evening, and certainly not wearing that dress. No, Anya Stroud, I want you to stand with me as an equal in shaping the world of our future."

Anya's mouth went dry. She wanted to protest that she wasn't cut out for that sort of role. Yes, she could perform all sorts of administrative tasks, and organizing Gears to hit objectives involved coordinating all sorts of resources, but she'd always been lower-level, dealing with a squad and the assets allocated to it.

Or assets I forced to have allocated to it.

"I'm not comfortable with larger situations," she said finally. "I mean, I have no experience with the big issues. All I've done is small-scale."

Jamila stroked her arm. "It may have escaped your notice, my dear, but the *world* is small-scale now."

That remark exploded in Anya's mind. *We've lost so much, so very much.* Certainly she had lost friends and felt that hurt keenly. Yet in that instant she saw how much the world had truly suffered. The people who died had taken with them all those things that held society together. Civility. Family traditions. Grandma's secret recipe for cookies or chicken soup. Many of them things that might never be recreated.

A wave of despair washed over her. For a moment everything seemed so hopeless. *To think I could do anything to change that would be arrogance.*

But to refuse to try? That's self-pity, and a complete waste of energy.

Anya took a deep breath. It was true. With the world having been reduced to such a small scale, she could do something. It wasn't a question of looking at how much the world had lost, but of how much of the world they still had with which to work. It would be a huge task, a daunting task, but one that had to be managed.

Humanity had no other choice but to deal with it.

"I will work beside you, Jamila, but with the understanding that I have no ambition to lead. We've lost so much that I don't

GEARS OF WAR: EPHYRA RISING

want to lose more. So I'm in." Anya drank down the rest of her wine. "I can't believe I said that sober."

"Sobering times, Anya, but a beginning." Jamila linked her arm through Anya's. "So let us get you another glass of wine, and I shall make a few more introductions. I'll let you size up the others we'll be working with—and then we begin to plan."

5: SHIN MUSEUM OF MODERN CULTURE

EPHYRA, SERA
15 HARVEST 18 A.E.

Marcus kept his face impassive as Hasterwith smiled, then the industrialist caught someone else's eye.

"Excuse me, gentlemen, do have a good evening."

Colonel Hoffman nodded. "And you, Mr. Hasterwith." As the gathering swallowed the industrialist, he glanced at Marcus. "Assessment?"

"His guns worked. Chainsaw bayonet, too."

"Sergeant, you're no longer a Gear. You've succeeded in your mission. Part of your new mission, whatever you choose that to be, will require you to use *all* of your words."

"I already do that, Colonel."

"You're being admirably low-key by avoiding the profane ones." Hoffman snagged a glass of red wine from a passing server. "I'm never going to apologize to you for things that got said or done during the war. I'm never going to tell you that secretly I liked you or was proud of you. You were, next to the grubs, the greatest pain in my neck. What I admired—what I still admire, Marcus—is that you kept going. You saw the war from your perspective, but from where I sat, lots of people just stopped. You didn't. Because you didn't, we can be here."

"I did what needed doing."

"And you went beyond that."

"Begging your pardon, Colonel, but why are you telling me this?"

Hoffman half smiled. "This new mission, your new life, it's going to require new things out of you. Since E-Day, since the Locust emerged and launched their assault, how many days have you been outside your armor, just breathing free?"

"Couple weeks, maybe."

"Uh-huh. And tell me, how many exits are there to this room? How many security personnel?"

Marcus looked Hoffman in the eyes. "Four, and not enough."

"Back to the wall."

"You said it made you comfortable, too."

"True." Hoffman drank. "The wars shaped us both and, for me, making the transition from a line unit to command, it took time. It's still a work in progress. Just remember that."

"Thank you, Colonel. I'll be fine."

"Do yourself a favor, Marcus. Don't keep telling yourself that."

Marcus didn't feel inclined to do more than grunt in response, but before he could do so, two women came walking up to them. The taller of the two spoke first.

"Colonel Hoffman, we just wanted to thank you for saving all of us."

"Yes, thank you for your service." The smaller one appeared skeletally thin, suggesting that wartime food shortages had seriously impacted her life. She smiled at Marcus. "And you, too…"

Hoffman smiled politely. "This is Sergeant Marcus Fenix. He led the team that put an end to the Lambent."

"Oh. Yes. Of course."

The taller one looked at her friend. "Wasn't he the one in prison?"

"I got time off for good behavior." Marcus attempted a reassuring smile, but given the women's sudden change of expression, his effort fell short. "I'm proud to have been of service."

"I should imagine you are," the taller woman said, but her opinion of Marcus had been set the moment she realized he'd done time. She returned her attention to Colonel Hoffman. "Colonel, we won't hold you up, but you simply have to come and dine with us some evening. I would love to hear of the war from your perspective."

Marcus wasn't surprised at having been excised from the conversation. She wouldn't have liked to hear about the war from his point of view, anyhow. Wiping blood off his face, picking strings of viscera off armor, combing fingers through his hair only to find chunks of brain tissue and bone fragments tangled there. *Using Locust intestines to tie a door closed because that was the closest thing to cord I could find.*

The women moved off into other knots of people and Marcus watched as news of who he was flew through the room. People began to saunter over, trying to appear casual, yet with fear in their eyes. They'd all open with the "Thank you for your service" line, then lower their voices, moving closer. They all had a question to ask, or a story to share.

One man approached and opened with, "So, I guess you saw a thing or two out there." He had thinning hair and enough excess jowl flesh to suggest that he'd been twice his current size, once upon a time. "You know, I once wanted to be a Gear. I thought about applying to the Academy, but my uncle owned Sunlight Chemicals. Big firm, did lots of Imulsion refining." What he wanted from Marcus was reassurance that he could have been a Gear, could have been a hero.

He would have been dead before his first clip was empty.

Colonel Hoffman patted the man on the shoulder. "The war made demands on all of us. Imulsion was what kept us going, so without people like you, frontline troopers never would have stood a chance."

"I just did what I could, Colonel Hoffman." The man snapped to attention and tossed off the sloppiest salute Marcus had ever seen. "Victors write the history."

Marcus scowled as the man walked away. "I'm not sure he understands what he just said."

"Nope, but he'll tell his friends, and they'll pretend it was profound." Hoffman shook his head. "They mean well. Some of them, at least."

A couple approached and, given their relative ages, Marcus would have guessed they were father and daughter, but the way they touched suggested otherwise. They just wanted to share their story of the miracle that brought them together. They'd lived their entire lives within a mile or so of each other, but neither knew the other existed. And then the Locust came and they both hid in the back corner of a basement. A Locust had been down there hunting them, but there was an explosion and part of the building collapsed and crushed it. The experience gave them a bond, and that grew into love and, "So you see, not everything that happened was evil. We're the silver lining in the dark cloud."

And you want us to tell you that just because you two found each other and true love, that your love somehow balances the deaths of hundreds of millions? Marcus had to stop his hands from curling down into fists. The image of Dom and Maria floated through his brain, and he would have traded a million of this couple for them to be back.

"Even in the darkest times, we had to hope there would be pinpoints of light." Hoffman reached out and shook the man's hand. "Thank you."

Marcus stared at the man's hand a moment before following suit, and had to restrain himself from just crushing it. "Yeah, thank you."

People continued coming over. Some wanted to know "What was it really like?" Others offered grand conspiracy theories, suggesting that the Locust were really an old biowarfare weapon from the Pendulum Wars, and that's why Jacinto had to be sunk because that's where all the records were. Several people looked Marcus up and down, assessing him, appearing rather intent on taking him to bed and adding another notch to their bedposts.

The stream slackened after Hoffman got called away and Marcus deepened his scowl. These people had no clue of the sacrifices the Gears had made for them, and that fact just raked cold claws through his brain. The war was all in the past for them, and they could return to what they had been before. It was a bad dream that they could forget.

Not an ongoing one that refuses to vanish. They faced the Locust horror when it came hunting them; they never went hunting it back. They never tried to exterminate it. *They never lost friends who chose to die so they would live—a brother I would have done the same thing for.*

Rage and sorrow burned in Marcus. He wanted to yell that they had no idea what it was like. They had no idea how unsafe they were. If the Locust erupted right here, they'd all be dead. *Sure, Hasterwith makes Lancers, but does he have one with him? No. He's dead. We all would be dead.*

Marcus felt the solid stone against his back, as if he were trapped between it and an invisible hammer. He slipped to the side and twisted away. He headed toward the eastern entrance, vaguely aware that Anya had last gone that way. Looked for her, but couldn't find her. He caught himself reaching up to activate his radio and call out for her, then slowly lowered his hand.

While looking for Anya he spotted another familiar face. *Aaron Griffin.* In an instant anger flashed through him. He wanted to fly over and brace the guy, closing the book on Marcus' last visit to Char. But he held back. *Not the time, not the place. No purpose in resurrecting that ugly bit of the past.*

He turned away from Griffin before the man noticed him. His anger began to fade, but he found himself surrounded by more of the people who had spoken with Colonel Hoffman. *They all look proud of themselves for having survived, but do any of them really understand what they survived? They want nothing to do with the reality, and instead just hope politeness can make it all go away.*

"They're kind of relentless, aren't they?" A slender man, dark-haired, about a head shorter than Marcus and a third narrower, nodded back toward the center of the gallery. "They want you to tell them they did all they could during the war, or that they could have done what you did during the war."

"Which class do you fall into?"

"Neither." The man jerked a thumb toward the refreshments table. "Let me buy you a drink."

"They're charging for drinks?"

"Figure of speech. I don't know if we actually have money anymore." The man shrugged. "Doesn't matter. I don't have any."

Something in the man's attitude separated him from the others. "So no retirement pay?"

"Probably not. Don't tell the others. A lot of them are hoping that bank balances from before E-Day will magically reappear." The man offered Marcus his hand. "Brandon Turrall. Don't even... we've never met."

"Marcus Fenix."

"I gathered." They shook hands. The man had a firm grip and looked Marcus in the eye as they shook. "I've seen plenty of your handiwork. Maybe not yours per se, but Gears'. Not everyone is a fan."

"That include you?"

"I've had moments." Brandon broke their grip. "Your house burns down, the firemen save as much as they can. Doesn't make much sense to be angry with them that they couldn't save everything."

"We tried."

"I know." Brandon led him over to a table where there was a mix of wine glasses. "Name your poison."

"I'm not a..."

"Connoisseur?"

"Never had time to develop the skill."

Brandon smiled at the young redhead filling the glasses. "Angela, yeah? Do you have that bottle set aside for Mr. Pendergast? Be a dear and pour us each out three fingers."

Marcus frowned. "Pendergast? On the board of Raven Aviation?"

"That was his dad." Brandon took two glasses half filled with whiskey and handed one to Marcus. "Tyrus Rain. Some of the best single malt left on Sera."

"Won't Pendergast be angry?"

"He'll get over it if he hopes to ever have any more of this." Brandon raised his glass. "To your health."

Marcus touched his glass to Brandon's, then took a healthy sip of the whiskey. He caught a lot of peat and smoke, but that disappeared as the liquor scorched the back of his throat. He swallowed and the burn coursed down into his stomach. He swallowed a second time, then shook his head.

"Finest single malt on Sera?"

"Finest I could find." Brandon swiped at the tears in the corners of his eyes. "Bottle said it had been aged eighteen years."

"Eighteen minutes, tops."

"True. I think some of it actually *was* Tyrus Rain, but what they cut it with was probably paint thinner." Brandon stared at the glass. "Though where they found that much paint thinner, it's anyone's guess. Don't worry. We'll have to finish the whole bottle before it blinds us."

"If you could target some specific memories, I'd take a gallon."

"If it could do that, this stuff would be the new Imulsion. The world would run on it." Brandon sighed. "You know, all those people who talked to you, they think they were in the thick of it, but they just had front-row seats. They're what historians would call witnesses to history. You, and Colonel Hoffman, you were making history. These folks won't ever see the difference."

"Which were you? Witness or a maker?"

"Depends on the day and who's telling the story." Brandon shrugged. "Fact is, I spent most of my time getting stuff for people. Made life interesting."

Marcus' eyes narrowed. Part of him thought Turrall was playing it coy so Marcus would ask him for details. The better part of him recognized the man was setting boundaries. He could respect that.

I'm sitting here behind nine rings of walls and a moat. Turrall wants to stay behind his walls, not my business to tear them down.

The Gear chuckled to himself. *I don't believe that. I want to know what's going on with Turrall. He's an outlier. He's a potential enemy. To leave him an unknown quantity means he remains a threat.* But if Marcus began to burrow in and question the man, Turrall would come right back at him. *I don't need anyone rooting around in my skull. He may think he knows, but he doesn't.*

None of them do.

"Marcus, I'm glad I found you."

Marcus looked over as Anya returned to his side. "Everything okay?"

"I think?" Anya turned and offered Turrall her hand. "Anya Stroud."

"Brandon Turrall." The man smiled easily. "I'd offer you what I gave Sergeant Fenix, but I'm thinking you deserve better, and he'd be a mite pissed if you felt obliged to drink it."

"Well, then, perhaps I'll just have another glass of wine."

Marcus plucked a red wine from the table and handed it to her. "Anything I need to know?"

"It'll keep." Anya raised her glass. "To a new dawn, and all the possibilities it brings."

"Brilliant notion." Turrall clinked his glass against hers. "To a new dawn."

Marcus nodded. "And possibilities."

Anya drank. "Let's hope we make the most of all of them."

6: STROUD ESTATE

NEAR EPHYRA, SERA

16 HARVEST 18 A.E.

Marcus could still feel the resonation of the glasses touching throughout the gallery, could still hear the echoing *clink,* could still see wine and whiskey sloshing, when the Locust erupted through the floor. Marble cracked. Splinters flew, along with people. Bodies spun lazily, gallons of blood splashing against the walls then dripping down over portraits and repainting peaceful landscapes into charnel fields.

The Locust—bulky, scaly humanoids—reached out and grabbed partygoers. They ripped off arms, bit off heads. More blood geysered. The invaders were awash with it, gore dripping from them, mixing with saliva. They wielded torn limbs as clubs, battering people, breaking them, knocking them aside as if they had no bones or mass. In an instant perfectly well-tailored and preserved clothes became rags.

Their roaring drowned out the band, which valiantly kept playing. For a time they managed even to stay in tune, then one

Locust Gnasher blew the flautist in half. Her insides sprayed over the outsides of the other musicians. The bassoonist discovered that his horn did not function as a shield, and then that it functioned no better as a weapon. The Drone snatched it away from him, then dashed his brains out with the instrument.

Not again! Marcus hurled his glass at a Locust, smashing it against the creature's domed head. He dashed past Anya and snatched a wine bottle from a terrified server's hand, then backhanded a Locust across the face, shattering the bottle. With the jagged neck in his right hand, Marcus stabbed the grub in the throat. Black blood gushed, steaming and stinging, but the Locust picked him up and hurled him halfway across the room. He smashed into the wall, smacking his head. Stunned, he slid to the ground and the painting that had hung above him tumbled down into his hands.

Somehow Marcus caught it. A landscape. He couldn't read the small bronze plate on the frame, but he knew the place. *The Stroud Estate.*

We will rebuild it. We will make it our future.

A clawed hand swept through the painting, reducing the canvas to ribbons. The Locust shook the frame off its hand, then grabbed Marcus by the wrists. It lifted him up, pinning his hands high against the wall, and using its body to trap Marcus' legs. Peering over its head he saw the reception drown in waves of blood, with heads bobbing and Locust wading through. A blonde woman in a green dress bobbed to the surface, grabbing at anything that would allow her to stay afloat. She clutched at a corpse, but her grip slipped. She went under again, red bubbles marking her disappearance.

He stared, waiting for her to surface again, but saw only the bubbles. Bubbles growing smaller and smaller with each passing heartbeat, and as they shrank, his conviction grew that he knew the woman's identity.

Anya!

His throat tightened, strangling off his shout. He got his feet against the wall, tried to push off, to knock the Locust away, but it just laughed. It opened its mouth, displaying gray needle-teeth, and bit into his stomach.

Marcus sat bolt upright in bed, throat aching, sweat pouring off him. He covered his face with his hands, thankful for the sweat burning his eyes. He focused on the stinging as the dregs of the dream melted. The ocean of blood flowed back into the floor and the people reassembled themselves. His chest heaved as he drew his knees up and rested his forehead on them.

Anya's hands settled gently on his shoulders. "Dom again?"

"Different dream. Same shit." He reached back with his right hand and found her knee, squeezing it. "I'm sorry for waking you. Let me just grab a blanket and…"

"No, Marcus." She leaned in and kissed his head. "If you want to tell me about it, I'll listen."

"No, it's… it was weird. Not from the war. Not entirely." He shrugged. "Dom got to rest easy."

"What happened?" Anya shifted around, sitting side by side with him, but facing him. She rested her hand on his shoulder.

"Locust, you know. At the reception last night."

"And not a gun in sight. No way to defend yourself." She nodded. "I have to say I felt that lack, too."

"So many people not understanding." He rubbed a hand over his forehead. "There was a portrait of this place, your family's home, and a grub shredded it."

"That's not a dream, Marcus, that's reality." Anya took his right hand in hers and kissed the back of it. "We have a lot of their handiwork to undo here."

"One brick at a time."

"Do you think you had this dream because of what Jamila Shin spoke about with me?"

"About organizing people, maybe making a government?" He gave her a wry grin. "Just because I don't like psychology doesn't mean I don't understand it. Sure, new challenges. Challenges where guns won't be useful. I was as useful as a toddler in a minefield at that reception. Shrinks would call it an anxiety dream, right?"

"I think that depends on whether you were naked or not." She glanced down. "If you don't think I should do this—"

He squeezed her hand. "Stop. I have always trusted you to make the right decision. I've bet my life on it, over and over. I'd be an idiot to second guess you."

"I'm glad you trust me, Marcus. I'm not sure I do. Not with this one. It's something bigger than me, massive, and I've seen what that can do to people. My mother." Anya swept her free hand around to take in the estate. "The reason I never spent much time here was that my mother chose to serve the COG, to devote herself to something bigger than herself. Her family hated it. I don't think they were right to do that, but that same devotion was what got my mother killed. And you and me, we've spent the majority of our lives dealing with something bigger than ourselves. We've devoted ourselves to it. I guess part of me thought we'd have the chance to step back, at least for a bit."

"Hey, I did, too." Marcus smiled at her, stroking her cheek with a finger. "To tell the truth, I knew it would be tougher for you than me. You have so much talent. How could anyone miss it? What surprised me was that it took them so long to come asking."

"It's not like there is that much talent left to choose from."

"Most of the folks last night wouldn't have shared your opinion." Marcus slowly shook his head. "We've seen it countless times. Folks who *want* to be talented, but..."

"Their only talent lay in the fact that their father owned something. Yes. Surround those people with enough competent folks, and you could prevent them from doing too much damage. At least it used to be that way, but now, with so much damage already done, society is so fragile." Anya raked fingers back through her hair. "Jamila Shin introduced me to a number of people, and I could see it in their eyes. Fear. They make a wrong step and the tenuous threads of civilization just unravel. Most of the people there would have walked away from the risk, but they knew that *if* they walked away, the grubs would have succeeded in destroying us, doing it from the grave."

Marcus felt tightness in his belly. "You see things the way they do, too?"

"You must, as well."

He shook his head. "I leave operational and strategic thinking to you and Colonel Hoffman. I'm tactics. You decide that we need a school, give me coordinates, a sketch of what you want, and I'll have it there for you. I don't need to know why. I trust that *you* know why."

She leaned in and kissed him on the lips. "Thank you."

"Welcome."

Anya sat back on her heels. "If I go to work with Jamila and get involved in rebuilding society, I feel as if I'll be abandoning you."

"But I don't." Marcus slipped from the bed and spread his arms wide. "You've taken care of me for a long time. Now I get to return the favor."

"You don't owe me, Marcus."

"I know, but maybe I owe myself." He pointed at the bedroom entrance—an eight-pane glass door he'd salvaged from the ground floor. "Wrestling that thing up here, replacing the broken panes, hanging it, that's the first constructive thing I've done in forever."

"What you accomplished with Delta wasn't nothing, Marcus."

"This is different. We agreed to come here, to build a future for us. You working on keeping humanity together, it will be part of that." He chuckled. "And you don't want to be around when I hit my thumb with a hammer."

"Like I haven't heard you curse before, Sergeant Fenix."

"True, but maybe *Mister* Fenix doesn't swear."

Anya tugged the sheet from the bed and wrapped it around her as she stood. "Mister Fenix. That's different. So you'll have my dinner on the table when I get home?"

"If that's what you want. You know, you don't have to be your mom. I don't have to be my father. We have a chance to decide who we want to be."

She walked over to him. He reached out, and she settled herself in the circle of his enclosing arms. "Well, I can't be my mother, since I'm well past the age when she had me."

"That doesn't mean you can't still be a mom, and a great one." Marcus kissed her forehead. "We've seen them, kids who need homes. So many people have died and left little ones behind."

"And non-swearing Mister Marcus Fenix will be the perfect dad, right?"

"As best I can." He lifted her chin so he could look into her eyes. "Of course, any kid raised under this roof will be plenty smart and all trouble, so I might backslide on that cursing thing. But our kid will be squared away."

"You'll have him saluting before he can walk, and making up a tight bunk." Anya laughed. "I can see it."

"And I'll be a better father than mine was."

"Marcus, Adam loved you…"

Tightening his hug, he just drank in her warmth for a moment or two.

"He did, in his way, but in that moment when he knew my mother was dead, when he knew I was going to need him more than I ever had before, he lied to me about her. Sure, to save me pain. To delay it. But I knew, and knew I couldn't trust him. It took Dom and Carlos and you to let me trust again. I won't do that to our children."

"I know, Marcus."

"I am serious, Anya. You'll see." He held her out at arm's length and smiled. "You didn't grow up here, but our family will and it will be great. We'll rebuild. East wing first, and the greenhouse in the garden. The main building only needs touch-ups, so we'll have time, but this will be a home for them, for us."

She caressed his cheek. "Don't take this as me doubting you, Mr. Fenix. I mean, I love our new door here, but how are you going to put the rest of this estate back together?"

Marcus scratched at the back of his neck. "Well, you're right, I've never built a building, but I have taken a few apart. I was thinking I would just reverse the process. That ought to work."

"Maybe you can reach out to Damon. He could help you with some of the finer points of structural physics."

"Anya, Baird will just talk the thing to death. And it will look funny."

"And probably blow up. Still…"

Marcus laughed. "It might keep him out of trouble for a while." Then, before the echoes of his laugh could fade, Marcus felt certain that Baird's visiting wouldn't work. *Not yet. I'd just bring him down. This is something I have to handle on my own.*

Marcus rubbed a hand over his jaw. "You're meeting with Dr. Shin today, yes?"

"Yes, she wanted to get organized as fast as possible. It's just… Marcus, there's so much we don't know, so much that's just out there."

"And no one better than you to handle it." He settled his arms around her again and hugged her. "I can't count the times, when pure insanity was exploding all around us, your calm voice came through the comms. You knew right where we needed to go. You were that link to sanity. That's what Shin needs. What Sera needs."

"How about you, Marcus? Is it what you need?"

"Always." He kissed her forehead. "More immediately, though, I need to know what you expect out of how I should be keeping your family estate."

She pulled back and looked up into his eyes. "You want a mission brief?"

"Reporting for duty, ma'am."

"Oh, you are *so* going to pay for that."

"If you can't do the time…" He smiled easily. "But I'm serious. Should I make you a lunch? What do you want for dinner?"

"You're going to perfect being a chef now, too?"

"There are depths to me you can only begin to guess at, Anya Stroud." He shrugged quickly. "I'll need to scrounge for some food, and finalizing the greenhouse repairs will be a necessity. I'll clear out as much as I can downstairs. Kitchen seems to be in decent shape, so probably start there. You know, securing a base."

"Okay, but don't use explosives."

"I'm saving those for plowing up some space on the south lawn, for planting. That's how it's done, isn't it?"

"Marcus, I think there's a reason the verb is *plow*." She stood up on tiptoes and kissed the point of his nose. "But I know you will do it all perfectly."

"Well, this place, it's a big part of our tomorrow. So, yes, perfect." He squeezed her again. "You fix the world, and I'll fix this corner of it."

7: MINISTRY OF SANITATION

EPHYRA, SERA

16 HARVEST 18 A.E.

Anya Stroud paused a moment at the foot of the stairs leading up to the ministry. They had seen the ravages of war. Chipped here, cracked there, with holes pockmarking the granite slope, they would require Anya to take a zig-zag route to reach her destination. She'd even have to backtrack in a couple of places and balance as she mounted a board someone had placed across one of the larger craters.

The landscape seemed an omen to her.

True, it reflected the state of Sera. The Locust and then Lambent had savaged the world. She'd seen so much destruction. *I contributed to it, most of the time unavoidably.* But she'd seen wounds close and heal among her friends. *That has to be my goal here, to help heal the wounds, the world.*

The Ministry of Sanitation building itself had seen better days, as well, but had managed to avoid too much damage from the Lambent. One stalk had twisted its way out through the facade.

It had shattered a huge glass panel, then curved up toward the roof. Dead, it reminded her of ivy, albeit monstrous and out of control. Still, it hadn't crushed the building's lines, and sunlight still glinted from intact windows.

Anya mounted the stairs and carefully negotiated her way to the plaza, then on into the ministry. Debris littered the marble-floored foyer, but someone had cleared a small path to the curving staircase that led up to the second floor. Anya followed that path up, and then along a relatively clean corridor deeper into the building. About halfway down a door stood open on the right.

Anya rapped on the office's doorjamb. The reception room contained a small desk and some cabinets, as well as a couple of tables someone had tacked together from bits of other furniture. A bunch of folding wooden chairs had been stacked in the corner, with one behind the desk and two others at the tables. In the far corner, on the outer wall, a door lay open to another office.

She encountered no one in the reception area, so she moved to the next door. In the office beyond, Jamila Shin—clad in workaday clothes, not the elegant fashion from the reception—steadied a portable blackboard as a young man with a wrench tightened a bolt. Anya quickly joined them, further stabilizing the blackboard, as the young man finished his final adjustments.

"Ah, Anya, I'd hoped to have things a bit more organized before you got here." Jamila gave her a quick hug. "Eventually we hope to have some computers up and running, but power is a bit spotty right now, so I thought hard copy would be good until we advance beyond the Stone Age."

The young man offered Anya his hand. "Thomas Ndara. Most folks call me Tom."

"Anya."

Jamila gave Tom a look. "This is Lieutenant Anya Stroud. She, and the rest of Delta Squad, put an end to the Lambent crisis."

Tom straightened up. "Pleased to meet you, Lieutenant. Thank you."

Anya held her hands up. "I'm just Anya Stroud now. Isn't that right, Jamila? We don't really have an army or a command structure."

"We don't have anything, Anya." Jamila scrubbed some dust from her left sleeve. "Right now we have Tom, who has been working like a dog to clear things up. He was educated with my son, Simon. He's practically a second son, and a dear."

Thomas smiled. "Simon says you like me better."

"There are times." Jamila laughed lightly. "Tom is completely trustworthy, and very resourceful, and throughout the city we have other people finding offices just like this, setting up their own space. Most of them you saw at the reception last night. A few may join us here…"

Tom smiled. "This ministry building suffered the smallest amount of damage, but it isn't that glamorous. There are a couple more offices on this floor, still in good shape, so you have your pick."

"At least it's suitable for cleaning things up, so it's good to my mind." Anya looked around for a clean surface on which she might sit, but a half-dozen computers and printers covered both desks and a long table, waiting for a jigsaw-puzzle genius to assemble them. "What exactly *are* we cleaning up?"

Tom handed Jamila a stubby piece of yellow chalk. She rattled it around in her hand as if it was a die she was preparing to roll. "To answer that, we have to break things down into goals. Primary needs would be food, water, and shelter. We'll toss basic sanitation in there, too, because having a disease rip through the population could easily finish off what the Locust started."

Anya nodded. "What are the estimates of the population?"

Jamila frowned. "We don't know—we have bad guesses, but no accurate estimates."

Tom scratched at the back of his neck. "Survivors are scattered all over. Because the Locust hit the big cities…"

"… while we hit *back* in the big cities." Anya winced. "You're telling me that people left to avoid places they thought the Locust were drawn to. And I already know the COG wasn't well loved out there. Still, if Griffin is here, there must be a good number of people in Char. Hanover, other big cities, must have people."

"They do, but we have no head count," Tom said. "I've been gathering as much data as I can for Dr. Shin, but everyone is jealously guarding the numbers."

Jamila had written *food, water, sanitation, shelter*, and *energy* on the board. "People are seeing their home populations as basic constituencies—even though we have no government, no system for voting, and certainly no votes to indicate the populace's confidence in us. We also have no idea if the people who have returned to the cities constitute the majority of the survivors, or if there are dozens of Stranded enclaves out there, which might outnumber us.

"The greater the population we have with us, however," she continued, "the greater the chances we have of rebuilding. It will be the concentration of knowledge and skill that will make it easier to pass those skills on."

"Right." Anya rubbed her forehead. "If there's a settlement out there, and no one knows how to put together a computer, they won't reap the benefits of having a computer to manage tasks. On a more fundamental level, we need bodies to work so we can rebuild."

"But with everything in survival mode—food being scarce, water potentially unsafe, and so many buildings structurally unstable—convincing people to return, to leave the safety of an enclave where they've lived in relative peace for the last two or three years, may be impossible." Jamila hugged herself. "And while I am in favor of Ephyra being where we rebuild, everyone has their own candidate. In some of those cases, there are people who are vying for power, which greatly complicates things."

"So we don't have a handle on vital pieces of information. And we're going to build from there?" Anya felt tension rising in her shoulders. "This is just a bottomless pit of fun."

Jamila nodded. "Now you see why I wanted you to join us. Thoughts?"

"A couple, maybe." Anya clasped her hands at the small of her back. "The situation calls for leadership, and I would be a fool to think there aren't a bunch of people believing that they alone should fill that role. They appoint themselves, gather some lieutenants to enforce their decrees, and pull people together—potentially against their will. Once they all start working in the same direction, they decide that their leader is right and start participating on a voluntary basis. Their area begins to prosper, and that draws more people.

"It could work, but based on my experience in the military, it has one core issue. Leaders like that tend to prioritize themselves and their desires ahead of those they govern. It seldom ends well."

"Those who hunger to lead seldom make the best leaders." Jamila smiled grimly.

"This leads me to think that we should skip the first step, and move straight to the benefit side." Anya spread her arms. "Ephyra's sanitation system should have included waste-water processing. What do we know about that?"

Tom folded his arms over his chest. "We don't know if the treatment plant was hit or not. There are leech fields and lagoons out there. The water isn't suitable for drinking, but irrigation, sure. Solid waste can be used as fertilizer and burned for fuel, if dried."

"I know that area. I saw the sewage plant when I was coming in this morning. Have you been out there?"

Tom shook his head.

Jamila's eyes narrowed. "What are you thinking, Anya?"

"The plant had laboratories for testing water—identifying biological agents and chemicals and so forth. I think it had its own power plant, too. If those facilities are still in good shape, I'd suggest we install people to make use of them. Damon Baird is a friend from Delta…"

"I know his name, Anya."

"Good. He's smart and inventive. He understands the tech we've been using, and is the sort of genius we need to recover information and skills we're at risk of losing." Anya smiled. "Don't tell him I said that, though. His ego will balloon up in a heartbeat. But he would be perfect for handling our needs out there."

"If you're confident he would agree, I think it's an excellent plan."

"Okay, so what I'm thinking is that if we take the water treatment plant, we can do a number of things. First, we can supply fuel and water—gray water can be made potable, and I'm sure the plant contained a small-scale purification system as part of the testing equipment. If not, Damon will be able to cobble one together. So what we do is give people water and fuel in return for some labor. Bring a bucket of debris, get a bucket of water. Rehab pipes and fixtures from ruins, you get access to running water when we make it work."

Jamila nodded. "Clearing projects will open up land which can be irrigated and planted. Building goes on near those fields we make usable. Sanitation we tie back into the sewer system, and to secure food you trade scrounged items for water."

"Until we can harvest what we've planted." Anya nodded back. "I'm sure Baird will have some suggestions on what else we can do to provide for people's basic needs."

Tom raised a hand. "Any clean-up is going to have to include dealing with the dead. There are bodies… *everywhere*."

Anya's heart sank. "There's no way to identify them, is there? As a Gear, we all gave DNA samples so they could sort our corpses out, but I guess that repository is gone—and few of these people would have been in the database, anyway. People will just never know."

The older woman added *identify bodies and deal with them* on the blackboard. "Practically speaking, mass graves and pyres make the most sense, but you raise a good point, in that we'll need to begin to track the dead and missing. In particular we'll need registrars for the dead. Perhaps Mr. Baird can determine what we'll need for samples, so we can keep traces that will be viable for analysis later."

"Right. We're also going to need to find anyone with medical training, identify a hospital we can get up and running again, and make that happen." Then Anya shook her head. "Sera was a big earthenware jug that got pounded to dust with sledgehammers, and we're going to rebuild it without even having glue."

"Oh, no, Anya, you've identified the glue, first thing. We offer the people the things they need. It's caring for them that will enlist them as our allies." Jamila wrote *service* on the board and underlined it twice. "Once they realize we are working for them, they will *want* to help out. They will join us and, if we listen, they'll tell us what else they need and how to satisfy that need."

"It's still a big puzzle to put together."

"But we will get there." Jamila tapped a finger against her chin, depositing a tiny smear of yellow chalk-dust. "There is one other thing we need to determine. It may seem silly, but could make or break our effort."

Anya raised an eyebrow. "What's that?"

"What will we call ourselves?"

"You mean us, or what we're doing?"

"Precisely. If people are going to join something, they have to be able to identify that thing." Jamila deposited the chalk in the blackboard tray, then rubbed her hands together to get rid of the dust. "Calling ourselves COG, or even New COG, would be to borrow a great deal of trouble. Likewise Coalition. Yet 'partnership,' or any variation of that, isn't grand enough to encompass what we want to do."

Tom nodded. "Anything that sounds military would probably hurt us, because of resentment toward the COG and, since we don't have a military, would leave us open to being mocked as weak."

Anya rubbed at her temples. Part of her couldn't believe they were even *having* this discussion when there was so much work to do. By the same token, she understood the need people felt to *belong* to something, especially if it was greater than themselves and the problems they faced. People would be trying to survive every day, and having a sense that they weren't alone would be important.

She looked up. "I think you already have it. We're here, in a building called the Ministry of Sanitation. We should just be the Ministry. It's not threatening. The building stands, so it works as a symbol. Sanitation is what we'll be doing, at least in part, so we're telling the truth. When others join us here, they become ministers in charge of whatever they're going to be doing."

"That works." Tom smiled. "And the chief minister coordinates everyone else."

Jamila shook her head. "Not chief minister, *first* minister. The first among equals."

Anya clapped. "Well said, First Minister."

"It's not a position I want. For the time being, let me do the work and worry about a title later. I would be happy to have anyone else be the figurehead, but because I organized the reception last night and will have to organize a subsequent meeting to bind us all together, I think I am stuck."

"You *are* the only one who can do it." Anya frowned. "So here's a question: how much of what we do will we share with the others? Griffin, for example, might find what we're doing useful in rebuilding Char. So do we share it with him, or force him to go his own way?"

"Excellent question. What do you think, Anya?"

"We share most of it, horse-trade for other things they have that we need. People will be suspicious. They'll think we're holding something back. So we will: the things we want to trade for. But in that scenario they'll trust the things we give away, and those things will be good for the people. As you wrote there: 'service.' We'd be stupid if we didn't try to help everyone."

Tom frowned.

"Something to add, Tom?" Jamila said.

The young man shook his head. "No, I think sharing is good. I suppose it will prevent folks from spending a lot of time trying to figure out what we're *really* up to."

"Good. We are agreed, then." Jamila returned to the board and retrieved the chalk. "Now we break everything down again. And then again. When we can't do that anymore, that's where we start rebuilding and give ourselves a world worthy of memorializing the sacrifice of those who have died."

8: STROUD ESTATE

NEAR EPHYRA, SERA
25 HARVEST 18 A.E.

Marcus settled into something of a routine.

He started by checking the estate's lands for more signs of squatters. Though he always carried a pistol and a shovel, he told himself that his main concern was that he might discover more people like the mother and child, and that he would do for them what should be done. He made his purpose a mission of mercy, because otherwise he would have admitted to himself that he was patrolling the grounds, much as he patrolled when fighting the grubs.

The Stroud Estate extended deep into the countryside. Beyond the hills where grapes grew, the land tapered down into woods. Marcus located a modest stone house half a mile into the forest, just beyond a grub-carved gash in the landscape. When he told Anya about the cabin, she explained it had been a gamekeeper's house, but that her great-grandmother had remade it into an artist's studio. She couldn't recall what sort of art her great-grandmother had created, and no sign of it remained.

Someone had clearly broken in, but the break-in didn't appear recent. He suspected squatters, but found no tracks outside to suggest which way they had gone when they left. A hundred yards downslope a brook cut through the property, so it had plenty of water, and the forest gave up lots of dead wood for fuel. The windows had somehow survived intact.

Their placement gives good fields of fire on all sides.

Marcus caught himself. *You're a civilian now. Fields of fire aren't things you need worry about.* Still, in the interest of safety, he spent several mornings cutting back the undergrowth—for fire prevention. But if there ever was a firefight near the cabin, the clear space would make approaching the building suicidal for attackers.

During his wanderings he saw very little sign of encroachment on the estate, and that surprised him. The lands had water, grapes, some vegetables that grew wild. The fields could clearly support anyone wanting to plant food and work, and weren't too far from the outskirts of Ephyra. While the two wings on the big house had taken damage, the main building was sound, the outbuildings even more so. It really made no sense that people hadn't moved in.

By mid-morning he'd completed the circuit and returned to the main house, but did whatever he could to avoid the kitchen. Therein lurked his nemesis. He knew it was ridiculous to think about it like that. He'd fought his way through life for as long as he could remember, and had killed legions of anything that opposed him.

All of my nemeses have died, which is the damned problem with this one.

He worked around the house, clearing up as much debris as he could. Scrap that might be useful went into one pile, debris he could burn for fuel went into another. He pounded nails straight, sawed boards down, knocked mortar off bricks he wanted to reuse, and even salvaged tiny pieces of a mosaic or two which had decorated the foyer. All the while he avoided the kitchen, and yet it lurked in the back of his mind, stalking him.

Finally, as the sun passed noon, he entered the kitchen and stared at the jar. It just sat there with a pasty-white blob in the bottom. He'd put a rubber band around the jar, marking the blob's level from the previous day. It had maybe risen an inch or so above that mark.

"You're teasing me, that's it. Just teasing."

Marcus scratched at the back of his head. In clearing up rubble he'd found a well-worn cookbook that had instructions for making almost anything. In a section called "Basics" the author described the simple joy of creating and nurturing a sourdough starter. All Marcus had to do was mix flour and water in equal measures and let the naturally occurring yeast in the air settle on the goopy mixture, and it would begin to grow and breathe and expand.

Just like it's fairy dust.

Once a day, as per the instructions, he'd throw half the mix out, feed it more flour and water, set the rubber band to the correct level, and wait. For bubbles. For the starter to rise. For something. *Anything.*

"Rise, damn you, rise!"

The starter just sat there.

Marcus pressed his hands flat on the table and forced himself to breathe. "This isn't Imulsion physics. You don't need to be Baird or your dad to do this." The book had said it could take as much as a week to get the starter going, and Marcus still had a couple of days to go. So he carefully discarded half of the starter, added water and flour, and stirred. He scraped down the sides and set the rubber band to the right height on the glass jar's exterior.

He stared at the jar again, and tried to figure out how to ask it to grow. He wasn't going to beg, and threats hadn't worked.

It's a living thing, Marcus. You can do this.

Maybe you can't. The doubt came to him in his father's voice. The voice of the man who had discovered that Imulsion was a living thing, the lifeblood of Sera. The voice of the man who'd had to destroy Imulsion to save the world and stop the Lambent.

Unbidden, the look on Adam Fenix's face came to him from the time when Marcus told him that he was becoming a Gear. Marcus hadn't understood it then, but he had been watching his father's hopes and dreams for him die. Hopes that Marcus might be able to avoid the military and put his talents to use alongside his father in a research lab. Adam couldn't tell Marcus that because of the fear that it would deepen the rift between them, driving them apart, perhaps forever.

Marcus' stomach began to flip-flop and he sat down on a wooden chair. He hunched forward, elbows on knees, and hung his head.

Would I have even listened to him? Would I have been a help to him? Or would I have killed his experiments the way I've killed that starter? The way I kill everything.

Memories exploded in Marcus' mind. The scent of Locust ichor, breathed in as a mist after a bullet blew through the skull. Or the pinpricks of bone splinters as he used the Lancer's bayonet to carve his way through an enemy. The screams of terrified civilians being cut short, and the slowly dwindling whimpers of a Gear too grievously wounded to survive. The crunch of bones underfoot, or slipping on some creature's greasy viscera. Days without showers or clean clothes. Days of not remembering when he'd last had a warm meal.

His chest got tight. *Is that it? Am I a creature so steeped in war and killing that killing is all I can do? Is killing the only thing I'm good at? I mean, Baird has his science and Cole is, well, the Cole Train, and Dom, he had his tomatoes... Dom and his tomatoes...*

Marcus smiled as tears began to leak from his eyes.

Damn Dom and his tomatoes...

He remembered his friend working hard to nurture the plants on the deck of a ship, just to have Lambent destroy them. *They were all Dom had left. And then...*

"Damnit, Dom!"

The world blurred.

Sunlight had faded by the time Marcus came back to being himself. That so much time had passed surprised him. The fact that he couldn't remember what had gone on during that time scared him.

If this had happened in the field...

Shivering, he forced himself to stand up.

He glanced at the starter in the jar. Thought it might have just barely crept above the red rubber band, just a little bit. But, more importantly, a bubble had formed. "You're still teasing me. I know that, but I'm going to win you over. I am."

Marcus grunted. *I may be good at killing, but I'm best at*

surviving and winning. Anya had her challenges and he had his. *And she's depending on me to carry my own weight.*

Anya was still in Ephyra, so he set out to check the snares and traps he'd set out around the estate. While he hadn't seen many signs of other people, rabbits abounded. Absent any natural predators—and he'd not seen a fox or a dog either—they'd bred out of control. Basic survival courses had taught him how to live off the land, and the rabbits didn't appear to be too clever or timid when it came to his traps.

Already he'd gotten two fairly plump ones. He snapped their necks, then cleaned them out and skinned them. He took the skins down to the barn, where he tacked them to a board so they could dry out, then took the carcasses back up to the house and built a small fire over which to roast them.

Being out on a patio just off the kitchen, under an open sky, with stars sprayed across the heavens, suited Marcus just fine. The kitchen had a full complement of appliances, none of which worked without power, and that was unreliably intermittent. Without dependable energy the appliances were just pretty hunks of metal. He figured that over the winter he'd try to harvest ice, store it in the barn, and use it to cool down the refrigerator in the warm months, since the insulation still worked.

That thought crystalized for him how much the world had lost. He'd taken survival courses, and they gave him the skills he needed to continue living. But those courses had been predicated on his being in a hostile environment with absolutely nothing.

That's how far civilization has fallen. People, most of whom had never been tied to the land or had ever killed anything, now had to learn those skills. *But who is teaching them? Who can they turn to?*

"Can they even survive?" He glanced at the greenhouse.

He'd replaced most of the windows and boarded up the few that remained. He'd patched up the planting beds and dug up what he hoped was good earth for growing things. But what he knew about botany he'd learned from Dom while helping him start his garden on the *CNV Sovereign*. He even had some seeds—tomatoes he thought—that Dom had sealed in a small bottle for him.

"Someday you may need to learn to feed yourself. I can't carry you forever." Dom had said it with a smile. Only his eyes had revealed the pain he felt at the loss of Maria's presence, of the death of their children and their family. Marcus hadn't seen it then, mainly because he didn't want to see it, but Dom had changed after Maria's death. He had lived for her, in hopes of finding her and saving her.

"You're right, Dom. Looks like today is the day I'll need to learn to feed myself." The tomato seeds would help, though Marcus remembered Dom swearing a fair amount as he nurtured the seedlings. He could do that in the greenhouse, and perhaps even get some fruit over the winter, but tomatoes wouldn't be enough to sustain even the two of them. Marcus didn't expect the Stroud stash of survival rations to last very long past spring.

It seemed to him that the reason he hadn't seen much evidence of people encroaching on the estate was that, as Anya had suggested to him, a lot fewer people remained than anyone cared to imagine. It seemed likely to him that those people probably had lots of arable land, so they didn't need the estate. Moreover, this late in the season, they'd have harvested any crops they'd managed to raise in the last six months, so he might be able to bargain with them for food and seeds.

Rabbit skins, if he could figure out how to cure them, could be worth something, and the vinegar, that might also be good for trading. He'd hang onto the good wine—the reception suggested how much that might be worth to certain people.

And there are grapes on the vines…

A stick popped in the fire. Sparks exploded in all directions.

Before Marcus realized it he'd dropped into a crouch and had drawn his sidearm. He glanced around, searching for Locust in the lengthening shadows, waiting to feel a Lambent stalk erupt from the ground. He could hear something moving out there, something rustling through leaves, but couldn't see it.

Then the fire popped a couple more times. A sparrow flew up from beneath a bush and perched on the edge of the roof.

Marcus let out breath he'd not realized he was holding. He lowered the pistol, but didn't slip it back into the holster. Sweat stung his eyes. He swiped at it with his free hand, then flicked droplets away. His heart fluttered in his chest much like the sparrow as it flew off. A wave of exhaustion washed over him.

Get it together, Fenix. He shivered as a breeze cooled his damp skin. He was sweating as if he'd been in an hour-long firefight. As he stood he felt awkward, since he didn't have his armor clinging to him. He felt naked. He went to shove the pistol home in the holster, but missed on the first try.

Deep breath. He slowed his breathing and became more deliberate in everything else, then flipped the rabbits over to keep them roasting on the other side. Picking up some wild greens he'd harvested from the garden, he washed them off, then put them in a bowl, which he placed on the table inside. He set the table, forcing himself to pay attention to what he was doing.

Then he turned around and looked at the jar of starter sitting there on the counter. A couple more bubbles had developed, and the mass had risen almost half an inch above the rubber band all the way around.

He smiled. "You're not my nemesis, you're an example. You get better day by day. That's the way I have to do it, too. For me, for Anya, for whoever is left. I owe that much to everybody who isn't here."

9: PEOPLE'S MARKET

EPHYRA, SERA
27 HARVEST 18 A.E.

Marcus' guts roiled as they used to do before heading into combat. Nothing debilitating, just an uneasy sense that reminded him that he was mortal. Traveling without armor, carrying a pistol hidden at the small of his back, intensified the feeling. He forced himself to focus and take things slowly, keeping to the fringe, scoping out exits and points which, if trouble was to come, he'd want to avoid.

He'd taken his first extended walk—*not patrol*, walk—the previous day, heading roughly toward Ephyra. He stayed off the roads, but let his course parallel them, and then on up to hilltops so he could better survey the area. He saw a couple of small farms: a house, barn, vegetable garden with some cold frames and maybe three or four acres under cultivation.

Whatever they'd been growing had been harvested, leaving the fields just brown dirt with cut stalks and leaves blowing about in the breeze. In terms of livestock he saw a fair number of chickens, a few pigs, but only one of the farms had enough dairy cows to be considered a herd.

He decided against approaching any of them and continued on. Occasionally one of the inhabitants paused and watched him for a bit. A couple of them waved, and he waved back. The people appeared cautious, but no one ran to fetch a gun, which he took as a good sign. The fact that none of them beckoned for him to come down and visit he took as yet another sign.

The fourth farm closely resembled the Stroud Estate in terms of having more buildings and some land dedicated to raising grapes. The main building, which was smaller than its Stroud counterpart, had taken little or no damage during the Locust War.

Or they've repaired it. They'd also found and hauled in a number of storage containers and an old bus. These they'd arranged in a semicircle to the northeast and dug into the ground. They'd used excess earth to build hills around them, and seeded it, creating bunkers. A couple of young kids played in the semicircle and for the first time Marcus saw some dogs— albeit curly-tailed mongrels.

He studied the farm for a bit and estimated the population at about twenty, including the kids. Mostly young, the population seemed split almost evenly male and female. Two of the women were pregnant, and one other had an infant she lugged around. An older couple appeared to know everyone and tended to be the center of attention, but Marcus didn't see either of them giving orders, and he also didn't see anyone wearing guns.

Most intriguing of all, they'd posted a big sign near the road.

1 Day to the People's Market.
All are welcome to buy or trade.

The number had been painted on a slat and hung on the sign, apparently being replaced each day as time to the market counted down. A couple of the men were scything the grass down on a patch of land near the sign, while other people hauled tents from the equipment barn and began setting them up.

Marcus continued his walk for a short while longer, then headed back to the estate. There he and his starter fought another battle in which the starter feigned resistance to his work, but did give off a faintly sour aroma.

Marcus' eyes narrowed. "You're not fooling me."

The starter chose to remain silent.

He pretended to ignore it and went to work continuing to clear debris from the estate's west wing. From the looks of things, with partial walls overgrown with ivy and the weathering of the hardwood on the floors, the damage likely had occurred early on in the Locust War. He didn't think Anya had been back in the last sixteen years, so there might never be a way of knowing.

Even as he cleared bricks and piled them up in the yard, he didn't find any trace of what had done the damage, though he'd seen enough in the past to know that a roving band of Locust could have easily blown through the wings and left the central building untouched.

They'd do it simply because it was in the way.

He found no sign of an eruption point, but hadn't expected to. If they'd come up through the estate, there would have been nothing left. The Locust could—and often did—appear almost anywhere. Still, the right combination of bedrock layers tended to deter them. They'd clearly come up somewhere else and had been roving. He knew he should try to find the egress point, but at that thought, weariness washed over him.

I've ventured into my fill of those holes. No more. The Locust are all gone. Imulsion. Lambent. Gone. Marcus straightened up, his back aching. The wars, the deaths, they seemed forever ago. They seemed almost unreal, and yet the pain of losing those who had fought by his side knifed him. Their sacrifices allowed him to be there, allowed him to survive. *To pretend—to let myself imagine the Locust were just a bad dream—betrays those heroes.*

He made another circuit around the grounds and checked his snares. He'd gotten one more rabbit, which he processed and, as dusk came on, began to roast over a fire. He sat by the fire, staring into the coals, attempting to look deeper. He felt the heat but it failed to warm him. As the flames guttered he remembered other fires. *So many other fires.* Fires that had consumed Locust and friends alike, reducing them to ash. *Leaving nothing to remember them by.*

"How much longer do you think for the rabbit?"

Marcus looked up, his eyes slowly adjusting to the darkness. "Yeah, sorry. How long have you been here?" He peered past Anya at the small table she'd set with their mismatched dishes. "How long have I been...?"

"Not too long. You were lost in thought, so I got the dishes, lit the candle." She came over and sat beside him, tossing another couple of sticks on the fire. "Penny for your thoughts?"

"You've made progress today, if we now have money."

She kissed his shoulder. "Offer to switch places with me. I'd rather be piling bricks. There's just so much to try to get through. So much we don't know. We don't even know if anyone *does* use money anymore, anywhere. There's a strong push to create currency, and redeem old bank balances with the new, but it seems ridiculous when the old economy is gone."

"A lot of money and power flowed with Imulsion."

"That's all gone, too."

He exhaled slowly. "There's an estate about seven miles as the raven flies northwest."

"I think that was the Hahn place. Farming, some wine grapes, and they used to raise horses."

"About two dozen people live there now, including some children. They're organizing a market tomorrow." He shrugged. "I was thinking of taking rabbit skins and some bottles of vinegar, see what I can get for it. Maybe learn what they do for an economy. Unless, you know, you want to eat rabbit for the rest of your life."

Anya gave him a hug. "I'd appreciate you doing that research, I really would."

"You don't like my rabbit?"

"I *love* what you do with rabbit. You have the char just right. Thyme or basil or rosemary would be wasted on it."

He gave her a sidelong glance. "You are the worst liar in the world."

"Which is why I'm not cut out for politics, but…"

Marcus stood and pulled her up with him. He encircled her with his arms and held her close. "You keep me sane, you know."

"Marcus, this world is insane, not you. We're in this together. I can't do what I do without knowing that you're backing me up."

"I'll be careful at the market. If I don't like what I see, I'll fade away."

"I know you will." She kissed his throat. "Give them a chance. For all we know, they could be the majority of the people left on the planet. We need to get along, or all the fighting was for nothing. We can't have that."

Marcus got up before dawn and pulled his gear together. He picked out four bottles of vintage vinegar, wrapped them in the rabbit skins and tucked them into a rucksack. He also tucked a few crystal baubles rescued from a crashed chandelier, as well as two empty glass bottles. He picked out a couple of packets of beef in lemon sauce from the store of survival foods, and hauled them along. Neither he nor Anya liked that particular meal, so it made for good trade bait.

As the sun began to peek above the horizon, and he buckled on his gun belt, Anya joined him, wrapped in a robe and with a blanket pulled around her. "Not the way I remember trips to the market."

"Just taking precautions. I have a list on the table there. What else do we need—I mean, if I can find things?"

Anya ran her finger down the list. "I see you've got eggs here. What are the chances you think we can get some chickens?"

"Not sure." Marcus frowned. "I'd have to learn how to raise chickens first, so just eggs this time. And I have seeds on the list. The greenhouse will help us grow plants, and seedlings or the fruit will be good for trade next spring."

"Right. Nails and glass?"

He nodded. "Probably won't be able to get much of those, but doesn't hurt to ask."

Anya pulled the blanket tighter around her. "Keep an eye out for what people are making themselves, versus what they've scavenged, and if they have a place to list things others want."

"Good thinking." Marcus donned an old barn coat and pulled the rucksack on. "Wish me luck. I'll have a full report tonight."

Anya gave him a kiss. "I cannot wait."

By the time he reached his previous vantage point, the People's Market had already begun to set up. A dozen white tents occupied the newly cut lawn and another two dozen people circulated between the stalls. The crowd had a good mix of ages, including a few kids, but no infants that he could see.

A few people appeared to have walked in, and the rest had gotten inventive with their transportation. An ox pulled the battered hulk of car. The engine had been yanked out and a metal chair welded in its place in the engine compartment. A couple of people had ridden horses, and others had accompanied dog- or goat-carts. One person had even hitched a team of sheep to his cart.

Marcus walked on down into the market and took his time. A half-dozen of the people there carried firearms, but there was only one Lancer and the man carrying it didn't have any spare clips in evidence. Beyond that most folks carried knives, but those seemed more utilitarian than military. No one wore any armor.

He stayed to the periphery for his first pass and was surprised at the variety of items on offer. Honey, cheese, eggs, and a host of different herbs and vegetables appeared plentiful. One stall offered ten- and twenty-pound sacks of flour. A couple of booths sold skeins of yarn in natural colors.

One booth had mounds of scavenged clothes and some luggage. That table belonged to the wizened old man who had the ox-car. While negotiating a trade with him, Marcus learned that in his youth the man had worked at the Ephyra airport handling lost luggage, and had recovered items from the warehouse where such things used to be stored. He traded for food and odds and ends.

People haggled, but in a good-natured way. People seemed to

understand that nothing had intrinsic value—it was worth what you could get for it, and desire would determine the price. Marcus traded some of the crystals for a couple of scarves and a pair of gloves for Anya. A bottle of vinegar earned him a jar of honey and ten pounds of flour. He traded others for cheese and eggs, then in exchange for his rabbit skins he got a basket in which to carry the eggs. The survival rations earned him some sachets of dried thyme and rosemary, and a chat with an older man he'd decided ran the Hahn estate.

"I'd be interested in seeds, especially for rosemary and basil. And peppers."

"Nope, won't trade rosemary seeds or basil seeds." The man shook his head, then cracked a smile. "Fact is, both grow easier from seedlings, and I have plenty in the cold frame. Name's Roger."

"Marcus. Thank you."

"You walked by yesterday, so you must be local." The man smiled openly, though the statement seemed more question than observation. "Whereabouts are you staying?"

Marcus jerked a thumb toward the southeast. "The Stroud Estate. I came with Anya Stroud."

"Helena's daughter." Roger chuckled. "She was the only one of them Strouds I could abide. I do believe a few of our grape vines may have grown from cuttings taken from that estate."

"Things are kind of wide open…"

"No, son…" The man patted him on the shoulder, "I stole those cuttings forty years ago in the dead of night. I did like Helena, though, and the way she didn't let the family bully her. Please pass my best regards to her daughter."

"Will do." Marcus took another look around. "How often do you have the market?"

"Every two weeks. Will 'til snow flies. But if you need anything, don't hesitate."

"Thanks. I'm probably going to have to learn how to raise chickens and such. I'd be willing to trade labor for the benefit of your wisdom."

"Walk with me, Marcus." Roger turned away from the market and strolled toward the main house. He lowered his voice. "I heard Helena's daughter became a Gear and fought the Locust, the Lambent. One look at you and I figure you might have been one, too?"

"Is that a problem?"

The old man shook his head. "Not for me, but there are some. I mean, we all lost people, but the sinking of Jacinto, for a whole city to vanish… A lot of people, Stranded, they liked to think that those who went missing were really alive and well in Jacinto. So in some of their eyes, COG and the Gears killed the city and all of their missing loved ones."

And I'm the one who's truly guilty. "What are you telling me?"

"Here on this farm, what's dead is dead. None of us want trouble. The world can't afford to have us fighting with each other." Roger pointed vaguely toward other unseen places. "Away from here, there are people who want to fight just because it makes them feel powerful in a very scary world. You're welcome here, Marcus. We'll trade fair and call you friend. Just be aware that ain't the same everywhere. Idiots will want to make you pay for the past. Here, we need you as a partner for the future."

10: WATER TREATMENT PLANT #101

EPHYRA, SERA
31 HARVEST 18 A.E.

Anya Stroud couldn't contain her joy as the blond man emerged from the water plant's front door. "Damon, we got your message and came as soon as we could."

Damon Baird swept Anya up into a hug. "Delta forever, right?"

Anya hugged him back, then broke free. "May I please present Minister Jamila Shin, and Under-Minister Thomas Ndara."

Damon shook hands all around. "Pleased to meet you. At Anya's suggestion I came out here and I've looked things over. I have some good news, and some slightly better news, but don't get your hopes up. Lot of work to be done and not just the work mere mortals can do."

Jamila nodded. "I assure you, Mr. Baird, that as much as we desire a miracle, we will be overjoyed at some simple and practical help."

"I think I can give you that." Damon held the doors open for the newcomers. "Let me give you a little tour first. You've doubtless noticed there's virtually no damage here. This site was selected because of the stone formation below—we're sitting in a natural stone basin. Its builders chose it in case the plant developed leaks, so toxins wouldn't flow into the groundwater. That same formation prevented the Locust from erupting through the place."

Anya nodded as they stepped into the lobby. Decorators had painted it a light blue and finished it with blond woods, making it all feel natural and open. Transparent pipes formed a twisting network above. Nothing flowed through them at the moment, but she imagined a time when clean water would gurgle through the pipes. The poured-stone floor had insets of mica and bronze fish, as well as other decorative elements making it look like the bottom of a lake.

"One other good thing about this plant was the influence of ecologists. They built it with solar panels. Those could only provide about ten percent of the needed power when the plant was running full bore—the facility drew power from the local grid for everything else. Good thing for us is that the solar cells appear to be in functioning condition, and should provide all the power we need for a while. When the moment comes, I'll work some of the patented Baird magick, up the output and buy us more time."

Anya and her companions followed Baird deeper into the building. They passed through several sets of doors and down some bare metal stairs to a massive underground room full of pipes and sand filters.

"This is the heart of the operation?"

Damon pointed to a massive black pipe halfway across the room. "That's where everything comes in—rainwater, run-off, industrial dumping, and household waste-water. Grates take out the larger debris, then we push it through a series of filters.

It comes out of them ninety-nine-point-nine percent clean, then moves on to chemical treatments and finally back into the water supply. Some of the water we divert back to flush the filters, and all that goes into the leech fields and containment ponds."

Thomas frowned. "Can you separate out the solid waste so it can be dried and made available for fertilizer or fuel?"

"Maybe." Damon considered for a moment. "To do that will require each batch to be chemically analyzed. If the water is pulling lead from pipes or is subject to some other contamination, we don't want that being burned. But I may have a solution for that, and a way to use human waste as a fertilizer without too much processing."

He waved for them to follow him. They descended to the filtering facilities floor and turned right. Through another set of doors they returned to rooms built on a normal scale, then passed into a large laboratory with wide windows overlooking containment ponds and fields beyond.

"Everything you can see from here is part of the plant, including those fields. There once were houses there, but the residents got moved because that was downwind of the plant. Not the sort of bouquet you want when having a weekend cook-out."

Anya pointed beyond the hills to the southeast. "I dimly recall a visit to the family estate when the wind was blowing in from the northwest. Ten miles away it was still a bit strong."

"When they took the houses out, they left the water system. We can irrigate all of that really easy." Damon held a finger up. "But that's not the good news. Look at that pool over there."

Jamila walked to the window. "The green, that's an algae bloom, is it not?"

"Well done, Minister." Damon smiled broadly. "In the past the plant would have chemically shocked the pond to kill the algae off. We'll introduce a different species of algae, then we'll harvest it. It's protein-rich and will substitute for meat protein. Plus, if we reconfigure one of the other pools, or build more, we can farm fish. More protein, and we can stock ponds and streams elsewhere. Best yet, the algae pellets can be used to feed the fish, and the algae has a fairly robust harvest cycle."

Anya's eyes tightened. "How many people can you feed?"

"I can keep maybe five thousand a day from starving, at least initially. More, if they have other foods and we're just supplementing their diet. As we expand, that number increases." Damon's smile faded, and he folded his arms over his chest. "This isn't going to be easy. I'll be building up a couple divergent technologies in one place. I need people. Good people. Smarter than me if you could find them. But, hey, look, I know you don't have any funding, since I don't seem to have gotten my last paycheck."

Anya smiled. "To be fair, Damon, we don't have a bank from which to draw funds, and you don't have one into which you can deposit funds."

"Okay, true. Fact is, however, I'll need good people and have to motivate them somehow to do highly stressful jobs. If we fail, people die. You know what that's like, Anya, but the folks I'll be using aren't Gears. That's a big ask."

Jamila lifted her chin. "Do you have a proposal, Mr. Baird?"

"I do." The smile returned. "Public-private partnership. You, the Ministry, will have a thirty percent stake, and your buy-in is giving me this facility and its lands. Damon Baird Industries will contract back with the Ministry for services at cost, forever, plus revenues going to the Ministry as they would to any stockholder. I will retain fifty-one percent, and the remaining nineteen percent I dole out to incentivize workers. The Ministry will have a seat on the board."

"The Ministry will need *two* seats on the board." Jamila stroked her throat. "In the event of bankruptcy or takeover, this facility returns to the Ministry or its successor."

Damon's brow furrowed for a moment.

Then he nodded. "Okay."

"Good. Thomas will draft the agreement. Is that a problem, Thomas?"

Ndara shook his head. "Happy to do it."

"Great to be in business with you." Damon rubbed his hands together. "So let me tell you one other thing. Anya, you remember Jack?"

"Remember? Absolutely." Anya turned to Jamila and Tom. "We had a support bot serving with us. Jack flew all over the place, doing all sorts of tasks, and sometimes helping out in a firefight."

Damon jerked a thumb toward the rear of the facility. "The city had a dozen or so non-military support units here for running through pipes, repairing leaks, clearing clogs, and such like. The robot shop even has some fabrication equipment for keeping the robots going. Based on the original plans and with the equipment here, I've worked up a design for a robot that can demolish, recycle, and reconstruct buildings. I'll test them building on-site housing for employees. If they work out, we can create more and have a lot of labor for rebuilding, including the dangerous part of checking structures for damage."

Jamila pressed a finger to her lips for a moment. "How long will that take?"

"Priority one is clean water and food, right?"

Jamila nodded.

"Month before I can work up the robots. Maybe less. Depends on who I get for help. I'll use the Jack units to check out pipes and make sure we can get a flow back into the city."

"Water will have to be for personal use," Jamila said. "Drinking and cleaning, no manufacturing. Not yet." Her eyes narrowed. "I do not want to use the availability of—or lack of—water as a political weapon. Until basic needs are met and food security is assured, diverting water to other manufacturing is ill advised."

Anya watched Damon's face. Her friend had always been the one to provide solutions for problems, as he was doing now, but political considerations hadn't mattered out in the field. Here he had to wrestle with the idea that his work, his inventions, would generate political power. Such power might be used in ways of which he did not personally approve.

How will you deal with that reality, Damon?

"It strikes me, Minister Shin, that expanding Damon Baird Industries' services and market would be a decision for the corporation's board."

"Quite so, Mr. Baird." Jamila canted her head. "A board which, I believe, would currently be comprised of yourself, Anya, and me. I merely address this as a concern for the board to consider. Anya?"

"Humanitarian needs have to be addressed, no doubt about it," Anya said. "We'll need to set priorities after that. Rebuilding has to be up there, especially with winter coming on." She frowned. "Other needs will have to be addressed as they come up."

"Yes, and there will be political considerations." Jamila spread her hands. "If Mr. Griffin asks for some of the construction robots to help in Char, we would want to help—in return for considerations. For alliances, *not* for domination. I think we all agree on that point."

Anya nodded, as did Damon.

"I'm glad we all concur there." Anya raised a hand to her throat. "What do you expect to exclude from the priorities list, Jamila?"

"Many things. Industries which manufacture peripheral items, items we don't need at the moment. Salad spinners and suitcases, most of the fashion industry." Jamila sighed. "Seradyne Industries manufacturing guns. I don't know that we need them."

Damon chuckled. "We always need guns."

"Do we?" Jamila arched an eyebrow. "There are more than enough in circulation—we manufactured millions, and I see no reason that anyone who wants one couldn't find themselves two or three. Aside from that, who will we be shooting? What is the threat we face? Do we need people killing each other right now? Can we afford to let anyone die?"

"I see your point, Minister."

"Let me be clear, Mr. Baird. The Locust were an existential threat to humanity, and they may yet win. We may not have the infrastructure necessary to keep people alive. One virus, one bacterium, could sweep through colonies of malnourished people and wipe them out in the blink of an eye. Our focus must be on keeping people alive, and reproducing at the fastest rate we can sustain."

Jamila stared out the window. "I have no doubt vast swaths of Sera will rewild and that it will take centuries for us to return to the numbers we knew before. Nevertheless, it is incumbent upon us to maintain the technological level we have now, to give humanity the best chance to thrive again. If we fail at that, we dishonor the sacrifice of all those who fought beside you, and those who died believing we would make a better future for everyone."

Damon nodded. "Makes sense, so an additional priority is

going to be medical care and fertility treatments. This lab has a lot of the equipment that can be used for that. We'll also need to secure a hospital, or build one from the ground up here. That might be a bit much for the first-generation construction robots, but there may be a way to speed up their learning in that regard."

"Very good, Mr. Baird." Jamila smiled. "You were right, Anya, he is a treasure."

Damon laughed. "Finally, someone who appreciates my genius."

"Just wait until she actually gets to know you." Anya shook her head and turned to the minister. "Because we're so close to the estate, I was thinking I'd stay here and head home after visiting with Damon a bit more."

"Excellent idea." Jamila headed toward the door with Thomas in tow. "We will have the agreements out to you tomorrow, Mr. Baird. Thank you for all you've done, and all you're going to do."

"My pleasure. Good to meet you both." Damon waited for them to head up the stairs and back toward the entrance, then exhaled heavily. "This is going to be a shitload of work."

"I wouldn't entrust it to anyone else."

"Thank you." Damon's eyes tightened. "It'll be interesting to see what sort of talent I can find out there, to make all this work. Anya, do you think Marcus would want to work on this?"

She arched an eyebrow. "You're that eager to take orders?"

"Well, I'd be the boss…"

"We're talking about Marcus."

"Shit, good point." Damon grinned and leaned back against the wall. "How is Marcus doing? Big change for him."

"It *is*, but he's embracing it. He talks about becoming domesticated, and his arch nemesis is a jar of sourdough starter. I mean, it *is* Marcus, so you know he'll have a nemesis. He's adjusting."

"That's good." Damon lifted his chin. "How about you? How does it feel to be in charge?"

"I'm not in charge, Damon. I don't want to be." She shook her head. "Jamila has brought all of this together, so she's our leader. She's very sharp, and the kind of leader we need. I like working with her."

"Easier to work with than Hoffman?"

"Same sort of toughness, just a different package." Anya sighed. "Having you here to make her visions functional takes some major stress off me. I can get back to what I do best, and make things work."

Damon gave her a thumbs-up. "Definitely a job for Delta, so we'll get it done. And, you know, if anyone gets in our way we'll deploy Marcus, and that will fix that."

11: STROUD ESTATE

NEAR EPHYRA, SERA

4 BOUNTY 18 A.E.

Marcus Fenix bent down, eying the planting beds he'd filled with soil and fertilizer. He'd mixed it all up well, the fertilizer being a cartload of horse manure that Roger Hahn had brought with him as a welcoming gift. He'd leveled everything off and given it a good soaking. He figured he'd plant peppers in half the beds—not because he liked them that much, but they were supposed to grow easily—and save the rest of the space for tomatoes and herbs.

Roger had been very helpful, offering advice not with a "You have to do this" delivery, but softening things. He'd say, "Well, smarter folks than me swear that if you…" in a way that would make it sound as if he was as clueless as Marcus.

Marcus had called him on it, but Roger had only shrugged. "Just hoping you can learn from my mistakes, son."

They'd walked around the estate for a bit. Roger had filled him in on details of how things had been before E-Day, and even back when he'd been a kid. There had been a bit of a rivalry between the Strouds and the Hahns, mostly because the Hahns had less money "and more pride, if you can imagine." He'd always thought the rivalry was silly, and said he was sorry to see the Stroud family all but gone.

Down near the barn Roger suggested that Marcus might want to eventually get a couple of horses, some dairy cattle, and some pigs.

"And goats. They'll eat anything, and will clear-cut old brush you don't want growing here. Just don't let them near your grape vines. Yours look in pretty good shape. Little late to harvest this year, but I'll swap you labor for labor to set them up and then harvest. Couple years from now we might have good wine."

"Thank you. That would be helpful." Marcus jerked a thumb at the barn. "What about a chicken coop?"

"To be honest, Marcus, we're only just now having much luck with ours. You have rabbits here, and though you might not see them, things that will eat rabbits. Those same things will eat chickens, and then there are the rats that like an egg as much as the next man. Back in the day we'd have a small pride of barn cats to keep that sort of thing down, but cats seem to have become relatively rare. Not sure if the Locust hated them, or liked to eat them, but…"

"I'll keep my eyes open for cats."

"Spend some of your spare time thinking up some good rat traps, maybe. Worth their weight in gold." Roger smiled. "Or honey."

"I think I have more use for honey. Once I master bread making, that is."

"I'd imagine dealing with Locust was easier."

"Little bit."

They shared a laugh and then Roger started back for home.

Marcus watched him go, fighting to keep a smile on his face because a sense of loneliness started creeping up on him. Roger was a good man, gentle in all the ways that Colonel Hoffman had been hard.

In a battle Roger would have been collateral damage, but in this world he's the kind of person who'll be a cornerstone for the future.

Marcus straightened up and smiled again, pleased with his handiwork in the greenhouse. Despite the fact that days had begun to cool off, the inside remained pleasantly warm. If it weren't for the pervasive scent of horse manure, he'd happily drag a chair in and bask in the warmth.

Someone rapped on the greenhouse door. Marcus had used the glass panel from it for repairs, and had replaced it with wood, so he couldn't see his visitor.

"Anyone home?"

Man's voice. Marcus' hand dropped to the pistol on his right hip.

"Door's unlocked."

The door swung out and a slender, dark-haired man filled the opening. He had his hands up, and a bottle of whiskey held in one of them. "Brandon Turrall. We met at the reception. Did I call at a bad time?"

Marcus released his pistol and crossed his arms over his chest. "You just happened to be out this way?"

"I found a better bottle of whiskey."

"Pendergast didn't want it?"

Brandon shrugged. "Doesn't deserve it. Hasn't earned it. But this repair work, this is good."

"Thanks." Marcus arched an eyebrow. "I suppose you want a couple of glasses?"

"If you're of a mind to share."

"Okay, let's go to the house." Marcus closed the greenhouse up, then followed his guest through the overgrown garden and onto the patio. There he scooped a pitcher-full of water from a cistern, poured it into a basin and washed the dirt and sweat off his face and hands. He dried them off on a threadbare towel, then slipped into the kitchen and grabbed two tumblers. Almost as an afterthought he grabbed a plate of failed experiments in bread making and brought them out to the table.

Brandon uncorked the bottle. "Now this, my friend, is Sera Dew. Original bottling from the end of the Pendulum Wars. It was never the smoothest, but at least it won't take the enamel off your teeth." He poured a couple of fingers into each tumbler, set the bottle down, and raised a glass. "May we bring into the future the best of the past."

"I'll drink to that." They touched glasses and drank. Marcus caught no hint of peat, but a fair amount of smoke. The whiskey flowed down his throat easily, with only the hint of a burn. "Oh, yeah, *much* better."

"Certainly the best I've had in the last five years." Brandon swirled the amber liquid around in his glass. "I know a man who claims he used to work at the Sera Dew distillery in Jacinto. He tells me that if I can find him a copper pot still, he can produce as much as I want. I half think he's lying, but one hundred percent hope he's not. That's a skill set we don't want to lose."

"Lot of those skills we'd not want to lose." Marcus glanced down at the brown disks on the plate. "Bread making would be another one."

"Oh, is that what those are?" Brandon reached for one, snapped it in half and broke off a smaller piece. He tasted it. After crunching for a bit, he nodded. "I like how you didn't burn them."

"I figure they're good for target practice. Or body armor." Marcus glanced back at the kitchen. "I have a sourdough starter that mocks me."

"It's an art, not a science." Brandon pulled a chair out from the table and sat. "I know some people who could help you out. Might even give you some of their starter. Lot of people survive on eating flatbread, and this is halfway there."

Marcus sat opposite him. "You seem to know a lot of people, people with information. And you find things."

"I move around a lot. I look for things. For people." Brandon set his glass on the table and leaned forward in the chair. "While you were running around saving humanity from the Locust, I ran around a lot, too. At first from the Locust, then, eventually, the Lambent. I managed to find things. I also found people— alive, or proof they were dead. The living I reunited. The things I found I traded. I've been doing that for about twice as long as I didn't need to."

Marcus sipped the whiskey and did some quick calculations. *He must have been a kid on E-Day. Eight, nine years old at the most. For someone that young to survive that long… And the first time we met he said he'd seen my handiwork, so he wasn't shying away from dangerous areas.*

"You must have been good at evading the Locust."

"Those that I could, sure. The others…" The man shrugged. "I managed to make their days unpleasant."

"You don't need to be modest with me."

"I'm not. I learned how to go places they couldn't, get through places where they'd get stuck, and to make it hurt for them to follow." Brandon sat back and sipped his whiskey again. "A lot of times all I had to deal with was wounded creatures you Gears had left behind. Locust, they can linger. Don't heal all that fast, but take a while to finally die."

"I won't begrudge any of them a hard and painful death."

"On that we agree."

Marcus drained his glass. "So why are you here? It's not by accident, you had to seek me out. Why?"

Brandon held the bottle out and refilled Marcus' glass. "First, wasn't hard to learn where you are. Stroud Estate was a logical choice. And then you went to the people's market. Remember the man selling old clothes and luggage? I've done business with him, and he recognized you from my description."

"So you're answering 'how' when I was asking 'why.'"

"Why's coming. Point is that I talk to a lot of people. I hear things, and one of the things I hear is stories of Locust still being out there. Loners. Small nests. Anecdotal reports. Probably stories mothers are using to keep kids in line." Brandon sighed. "Some of the people I know, they've asked me to check out those stories."

Marcus' flesh puckered, and it was more than the cool autumn breeze rustling through the garden. *No, we had to get them all. If they can breed...* He rubbed a hand over his forehead.

"If news got out..."

"Panic. Anarchy. People are just getting over being terrified, and to be plunged right back into horror..." Brandon shook his head. "And there are people who would take advantage of the rumors. Pendergast is a huge dollop of idiot, but he has people around him who would push King Ravens as the only line of defense, and try to organize people for their own safety, if you catch my meaning."

"Right." Marcus remembered Raul Hasterwith, and could see him pitching Lancers in the same way. *What does he know? Was he*

*thinking of this already, and that's why he offered me a job? Would
he use me to build a cadre to stave off the threat?* "So what do *you*
want from me?"

"Marcus, I can track the stories down. I can get us to the places
we need to go, but I don't have a soldier's eye. I can't assess the
threat level, and I sure as hell can't deal with it the way you can."

"You're getting a little ahead of yourself. How reliable are
these stories?"

"Good enough that I think they need to be checked out."
Brandon frowned. "The Stranded, they've organized themselves in
all sorts of ways. There are a bunch of nomadic bands wandering
around. There are camps in cities…"

Marcus nodded. "I've seen some of those."

"Of course. People have formed settlements out there, in
the middle of nowhere. Ted—the luggage guy—he circulates
between them on a circuit that takes him a couple of months.
And the wanderers, they visit settlements to trade. For every
group I know about, I imagine there are two or three that I don't.
People are just scattered in tiny pockets, and these stories filter
out through them."

"But no hard evidence."

"Not yet. So when there's a story of a couple of kids going
missing, that could be runaways, it could be Locust. But we have
to know the truth, right?" Brandon stood and opened his arms.
"Look, I see what you have going here. You and Anya, the way she
looked at you the other night, that's something real and special.
You're making a life here. You're doing what you fought for. I
wouldn't blame you if you told me I was crazy, and that I should
never darken your doorstep again. You've earned this, and I mean
that, sincerely."

Marcus scratched at his jaw. "If I send you packing, what will you do?"

"I'll keep looking. I have a line on a woman who says she served with Gamma Squad. She only has one leg, but I think I've found an artificial one that will fit her."

"'Says she served…?'" Marcus shook his head. "Why are you doing this, Brandon?"

"It's what I do?" The man tossed off the rest of his whiskey. "I don't know any other life. I don't *want* to find Locust, but if they're out there, if they're stopped so no one else has to lead the life I did, then maybe things will get better. Maybe I'll find some peace. That make any sense?"

Marcus sat back and stared down into the glass he held in both hands. "I hear you. Okay, you're right. I'm making a life here for me and Anya and, you know, kids. It's a life I want. Maybe I *have* earned it. Anya certainly has, and she's now doing more. And while folks may think I've earned a rest, I don't know that I'm tired yet."

"It's the sense that there's something more out there, right?"

"Yeah and, maybe, some things aren't resolved in here." Marcus rapped his knuckles against his skull. "I have to think about your offer. I have to talk with Anya. And if I do agree to go, it'll take me a few days to set things in motion so I don't lose the start I made here."

"That's fair enough." Brandon put the cork back in the bottle but left it on the table. "Is there anything I can do to help with preparations?"

Marcus grinned. "Find me a cat? Pregnant."

Brandon's mahogany eyes narrowed. "Not the oddest request I've had in the last week."

The Gear looked up. "One other thing. You said 'people' had

asked you to look into the stories. Who are those people? People you work for, like Pendergast?"

"I work *with* Pendergast, not *for* him."

"Then who?"

"No one you'd know."

"We're going to have to trust each other, Turrall."

The smaller man held his hands up. "Right. I got you. You agree to go, first thing I do is introduce you to my people. You decide to back out after that, I'll get you home again and you'll be growing green things in no time. As a bonus, I'll have someone come show you how to make bread."

Marcus stood and set his glass on the table. "I think I'm going to need you to throw in the bread lessons, no matter which way this goes."

"Done and done." Brandon offered his hand. "I do believe, Marcus Fenix, we have a deal."

12: STROUD ESTATE

NEAR EPHYRA, SERA

4 BOUNTY 18 A.E.

Anya Stroud had the Ministry car drop her off at the end of the long drive into the estate. The grounds had once been impeccably maintained, with vast lawns spreading out on either side of the tree-lined lane. The fields had long since grown up and turned golden with the autumn. The trees had lost most of their leaves, and gaps in the line revealed where some had been harvested and others had fallen over.

She'd been very young when she'd first seen the estate—not much more than four years old. She'd joined her mother when Helena had gone to inform Anya's grandfather that, contrary to his wishes, she was *not* resigning her commission. She would, instead, be accepting a promotion. Her mother had practiced her speech in front of a mirror, and Anya remembered it. She'd never detected nervousness in her mother's actions, and now admired her mother for how well she had handled it.

The estate, then, had seemed as big as the whole world. A

massive stone pile, it had two wings which had since crumbled, and the main house which had somehow weathered the Locust assaults. She hoped that she and Marcus could rebuild it, but not out of any desire to capture past glory or assert privilege. Instead she wanted it to be a place for their family, and a sign of hope—a symbol suggesting that a return to the normality of the past was achievable.

There are so many things we have to get done before that.

Jamila Shin had joked that they were getting into the "R&D" portion of the job. Anya thought that meant *research and development*, but Jamila corrected her. *"It means requests and demands."* Both of those had begun to inundate the Ministry. Requests generally came cordially and asked for things that any governmental body would normally supply. This included fresh water, housing, food, and medical facilities. The Ministry had made all of those priorities, and Damon Baird's work progressed as fast as humanly possible. They'd found him some aides and he was putting them to work at DB Industries.

The *demands* most often came from those who had once known privilege. They wanted the same things everyone else did, but they wanted to be *first*. More often than not Anya faced angry people who had nothing *now*, and were outraged that they weren't given something before others who *never* had anything. *"They are used to having nothing, you see, which is why we shouldn't have to wait in line."* That to them this seemed perfectly logical and proper horrified Anya—made worse by how easily they offered such arguments.

Her first inclination was to open up and blast them, verbally at least, but Jamila had cautioned her against that.

"You see, Anya, they wouldn't understand that they are no different from anyone else, because without believing in their own superiority, they are nothing. Their self-conception would crumble and cease to exist. In fact, it might be more merciful just to shoot them."

Then Jamila's eyes had tightened. "The fact is that right now *we* have nothing, either, but we cannot let them know that. We will need them later. When we reorganize society, we'll do it along the principle that all people are necessary and equal. We need these people to buy in, and if we need to humor them, implying that they are first among equals, then we do that. So when they demand something, we tell them we understand and we have a 'special list' for people who, 'you know, are worthy.' Some of them may even see through the ruse, but the leaders among them will understand why—and those are the people we really need to have backing us."

Anya found that sort of nonsense annoying, but it wasn't as if her life—even as a Gear—hadn't involved such demands. Life always forced compromises. A quartermaster might like coffee on her desk by the time she came in. If that kept her sweet, it made getting ammunition that much easier. *And sometimes, the conflicts are just so petty and stupid that they're not worth the energy it takes to win.*

What was important was to remember the greater goal: rebuilding a society where humanity could flourish. *Claw out the immediate wins, and build toward the tomorrow we all want.* A shiver ran down her spine as she remembered the word *tomorrow* —the word she had uttered on the day the Locust threat had died. She'd been exhausted and hurting and sad, and yet there had been a note of hope when she said it.

Tomorrow was a reason for living, for pressing on.

And that's what I'm doing. Anya smiled. *That's what* we're *doing.*

She entered the darkened house and headed straight through to the kitchen, then the patio beyond it. She paused in the shadows, just shy of the doorway. Her smile grew and her heart began beating faster. *As if I'm still a schoolgirl with a crush.*

Marcus sat there in the light of a dancing fire. He'd pulled a blanket around himself and stared into the flames. Two glasses and a bottle sat on the table beside him. He was motionless, his expression serious and yet without worry. The concern which had consumed him had vanished.

Apprehension gone. Good.

She stepped forward and leaned against the doorjamb.

"You had a visitor."

He nodded. "I washed the glass out and left it for you. The bottle is Sera Dew."

"Sera Dew?" Anya stepped forward and examined the bottle. "This is what Dom would drink when he was in a reflective mood."

"Said it helped calm his mind so he could sort through things."

"Does it work?"

Marcus smiled and looked up. "Seems to."

Anya poured a couple of fingers into her glass, and touched it to his.

"To Dom."

"To Dom." Marcus sipped the whiskey and remained still for a moment. "I didn't hear the car."

"I walked in from the main road." She pulled the other chair around closer to the fire and sat. "Long day, and I wanted to shed a lot of it before I got to you."

"You know I'll listen, and be angry on your behalf."

"Yes, darling. Maybe later." She laid a hand on his. "Who was this visitor? Damon?"

"He never had that good taste in liquor." Marcus chuckled. "No, it was a guy we met at the reception. Brandon Turrall."

"He stopped by out of the blue?"

"Not really." Marcus leaned forward, firelight flickering over his features. "He claims he's heard stories that there are still Locust out there. Maybe bogeyman stories. Maybe nothing. Maybe folks talking nonsense before, but now thinking it's real. He's going to go looking for them, and asked if I wanted to come along."

"Do you?"

"It's not that simple, Anya." He looked at her. "I like what we have here. I see it working. The greenhouse, and I *will* get bread made. Get some chickens. Some goats. We'll make wine. We'll make cheese. We'll make this into our home, and bring in kids who need a place to grow up."

Anya's breath caught in her chest. *Children, here.* In a heartbeat she could hear their laughter and see them running around. She could hear Marcus telling them to mind the fire or police the area. The estate needed a new generation, and even though she couldn't have children herself, Anya and Marcus would make it happen. "Right. Wine. Children. Cheese. Yes. We need that. All of that. Not just you and me."

He took her hand in his and squeezed it. "My dad wasn't much of a dad, but Dom and his kids… We fought so hard to make sure there would be a future."

"You'll be a great father." Anya laughed. "And a terror for anyone who wants to date our daughters."

"I can live with that." Marcus slowly smiled. "I won't lie to our kids, either. Or to you."

"I know." She shifted in her chair. "You want to go, don't you? With Brandon."

"It's not something I *want*." He frowned. "Everything ended so fast. For the first time in forever there wasn't something jumping at us or bursting up through the ground. It doesn't feel real. Lacking the sense of being hunted, it makes all this feel like a dream. The entire time I've been waiting, thinking something was lurking. A sense of impending doom."

"So when Brandon told you what he wanted to do, it made sense?"

Marcus nodded.

"I know how you feel." Anya sighed. "All the work I'm doing now, it's bracing for what I *know* will come. Not Locust—God, I hope not Locust—but what if we put people into a building, and it burns down? What if a water main breaks? What if the food supply collapses? What if folks start getting sick? Problems that wouldn't have amounted to anything even ten years ago could wipe us out today. It could finish what the Locust started."

"Anya, what can I do to help?" He pointed off northwest. "I can talk to Roger Hahn and get some of his people to help out here. I can join you at the Ministry and…"

Anya covered her mouth with a hand, stifling a laugh.

"…what's so funny?"

"Oh, no, Marcus. You in the Ministry? Never. It is all the things you hate about organization. In triplicate. People whining about trivial things. Imagine that reception, but with folks not nearly on their best behavior. It would kill you. No. You are so sweet for offering, though."

Setting her glass aside, she took his hand in both of hers. "Marcus, I know you. I know that in your head you know that you did everything anyone asked of you. You did everything you could to end the threat to humanity but, deep down, in your heart of hearts, you feel as if you need to do *more*. I understand that. It drives me, too—to do more. At least, for a while. Long enough to get things back up and running. Then you and I, we come back here, we build our family and our wine and our cheese; then our kids have *their* children and we give them the tomorrow that we won for them."

His eyes closed. "I don't want to abandon you. I look forward to your coming home to me. You look forward to the same thing, right?"

"I do, very much." She raised his hand to her lips and kissed his palm. "You won't be abandoning me. In fact, you'll be doing me a great service."

"How so?"

"The fact is, we're trying to build a world for everybody, but we have no idea of how many people and what their needs are. You can be my eyes and ears out there as you and Brandon chase down these stories. You can tell us what other places are doing—what people like, and what they don't. We're in a bubble here, and overwhelmed just dealing with the people we know about. We don't have the time or resources to look outside that bubble."

His eyes opened again, but only narrowly. "I can do that. I can send you reports. People, places, things, the basics. But economic development, that sort of stuff, not sure I'm your guy."

"That will be perfect." Anya nodded. "It'll really help."

"Anything I can do to make your life easier, just ask."

"About that." Anya stood and tugged Marcus to his feet. "Bring the bottle."

She took him by the hand and up to their bed. She sat him down on the edge of it and tugged off his boots. She looked up at him and smiled. "Make love with me, Marcus. Let's do this for *us*. To remember until you return home, and to recreate when we're together again; never, ever, having to be parted."

Anya slipped out of bed, pulled on a robe, and made her way down to the kitchen. She gave the jar of starter a reproving glance just because it deserved it, then kindled a fire in the small tornado stove on the patio. Quickly she heated water then made two mugs of tea, which she brought back up to their bedroom. Placing one on the table at Marcus' side of the bed, she slipped back in beside him beneath the sheets. She pulled herself up against the headboard and sipped her tea while watching him sleep.

I would wish this sort of peace for him always. Marcus carried the weight of the world on his shoulders—always had, if what Dom had said was true. Always responsible and accepting the consequences of his actions. Accepting the burden of other people's tragedies. That responsibility etched the lines on his face, traced every scar on his body.

But now, as he slept, the tension had eased. He'd set the burden aside. *He can't reach the future while hauling all of it around.* It would take time for him to slowly let it evaporate, but that peaceful sense told her it would happen. And, she hoped, going out one more time would help. Finding one more battle to fight would give him perspective, and permission to go after the future they desired.

His tea had gotten cool by the time he woke up. Marcus stretched and then smiled openly at her.

"The most beautiful sight I could imagine."

"Stay out of my mind, Marcus Fenix." Anya brushed hair

from his brow. "Just wait until we have a couple of kids rolling in here, jumping on the bed, wanting their dad to make fresh bread for them."

"You have a full fantasy life, don't you?"

She leaned over and kissed his forehead. "You're the center of it, so, yes."

He sat up and tucked pillows behind his back. "That'll be a wonderful day. What do you figure? Seven, eight kids?"

"Let's start with one, maybe two. Boy and a girl, I think."

"I'll keep my eyes open when I am out there." Marcus grabbed the mug of tea from his table and drank. "Thank you. You could have elbowed me so it would have been hot."

"I like watching you sleep." She set her cup aside and rested her head on his shoulder. "I have a question for you."

"Sure."

"Have you reached out to Baird at all?"

Marcus shook his head.

"Why not?"

"From what you said he's really busy, so I didn't want to interrupt him." Marcus sighed. "You know how he is. He'd explain to me about yeast and tomatoes and setting up a still or something else, and I wouldn't want to be ungrateful, but…"

"He could be a bit much to take right now?"

"Yeah. I have his info. If I see anything out there that he'd be interested in, I'll reach out to him." Marcus glanced at her. "Why are you asking?"

"He asks after you. It's not like he's hurt that you haven't said anything, but…"

"Got it. I'll remedy that, I promise. But there's something else, isn't there?"

"Yes." Anya nodded. "You've pretty much been here all alone, yet you're willing to head out with someone you just met. Why?"

"That's a good question." Marcus scratched at his chin. "You. Baird. Cole. You've all been there. We understand each other. Don't need words sometimes. I like that. With you, I like it a lot. Turrall hasn't been where we have, but he's been out there. He's got a different way of seeing the world. I guess I need that."

She nodded. "Halfway between a Gear and a civilian? I can see it. In addition, apparently he knows where to find the good whiskey."

"That doesn't hurt." Marcus shook his head. "I'm just hoping we can find the truth behind these Locust stories. Put them to rest, and then it's back here to the serious work of building our family."

ACT 2

1: STROUD ESTATE

NEAR EPHYRA, SERA
8 BOUNTY 18 A.E.

"**D**amn, Marcus, you know how to dress for war."

Marcus turned as Brandon came on through the house to the patio. "You look like you're going birding."

Brandon shrugged. "That's not much of a hobby anymore. You think Locust hated birds, or that the general environmental devastation is the culprit?"

"Outside my area of expertise." Marcus shook his head. The younger man wore a light jacket half zipped up over a collared shirt, and casual slacks. The jacket and shirt had clashing plaid patterns, and the pants were a comfortable beige. The only concession he had made to the nature of their Locust-hunting mission appeared to be a sturdy pair of combat boots. "But seriously, aren't you underdressed?"

"I have more kit out front." Brandon shrugged the remark off. "But, here, I brought you this."

He tossed Marcus a maroon and black jersey featuring a rearing stallion with a fiery mane and tail. It had the number 56 front and back. Marcus caught it easily. "Char Hellions? You expect me to wear this? Couldn't find a Cougars jersey?"

"It's easier to find good whiskey than one of those." Brandon smiled. "Ted, the luggage guy, he found it for me. I figured you might want to wear your armor, and this will make you more presentable."

Marcus scratched at the back of his head. He'd felt great pulling on his old kit. He'd even taken some time to touch up some of the paint and scrub away spots of blood that he wasn't entirely certain were there. Feeling its weight again, hearing the click of the fasteners and the rasp as he tightened the straps, made him feel closer to whole than he had been in a long time. Pride had swelled in his chest.

But then he'd seen the shock on the faces of the two guys from the Hahn estate who'd taken up residence in the stables. They must have known he'd been a Gear, but seeing him in armor had surprised them.

It reminded them the war was real.

He held out the jersey and looked at the name written on the back. "Who was Foster?"

"Defensive back. Only guy he couldn't stop was the Cole Train."

"Cole will like that." Marcus grunted. "Maybe I *will* lose the armor, at least for now."

"Where we're going, not everybody is a fan of Gears." Brandon shrugged. "You'll have plenty of time to kit up before we get anywhere near the sightings."

"I'm not inclined to lose the sidearm."

"Right there with you." Brandon unzipped his jacket to reveal two small pistols in shoulder rigs.

"Anything heavier?"

The smaller man jerked a thumb back toward the house. "I see you've got a Lancer. That should cover us. I have an old hunting rifle, over/under, twelve point five millimeter. It's in a saddle scabbard."

"Saddle?"

"Yeah, c'mon." Brandon disappeared back into the house and out through the front. Marcus followed, picking up a small duffle to which he'd strapped the Lancer. Out in front of the estate, four horses cropped grass. The two larger ones had chocolate-brown coats with black manes and Demi-lune horns of a lighter color on their brow. Brandon hauled himself up into the saddle of a lighter brown horse with a brown mane and darker horns. The pack horse behind it had a white coat with big brown spots. As reported, the walnut butt of a rifle peeked out of a saddle scabbard on the first horse's right flank.

Brandon smiled down at him. "You've ridden before, right?"

"Sure." Marcus didn't feel inclined to mention that it had been back when he was twelve, and his *only* lesson in riding. He shucked his rucksack and attached it to the pack saddle, then hitched the duffle to the other side. "Been years."

"I'd have preferred a truck, but horses don't run on Imulsion, and given that the world's run out of it, we'd be moving slow." Brandon rode over and grabbed the bridle of Marcus' horse. "Left foot in the stirrup."

Marcus bit back a sharp remark simply because he didn't hear any judgment in the man's voice. He swung himself into the saddle, struggling to retain his balance, and set his other foot in the right stirrup. He recalled enough to refrain from jamming his foot fully into the stirrup, so he could kick free if he fell from the saddle. He took the reins up in one hand and patted the horse's neck with the other.

"We might want to go slowly. Just to let me get used to riding again."

"We don't have that far to ride and we don't need to hurry." Brandon looked toward the house. "Anya going to see you off?"

"She headed into the Ministry at dawn." Marcus made no attempt to hide a grin. "We said our goodbyes already."

"Glad you got the chance."

Marcus reached back and tapped the duffle bag. "Anya got some communications gear from Baird—Damon Baird. We have one of the Ministry's few satellite phones. Works with MilNet and maybe the old commercial networks. Charges off a solar panel."

"Good. If the stories are true, we'll want to get the information to the right people fast."

"And Anya is the right people." The Gear nodded once. In saying their goodbyes, he'd held Anya close for a long time that morning, drawing in her warmth, remembering how her hair smelled, how it felt as he stroked it. His heart already ached for her. Seeing her, hearing her voice, feeling her move against him in the darkness made him smile, and when they made love, their intimacy gave him a sense of being part of something greater than the two of them separately. It carried him beyond all the horror they had shared and made new, stronger memories.

They rode slowly, letting Marcus get used to the horse's gait and how he had to shift his weight to accommodate the animal's movements. He fell into the rhythm, and soon was moving easily with it. He hadn't ridden in forever, but now, as an adult, he found he enjoyed it. Not only did it feel right, but it was so different from traveling in vehicles, King Ravens, or on ships. This helped distance him from the firepower sprints through a Locust-clogged landscape.

Slow, but natural. The pace at which the world will recover. Marcus smiled and patted the horse's neck again. *This isn't bad at all.*

They rode west for a couple of hours, cutting across fields with grasses high enough to brush their boots, or riding through forested lanes. Buildings—some pristine, others in ruins reclaimed by ivy and saplings—lined the stretches of road they traveled. Here and there crows heckled them as they trotted past, and rabbits darted across the road ahead of them.

Jagged tracks of destruction cut across fields and erupted beneath roadways. A Locust track could pass between a homestead and a barn, disturbing neither, then a bit further along it would look as if Locust had gnawed their way through anything wooden and a few things made of concrete or rusted metal.

The world appeared exhausted and unkempt, lonely, and yet terrified of being rediscovered.

Marcus glanced at Brandon. "Lots of signs of where people used to be, but no people. Not even laundry drying on a line."

"Lot of these places were abandoned even before E-Day. The Pendulum Wars meant jobs in the cities, so farm kids abandoned the old homesteads. Folks like the Hahns and the Strouds just expanded their estates." Brandon shook his head. "The grubs, the sinking, the glowies, they didn't leave many folks alive, and few of those who survived ever knew places like this existed. World overpopulation isn't much of a worry these days."

"Wouldn't people want to find a place like this and make a life?"

"Hey, I think you and Anya have got the right idea, but you're survivors. You've spent a decade-plus working with nothing and making it into something. Lots of people have spent that same time just dealing with subtraction. They've lost family. They've lost homes. They've lost the only lives they've known, and while they're shell-shocked, they've had well-meaning folks telling them where to go, maybe handing them food and blankets. They've become so reliant on others that they've abandoned their decision-making."

Marcus wanted to disagree, but as he thought about what he'd seen fighting the Locust, he understood his companion's point. *People have always sought leaders to make decisions for them, to absolve them of making mistakes. I thought that was because they agreed with the leaders, but being swept along because they couldn't make decisions on their own, that also tracks.*

He ran a hand along his jaw. "Makes me glad Anya's working with Jamila Shin to provide some leadership."

"It's definitely a cause for hope." Brandon pointed toward a distant hill. "Just over that hump and we're home. Don't have any whiskey there, but I can guarantee some good bread."

"Let's go."

After an hour they crested the hill. A shanty-town stretched out below them. It reminded Marcus of the Hahn estate, because people had converted cars and buses into homes. Those were the lucky folks. Plywood scraps, cinder blocks, ragged canvas and corrugated tin sheets united at discordant angles and into odd shapes made up the rest of the dwellings. Toward the center things had been arranged on a grid, but then concentric circles of makeshift buildings surrounded the camp. Gray smoke from cooking fires drifted lazily through the air. Beyond the buildings a number of acres had been cultivated, but all that had been harvested, leaving brown earth and chaff.

"What is this place?"

"Started as a Rack—a 'resident accommodation' camp. Back when the COG functioned they brought in food and clean water. Then that stopped. Diseases swept through, killed a bunch. Now folks drift in." Brandon shifted in the saddle. "It's been my home since I was small enough to hide in these grasses."

He led Marcus down the hillside. A couple of dogs barked at

their approach, then a couple of children emerged from makeshift shacks to watch them. Most retreated when adults yelled at them, but a few headed out to greet the newcomers. A knot of men and women formed up, looking as if they expected trouble. Their number shrank by half as Brandon waved and some folks waved back.

"Why do they stay here?" Marcus asked, glancing warily left and right. "You've told them about other places, right?"

"They don't *trust*, Marcus. The Coalition brought supplies, then just stopped. The government sank Jacinto. And the Hammer of Dawn strikes still generate nightmares. The people are sure that if they go out and take over an estate, someone will show up and kick them out or fire will descend from the sky and roast them. Better the devil they know..."

"I had no idea."

"This is their world, Marcus. They do what they can, just waiting for the Locust to come and get them... Most of them, anyway." Brandon shrugged. "Some get away, but not many. Come on. There's someone I want you to meet."

Brandon cut back along the face of the hill and headed toward one of the larger tents—one which also appeared to be in good repair. A couple of teens came out and took the horses' reins as the men dismounted. They led the animals off and Brandon held the tent flap open. Marcus entered and gave his eyes a moment to adjust to the dim light. Brandon came in on his left and a dark-haired woman came through an opening on the right.

Brandon swept the woman into a hug. "I told you I'd be back without a problem."

"This time, Brandon, but it won't be forever." The woman freed herself from Brandon's embrace and offered Marcus her hand. "I'm Adira Turrall."

"Marcus Fenix."

"Pleasure to meet you. Brandon is my little brother."

"She got the brains in the family, I got the looks." Brandon draped an arm over her shoulders. "Adira was in her first residency after medical school when E-Day happened. The COG made her the chief medical officer here, and when they went away, she was pretty much the only authority figure left."

She tucked a lock of hair behind her right ear. "You saw it riding in, I bet. This place isn't going to be viable much longer. We're lucky the well works, but we're shy on food, and my medical supplies are whatever Brandon can find or trade for, so a bad pox will kill half the people. We need to get everyone to move…"

Marcus nodded. "…but they've heard there are Locust out there."

"That's the long and the short of it." Adira's brown eyes narrowed. "Brandon says you're the man for the job."

"I've killed my share of grubs."

"You're a damned Gear. You've killed your share of *us*, too." An emaciated man stood in the entrance. He pointed a quivering finger at Marcus as two more held the tent flaps wide, and a half-dozen other people stood behind him. "We don't want him here, Doctor. It ain't safe. Where Gears go, the Locust show. True in Char. True in Hanover. Gonna be true here."

Marcus shook his head. "It's not like that."

"Not for you, maybe, all big and strong and in your armor. We ain't that. Our kids ain't neither. You couldn't keep us safe, and you damned sure ain't killed all the grubs. They're out there. We know."

Marcus' hands curled down into fists. He wanted to yell back at the man. *You're not the only one who lost people, people who should have lived.* The fireball that consumed Dom blossomed in Marcus' mind again. A lump rose in his throat, choking off any words.

Adira marched over, eyes blazing, and stabbed a finger in the man's chest.

"Bert Stanfield, how *dare you*? You haven't managed to do a damned thing in this camp for the last ten years, other than eat and complain. You don't farm, you don't scavenge, you don't help teach the kids, you don't do anything. This man here, he's come to help us. You're afraid the Locust are going to eat you? This is the man the Locust are afraid will eat *them*. And frankly, right now, if he wanted to stake you out on a hilltop as bait for them, I'd hand him the rope and sharpen the stake.

"And the rest of you know better, too." She gave the crowd behind the old man a hard stare. "Locust don't show up where the Gears are, the Gears go to where the Locust are. Now, are there really Locust out there, or are they just the foolish stories you tell each other because being afraid of Locust is easier than dealing with what's outside this little valley? I don't know, but he and Brandon are going to find out. So, if you want to act like children, do it somewhere else."

"I… I… I…" Bert Stanfield retreated, his face red.

Before he could express a wholly coherent thought, a small boy walked past him and up to Marcus. The child reached out with both hands to tug at Marcus' fist.

"Hey, mister. Are you a Gear?"

It took Marcus a second as he looked down at the boy's dirty face, and the earnest expression on it. "Yes. I was… yes, I'm a Gear."

"Really?" The boy's expression opened.

"Yes, really."

"Good." The boy nodded solemnly. "Then you're the one who's gonna find my sister."

2: HIGHWATER AUDITORIUM

MINISTRY OF SANITATION, EPHYRA, SERA

8 BOUNTY 18 A.E.

It struck Anya that she'd seen the same sort of factional uneasiness before. Back during the war, when command had brought together multiple units for a combined operation, each seemed to feel that everything hinged on its performance. Those same units would be convinced that all the other units would buckle under the pressure. The same sentiments flowed within the various groups assembled in the auditorium.

They'd come at Jamila's invitation. Thomas had stood the folding chairs in a semicircle in front of the stage, with small groups of them on each wing, and a wedge of general seating in the middle. He sat off to the right, along with Anya. All the way across the floor, Aaron Griffin and some aides sat facing her. Raul Hasterwith and Nathan Pendergast sat with their contingents on that side of the room, as well.

Closer to Anya sat Diana Egami from Hanover and Cara Lima, who appeared to represent several Stranded settlements in the

Timgad Valley. Anya herself nominally represented the Westmarch district of Ephyra, and Jamila the City district. The rest of the people in that middle wedge had come as observers, many of them from small settlements or neighborhoods within Ephyra.

Jamila mounted the stage and took her position behind a podium. She graced everyone with a smile.

"Welcome to all of you. I am very pleased you were willing to accept my invitation to attend, much as many of you did at the museum nearly a month ago. The series of catastrophes which has beset our people threatens our very existence. It is my wish that through frank and open discussions we can identify the problems we face, and find a way to work together to rebuild all we have lost."

Immediately Aaron Griffin rose. "What's this *we*? My home is Char. What can be done in Ephyra that benefits me and my people?"

Jamila appeared unfazed by his question. "You raise a very good point, Aaron. As yet, I do not have an answer for you. However, I would hope all of you will agree that we have problems in common, whether here in Ephyra or in the outlying cities and settlements. We seek solutions to those problems, and the ones you find workable may well apply elsewhere. The first order of business for all of us, it would seem logically, is to assess and stabilize the current situation."

Nathan Pendergast II stood. "I think it's patently obvious that the critical issue is one of economics. Not only did the Locust kill billions of people, but they wiped out untold trillions in wealth. Without that, we have no ability to rebuild. We need to reestablish the monetary system and reinstate the wealth that was lost. Then we can move forward with establishing credit, property rights, taxes, and the ability of the people to band together and rebuild."

Cara Lima, a tall, rangy woman with her dark hair plaited into one long braid, shook her head. "Speaking for people who have been carving something out of nothing, *money* isn't the issue. We work, we barter, everyone gets what they need. If someone needs a house or a barn, we get together and pay for it with our sweat. What concerns us more is making sure that we have power, water, food, and getting our children educated so they can do more for the world than we ever did. That's more important than you having a bank balance that means none of your family ever has to work again."

"In Hanover we have basic services and eat well because of the fishing fleet." Diana Egami uncurled from her chair. "We're cleaning up the city, but our medical infrastructure is nonexistent. Diseases we could have cured with two weeks of pills will now kill folks. We're back to the days of bloodletting, leeches, and plucking flowers under a full moon, as far as medicine is concerned."

"Exactly." Pendergast nodded vehemently. "But rebuilding a pharmaceutical factory isn't a cheap proposition. If we don't have an economy, how will companies invest in development?"

"Nathan, you're still out of touch, just like you've always been." Raul Hasterwith waved his colleague to his chair again. "People made pills and researched cures well before venture capitalists ever existed. Barter functions perfectly well. Instead of getting paid in gold and then going out to buy food, you get paid in food. Now, do we need medicines? Absolutely. Would it be helpful to have a factory to mass-produce pills and vaccines? No doubt. But, as Ms. Lima suggests, microeconomies already exist. The trick will be in making certain they can communicate and trade with each other. Communications will require power, and since Imulsion is no longer an option, energy production would seem to be a high priority."

Aaron Griffin gave Hasterwith a thumbs-up. "Communication makes it all good."

"Precisely." Hasterwith sat forward. "Seradyne Industries has a number of facilities that survived, and have been brought back online. Even with a limited power grid, we've established links to a variety of radio and television broadcast centers and the repeaters that relay the system. Many were part of our entertainment network. We are working to bring more online to provide the best possible coverage to communities as we become aware of them. We would be most pleased to provide people who are involved in leadership positions with the equipment necessary to work with the system."

Jamila smiled. "That's most generous, Raul."

"We are prepared to go even further, Jamila." Raul stood slowly, clasping his hands at the small of his back. "We have all suffered most grievously. So many dead. So many missing. What we are prepared to do is to use the computing power of our biggest surviving facility, located halfway between here and Hanover, to serve as a clearing house for people who are looking for loved ones who have gone missing. Likewise for people to report on the dead. Our medical insurance database is set up to handle the data, and has a great deal of it already input."

Aaron Griffin looked over at him. "That ain't gonna be free. What does it cost us?"

"Participation, Aaron—nothing more."

Anya tugged at the cuff of her dress uniform jacket. *And it will give you a wealth of information about how many people exist, their locations and status.*

She made a quick note, then rose at her place. "That's a very generous offer, Mr. Hasterwith. Connecting people and easing their minds would be very helpful. It strikes me, however, that such information would be valuable in so many other ways. Will we be provided direct access?"

"That would depend on what your intentions would be, Lieutenant Stroud. Are you looking to recruit people to rebuild the military? What then? Reestablish the Coalition of Ordered Governments—the COG that burned the surface of our world, and then sank Jacinto? I think anything as drastic as that would necessitate that we all agree. But perhaps you think otherwise. That you would appear in that uniform certainly suggests it."

Anya blinked at the directness and bitterness of Hasterwith's accusation. Her hands snapped down into fists, but she caught herself before she exploded. "Yes, I'm wearing my uniform. I was a Gear. I served proudly. I killed my share of Locust. But it's not with the thought of reestablishing *anything* that I dressed this way." Anya looked around the room. "When Jamila invited me to participate, I realized what a momentous occasion this is. I chose my uniform because it's the nicest clothing I own. It also reminds me of all the friends who died guaranteeing that we could be here today. So it's not a challenge or an insult, it just marks how seriously I take what we're here to accomplish."

Hasterwith pressed his hands together in an attitude of prayer. "Forgive me. It appears I misjudged our colleague. I let my unease at the thought of returning to the days of COG's wanton slaughter blind me to the fact that, clearly, such horrific decisions were made well above your pay grade. It's unfair of me to hold you responsible for actions over which you had no control and with which, perhaps, you did not even agree. At another point, however, when we discuss mutual defense, it will behoove us to guarantee that the military is aware it serves the *people*—and that if line personnel perceive an order to be in violation of such a dictate, they are within their rights to refuse to carry it out."

Anya sat slowly, emotions churning within her. Part of her

ached at the losses inflicted by the Hammer of Dawn. *So many people, so much destruction, in the blink of an eye.* Had there been any alternative, she would have fought for it, but at the time—facing that threat—the Hammer was the only thing keeping mankind alive.

As much as it saddened her to remember that agonizing time, she also wanted to walk across the floor and drop Hasterwith with a straight right hand. If it weren't for what she and all the people represented by her uniform had done, no one in the room would even be alive. The Locust would have destroyed everything.

In the face of that stark truth, Hasterwith's petty comments and Pendergast's misplaced concerns seemed laughable.

Part of her recognized the greater meaning behind Hasterwith's attack. His goal was to remind everyone about the horrors of the war. In doing so, he hung it firmly on Anya. To hobble her, to cripple any plans she had, he'd evoke the war again. The blood of anyone who died during that time would forever stain her hands in the eyes of others.

Part of her was tempted to walk out, to leave the politics behind. She resisted the temptation because she recognized the seriousness of the issues facing humanity. She had been in the trenches. She'd fought Locust. She'd been anointed with their blood and she'd held the line against human extinction.

That again is my job here. If people didn't get the things they needed, humanity would cease to exist. She wasn't going to let Hasterwith or Pendergast or Griffin court disaster for people just to ease their minds over their selfish concerns.

Jamila moved out from behind the lectern and opened her arms. "Raul, thank you for your apology. We must all remember that we are gathered here to look forward. Our views will be tempered by our experience of the past, no doubt, but we cannot let our fears cripple our efforts to make the world a viable place. For my own part, I have worked the last weeks very closely with Anya Stroud. She has a first-class analytical mind. Anya is responsible for the Ministry's ability to deliver fresh water and take away sewage in many of the city's precincts. She and my aide Thomas have studied and collected recommendations for much of Ephyra. These recommendations have been compiled into a report which can serve as a basis for our further discussions.

"Her devotion to duty and ability to focus on details stood her in good stead as a Gear, and those same traits have made her invaluable to the work we have begun."

Aaron Griffin folded his arms over his chest. "Okay, clean slate. Give us the goods, Lieutenant."

"Please, just Anya." She stood and took a deep breath. "Back during the Pendulum Wars and in the Locust War, the COG initiated a couple of doomsday scenario programs. They established shelters and stockpiled them with food, medicine, other necessities. We've been digging through records and have located a number of these secret stockpiles. I hope, my friends, there will be enough medical supplies to fill in until we can get some small-scale production facilities up and running.

"Another part of the program secured stockpiles of seeds for a wide variety of high-yield plants which we can use to boost agricultural output. Some of these facilities include frozen eggs and sperm for establishing and improving herds of domesticated animals. The reports you'll be given show where the stockpiles are located, and suggest ways to use them to guarantee that everyone benefits."

Cara Lima frowned. "How are we going to determine the ways

these resources will be allocated? Do we go by actual head count? How are the tiny settlements—the ones that need the most help—going to even know about this stuff, if they don't have people here to represent them?"

Raul nodded. "This goes back to my point about communication."

"This is why we are here." Jamila returned to the lectern and consulted some notes. "This is a matter for people who understand logistics, and can estimate need. Both Cara and Diana have expertise in this area. Aaron, I might suggest that you and Anya join them to figure out a plan for allocation. Nathan, if you have any King Ravens or other transportation which could help, I would ask you to get us an inventory, as well as a list of needs at your end. Raul, your communications network will be vital in assessing the needs of outlying communities."

"I have a question for Lieutenant Stroud." Hasterwith picked an invisible bit of lint from the sleeve of his black jacket. "You've not mentioned weaponry in conjunction with these repositories. Would you have us believe that there is none?"

"No, sir. The COG did establish munitions dumps—many of them, on a much smaller scale. However, that data was compartmentalized and heavily encrypted." Anya glanced at Thomas. "We have yet to succeed in decrypting what little of the information we can find. We must bear in mind, as well, that if the sites still exist, some of the weapons date from well before E-Day, and the munitions may have deteriorated to the point of no longer being useful."

"That actually makes a great deal of sense." Hasterwith jotted down a note. "Fortunately, Seradyne will be able to manufacture a limited number of weapons and ammunition, should it become necessary to arm people for their mutual defense. I would hope,

Cara, that your people would see the wisdom of returning to central locations, simply because a concentration of people will be easier to secure. I think all of us are aware that out there, we will find people who have no desire to recreate civilization. The takers. Bandits, that sort of thing, those who want their needs met without being willing to work on their own behalf. It would pain me greatly were people to be unable to defend themselves against such animals."

Cara began to respond, but Jamila held up a hand to forestall any protest. "If I might, Cara... Only through the fully frank and open discussion of issues are we going to be able to pull the world together, heal its wounds, and move into the future. These stockpiles will help us address immediate issues. Let us work together, now, to make these resources available to our people. If we do it well, *then* will be the time for us to address more... politically sensitive issues."

And if we fail... As the meeting came to an end, Anya watched Hasterwith go over to shake Pendergast's hand. *...we'll be fighting to see who will command the tattered remnant of humanity, and watch it die.*

3: RESIDENT ACCOMMODATION CAMP #2709

JACINTO PLATEAU, SERA

8 BOUNTY 18 A.E.

"Your sister?"

"Yes." The little boy nodded matter-of-factly. "Her name is Sierra." He reached up as high as he could and got on his tiptoes. "She is this tall. She has black hair, and is funny."

Adira turned from the scarecrow of a man standing at the tent's opening and moved over to crouch by the boy, giving him a hug.

"Nick, we've talked about your sister."

"And this Gear will find her." The boy, his eyes glistening, looked up at Marcus. "You will, won't you, mister?"

Marcus dropped to a knee, so that he was eye to eye with Nick, and rested his hands on his shoulders. "I will. I'll look for her, and do all I can to find her."

"Okay." The boy smiled and stuck his hand out. "Shake on it."

The big man's hand engulfed the boy's. As they shook, Marcus looked up at Brandon, who wore a haunted expression. *This will be trouble. But it's not the first time I've had trouble.*

"Okay." Nick gave Marcus a solemn nod. "I'll go make up a bed for her. Thank you." He turned and marched straight out of the tent, past Stanfield and the other adults.

Marcus stood again. "What's the mission brief on that?"

"Not good." Brandon scratched at the back of his neck. "Nick came in with a half-dozen people about six months ago. They said they'd found him in a farmhouse ruin. Nick said his sister had told him to be quiet and wait until she got back, but he'd been on his own for a few days."

Marcus glanced at Adira. "How old is he?"

"Six, I think." She folded her arms over her chest. "Malnutrition has him smaller than he ought to be, but language and reasoning put him there. He does well in the school we have. He's learned his letters and is good at math. The problem is that the people who brought him in saw no signs of anyone else, so we don't even know if Sierra exists."

"I've asked after her—a girl so tall, dark hair, perhaps worried about her little brother. She's got to be at least early teens." Brandon shook his head. "I've come up empty. Maybe Locust got her. Maybe... It won't surprise you to know there are human predators out there."

"Slavers?" Marcus' eyes narrowed. "Cannibals?"

"And things not quite so extreme." Adira sighed. "Lots of little communities have organized themselves to preserve what they've got and to live up to a particular code of conduct. Polygamy, polyandry, tradesmen adopting kids to teach them a skill. Things that have worked in the past, but not everyone agrees with. If a group like the one that brought Nick in gets too big, they might drop people with another settlement. If that settlement really needs young people, or someone wants children to raise, and they make a deal..."

"Right." Marcus scratched at his jaw. "If it's for survival, they don't see it as exploitation?"

"And then there are the times when it might be in a person's best interest to go, but they don't see it." Adira shook her head. "We have families come out here from time to time, looking to adopt kids. Brandon or someone else will check them out, see what they have going on, and we'll make the best call we can. While we've taken food from the farmers who adopt kids, we've never *sold* children. We're not turning down help to keep others alive. It's a terrifying world out here, and an ethical quagmire."

"That you pay attention to it counts for a lot." Marcus frowned, then looked at Brandon. "Is there anything else we know about Sierra?"

"Aside from the fact we don't even know if she exists? We don't know if she's his biological sister, or someone he just called sister and, you know, at his age, he probably thinks she *is* his sister, regardless." Brandon opened his hands. "With the 'dark hair and this tall' description, chances of finding her are slender."

"For that matter, she might be dead." A vision popped into Marcus' mind, of the woman and child he'd buried. He glanced at Brandon's sister. "Is there anyone here who Nick counts as family, Doc?"

"Only the whole camp." Adira smiled. "Kid with a story like that breaks a lot of hearts, but his little smile mends them right back up again."

Marcus popped the buckles on his armor and pulled it up off over his head. "Good. Now, let's see about gathering together the siting stories on Locust, and maybe a map of where folks found Nick. We're going to be looking for things I don't want to find, so we might as well look for someone I do."

One woman in the camp had previously been a surveyor, and knew the local area pretty well. She'd collected a variety of charts and maps, and had become skilled at drawing the same freehand. She provided them a specific map for the Ephyra district, and a copy of a map she'd made that included approximate locations for settlements she'd heard about from travelers. For those, she included anything with at least a dozen people, so the Hahn estate showed up on her map, giving Marcus a point of reference that locked many other things in place.

Marcus worked with Adira and Brandon well into the night, then crashed on a cot in one of the wards. He lay there, staring at the canvas above him, hands behind his head. The occasional dog barking or someone trudging past to use the latrines sounded normal. He felt as if he was back in some bivouac with the other Gears, just waiting for King Ravens to carry them off to places where they'd unleash hell on nightmare creatures.

He had so hoped those days were over, that they'd finally destroyed all the Locust, but something inside him said there had to be a spark of truth behind the rumors. If so, that meant he had failed.

We failed, and Dom's sacrifice was for nothing.

He stopped himself from spiraling down into despair by deciding that he should apply the same standard to Nick's story. Marcus decided that Sierra actually did exist, that she did have black hair and that she was "this tall." If he was going to accept that horror continued to exist in the world, he'd balance it with a touch of hope. He would find Nick's sister, or he'd find out what had happened to her—and deliver unholy hellfire to whomever had taken her away from her brother.

Yeah, you're doing you, Marcus. Set an impossible goal, and wonder why things don't work out the way you think they should. He exhaled slowly. *But, you know, making this world work, that's the biggest, most impossible goal. I'm just knocking off a small piece of it. I'll get this win, and worry about the rest of it later.*

Finally he felt the day's exhaustion catching up with him. If he'd been forced to bet, he'd have put his money on a nightmare where grubs burst into the camp, swallowed Nick whole, and devoured everyone else in great, gory bites. Surprisingly, malignant dreams remained at bay, and he got the rest he had earned on that long ride.

Marcus got up early, feeling rested, washed his face and pulled on the Hellions jersey in lieu of his armor. He only recalled his dreams in snippets. Somehow they involved his fondest memories of time spent with his father, but *he* was the father and Nick was his son. The sun shone, flowers bloomed, and Nick laughed at all sorts of nonsense.

One of the camp's residents brought him a piece of flatbread with beans spread over it and rice piled on top. A steaming cup of some herbal tea accompanied it. Marcus used his boot knife to substitute for a spoon until the rice mound had shrunk enough that he could tear the bread up and finish his meal that way.

"Hey, Mister Gear, I found you a rock." Nick trundled over, holding out a smooth stone disk the size of the boy's palm. "Sierra said these rocks are lucky."

Marcus took it and inspected the gray stone carefully. "I've heard that."

"It's a good one."

"I can see that."

"Tell Sierra I gave it to you." The boy smiled. "When you find her."

"Okay, Nick." Marcus slipped the stone into his pocket, then offered the boy some of his breakfast. "You hungry?"

The boy nodded and tore off a small piece of the bread. He made a great show of chewing it thoroughly. Then a perplexed expression crossed his face. "Is it tough to be a Gear?"

"It can be."

"Maybe I can be one. When I grow up. And help people."

"Helping people is a good idea, but you don't have to be a Gear to help." Marcus nodded over at Brandon emerging from the clinic tent. "Brandon helps and isn't a Gear." *And I hope like hell, son, that your world isn't going to need more Gears.*

Brandon rubbed some sleep sand from his eyes and wandered over. "Nick, do me a favor? Tell Ben we'll need our horses saddled right away."

"Okay." Nick waved. "Bye, Mister Gear."

"Bye, Nick." Marcus held the remaining half of the flatbread out toward Brandon. "Help yourself."

Brandon shook his head. "I'll head over to the mess tent to get my own. Couple of people I have to talk to before we head out. I'll catch up with you."

"Roger that." Marcus finished his breakfast, then returned to his cot to tidy it up. He also bound his armor up to tie it more easily to his pack horse's panniers.

Adira appeared and handed him a leather satchel. "Bandages, some ointment, needles and thread. Can't spare painkillers, but this ought to be enough for cuts and scrapes."

"Thanks." He looked up at her. "Brandon was eight or so on E-Day?"

"And a half. I was the firstborn in our family, he was the surprise. We have—had—two more brothers and a sister in the middle. Nearly as we know, they and our parents are dead. I ended up here and about a year later he showed up, traveling with Ted in the luggage cart." She smiled at the memory. "He travels a lot, but always comes home."

"Seems like he's seen a lot."

She shook her head. "I don't know. He leaves all that outside the valley, but he does have scars. I think he's happy to leave what's happened outside on the outside."

"He's not alone there." Marcus stood and hefted his armor onto his back.

Adira rested a hand on his shoulder. "Just so you know, Brandon usually travels alone. Always comes back with people or things, but heads out by himself. For him to have recruited you means he trusts you. So, please make sure he gets back here."

He patted her hand. "You have my word."

"Thank you." She sighed. "And look, it would be a miracle if you even caught word of Nick's sister. Nobody expects…"

"Nick does. That's mission critical for me." Marcus gave her a grin. "So it's a miracle. I've lived through a bunch of those. There ought to be at least one more out there with my name on it."

Adira followed Marcus from the tent and helped him tie the armor onto the pack horse's back. They had the four horses with which they started out, but switched to riding the mounts that had carried the kit the day before. Brandon tied a canvas bag to his pack horse, hugged his sister, and mounted up.

A small crowd gathered to see them off. Nick stood with

Adira, waving heartily. Others surrounded Stanfield and appeared happy to see the back of them. Marcus, whose hind end hadn't quite become accustomed to the feel of the saddle, waved back and then caught up with his companion.

"Stanfield usually watch you go?"

"Nope. Mostly isn't up before noon. The Stanfield clan had a family reunion in Aspic Park on E-Day. He had the better part of a case of beer inside him when the Locust erupted. Of a hundred twenty-three people, five survived. His daughter, a sister-in-law he hated, a nephew, and someone's infant. Some people just can't recover, have no resilience. His daughter got tired of it eight years ago or so and left. I don't think he's heard from her since." Brandon shrugged. "Confronting you was the most active thing he's done since I've known him."

"During the war, we saw lots of people like him. Scared. Looking for someone to blame." Marcus twisted around and made sure his armor remained securely attached to the saddle. "They always wonder, 'If we saved *them*, why didn't we save everyone?'"

"No one's immune to wondering that." Brandon threw his shoulders back and stretched. "So many people *almost* made it. Just another inch…" His hand closed as if trying to grab at a phantom.

They haunt us all. Marcus stared straight ahead. He saw Dom's face. Maria's. His father's, and so many more. Faces of the living as they died. Faces of the twisted and broken. The charred remains of those that the Hammer of Dawn tagged as collateral damage. *So many gave their lives. Some willingly. Some because they were in the wrong place, wrong time. And I wasn't fast enough to save them.*

If only… if only… Those two words echoed in his skull, a recursive chanting that drained him with every repetition. The bullet that would have saved someone. The bit of cover that they didn't hide behind fast enough. The ground collapsing beneath someone, or something, or a sinkhole swallowing whole buildings. Whole blocks.

"Marcus? Sera to Marcus… come in please."

"Yeah, sorry."

"You good?"

"Yeah, you know, just… thinking." Marcus rubbed a hand over his forehead. "What was it you were saying?"

"Couple miles is where we decide to head straight for the coast and along it to Hanover, or cut up, make for the place where they found Nick, and then hook around to come at Hanover from inland. You have a preference?"

"We can reach the farm by nightfall, yes?"

"Might even have some daylight to look around, though after four months…"

"I don't expect to find anything, but…" Marcus nodded. "After that, I think Hanover is the right choice."

"Yeah, some reports of weird sightings coming through there."

"Good, that, but it's not what I meant." Marcus fished the flat stone out of his pocket. "Nick gave me this. He said Sierra claimed stones like it were good luck. These are the kinds of stones you see around lakes or oceans, worn smooth, great for skipping. Makes me wonder if they weren't from there." *If they weren't fleeing the Lambent that attacked when we were last there.*

"That's a good idea. I like how you're thinking."

"I'm going to need you to tell that to Colonel Hoffman at some point."

Brandon smiled. "You think that'll get you your old job back?"

"Nope, not at all." Marcus laughed. "But it might explain to him how I managed to live through all the fighting. I'm pretty sure he's just put it down to dumb luck and stubbornness for all these years."

4: COUGARS' STADIUM

HANOVER, SERA

15 BOUNTY 18 A.E.

Marcus and Brandon located the farmstead where the travelers had found Nick. One of the two tall trees that had been described to Brandon as flanking the house had since fallen down. The tree split the house front from back, with the back half falling away and the front just sort of sagging in. They took a quick look inside, but found nothing of true significance. Marcus spotted a couple of flat stones piled one upon the other near the door, but they were the size of dinner plates, so he discounted those as being connected to Nick and Sierra.

They expanded their search for a hundred yards in all directions, but again came up empty. At least they found no signs of Locust, nor any secluded camp sites.

The farm's well still worked, so they were able to water the horses and let them graze the fields. As night arrived the two men built a fire and, despite the seasonal chill, slept out under the twin moons.

In the morning Marcus took another look around, but found nothing.

The rest of their journey to Hanover remained uneventful. Marcus began to relish the simple demands of travel and the slower pace of life. During the war everything had been hurry-up-and-wait, with action taking place at hyper speed. Everything had to be done immediately, or disaster would ensue. The unrelenting pressure stressed everyone to the point where they thought that if the Locust didn't kill them, the tension just might.

The uncomplicated routine on the road didn't take any thought. Set up camp, take care of the horses, sleep, break down camp. Saddle up and push on. Far from being boring, the repetition felt reassuring. Marcus made certain to check and care for his weapons and remained aware of his surroundings, but he didn't have that sense of catastrophic doom dogging him relentlessly.

It helped that Brandon didn't seem to mind traveling without unnecessary chattering. By the end of the second day out, they'd gotten so used to each other that pointing at something would earn a nod in response, and that would be sufficient. They divided labor evenly, laughed easily, and didn't complain too much about each other's cooking.

It took a week to reach Hanover. The city—once a coastal jewel—largely lay in ruins. Much of it had burned, but the fires had died out long before. Still, tendrils of gray fog drifted between jagged buildings which thrust up into the air like broken teeth. Lambent stalks twisted in and around them, threading their way in and out of gaping holes. The city, from that perspective, appeared to have rotted through.

Yet, without active flames and smoke drifting over it, the place seemed somehow peaceful. The stadium had indeed taken damage, but hadn't completely collapsed. Thinning fog revealed that through the summer, plants had continued to grow and much of the war's damage lay hidden beneath a blanket of evergreen ivy. It had even grown up around a few of the Lambent stalks.

What surprised and impressed Marcus was the way the people remaining in Hanover had organized themselves to clean up and rebuild. Recovery near the docks was furthest along, and worked its way toward the city center. At the same time, it appeared as if people from the stadium district had begun their own clean-up, and worked down toward the center, thus creating a clean band across the metro area. They'd torn down Lambent stalks, cleared rubble, and long ago collected the dead for burial.

People paid the riders little mind as they approached the stadium. A few wore sidearms, and each work area had a couple of sentries with long-guns, but fairly often those guns had been laid aside to free up hands needed for clearing rubble.

Marcus pointed toward the stadium. "A buddy of mine was from Hanover and, I think, returned here after the war. He'll be at the stadium, or people there will know where to find him."

"Augustus Cole?"

"You know him?"

"I know *of* him. Who doesn't? Before all this Locust stuff, I wanted to be him when I grew up. He's a legend, as much for Thrashball as for being a Gear."

"Whatever you heard, double it. He's as good as they come."

They rode on toward the Stadium, through areas that hadn't yet been cleared, threading their way between rusted hulks and past ivy-swathed Lambent stalks. Where the Lambent had exploded up from below, not much grew, and what did appeared stunted and diseased. Fragments of hard crystal shell crackled beneath the horses' hooves, residue of the Locust killed by the Imulsion Countermeasure. This, too, appeared to stunt plant growth, and breathing the dust left a bitter taste in Marcus' throat. His horse didn't seem to care for it either, picking its way around the chunks. Marcus stroked its neck.

They emerged into another reclaimed zone and the horses calmed down. Work crews here were engaged in reconstruction as they had been in the city center, but were markedly different from the people the pair had seen previously. Generally speaking, the Stadium district's workers were younger and very fit. It struck Marcus that if he had been looking to recruit Gears, he'd have started here. These people clearly had access to food and water, appeared clean, and kept their clothes in good repair.

Marcus and Brandon, on the other hand, had spent a week living rough, so they definitely looked out of place. They rode toward the Stadium and headed for a gate labeled "Cougars' Plaza," where two well-dressed young men stood, one pale, the other with dark skin, and both muscular. These guardians looked them up and down, then stood there and gave them a stone-faced expression that told Marcus they weren't getting past.

Marcus reined up short, but didn't dismount. "I'm looking for Augustus Cole."

The white guy shook his head. "He's busy."

"I'm an old friend of his."

"No, man, you're not." The black man opened his hands. "Just because he did an ad or something for what, your sandwich shop back in the day, he don't know you. This isn't a charity."

Marcus pointed. "Why don't you use that radio and tell him that Marcus Fenix is here."

The two guards exchanged glances. "Oh, *hell*, why didn't you say? Marcus Fenix. Charlie, you got Marcus Fenix on the list?"

The white guy pantomimed checking an invisible list. "Nope, no Fenix on the list. But, Dexter, isn't he the third Marcus Fenix this week?"

"Fourth, and the most broken-down one yet." Dexter sneered at Marcus and waved him away. "Beat it, old man. Get your sorry ass out of here."

Brandon leaned over and took the reins from Marcus. "Do what you have to do."

Marcus swung from the saddle and balled his fists. "Just use the radio."

"Or what, old man?" Dexter shifted his shoulders and widened his stance. "How about you take it from me, and call up there yourself?"

"No." Marcus slowly grinned. "I take it from you and shove it so far up your…"

The radio on Dexter's belt crackled. "Dexter, take a knee, son." It was a familiar voice, and Marcus let himself relax.

Dexter plucked the radio off his belt and hit the switch. "Nothing to worry about, sir. Just the usual kind of crazy."

"Oh no, baby, that man's gonna tear you in half, then strangle Charlie with your guts. Let Sergeant Fenix pass."

The eyes of both guards grew wide, and Marcus let his grin broaden. He stepped forward and snatched the radio from Dexter's hand.

"Cole, you're ruining my fun."

"And you're gonna ruin my secondary. I'm sending someone down for you. Give the horses to Charlie. Charlie, you take care of them like they was mine."

Charlie fumbled with his own radio. "Yes, sir. Like they were yours."

Brandon dismounted and tossed him the reins. "When you brush them down, see if you can get the burrs out of their tails."

Marcus handed Dexter back his radio and lowered his voice to a whisper. "Cole wasn't kidding."

"No offense intended, sir."

"You might work on your delivery."

Another well-dressed young man emerged from the stadium into Cougars' Plaza, smaller than his compatriots and smiling. "I'm Roberto. I work with Mr. Cole as his administrative assistant. Let me take you to him."

Marcus grunted, and kept his face impassive. The Augustus Cole he'd fought with side by side would have laughed at the idea that he'd ever have an administrative assistant. People with that sort of job served as a buffer between important people and everyday folks. Cole never would have wanted that. He'd always been a man of the people, happy when they remembered him, and overjoyed when he stopped the monsters trying to kill them.

Roberto led them across a vast lobby to a lift. "Despite the damage the stadium suffered, the geothermal power plant that was part of its construction survived nearly intact. We made the necessary repairs, and that has supplied enough power to accelerate recovery in this district. Mr. Cole has been instrumental in inspiring the people to assist in recovery throughout the city. He's been working closely with Captain Diana Egami in this regard."

The lift rose smoothly as Roberto spoke. It stopped on level five and opened into an office with a wall of windows looking out on the city. It boasted wooden paneling, and nice furniture filled it, save for a single, battered locker off to the side. The carpeting had been stitched together from remnants, but covered the floor from wall to wall. The wall opposite the windows was curtained.

Augustus Cole sat in a chair behind the desk. He rose, a massive smile on his face. "As I live and breathe. Damn, Marcus, you are a sight for sore eyes. Come here!"

They met halfway and hugged. Cole squeezed him so tightly Marcus expected ribs to crack. He pounded Cole's back and didn't want to let go. Just seeing him and hanging on to him brought another layer of reality back to the world.

"Damnit, Cole, you are a sight for sore eyes. Anya sends her love."

"Of course you missed me, baby." The big man released him and turned to Brandon, offering his hand. "Augustus Cole."

"Brandon Turrall. Pleasure's all mine."

"Come you guys, sit." Cole looked past Marcus. "Roberto, you can take off."

"Yes, sir, of course, but you do have a seven o'clock."

"Calling an audible here. Push it to tomorrow."

Roberto nodded. "As you wish, sir."

"And bring us something to drink. Good stuff, okay?"

"Of course, sir."

Marcus moved to a chair and watched Roberto exit the office. "Never thought I'd see the day…"

"I know, but the Cole Train is back, baby." Cole's wide smile shrank a bit. "Brother, I didn't know what I'd do when I separated from Delta. I came home and things started moving—slow at first, then faster in the last three months. Marcus, they even want to start the League again. We're reviving the Cougars. I'm an owner-player-coach."

Marcus arched an eyebrow. "Aren't you a little long in the tooth for Thrashball? You're still in great shape but…"

"The Cole Train is eternal, baby." Cole sat back. "Fact is that all the kids who want to play never really have. For the last sixteen years there haven't been games, leagues, training programs, nothing. I hold my own against them. But there are so few athletes we'll start playing eight-on-eight."

Brandon frowned. "It's a great idea, but I'd have thought organized sports would be lower on the list of things that need doing."

"Me, too," Cole admitted. "Took me by surprise, but they explained it like this: people don't know what to think about who they are or whether or not we'll ever be normal again." He interlaced his fingers. "To give people identity and unity, Seradyne Information Services wants to broadcast games to every town and settlement. The idea is to get a big screen in every settlement so they can run news and sports and anything we can recover. We won the war, but so many people lost so much. Having their favorite teams come back gives them something to be proud of, and the Cougars will start all that."

Marcus' eyes narrowed. "Who did you talk to at Seradyne?"

"Raul Hasterwith, why?"

"No reason. I met him a month ago, and he offered me a job."

"Oh hell, Marcus, you want a job, baby? I'll give you one. You name it, anything you want."

"You're a good friend, Cole. I'll remember that." Marcus sat forward, forearms on his thighs. "I sort of have a job now. Brandon and I are tracking down reports of new Locust sightings."

Cole didn't seem surprised, and he nodded slowly. "I hear stories now and again. Nothing panned out. Certainly not in the city. Last rumor put one north and west of here, maybe a month ago."

"You're not giving those stories any weight?"

"It's all ghost stories, Marcus. Last one was a small group

of folks coming here—said they were camping at night. Heard something. Had something rush the camp. They said they scared it off by banging spoons on pans and throwing rocks. That's not any Locust I know."

"Sounds off to me, too." Marcus rubbed a hand over his unshaven jaw. "Another thing, another long shot. We're looking for a young woman named Sierra. Black hair, about this tall."

Cole shook his head. "Not someone I know."

Brandon shifted in his chair. "There's a chance she was taken by traffickers."

"They're a problem. They're shoot-on-sight in town." Cole opened his arms. "As for the problem with refugees, come here, take a look." He got up and led them to the office's curtained rear wall. He drew back the drapes, revealing the rebuilt stadium. Cots lay in even rows over the playing surface, with a wide gap cutting across the field's midpoint. Curtains separated the cots into clusters of twenty. High above the field two rows of luxury suites appeared in good repair, and a number of the balconies had clothes-lines hung with laundry.

"We're using the stadium for more than just playing our games. We've been repairing the suites and we're housing families in them. The cot dormitories hold lots of single folks. The catering kitchens provide meals, so we have a whole community that works, eats, and sleeps here. We fixed the plumbing, so the old locker rooms let everyone shower at least once a week."

Marcus patted Cole on the back. "Damned fine job you've done putting this together."

"Thanks, man." He rested his hands on Marcus' shoulders. "All the things we saw, all the things we done, this here is some of my best work."

Marcus smiled. "Feels good to be building something up, instead of tearing it down, right?"

"You know it, Marcus. Lots of the folks living on the field, they're the ones the traffickers would be taking. I'll have Roberto ask around about your Sierra. Maybe you'll get lucky."

"I'd rather Sierra does, you know."

"Sure, man." Cole playfully slapped at Marcus' stomach. "Who is this girl?"

"Her kid brother asked me to find her."

"Anything I can do to help, you know that." Cole shook his head. "Can you believe it, Marcus, that we made it all the way through?"

"Why us, when so many of them didn't?"

"I don't know, brother." Cole hung an arm over Marcus' shoulders. "I just always had it in my mind that I'd be here. I'd be the Cole Train again. Unstoppable. And see that suite over there? With the Delta crest? That's for Delta. Any time, any event, Delta is in the house. And maybe Colonel Hoffman, too, if we decide."

"Maybe." Marcus smiled. "Looks like you're doing good here, Cole. Everyone would be proud."

"Wish more were here to see this, but yeah, baby, I love it." Cole nodded. "We'll make something that will last, create some good memories."

"Amen to that." Marcus nodded toward the cots on the field. "Got room for two travelers for a night?"

Cole arched an eyebrow. "You look like rough customers."

"Don't come any rougher."

"We'll fix you up." Cole laughed, the warmth of his mirth filling the office. "Not for old time's sake, Marcus, but for building a new future."

5: DB INDUSTRIES WATER PLANT #01

EPHYRA, SERA
16 BOUNTY 18 A.E.

Anya Stroud waited in the doorway of the water treatment plant's laboratory, a bemused smile on her face. Damon Baird had managed to twist himself into an uncomfortable shape as he'd crawled partway inside the chassis of a humanoid robot a little larger and bulkier than a person. Sparks flew out here and there, along with a sibilant stream of profanity. The sparks stopped—the cursing did not—and a gloved hand blindly groped for a spanner on a nearby table-top.

Anya walked over and placed the spanner in Damon's hand.

The hand froze for a moment, then grasped the tool and withdrew into the chassis. A couple of clanks later, Damon reemerged. He pulled off the welder's goggles, leaving two clean circles on a besmudged face. He shielded his eyes against the light, then smiled.

"Hey, Anya, I thought I was going to see you tomorrow. Or is it tomorrow already?"

"No, tomorrow is still tomorrow, and the various ministers are looking forward to the tour of the plant."

"Ministers, is that what we're calling you now?"

She nodded. "'Counsellors,' 'facilitators,' and 'coordinators' all had their proponents, but 'ministers' won out in the end."

"Sure, more legit for people who are rebuilding a government, and avoids the corporate stink of 'chairman.'" Damon set the spanner on the table, then shucked his gloves. "Actually I'm glad you came here to remind me. There's some stuff I'm going to want to hide. Like the lab and this beauty." He gestured to the robot.

"Is that…?"

"The idea I told you about the last time you were out here? Yep. Working title is DeeBee X1. Pretty slick name, right? Came up with it on my own."

"I never would have guessed, Baird."

"Okay, maybe a little obvious. Anyway, the DeeBees: I put the guts of an old Jack unit into a body with arms and legs. I even slapped on Jack's face, for the personality. Cool thing, we can change the arms as needed and attach tools, so we could have, for example, a DeeBee with a rotary blade for cutting through rebar, and another with a jackhammer. We set them on a ruined building, they break it down, haul the parts somewhere else, and build something new—same as folks are already doing for housing, but no worries about an unstable structure collapsing and killing someone."

"When will the prototype be operational?"

"A week?" Damon shrugged. "Maybe longer. I won't be ready to go public with it until I have a few working models, but I was thinking I'd run a field test at your estate, cleaning some things up and rebuilding the wings. I can make the arrangements with Marcus when he gets back."

"Anything we can do to help, of course, we'll do." Anya appropriated a chair from one of the lab stations and sat. "He called this morning. He's in Hanover. Cole sends his best wishes."

"Glad they connected. I'll give Cole shit for not letting me know." Baird chuckled to himself. "No idea when Marcus is going to be back?"

"They're chasing down insubstantial stories, so there's no real timetable. I'll tell him you asked after him when we talk next. Hopefully we'll get more time on the connection."

Damon jerked a thumb at a satellite phone recharging near the door. "Depends what satellite you hook into. Seradyne's has a couple that are easy to locate but the carrier is dirty, or so it seems to me. Conversations frag a lot. You were using the old MilNet, though, right?"

"Working it is second nature."

"And teaching Marcus a new way of doing things..."

"Hush. If it works, there's no reason to complicate things." Anya glanced down at her hands. "You said Seradyne's carrier is unreliable. What about the rest of their equipment. How *secure* do you think their system is?"

"As secure as anything on the planet, I guess." Damon scratched at the back of his head. "I don't imagine they have much in the way of programmers specializing in security, but I'm not sure there are any hackers out there trying to get into their stuff. Definitely less opportunity to do that sort of thing, since we really have no networks and no centralized databanks. Why do you ask?"

"Just a hunch." Anya sighed. "The ministers are trying to assess resources and needs, in order to provide for as many people as we can. Seradyne is being very generous with their Information Services assets. They want to put television and radio repeater units close to every village and township and settlement they can find. They want to get people news and allow them to communicate with each other. If Redland Hills has surplus wheat, and Whitefish Bay has a bunch of dried fish, they can work a deal. They're providing the service at no charge, but once we figure money out, I expect charges will begin to accrue."

Damon frowned. "How would that deal work? Redland Hills radios out a bulletin that they have the wheat, then Whitefish Bay reaches out and says they'll trade fish for it? So many ways to abuse that sort of a system. Seems as if someone—Seradyne most likely—would have to be the escrow agent for all such trades. Anyone who doesn't deliver what they promise gets cut off."

"Which gives Seradyne a lot of power, because they control the information."

"Information and the economy." Damon opened his hands. "Right now, if two towns cut a deal, things are settled in person, when they make the exchange. But it would be easier, right, if there was a central market where trade could take place. Those repeaters could broadcast on a variety of frequencies, so Seradyne could set up a premium trade channel and they'd be the market."

"Exactly, Damon. We have a small trader's market over at the Hahn estate every couple of weeks. Something like that, but on a larger scale."

"But this would be massive, Anya, and virtual. Whitefish Bay can't be hauling dried fish to Char and Hanover and Ephyra, but they *could* send it to a central location—a place that Seradyne provides. Seradyne gives them credit for the fish, and Whitefish Bay orders up a bunch of things to be shipped back to them. Seradyne's credit becomes the fiat currency for the world."

Anya nodded. "And once they control the market, they control the price of every item in it. Redland Hills and Whitefish Bay might agree on a price if they trade directly, but Seradyne could raise the prices to both parties. Even if there was an assigned middleman, Seradyne could decide to cut them out and refuse to trade with them, crippling them.

"I don't want to think anyone would do that but..." Anya hugged her arms around her middle. "It's not just a question of Seradyne sinking its claws into the world, but of Seradyne being the trellis upon which the world will regrow. We have to reestablish society, and the information technologies that Seradyne provides are critical for that, but that's a lot of power to put in the hands of one man or one corporation."

"It's the sort of vital service that might be nationalized, except..."

"Except we have no nations and no army with which to seize control of the network." Anya shivered as a cold tingle ran down her spine. "As you said, they could create multiple layers to the communications network. If one group and their allies get information faster than another group, that comes with a distinct advantage. And if proprietary information gets revealed..."

"Or news just gets spun with a certain angle." Damon pointed in the direction of Hanover. "Take Marcus' hunt for Locust. You want to keep that quiet so people won't panic, which is understandable. Why yell 'fire!' if it turns out there are no flames? If Marcus and Brandon find nothing, great.

"But follow me here, Anya: Seradyne could spin the story about there being a hidden danger that the Ministry didn't want to let people know about. That begins the erosion of public trust. Then, if they find some Locust but put them down, the threat turns out to be real and again the Ministry is withholding information. Maybe it turns out well this time, but the people wonder how many more instances there are, and…"

Anya nodded. "Moving against Seradyne now is impossible, because we need what they're offering."

Damon nodded. "Still, someone is going to have to keep a close eye on them, and limit their power. If Hasterwith decides he wants to be top minister or supreme minister or whatever you're going to call it, he'd be in a position to thwart any attempt to prevent Seradyne from becoming not only the trellis, but the greenhouse and everything else."

"No, you're right." Anya tapped a finger against her chin. "I'll bring all of this up with Jamila. She's the politician. She has the connections and the way to make people see what's going on without getting anyone too alarmed."

"And what's your Plan B, Anya?" Damon's eyes narrowed. "What if Jamila doesn't turn out to be the person for the job. From my perspective, I think *you're* going to have to be our Plan B."

"No. I am not, nor do I want to be."

"Shin brought you into the Ministry for a reason."

"Yes, because of my logistical and organizational skills. And in the first meeting of ministers I got ripped into because I was wearing my uniform, suggesting I wanted to recreate the COG and establish a military hegemony."

Damon chuckled. "How's it gone since then?"

"Well, I think it's been okay. I'm getting to know folks, and I think they're coming to trust me." Anya sighed. "Okay, you might have a point. Maybe we do need a Plan B, but I'm adamant. I do *not* want to be a politician."

"Yes, Madam Minister." She balled a hand into a fist, and he cringed. "Now, what do your logistical and organization skills suggest?"

Anya gave him one of those I-really-hate-you-right-now stares, which only broadened his grin. "Okay, diversionary tactic. If Seradyne is looking to lock up the economy, then we diversify it. When ministers tour here tomorrow, show them the algae ponds. They should be able to recreate that technology pretty quickly, right?"

Damon nodded. "Which means each settlement can become food secure, taking food trade from a necessity to a luxury, making it harder for anyone to manipulate prices. What else?"

"We suggest an ancillary aspect to rebuilding. Every block of buildings will include space for community events, education, and the preservation of traditional cultural items: food, holidays, artwork, hobbies, games. We use those to build local pride and identity, then work to share the recovered arts between settlements. It will bring people together, and make it more difficult to divide them later."

"Good angle, Anya. Seradyne ought to like that because the educational centers could be where their big screens and communications nodes get located. It would put them *in* the heart of every community, but not *at* the heart of every community." Damon smiled. "This is the Anya Stroud I remember—the rebellious streak surfaces."

"Flatterer." Anya chewed her lower lip for a second. "With your DeeBees, could you get started on building a prototype settlement and community center?"

"Sure. I'll toss in exterior walls that will make each settlement a little fortress. You can put murals and other art on the inside walls so it won't seem so sterile, but it'll also be a hedge against disaster if there *are* more grubs out there."

"Great." Anya looked down at her hands again. "Now here's the heavy lift. Can you hack into Seradyne's systems, look around, see if any of what we've discussed is actually going on?"

Damon looked at her, his face slack, eyes blinking. "I think it would be very ill-advised for a member of the Ministry to ask me to commit an act of industrial espionage."

She raised an eyebrow. "You realize we don't have laws against that yet."

"Regardless, to request an attack on the personal property and business of another minister, if revealed, could have all sorts of negative blowback."

"So you won't do it?"

"This is me, Anya." Damon shook his head. "I've already done it on a local facility. Had to crack their systems so I could figure out how to defend myself when they come after mine. I'm in. Everything seems legit. Their encryption of communications between branch offices is pretty robust. Only important things go out in those encrypted radio broadcasts. The rest is slow, over reconstructed copper lines. I bet they courier a lot of info, too."

"You could have mentioned this earlier..."

"Plausible deniability. The good thing is that we still can use the MilNet as a secure line of communication, as needed. And since we suspect Seradyne is going to be weaponizing data, might I suggest we prepare to give them false information to contaminate their data pool, should the need arise."

Anya rubbed a hand over her forehead. "As much as I wasn't a fan of the terror, blood, and death, there was a simplicity to fighting Locust, as opposed to dealing with other human beings."

"Locust were the prelims, and humanity won. Now we get to fight humanity for the championship."

"Why can't we just remain focused on rebuilding?"

"Because the survivors don't realize how close we were to

losing it all—and, the fact is, we're not wholly in the clear yet." Damon waved her over to a small hydroponic gardening station. "When the last of the grubs and glowies died, they shelled up, right? There's crystal residue all over the place." He pointed to the experiment. "Plants on the left are getting a five percent infusion of that. On the right, soil that's clean and conditioned."

Anya studied the plants for a minute, but even the most cursory glance showed a marked difference. The tainted plants rose to three-quarters the height of the others. They weren't as deeply or brightly colored, and the leaves had all become desiccated, curling up along the edges.

"Is it too soon to know if they will bear fruit?"

"I'm not even sure they're going to blossom. Root balls are shallow, so while they can live here in the lab, outside, in the soil, a good stiff wind will tear them out of the ground." Damon nodded toward another part of the lab. "I'm also going to run similar tests using mice. I've been breeding some strains from field mice, so we'll need new baselines to evaluate the results. But I'll see what the crystal will do to them, and then see how much crystal gets through into the food chain. This is another reason why the algae food program is so important in the short term."

Anya pressed a hand to her throat. "Is there any way to clean the soil?"

"Too early to tell. Clean soil I'm using here was already stored at the facility."

"Okay. I know you don't want anyone in the lab tomorrow, but this is vitally important. Can you have these samples set up someplace where you can explain this to all the ministers? This is a legitimate crisis, and we need to get everyone united in making sure they remove the toxic soil as they rebuild. They can help search for a way to clean it, too. This will bring home the harsh reality that we're not out of the woods yet."

"And perhaps sow a bit of concern about trading food with other places before they've agreed to protocols for growing it clean?" Damon smiled. "Cutting into that central market idea, yet again."

Anya smiled back. "For a Plan B constructed on the fly, I think it will work. Jamila can make it work."

"Work quite well, I hope, Madam Minister." Damon nodded smartly. "And in this, I am most pleased to be of service."

6: GRANITE GORGE

HANOVER, SERA

16 BOUNTY 18 A.E.

arcus held up a gloved fist as he crouched. He'd seen
something through the brush, in the late afternoon light. He
pointed in its direction, then at his own eyes, and back toward
the shadow.

Brandon, who had stopped at the first hand signal, cut off to
the right and began to loop his way around toward the target,
bringing his rifle to hand.

Marcus, encased in his armor, raised his Lancer and covered
the dark blob. His breathing remained steady and he locked in on
the target. Until he knew what it was, he wouldn't pull the trigger,
but if it moved aggressively at Brandon, he'd burn it from existence.

Brandon came back into view about five yards beyond the
unknown target. He stared for a moment, then slung his rifle over
his shoulder and waved Marcus forward. Brandon advanced and
dropped to his knees.

"It's okay, son, we got you."

Marcus cut straight through the brush, ignoring the branches scourging his arms, bracken and brambles tugging at his legs. He kept his eyes scanning for anything beyond the small clearing where Brandon knelt, but saw nothing. Then he reached Brandon.

"Oh, shit."

Brandon rolled a young man over onto his back. The kid couldn't have been much more than twelve. He'd had his hair shaved off and he was nothing but skin and bones. He wore a ragged loincloth and a threadbare sweatshirt which had lost one sleeve and most of the lower half. The kid hadn't washed in a long time, and had new and livid welts over his thighs and stomach.

"Easy." Brandon lifted the kid's head and got him to drink a bit from his canteen. "Who are you? What are you doing out here?"

The young man stared up at them, shivering and whimpering.

Marcus lifted the kid's left arm, the bare one. "Ligature marks on the wrist."

"I saw. This wrist and the ankles, too."

"Right, but this is the weird thing." Marcus rotated the kid's wrist, exposing a curved line of round scars. "That's a grub bite."

"You kidding me?"

Marcus shrugged. "Well, never seen a bite healed over like this, but I've seen the mouths up close, and I'd bet on it."

Brandon rubbed his thumb over the round scars. "That looks fairly fresh. I heard stories of grubs kidnapping children, just didn't think they were real."

"Yeah, stories to keep kids in line. Also unfortunately true." Marcus glanced over at where a piece of the sweatshirt had caught on a branch. "Can you keep him quiet?"

Brandon nodded and scooped the boy up in his arms. He pulled back as Marcus advanced. The Gear moved to the tree, keeping the trunk between him and the kid's line of approach. No mistake about the cloth, it had come from the sweatshirt.

Kid was running, caught his ankle there on that deadfall and crashed down where we found him. Too exhausted to run anymore.

Something moved out in the lengthening shadows. It covered an arc that cut across the kid's path, then went further, traveling downwind. Marcus couldn't see it, save in shadows. Low and bulky, it moved with a herky-jerky gait that suggested it was broken or wounded, but it made no sound. And every so often it crossed the space between trees, very quickly. He couldn't remember ever having seen anything like that, and with a chill cutting at his spine, he glanced down to check how many bullets he had in the Lancer.

The thing stopped moving, then rose on hind legs. The shoulders canted unevenly and for a heartbeat he expected it to fall over. Then it launched itself forward, clawing at the ground as it came. It slammed into a small tree, snapping the trunk, then bounced off a larger one—which pointed it straight at Marcus.

Without thinking Marcus brought the Lancer's muzzle up and hit the trigger. Shell casings arced out in a smoking chain. The rifle lipped flame. Bark exploded from trees. Splinters flew in sharp shrapnel clouds. The shadow beast grunted and jerked, but didn't slow down. It burst through the trees into the small clearing.

The grub roared and leaped toward Marcus.

He continued firing, the bullets chewing their way through the creature's pale flesh. Still, the gunfire wasn't stopping it, so Marcus triggered the chainsaw. The bayonet's scything blades whirred. The Gear lunged upward, impaling the grub through the sternum. Blood spattered, acrid mist stinging Marcus' nostrils. He twisted, using the grub's momentum, and slammed it into the tree, snapping its spine. He lunged again, stabbing the bayonet down into the grub's vitals, then ground it up and down before sawing it out through the thing's belly.

The grub slid to the base of the tree, its guts splashing out over gnarled roots. Marcus pulled back, already slapping a new clip into the Lancer when something hit him hard in the chest. He flew back, smacking heavily against another tree. He saw stars, then heard the rifle report. He couldn't breathe, and the Lancer had bounced away four or five feet to the left.

A skinny man carrying a rifle came running forward. Horror washed over his face as he looked down at the dying grub trying to claw its guts back into its body.

"Oh, hell, why did you have to go and do that?" The man, whose commitment to personal hygiene made the child look positively pristine, stomped his feet and pointed the rifle at Marcus' head. "Daddy's gonna be so angry. He's gonna... Oh no, ain't my fault. Dodger, he'll be mad, but he'll like that armor you got there."

He raised the rifle and took aim.

Then his head exploded. Everything from the bridge of his nose up sprayed out in a glistening gush that painted trees, leaves, and even spattered the grub. The man's corpse remained erect for a moment, then pitched forward, falling at Marcus' feet.

Brandon ran over, his hunting rifle's upper barrel smoking.

"How bad?"

"Barely bruised. Armor." Marcus pulled himself into a sitting position against a tree. "Nice shot. In half-light, too."

"Guy once told me to make the first shot count. Might not get a second one."

"Words to live by." Marcus recovered his Lancer, shook blood off the bayonet, and the two men approached the grub. "Careful. Some of them take a bit of time to die."

"Noted." Brandon poked the grub's foot. "I think you did the job on this one."

"Had enough practice." Marcus pulled a small flashlight from a pocket. He played the beam over the grub. Of all the Locust he'd fought, this one fell at the lower end of the size scale, almost as if it was an adolescent rather than a full adult. It lacked the muscle mass of most, not making it lean as much as undernourished.

And there is more. "Okay, that's real odd. See there at the hip, Brandon, extending to the back, what does that look like?"

"Burn scars. Healed up."

"But how? The Imulsion Countermeasure should have just burned all the way through it. It burned up all Imulsion-contaminated cells."

"I remember. A hell of a light show." Brandon shrugged. "Humans weren't poisoned with enough Imulsion to become candles, though."

"Most weren't." A vision of Adam Fenix flashed through his son's mind. "Relevance?"

"My point being, what if, somehow, some of the Locust weren't poisoned *enough*? What if something in their diet helped chelate the Imulsion, or something else?"

"So, what, the ICM banged them around, and they got better?" Marcus ran a hand back over his head. The grubs were all dead. They had to be. *Because if one survived, more could have survived. They could be breeding.* He pressed a hand to the ground waiting to feel tremors as a prelude to the Locust bursting up through the ground.

That hand tightened into a fist. *Slow down, Fenix. This is one grub, not a maternity ward.* He took a deep breath, then looked over at the dead man. "Could this idiot have found a dying grub and nursed it back to health?"

"They were traveling together, right? I mean we have to figure they were trying to track the kid down."

"Yeah, well, we made enough racket that this fool's daddy is going to come check things out. We better move."

Brandon pointed his rifle at the grub's head. "Think they have any more of these at home?"

"I sure as hell hope not." Marcus checked the Lancer's ammo level. "But if they've made a puppy mill into a grub factory, I think we know exactly what we'll do about it."

Heading out from Hanover, Marcus had figured the stories they were tracking down were just campfire tales meant to scare kids. A lot like the stories of grubs snatching children. Descriptions of the Locust had been sketchy—things only seen in shadows, and no grand slaughters to leave evidence of Locust living in the area. Most of the reports could have applied to a wounded bear—if any of them had survived the last decade and a half. As nearly as Marcus could tell, the stories all sounded so similar that they likely originated from some years-old incident, the details of which travelers picked up in Hanover or Mercy and shared wherever they landed.

Finding a living grub changed everything. If news got out about a confirmed Locust sighting there would be no controlling the panic. As haunted and exhausted as the people were just six months after the war, they'd not have the energy to deal with such a new crisis, and the general population's morale would plummet.

The Gear shook his head. *We don't have enough information yet to raise a general alarm. Was that grub an outlier? A relic that hadn't died yet?* Marcus set his jaw. *It's just like back in the war. Recon, analysis, planning in action. Right now it's recon.*

Marcus located a small ravine where they hobbled the horses and secured the kid in a makeshift canvas shelter between two trees. They wrapped him up in a blanket, left him water, then headed out to parallel the trail the gunman had used to track the boy. About a mile and a half on they crossed a dirt road that angled down to what was once a large gravel quarry.

The buildings all shared the same wood and corrugated tin construction. The largest sat in the middle of an oval space, with the road entering at the narrow end, and a stream cutting through at the larger. Four smaller outbuildings, each more ramshackle than the next, lay at the base of the hill that had been cut away long ago when the quarry was still active.

"Marcus, between the two middle huts there. The wires and fence."

The Gear studied it for a moment. "In the old days, that would have been a kennel. Now, a slave pen."

"The kid?"

"Or the grub. Or both."

They made their approach through the woods on the far side of the road and worked their way down to the nearest of the smaller buildings. Marcus peered through a dirty window and instantly recognized the copper coil and big cylinder. "It's a still. They're making alcohol."

"No guards?"

"I think we killed him. *Them*. The grub must've just been a big guard dog. The scars on the kid's arm—I bet it dragged him back previously."

"Poor kid." Brandon nodded toward the big structure. "How many you figure in there?"

"Half-dozen, maybe more." Marcus pointed toward a wagon crafted from the back half of a pickup, parked over by the main building. "If you can get over there, I have an idea on how we get them into the open without getting ourselves killed."

"Okay. What'll your signal be?"

"Trust me, you won't miss it."

When the flames brightened the distillery's interior, Marcus yelled "Fire! Fire!" and shot the Lancer into the air a couple of times, then repeated his cry.

Faces appeared in the windows of the big house, then the front door flew open and a heavyset man waddled out into the yard. Four men and two women poured out after him. They all stared at the fire and smoke billowing through the ill-constructed roof. The subordinates milled around for a second, then turned to their leader, whom Marcus took to be Dodger.

He pointed. "Well! Put it out."

Marcus stepped out of the shadows. "Not going to happen. On your knees."

Brandon appeared from around the corner of the building, both of his pistols drawn. "You heard the man."

Dodger posted his fists to his hips. "You have no idea…"

"Your grub is dead. His keeper, too, and we have the boy."
Marcus triggered the Lancer for two short bursts. "I'll happily
drop all of you."

Two days later they arrived back in Hanover. Approaching the
city through the Stadium district they got a quick escort and a lot
of strange looks. They had a seven-person team chained together,
pulling the wagon. The wagon contained three children and
seven women, two of whom were pregnant. The boy they'd first
discovered rode on Marcus' pack horse, and two more women
rode on Brandon's.

Roberto greeted them and security hauled the slavers off. The
stadium's original design had included a satellite police station
with a half-dozen cells for unruly, drunken fans. Other people in
the Cougar organization gathered the rest of the travelers to get
them checked out by the team's medical staff, and then fed and
housed. Once they'd headed into the stadium, Roberto conducted
Marcus and Brandon to Cole's office.

There they explained everything to Cole, beginning with
killing the grub and then on to what they'd discovered in the
compound. Cole, visibly agitated by the news, found a map of
the area, rolled it out on a desk, and Brandon tapped the quarry's
location with a finger.

"Yeah, this is it. Their leader's father had worked the quarry
back before E-Day. The guy knew the area, did a lot of scavenging,
poaching and, through the years, robbed a lot of people. He'd kill
the men, take the women. The ones he liked he'd keep as breeders.

The youngest of his gang were twins—boy and a girl—who grew up in that system. The women he didn't care for he'd use for trade."

"For trade? Damnit." Cole's expression darkened. "Not down here. We don't play like that."

Marcus slapped his friend on the shoulder. "We know. That's why we brought them here. No, this guy had a circuit out toward Mercy and the settlements up that way. We're going to follow his old path and see if we can find Sierra. His prisoners remembered someone who might have answered to her description, but nothing definitive."

"Where did he get the grub?"

"Don't know. He's not talking." Brandon shook his head. "However, he had ledgers and I'm hoping they'll point us in the right direction. Names, dates, other details. Hopefully we can backtrack. The one thing we do know is that he's only had the grub for six months or so."

Cole nodded. "After the countermeasure."

"Yeah, and the scars on the thing make me think it was hurt badly, but recovered." Marcus shook his head. "Clearly brain damage. It might as well have been a dog, the way it obeyed them and kept the captives in line."

"Damn, Marcus." Cole leaned heavily on the table. "We spend years fighting to stop Locust from ending humanity, and people do this? How?"

"All too easily, brother." Marcus shook his head. "Makes me want to grab Anya and haul her away to an island where we don't have to deal with it."

Cole shook his head. "Do you think there are more grubs out there, or was this a one-off?"

"Don't know. Don't really want to consider the reality if there are."

"I hear you, brother. I just…" The man's voice faded. "You know, just when you start to see hope on people's faces."

Marcus patted Cole on the shoulder. "That's why we have to scope out the problem. Panic will kill more folks than the grubs. At least we have a trail to follow."

"Happy hunting, and save me a spot on your island, baby." Cole glanced up. "How's next Tuesday for move-in?"

"I love it, but first I gotta find the E-hole the grub crawled outta." Marcus gave his friend a smile. "After that, first boat I can find."

7: FLORES FAMILY CEMETERY

MERCY, SERA

24 BOUNTY 18 A.E.

Marcus gazed down at the kneeling angel, its head bowed and hands pressed together in prayer. It knelt atop a pedestal with the name Flores carved onto it. The crest of one wing had broken off, but otherwise the angel retained its granite immortality.

Around its neck hung a necklace that had belonged to Maria Flores Santiago. Intertwined with it was Dominic Santiago's COG identification tag. Marcus lifted the tag, felt its weight. On their last visit, Dom had taken time at the grave and, unbeknownst to Marcus, had placed his COG tag on the memorial.

Dom knew. *All the things that had worn him down. Everyone he loved, gone.* A lump rose in Marcus' throat. *Everyone but Delta, and he made sure we would continue.*

Marcus let the COG tag lie heavy in his palm. *I miss you, brother. So much.* He closed his hand around the tag, holding on tight, then gently laid it against the angel's breast. *Rest well. You've earned it.*

— 179 —

He half turned toward Brandon, who waited a dozen steps back. "Dom Santiago put this here. The Flores were his wife's people. Necklace was Maria's."

"She buried here, too?"

"No." Marcus started to explain what had happened, but caught himself. He felt the pain keenly in his chest—the pain Dom had experienced when he let Maria know peace. "Dom and Maria had two kids, but Locust got them early on. They got Maria later. Dom… Dom died some distance from here, saving my ass."

"I'm sorry you lost your friend."

"Really my brother—more than just being part of Delta. We were brothers in arms, and the shit we got up to out of uniform, well…" Marcus' mouth wanted to smile, but his throat tightened more fiercely and his vision blurred. *So many memories.* Most poignant of them was Dom confiding in Marcus that he was going to be a father for a second time. The look of sheer joy on Dom's face went unrivaled in Marcus' mind until he recalled his friend holding his newborn baby girl. *The light just shone from him then. So proud, so thankful, so sure of what the future had to bring.*

The same sort of light that engulfed him at the end. Dom had died to give Marcus and the rest of Delta a way out of a deathtrap. Formers from one side, glowie grubs from the other, Locust swarming the tunnel entrance. *If not for Dom's sacrifice…*

Marcus walked around to the statue's right side and picked up the broken bit of wing. He put it back into place and it remained there because of gravity. Marcus figured it would take a stiff wind to knock it down again.

"Dom… I think Dom put his COG tag here because Mercy was where his heart was. He used to tell the story about when he decided to ask Maria to marry him, he decided to do it properly. He came all the way up here to ask her great-grandfather, the Flores patriarch, if he could have her hand. I think the old man is buried right under this angel."

The Gear's hand rested on the statue's head. "Dom knew it wasn't going to be easy to make his case because their first child was already on the way. Dom confessed all of that, and that he really loved Maria with his whole heart. The old man, white hair, big white mustache, listened solemnly. Sat rock-still, stared into the distance. Finally he looked Dom in the eyes. 'It takes a quality of man to come here and explain this. I believe you. I trust you. I give my Maria to your care. Cherish her. Love her always,' he said, then shook Dom's hand. Dom always said after that he already felt married, everything else was just for the pictures."

Marcus shook his head and chuckled.

"What, Marcus?"

"Dom, he might make a mistake, but he never shirked responsibility; never shied from hard work, and loved his family so fiercely..."

"I'm sorry I never got to meet him." Brandon nodded. "Take all the time you want."

Marcus took a knee in front of the statue, imagining the old man Dom had described standing there. "I give Dom to your care, now and forever. Rest well, my brother, rest well." He lowered his head and knelt there in silence for a bit, then climbed to his feet.

"Thanks."

Brandon gave him a quick nod.

"You have more addresses in Mercy we have to check out?"

The slender man consulted a notebook into which he'd copied relevant information from the ledgers Dodger had kept.

"All these addresses are a composite of his last three years, and nothing in town itself since the Imulsion Countermeasure. The people here now appear to be Stranded that came to pick things over, and stayed for the view or got out of Char and decided living on a mountain was it for them."

"So that's it? Dead end?"

"One last one, but odd address. '807 Char Highway North 2'" Brandon's brow crinkled. "Highway is the main drag, and 807 would put it about four blocks that away, hanging in mid-air." Marcus looked at the location Brandon pointed out, then shook his head.

"Can't be it, so we go the other way."

"That's where things are blown to bits."

Dom... Marcus exhaled heavily, and gestured. "There's a crater off that way. That's where Dominic Santiago drove into a tanker full of Imulsion. Blew the hell out of glowies, Formers, and Locust. He sacrificed himself."

"You didn't say anything when we rode past coming in."

"I didn't..." Marcus walked to their horses and pulled himself up into the saddle. "I saw him die, but I didn't see *him*, you know. The explosion and fireball. Anya held me back or I'd have plunged in there to get him out. So riding in, I really didn't want to look. I didn't. I didn't look close. I was afraid I'd see something that would remind me that I failed to save him. That I *could have* saved him. Does that make any sense?"

Brandon stroked his own horse's neck. "People will tell you it's 'survivor guilt.' You wonder why you survived and Dom didn't."

"I know why Dom didn't survive."

"Yeah, then maybe what you're wondering is why he did that for you. You're wondering, what did he see in you that was worth the price he paid, and you're wondering if you can ever live up to that vision of yourself."

Marcus looked sidelong at his companion. "You aren't talking about me right now, are you?"

"Nope."

"Who did you lose?"

"Nobody. The pain's not mine." Brandon reined his horse around the twisted chassis of a mangled car. "I've never let anyone get that close to me. Except my sister."

"Then how...?"

"My sister. She's birthed kids, she's kept people healthy. When the grippe runs through the camp, she's tireless, but sometimes people die. There's nothing she can do. No matter how hard she works, they die. But the loved ones of that patient, they praise her and thank her. They're seeing her as a miracle-worker who did all she could, and they're sad that their friend or their brother or daughter died, but they're not angry with her—but she is with herself. She wonders when people are going to see how powerless she truly is, when they're going to figure it all out. Figure her for being a fraud. So for her, trying to reconcile how people see her and how she sees herself slowly drives her insane."

Marcus scratched at his throat. "What does she do to handle it?"

"For better or worse, there's always another person to save, so she distracts herself with duty." Brandon shrugged. "I think that works for her because she racks up another victory as a hedge against the crushing defeats. The wins let her live up to other people's vision, at least for a little while."

Maybe that's it, Marcus thought. "Maybe that's what I need to do—live up to the man Dom saw as worth saving."

"I suspect you already do."

"I can do more. Raise tomatoes. Kill Locust." *Become a good dad—living up to his example.*

"Both of those will work." Brandon glanced at the side of the road for a moment, then looked over at Marcus. "Hey, I said '807 Char Highway,' right?"

"Uh-huh."

He pointed off to the shoulder. "That's mile marker 813. We're four miles from 807."

Marcus smiled. "Right, and then we head north for two. That ought to put us somewhere in the saddle between Mercy and the next mountain east."

"Be there well before nightfall." Brandon glanced further down the broken highway. "If you want, to pass the time, you can tell me more about your friend Dom."

Marcus thought for a moment, then surprised himself by smiling. "Dom, he could be a handful, but was the best man I've ever known. There was this time, when we were kids…"

A little more than a mile north of mile marker 807 brought the travelers to a gravel road winding up through some trees to a small, elegantly built hunting lodge. Unlike the one on the Stroud Estate, for this home the builders had drawn inspiration and raw materials from the local area.

Flat slate slabs covered a patio to the front. The logs for the cabin all glowed with a honey-colored varnish, save for the darker ones with the bark still on, which had been inserted into the pattern for decorative purposes. Large enough to house a dozen people easily, it also had a carriage house and stable, a smaller building housing a generator, an icehouse and a couple of cozy cabins, likely for extra guests or overflow staff.

As they rode up an older man sat on the steps halfway between the front door and the patio, with a shotgun across his thighs.

"That's about as far as you want to be coming up here without an invite."

Brandon let his horse take a couple more steps. "If you have the time, we'd be obliged if you could answer a couple questions for us. I'm Brandon Turrall. My associate is Marcus Fenix."

The old man's gray eyes hardened. "Fenix. You went to prison, that right, for slugging your CO and disobeying an order?"

"That was me."

The old man chuckled. "I did two years for the same thing a whole lot of long times ago. What do you want to know?"

"Guy calling himself Dodger from near Hanover used to trade out this way. He had your address in a ledger."

"Yes, that's right." The man jerked a thumb toward the cabin. "Griffin Imulsion Corporation down to Char owns this place and they got me caretaking it. Have for the last twenty years. Used to have sales meetings up here and the like. Used to be if I needed something I sent an order down the hill to Mercy or Char and I'd get a delivery.

"With the grubs crawling all over, deliveries stopped. Dodger, he'd always have a thing or three I needed. I'd trade for that and maybe hire some of his boys to help out around here. I know they weren't no good, and I might not have questioned where they got some of the things I bought off them, but they didn't give me no trouble."

Marcus rested his hands on the saddle horn. "They had a grub they used as a watch dog. You ever see it?"

"No, but I know a bit about it." The man scratched his unshaven jaw. "Not too long after the big explosion down to Mercy—month later, maybe two—I started hearing things at night. Seem to come from Fletcher Bend, just down the hill and around north a bit. Long time ago they did mining down there, but that's all abandoned. Dodger came through and I had him and his boys take a look. They never did come back to me, but lit out from there."

"So you don't know what exactly they found?" Brandon frowned. "Whatever it was ended the noises you heard?"

The old man spitted Brandon with a stare. "I ain't so foolish as I'd go after a grub by myself with this scatter gun, but I do my fair share of hunting up here and I can read a track. I backtracked them to one of the abandoned mines. They didn't go very deep, but I read grub signs there. I did some looking after they left and… Well, wait here for a bit."

The old man stood and headed back into the cabin.

Brandon looked at Marcus. "Just a coincidence that Aaron Griffin owns this place?"

"I'm sure he has plans for it, too, but I think he has a hate on grubs after all the damage done in Char." Marcus shrugged. "He doesn't like Gears very much, just so you know."

"So I've heard."

"Here, I found it." The old man descended and tossed Marcus a black plastic box about the size of a playing-card deck, but twice as thick. It had been scuffed up and cracked open on one of the narrow ends. He looked inside but only saw black char and caught the faintly acrid scent of melted circuitry. The baseplate had four protruding screws, one in each corner, two of which had flattened fasteners on them. Two wires also protruded from the box, one being twice as long as the other, and Marcus felt certain they'd been snapped off.

He tossed the unit to Brandon. "Take a look at the bolts."

The slender man peered closely at them. "Looks like drywall fasteners. Push these into the wall and turn the screw. They expand, locking things up tight. But there're scraps on these. Is that tissue?"

"I think so. Grub hide."

Brandon glanced at the caretaker. "Will you take us to where you found this?"

"I might could do that." The old man nodded. "Not 'til morning, though. Now, how you going to make it worth my while?"

Marcus smiled easily. "We can get a message to Aaron Griffin letting him know you're still here and the place is in great shape."

"Well, that would be plenty nice of you." He scratched at his throat. "Or you could tell him I'm dead and this place is a complete loss. He's got enough to worry about down in Char, I figure."

"I believe we have a deal." Marcus swung from the saddle and felt the flat stone in his pocket. "One more thing. We're also looking for a girl. This tall, black hair. She's funny, sense of humor. Answers to Sierra. We think Dodger might have gotten his hands on her about the same time he'd have been around here."

"No. I don't recall a girl with them, then. I do remember Dodger getting into his cups one night, said something about how he liked bringing me salvage parts because when their cargo had to be pretty, he had to be careful. 'Junk don't scream when I drop it,' he told me." The old man scratched at the back of his head.

"Now I do recall a time when Dodger headed up north from

here. Had a couple women with him. He went west, sent one of his boys riding hard back here and traded me for a set of silverware. It was one of about a dozen, so I didn't think anyone would notice it missing. I don't know why they'd want it and I ain't seen it making food taste better, but weren't no bother of mine. That was about a year ago, maybe two."

Brandon glanced to the west. "How many settlements out there, do you guess?"

The caretaker shook his head. "Don't know. Haven't really paid it any mind, but you boys find anywhere they're wanting silverware or fancy things like that, we can do some business."

"We'll bear that in mind." Marcus heard the words and about a second later realized he was the one saying them. *Is this the future we're reduced to? Trading people and artifacts from the old world until it all collapses into decay?*

"Well then, gentlemen, take the carriage house to make yourselves at home in." The old man gave them a gap-toothed grin. "Tomorrow morning, I show you the hole where I found that box, and might even load you up with some silverware as traveling samples. Mr. Griffin don't ever need to know."

8: MINISTRY OF PUBLIC WORKS

EPHYRA, SERA

25 BOUNTY 18 A.E.

Anya sat on the Ministry steps finishing the bread, butter, and sun-dried tomato sandwich she'd brought in for lunch. She made it last because while she missed Marcus fiercely, the folks Roger Hahn had sent over to work on the estate brought bread-making skill and a generous supply of food which had been preserved from that year's harvest. Roger had said it was only fair that they share, and that if Anya wanted to keep accounts and settle them when harvests came in next year, that was fine by him.

The sun was warm but the air was cool, and as she ate she watched crews of volunteers clearing the streets of crystalized Locust remains. Damon Baird's reports about the effects of the crystals on plant growth and animal development had stunned the other ministers, moving clean-up to the top of their priority lists. Gloved and masked workers dug the corpses up and loaded them into carts. Other crews cleared the holes of contaminated dirt. The corpses and crystal shells and dirt got hauled off to dumps or to fill in E-holes, which were then sealed over to prevent leakage.

"It is fascinating to watch them work so hard on this project, as if their lives depend upon it."

Anya turned and looked up, seeing only a silhouette with the eclipsed sun as halo, then shielded her eyes with a hand as the figure descended a few more steps to the street level.

"Minister Hasterwith, what a surprise."

"I could say the same of you, sitting here as if you were a normal person, spectating."

"But I *am* a normal person." She brushed some crumbs off her lap. "Had you come sooner, I would have offered you half of my sandwich."

"A generous offer, to be sure." The man turned toward the street. "It's remarkable that people, when told of a danger in an authoritative voice, fail to question the veracity of the fact. As well you know this is simply because danger invokes fear, triggering an emotional reaction. Emotions, in turn, deny access to critical thinking. So fear trumps logic, and prompts people to act without thinking."

Anya stood, pulling her jacket tightly around her. "Are you saying that you doubt the research concerning the Locust dust?"

"You and I both know it is preliminary, and that we have no solid data despite the fact that we've been killing Locust and the Imulsion-derivative toxins in their tissue have been leeching into the ground for well more than a decade." He gave her an indulgent smile. "And by *we*, of course, I mean *you* and the other Gears. And *that*, Minister Stroud, is why you are not even close to being a normal person."

Anya's eyes narrowed. "I can't tell if you mean that as praise or condemnation."

"Consider it a token of my respect for you. While I might philosophize about what the effort to clean up the Locust dust tells us about the nature of mankind, I do admire your organizational skills and drive to deal with this issue. Those are assets which I should hate to see squandered."

She caught something in his manner, the way he turned slowly to face her, that sent a jolt running up her spine. "How would my skills be squandered?"

"How well do you know Jamila Shin?" Hasterwith's smile diminished ever so slightly. "You were her invited guest to the museum gathering, and she chose for you beautifully from the clothing collection. Surely you noticed that not everyone was so perfectly accommodated?"

"I'd not met her before the reception. Her family and mine were acquainted, but my mother was estranged from the family." Anya glanced back at the Ministry building. "I believe Colonel Hoffman recommended me to her, and I have enjoyed working with her."

"What do you think her goal is in all this?"

Anya frowned. "What are you expecting me to say? I think she has been transparent in her goals. She would like to organize things so mankind can survive."

"Can you possibly be that naïve?" Hasterwith looked at her closely, puzzlement opening his expression. "You think something like this, like cleaning up the streets, is her end goal? My, my, Minister Stroud, can I have overestimated you?"

Please believe you have overestimated me. And let me help you.
"Minister Hasterwith, I accept her at her word that she is working for the common good, to get us through this winter. I haven't looked past stabilizing humanity. My goal is our survival. Once we

are on solid footing, then I look forward."

"Ah, yes, of course." Hasterwith tapped a finger against the point of his chin. "You were always an operational person, then tactical, never *strategic*. This makes sense."

Anya arched an eyebrow. "And *you* are a strategic thinker?"

"When running a large industrial firm, one must be. So, yes, I am, and a rather good one. Thus is it my want and desire to contribute to the solutions of the immediate problems and, simultaneously, anticipate problems so I can pivot to deal with them most effectively. Take for example the discussion of money."

Hasterwith lowered his hands. "Granted Minister Pendergast has focused too much on the nature of the currency, what it should be called, who should be represented on it, all under the guise of needing cash in the short term. And—to give the man his due—wanting his father on a coin was to be expected, but that led to a discussion which, frankly, overshadowed the reality of our existence. If we are to survive, we will need a currency so goods and services can be paid for. Bartering for vegetables and eggs has an expiration date, as such things spoil or are consumed."

Anya tucked a lock of hair behind her right ear. "So having a pocket full of gold coins is the solution to our problems?"

He swept a hand toward a team of four men, levering a cluster crystal containing a half-dozen corpses out of a shallow depression in the ground. "Which will run out first, do you think, Minister Stroud? Locust crystals, or the volunteer enthusiasm to dig them up? I will tell you that the winter, with its snow and bitter temperatures, will arrest the enthusiasm almost immediately. And then next spring, as we need to be plowing fields and tending to crops, people will be consumed with their own short-term survival. They'll clear crystals from their fields. They'll make walls out of them or maybe even repair homes with them. Getting them to return to the backbreaking labor they're doing now will be nigh unto impossible."

"Yet you think that giving them coins will motivate them to return to clearing the streets?"

"You would be surprised at how much motivation a bribe can be, Minister. Now, we would have two choices: either we pay people money to do this sort of work—any work, really—or we coerce their cooperation by denying them things. If they do not work, kick them out of housing, deny them water or access to medicine. Not humane in the least, no. Horrifying, if I read your expression correctly. By organizing an economy, not only can we provide for the people, but we can curb anti-social behavior, and we can encourage people to innovate in rebuilding humanity."

Anya shook her head. "But this leads us to the issue of reestablishment. To whom do we give money, and why? Do we start with a pool of a million credits and parcel them out evenly among people?"

"Money is a tool. You give it to those who can do the most with it." Hasterwith smiled. "You do not give a toddler a hammer."

"There're not many adults I'd give a hammer, either, Minister Hasterwith. Look, Pendergast clearly backs a plan that would see everyone restored to their relative levels of wealth from some arbitrary point in the past. You, Pendergast, Griffin…"

"…and Jamila Shin…"

"…and Doctor Shin, would all fare very well under that system. But what about people who have lost everything and have no records of how much they had, how much they lost? How can you justify condemning them to a life of poverty?"

"Poverty is relative, Minister Stroud." Hasterwith smiled.

"Take your case. Your family had money, but you grew up modestly. Denied your family's wealth, you will do quite well because the standards you have set for yourself are modest. Pendergast, Griffin, myself, have worked hard to earn what we had, and much of our work involved making investments to grow the economy. This is what we understand how to do. We are wealth creators. With prosperity comes opportunity, and it's opportunity which we sincerely need at this time."

Anya shook her head. "I understand what you're saying, but I do not agree with it."

He pointed a finger at her. "And there, Minister Stroud, is how your talents will be squandered. You are very good at what you do. You make operational some very difficult tasks. Aspire to more, aspire to power, and you will find yourself without the skills and resources to succeed. I do want you to succeed, Minister. Do that at which you are best. Let others worry about the rest."

"Or?"

"Whatever do you mean?"

"The implied threat. Usually when someone gives another person a directive, there's a punishment for disobeying. Care to elucidate?"

Hasterwith laughed. "Oh, Minister Stroud, if that's the impression I've left on your mind, please forgive me. I would never threaten you. I'm merely pointing out that within the realm of politics, one swims with the current, or one drowns. We can't afford to have you drown. You are far too valuable to us for what you do. Were you to stray from your lane, I simply think you would be unsatisfied, so I suggest that you avoid making such a foolish decision."

"Well, then, thank you for your concern." Anya mounted

the steps. "If you have other insights, Minister, don't hesitate to share them."

"Of course." The man sketched a bow. "To the betterment of mankind."

She continued up the stairs and to her office within the Ministry. The game Hasterwith had been playing at was one hundred percent the reason she hated politics. He clearly wanted to influence the future for his personal benefit. He didn't care who would get hurt to fulfill his ambitions. She had no doubt he would employ whatever means he could to get his way, and that he'd already had talks with other ministers to warn them against standing in his way.

"I haven't seen a look that dark on your face since the day you decided you had to join us in the trenches."

Anya looked up and smiled as she entered her office. "Baird, I didn't expect you. Did I miss a call?"

The blond man shook his head. "I didn't want to entrust this to devices, and I needed to get out of the lab."

"Sounds serious."

"It is, but so is feeding my towering genius."

"I believe the word is pronounced 'ego'."

"Sharp as ever." Damon pulled a chair around to face her desk. "First thing, I've looked at the photos Marcus sent to you, of the plastic box. Definitely circuitry, but there's not a hope in hell of telling what sort of programs the chips had burned into them. However, given that it was bolted to the skin of the grub he made a mess of, I'm going to hazard a guess it's some sort of training device. The sort of collars people used to put on dogs to stop them barking or wandering too far from the control unit. They used to call it an invisible fence. As the animal wandered, the pain increased."

Anya sat behind her desk. "But a shock wouldn't even slow down a grub."

Damon shrugged. "The Imulsion Countermeasure killed most of them, but clearly not the one Marcus ran into. The pictures he sent of it aren't good enough for a definitive analysis, but the burn scars have me thinking along these lines. The grubs that survived might have been sickened, but like getting sunstroke and a bad sunburn. When your skin is so badly burned, hot water will be agonizing. Maybe the ICM made them more sensitive."

She rested her elbows on the table. "If someone got far enough along to be bolting these things onto grubs, chances are that this wasn't the first one someone had tried to control. Do you know of any research...?"

"Nothing I've ever heard of, but there could have been a black-op somewhere that tried to develop grubs as weapons to hunt down other grubs."

"Those could have been useful."

"Sure, until the other side figured out how to jam the control signals. Things would get ugly for the home team really fast, in that case."

"Any idea where they might have been doing that research?"

"No." Damon shook his head. "But I dug through some tax records, titles, deeds and the like, and up popped small, isolated plots of land which some of the larger corporations had owned. Ran them like company towns—essentially what Mercy was. Harkness Ford on the Whiteash River is one. Razek Industrials owned it. Marcus should be really close. He might want to look at what's there."

"I'll suggest it. Thank you."

Damon sat forward in his chair. "Now, what was it that had you scowling so much when I came in here?"

"Nothing, really. Just someone talking a lot about the future he wants to see, and he warned me off trying to interfere."

"Thereby alerting you to the need to interfere?"

"That landed on target." Anya chuckled. "I don't want to be doing any of this politics business. I leave that to Jamila. I'll just have to make sure I give her all the ammunition she needs to deal with the battles of the future."

Later that evening, when she was back at the estate, Marcus called her on the sat phone, using the MilNet connection.

"I'm not calling too late, am I?"

"Not at all." She smiled, cradling the handset between her shoulder and ear. "I love when your voice is the last one I hear at night. How was your exploration?"

"Good. E-hole wasn't much. Twenty yards in it had collapsed, so the grub was using it to live in. Probably felt familiar. No evidence of any others."

"Good. I talked to Damon and he thinks that this wasn't the first attempt to control a grub."

"Roger that. We've been operating on the assumption that where there's one, there could be more. We're going to head west. Brandon has some settlements on his list where we'll ask questions."

"Is Harkness Ford one of them?"

The sound of paper being folded back and forth came through the receiver faintly. *"Not on this map."*

"It's on the Whiteash River."

"Got the river here, and there's only one or two spots where it could be. We will take a look."

Anya smiled and wished Marcus could see her expression. *And that I could see his face.* "Any luck finding Sierra?"

"*Not so far.*" Marcus fell silent.

"What is it?"

"*I'm going to find her. I'm not going to stop until I do.*" Weariness crept into his words. "*But finding her isn't going to solve Nick's situation. Bringing her to the camp won't. So I've been thinking... Maybe we bring them to the estate.*"

"Jumpstart our family." A flutter ran through her stomach.

"*I know it's a lot to think about, Anya. We've never been parents and...*"

"Yes, Marcus."

"*What?*"

"I said yes." She couldn't help smiling again, her stomach settling down. "It's a brilliant idea."

"*Really?*"

"My love, today I had a conversation with a man who said I wasn't looking far enough into the future. He was probably right, but for all the wrong reasons. Inviting Nick here, inviting Sierra and whomever else we need to, becomes a way not only to look to the future, but to build to it, too. And, yes, it might be earlier than I was thinking, but it's our tomorrow, thus we jump in. So, yes, that mission is a go."

"*Thank you, Anya.*" Relief threaded through his reply. "*I love you. Sleep well, and I'll report anything good I find.*"

9: HARKNESS FORD

SERA

27 BOUNTY 18 A.E.

Marcus rode up through the main street of Harkness Ford, heading west toward the bridge. The town had been built in a narrow canyon through which the Whiteash River flowed. It had consisted of a half-dozen buildings on the eastern side of the river, straddling either side of the road. One cross street contained a few houses, but the road had never been paved and neglect had left it pitted. The mountainside extending up above the town and again below it had once upon a time been clear-cut, but trees had grown up to replace those that had been harvested.

Harkness Ford itself had died at least a dozen years previously. Broken windows, splintering woodwork, sun-faded signs, and well-weathered pavement showed neglect and decay. The laundry sagged to the left, resting its upper story on the general store, and the mechanic's shop on the other side had begun to sag inward. The hotel, which had risen to three floors, appeared to be in the best shape, but the attached restaurant had lost half its roof at some point. The tavern—probably the oldest building of the lot—had survived the best, but it still had a tree growing into one corner, cracking the wall and foundation.

"What do you figure, Marcus? Logging town a century ago, good spot to get lunch when driving through the mountains after that?"

"Seems like." Marcus spread his arms and stretched. "I'm not sure why Anya thought this would be of interest. Nothing here but firewood waiting for a match."

"I don't see any E-holes or signs that the Locust ever got up here." Brandon looked around. "I don't think I want to be spending the night in any of these firetraps. Maybe we should just keep going."

"Sky looks clear, so it's going to be cold." Marcus pointed toward the bridge. "Let's continue west, find a place sheltered from the wind, and make a camp."

"Sounds good. Maybe we find a pool where we can convince some fish to come to dinner."

Marcus nodded, a smile teasing the corners of his mouth. So much of his life had been about rushing into danger, about firefights and a cacophony of explosions big and small. At times it had seemed like the only life he had ever known. Getting a peaceful share of rack time had been a luxury. It was an anomaly in his world.

Traveling on horseback, letting the animals set the pace and letting conditions determine how long they'd travel, seduced him. Yes, the Locust had torn Sera apart. They had destroyed so much of what man had wrought, but nature had resumed its endless cycle when the Locust retreated. The world had already seen part of the spring and the whole of a summer. Life had fought back and, depending upon where he chose to look, he could easily imagine seeing the countryside as it had been when Harkness Ford first was settled.

They mounted the bridge and Marcus openly grinned. Dark water flowed down from above, churning to foam as it raced between rocks and washed over submerged obstacles. Bushes grew down to the water's edge, and reeds grew up in brackish back channels. Insects buzzed over the water and shimmering trout leaped into the air trying to catch them.

Wait a minute.

Marcus pointed to a flash of red bobbing up and down in an eddy. "What's that?"

Brandon looked right. "I can't tell. Just a minute." He rode to the bridge's far end, then tied his horse to the tension cable. Scrambling a dozen feet down the riverbank, he managed to avoid falling in and reached for the red splotch.

"It's a hat."

He clambered up the hill to the end of the bridge as Marcus slid out of the saddle. "Visored cap. Log cabin, rifle crossed with a fishing rod for a logo. Says Razek Lodge." Brandon turned it over and grabbed the tag. "Proudly COG made."

Marcus stared intently at the cap. "Wasn't there a company called Razek Industrials?"

Brandon shrugged. "I may have seen that on some salvage. Oh, wait, yeah. Yeah, I remember getting my sister a couple cartons of vintage gauze sponges. They were from Razek Medical, but the cartons had a Razek Fiber logo on them."

"Okay, that makes sense." Marcus pointed back at the town. "And now I know why Harkness is teasing the back of my brain. There was a company, Harkness Paper, that would have logged this place for paper pulp. Razek Industrials bought them, then merged with some of their competitors, then bought up a bunch of their customers. So this place must have been something they acquired in the original deal."

"And the lodge?" Brandon wrung water out of the cap. "I don't know if it's occurred to you, but this cap doesn't look that old. Is it possible that Razek kept this lodge the way Griffin kept North 2?"

"Well, we know that cap didn't flow upstream. Let's see if we can find a trail going higher." Marcus swung back into the saddle. "Worse comes to worst, we might find ourselves new hats."

About a hundred yards past the bridge they found a nearly overgrown cart track heading off on the downhill side of the road. They rode along it, proceeding up a switchback trail to the bottom of a ravine. A small stream trickled through the ravine and the cart track continued past it, then turned abruptly uphill. They continued following it and passed through a large underpass that served as a runoff channel for rain, which avoided the water undermining the road above. Brush and trees on either side wholly obscured the road above, and only allowed dancing motes of sunlight.

The track led upward through a couple more switchbacks onto a slightly broader track curving around the mountain above Harkness Ford. It leveled out, then passed between two peaks, revealing a high-mountain valley.

They crested a small rise and caught glimpses of several buildings and a small lake in the hidden valley. They started their way down and two hundred yards further on a man emerged from a small watch post nestled back in the trees. He carried a Lancer, but didn't level it at them. He also wore one of the caps, as well as a red shirt with the same logo over the left breast.

Marcus reined up. "We're not interested in trouble."

The guard smiled. "Good, that would be two of us. Can I have your names?"

"I'm Marcus Fenix, and this is Brandon Turrall."

"Fenix with an F, right?"

"Yes."

"Okay, just give me one second." The man returned to the watch post, leaning his gun against the exterior wall, and appeared to consult a list on a clipboard. He set the clipboard down, then held a phone receiver to his ear. He cranked furiously in a circular motion with his right hand, then waited.

Marcus looked at Brandon. "Is this making sense to you?"

"No, but he has a clipboard. That means it's official, right?"

The man in the shack nodded emphatically, then put the receiver down. He grabbed something off the surface the phone was on, then came jogging back toward them. He didn't so much as glance at his Lancer and had a big smile on his face.

"Hey, sorry this took so long. These are your visitor passes. Just clip them on and stop at the Hospitality House—it'll be the first building on your left. Can't miss it. They'll give you new name tags and everything. Welcome to Harkness Glen."

Marcus accepted the white, rectangular pass and fastened it to the collar of his jacket. "Thank you."

"You're welcome, sir."

Brandon took his tag and clipped it to his jacket's zipper. "Is there anyone we should ask for?"

"Isadora will take care of you." The man waved at them and walked back to his shack as they rode past. Neither of them spoke until they were well out of the guard's earshot, and then they kept their voices low.

"What was that, Marcus? ID tags? I don't know... it's... weird."

"Just keep on your toes. For all we know they're cannibals, and we're a food delivery."

At the bottom of the hill the trail opened out, giving them a better view of the hollow. A wide stream ran through the middle and appeared to have been dammed further up on the high side—creating what Marcus had seen as a lake before. The water in the reservoir clearly went for living, irrigation and, if Marcus wasn't misreading things, provided electricity through a small hydroelectric plant.

Workers had terraced the sides of the valley, providing land for growing crops and grazing animals. Marcus spotted cattle and a fair amount of both sheep and goats, with the barns and stables maintained in the lower reaches, but back on both flanks. A number of large log cabins occupied top tiers here and there, but the vast majority of buildings were smaller and grouped in lots of a dozen. The "Hospitality House" appeared on the left, and in the center stood a larger building that immediately struck him as being the settlement's heart.

As they drew closer to Hospitality House a series of less elegant buildings came into view beyond it. A thin screen of trees tried to hide them, but a dark gash of a road led to them and appeared well traveled. Plumes of smoke rose from a variety of locations on the hillsides, back in the woods, suggesting other buildings being tucked away more successfully.

The two travelers rode up to Hospitality House and tied their horses to the porch railing. As they dismounted, the twin doors sprang open and a vibrant young woman wearing a bright blue dress with a white belt emerged. She had a matching blue bow in her black hair and displayed dazzlingly white teeth in a wide smile.

"Welcome to Harkness Glen, gentlemen. We are so very glad you've chosen to visit. Here, let me take those nasty visitor tags. Mr. Turrall, here you are. And I hope you don't mind, but I presumed and put your rank on your tag, Sergeant Fenix."

"I'm not really a Gear anymore... Isadora?"

"I can change it if you wish. You see, we set great store by tradition here and what you have done for all of us won't ever be forgotten." The woman handed Marcus a golden name tag. "Now, we're going to put you in The Birches East Two. I know it will be a bit small, but you'll have your own rooms and we have a couple of the help preparing things. It has a wonderful view of the reservoir, and if you want to do some fishing, we'll gladly get you any equipment you need."

A couple of gunshots rang out toward the east. Marcus slid his Lancer from the scabbard and Brandon had his fist full of pistol before the echoes died.

"Oh, my, look at you both. So fast." Isadora's eyes had widened, but neither her expression nor voice suggested any fear at all. "If you want to go shooting, we can arrange that, too."

"The gunfire doesn't concern you?" Brandon frowned as a few more shots followed the first, the sounds coming in pairs.

"Well, one gets used to it. That's just the boys at the club. You know, shooting their disky thingies. 'Pull' and *blam*." She lowered her voice to a stage whisper. "I think half of them, Sergeant, are pretending they're you, shooting grubbies."

"'Grubbies. Yeah." Marcus' flesh puckered. "Isadora, we found Harkness Glen almost by accident. Can you...?"

"Thank you, Isadora, I'll take over now."

"Yes, Ms. Razek." Isadora bowed her head, then retreated back into Hospitality House.

The woman who'd spoken had walked down from the central building. About Marcus' age, she stood tall, had sharp, handsome features and wore her black hair up. Her amber-eyed gaze swept over both men, then she offered them her hand—albeit without stripping off the black leather glove.

"Karima Razek. I'd be the fourth in the line to run Razek Industrials, but my father only produced daughters—at least with my mother, that is."

Marcus shook her hand, finding her grip solid and strong. *Her versus a grub barehanded, I'd give her the edge.* "Pleased to meet you."

"And the both of you." Karima watched them closely. "Let me answer what you were going to ask Isadora. It will be easiest if you come this way." She started walking toward the buildings beyond the screen of trees. "Harkness Glen was designed to be an idyllic example of how my great-grandfather thought life should be after he came here from Kashkur. When he sought to harvest the trees in the region, he left this section unspoiled. In his day he constructed a few cabins centered around the Clubhouse, and would invite friends, family, board members, and business prospects here. When my grandfather took over, he expanded on his father's vision. He put in the buildings we will see now."

She led them to one end of a long complex, into a wide corridor. Its left wall was glass, allowing them a clear view of the facilities below. "This complex represents most everything that Razek Fiber does. Here, for example, we're taking wool, cotton, and other natural fibers, washing, carding, and spinning them into thread. Here we have looms to produce cloth. We dye it—our palette is a bit limited at the moment, you understand—and then you can see the sewing stations where we make all the clothing. There we have all the medical cloth, towels, sheets. Again, we are short of plastic and cardboard packaging materials here, but we do have the capability of producing paper for all purposes, including insulation."

As she spoke she led them along the corridor. They looked down on the various processing stations. Automation handled most jobs, but the few people working the floor saw them and waved happily. One person wheeled a bin containing the sort of red hats that they had found.

"My grandfather's goal in creating this, and my father's in expanding it as we acquired more companies, was to treat the Glen as the world in microcosm. We grow our own food, we harvest our own raw materials, and do it in a responsible and sustainable way." Karima sighed. "This has not been an easy burden to shoulder, in such times as these, but I share the Razek ethos that says we never surrender."

"That's good." Marcus gave her a nod.

Brandon lightly tapped the window. "Who exactly are you making all this stuff for?"

"Our residents primarily, but we trade with outsiders."

The younger man nodded. "And your residents are?"

"Family. Board members and their families. Other acceptable guests." She smiled. "You, Sergeant Fenix, for example. My family has always supported the Gears and the sacrifice you made to defend us. Now you, Mr. Turrall, I don't know, so you are being judged by the company you keep. Favorably, I might add. Were you to desire to stay, we would find a suitable place for you."

"Thank you, I think."

"Honesty and forethought. How welcome." Karima clapped politely. "But gentlemen, we are truly happy to have you here.

Toward this end, we invite you to join us for our weekly residents' dinner in the Clubhouse. Six this evening. You'll find suitable attire in Birches East Two."

"I'm honored," Marcus said, "but I'm still trying to wrap my brain around what you have here."

Karima smiled politely. "How can I ease your mind?"

"Well, so many things…" His eyes narrowed. "You've more here than we've seen in any other community we've visited. You appear to be self-sufficient."

"We are, thank you."

"Then what is it you trade for?"

"The most precious resource of all, Sergeant Fenix." Karima Razek spread her arms. "People."

10: MANUFACTURING CENTER

HARKNESS GLEN, SERA

27 BOUNTY 18 A.E.

"**Y**ou trade in *people*?" Marcus stared at Karima as they exited the building. "Did you mean to say that?"

Karima's hands came up. "Please, Sergeant, I did not mean what you clearly believe I meant. I shall explain as we walk to the Birches."

Marcus and Brandon unhitched their horses and led them along. The trio traveled across the long lawn that bordered the main building, bearing toward a small knot of cabins near a birch grove. The two men exchanged wary glances. Marcus didn't like that their journey took them closer to where people had been shooting.

"Let me assure you both, Harkness Glen has nothing to do with human trafficking," she said. "My comment was... aspirational. As nearly as we can tell, we have here one of the very few industrial plants that still works. Yes, it is tiny, but we are able to turn out a number of items which other settlements find very useful. Primary

— 209 —

among them are bandages, other medical supplies, blankets, and clothing. What we have a severe shortage of is labor.

"Thus we hire people from other settlements to come here and work for us, on a seasonal basis or longer-term contracts. Isadora, for example, is from Westbrook and has been part of my staff for three years now. In addition to room and board for her, Westbrook—where her mother, brother, and his family still live— gets clothing and medical supplies as per the details of her service contract. Isadora is free to terminate her contract with a month's notice, and gets an annual review with an increase in wages."

Brandon frowned. "She contributes to the community, so is she part of Harkness Glen?"

"You mean to ask if she earns an equity stake."

"I mean there's a difference between being fired from your job and exiled from your home community."

Karima's smile faded. "What do you know of Razek Fiber— the company's history?"

Marcus shook his head. "Nothing."

"Less than that in my case." Brandon shrugged.

"My great-grandfather, the first Karim Razek, came here, created and built the company from the ground up, but he always gave the employees an opportunity to invest. This is a tradition we continue, though it is difficult without currency. We keep track of contributions to our success, so Isadora and others are earning equity. After five years of service they become vested and earn the right to live here permanently. If they choose to leave, their equity stake is converted into real assets which we pay out in bulk or over time." Weariness crept into Karima's voice. "We have really tried to continue the traditions from before."

"How many people do you have here?" Marcus looked around,

taking in at a glance a group of older individuals playing some sort of lawn bowling game, and a number of younger people serving them drinks. "Does everyone work, or—?"

"Again, we're trying for an equitable solution." Karima waved a hand toward the lawn bowlers. "We have families here who have invested substantial amounts of money in Razek Fiber."

"But that was *before*, yes?" Brandon frowned. "Do they get a couple weeks a year to be pampered, then join the workforce like everyone else, or are they getting a free ride?"

"It's not a free ride, Mr. Turrall. These people worked very hard for most of their lives. They helped build this place. Can a society that denies people credit for their past contributions truly provide fairly for everyone else? If not for these people, none of this would be here. Ultimately, everyone who is a part of this community will have an opportunity to enjoy the fruits of their labors in the same manner, once they earn it."

Marcus held a hand up. "We're not here to pass judgment. We've traveled a lot. Not every settlement is doing as well as this one is. I've seen a refugee camp that is overcrowded, with a medical system that is overtaxed and a marginal harvest that will lead to a lot of hardship. A bad flu would devastate them, and I'm pretty sure I'm understating how close to the edge they are."

Karima chewed her lower lip for a moment. "I was here with our board and their families for a retreat on E-Day. Why and how the Locust never found us I don't know. We do have some people who think our being spared suggests some moral superiority or divine favor, or both. Some of the children who have grown up here have no idea how bad it was. Perhaps you'll see this evening."

"You're afraid that their unrealistic view will spell disaster, if the bubble is ever burst."

"Yes, Sergeant." She hugged her arms around herself. "It's my duty to hold everyone together and keep everyone safe, but when people don't think they need to be kept safe… It makes the job more difficult."

Karima scratched at her forehead. "The main building is the Haven Club. We will be expecting you in two hours—six o'clock, to be exact. Punctuality is appreciated. I've assigned Otto from my staff to attend you, and we'll have staff from the stables take care of your horses."

Brandon smiled. "That's much appreciated."

She led them to their modest cabin. It featured wood-shingled walls, rough-hewn pillars and railings for a porch which wrapped two sides of the building. The handmade chairs and table on the porch matched the cabin's esthetic.

They hitched their horses to the porch railings, climbed the steps and entered. The door opened into a small sitting room to the left, a set of stairs leading up in the center, and a small kitchenette to the right. At the upstairs landing two doors opened to the right and left.

Karima smiled. "Please accept our hospitality. Though we are isolated here, we've learned through outsiders what you and your Delta Squad did, Sergeant Fenix, to keep us all safe."

"Thank you, Ms. Razek." Marcus walked her out and pulled his saddlebags and Lancer from his horse before attendants led it off. Brandon did the same, resting his rifle on a pair of pegs over the mantel in the sitting room.

"Does this make it feel homey?"

Marcus shrugged. "Back when the world made a bit more sense, when I heard people use words like 'retreat,' I thought they were out of touch with reality. To think there's a whole settlement that escaped dealing with grubs..."

Brandon waggled a finger. "No, Marcus, they're 'grubbies' here..."

"...'grubbies,' whatever, because they were on a retreat. It's just... it makes it even more surreal." He stretched his arms out and pulled them back until his spine popped. "You think Razek has her head screwed on straight?"

Marcus' companion sighed. "You know, I heard a lot in her voice that I hear in my sister's. I just..." Brandon fell silent for a moment. "I just don't like the idea that some of the people aren't working as hard as everyone else. I mean, look, sure, it's great that Isadora can earn her way in here, but for others to be living out a perpetual vacation, just because of things they did in a previous life, that doesn't seem right. That world simply doesn't exist anymore."

"But the fact is, it *did* exist. Look, your sister has medical knowledge from that time, right? So she brings it forward. Maybe some of these people are bringing their previous experience to bear. That's got to count for something." Marcus groaned. "I don't know. This sort of thing is why Anya is rebuilding society, and I'm out here hunting grubs... grubbies."

"Maybe you're right." Brandon shook his head. "The best solution is where folks do what they're good at, and hopefully that covers for others who aren't able to do so. A society based on altruism has to be a good thing, right?"

"Beats the alternative by a mile or three."

A man in the cabin's doorway cleared his throat. Middle-aged, with a shaved head and hint of paunch, he entered bearing armloads of towels and bedding.

"Gentlemen, I am Otto. Back behind the stairs you'll find the bathroom and shared shower. I'll put the towels in there. Soap in the drawers. You should have enough hot water to shower and shave."

Brandon arched an eyebrow. "Shave?"

Marcus ran a hand over his jaw. "I'm kinda getting used to this beard."

"You're guests at the Haven Club this evening, gentlemen. You'll want to be presentable. A *trim*, sir, might be in order." Otto looked them up and down. "Those clothes we can launder or burn, your choice. I will return with suitable clothing in the correct sizes."

Marcus half smiled. "How long have your worked here, Otto?"

"I have been on Ms. Razek's staff for twenty years, sir."

"So you've earned your own place here. You could be at the Haven Club, yes? Lawn bowling?"

"Yes, sir."

Marcus' eyes narrowed. "Then why still work?"

"Because I don't like lawn bowling, sir, and I enjoy working." Otto grinned easily. "What some find entertaining, others find burdensome. Now, if you gentlemen will excuse me."

"By all means, Otto." Marcus nodded. "Last thing I want is to be a burden."

If you can't remember when you last had a hot shower, it's really been too long.

When he'd been serving as a Gear, showers had been a luxury; and a long hot one an extreme privilege. Marcus took the opportunity to scrub every inch of himself, rinse off, and start all over again. Water dripped from his beard to his chest and down his back as he stepped out. He wrapped himself up in a towel and it felt almost as good as a lover's embrace. Harkness Glen might have been a tiny oasis in a nihilistic, entropic nightmare, but that towel was a monster of pure pleasure. He started plotting on how he could steal two—one for himself and one for Anya, and how he could keep the secret from her in the event he could only get away with one.

No, this is too good. I'd share.

Slipping from the bathroom, he noticed his clothes had vanished. Upstairs, in the bedroom on the left, he found underwear, socks, a black, knit, short-sleeved shirt and tan slacks. The shirt had the Harkness Glen logo over the left breast, and the word "Fenix" embroidered in gold above the logo. The moment he saw it he smiled, then thought it was incredibly cheesy—the sort of thing public relations folks did for VIPs.

Then it struck him that in this place, at this time, expending their resources to embroider and personalize a shirt probably marked a high honor.

He emerged from his room fully dressed, save for his boots. He spotted them, and saw that Otto or some subordinate had done his best to knock off all of the mud and wipe away the grime. Brandon stood in the sitting room, where Otto assisted him in hanging a thin sweater around his neck and knotting the arms at his throat.

Brandon caught his eye. "I'm told that this is the fashion, and my shoulder holsters are not."

"It is the fashion for this season, Mr. Turrall." Otto nodded solemnly. "The Fashion committee voted. We have darker colors for the fall, hence you are in a burgundy and this is for Sergeant Fenix." He picked up a black sweater and approached Marcus.

The Gear took the sweater from him. "I think I can handle it myself, Otto. Not my first time."

Brandon looked at him. "You've worn a sweater this way before?"

"Yeah." Marcus twirled it on like a cape. "Once. I was twelve."

"Oh, an expert, then."

Marcus tied it and turned toward Otto. "Pass muster?"

"Perfectly, sir." The… manservant?… clapped his hands. "I'll have your beds made up before you return, and your cleaned clothes returned by morning."

"That's great. Thank you." Marcus headed out onto the porch, and Brandon followed. They walked through the birches to the Haven Club. Evening had fallen and strings of lights decorated the building's broad, wraparound porch. Men and women of various ages chatted with one another, the men all similarly attired with the sweaters over their shoulders, despite the chill evening air. The women wore long, ankle-length sweater dresses with broad stripes of autumnal color and big wooden buttons holding them closed.

"Any of this scare you, Marcus?"

"Scare?" Marcus shook his head. *Given what I've seen…* "Unsettle, maybe. What's setting you off?"

"I guess I expect to be judged, and that shouldn't bother me, but…"

Marcus laughed. "Look, I've been judged and often hated by everyone up to and including the chairman. Fact is, we all breathe the same air and bleed the same blood. Anyone who thinks they're better for 'reasons' is a fool. Ignore them."

"That actually work?"

"Sometimes. Pisses 'em off, though." Marcus looked at his companion. "You *know* what you've done. The good, the bad. The things you take pride in. They don't. Just take comfort in knowing that people you respect will respect you back. Can't really ask much more out of life."

"Sounds like a plan." Brandon laughed. "It's still weird, though. I'd feel more comfortable walking into an E-hole than this place."

"We got through the museum reception. This'll be nothing compared to that."

They reached the Haven Club and conversation stopped among those nearest the broad stairs. The two of them ascended and the double doors opened. Karima Razek swept forth, her red sweater flaring out as she strode forward. "Sergeant Fenix, Mr. Turrall, welcome to the Haven Club. Please, let me show you around."

The bystanders' expressions changed from wary or curious to smug or politely pleased—and did so often. Their hostess shepherded them into the foyer. Two stairways went up, one on each side of the entryway. Beneath them hallways opened into the wings, while another passage ran back to what appeared to be a large dining room. Everywhere the eye could see, more people circulated, accepting drinks and tidbits from silver trays held by young men and women.

Karima steered them to the left. "The club began as the main building for the Glen, where guests would meet to share meals. It was a hunting lodge and, as you can see, our members did enjoy their hunting."

The room she guided them into had furnishings gathered into various conversation nooks, and featured large portraits on each wall of people Marcus took to be Karima's forebears, each dressed for hunting or fishing. The rest of the decoration consisted of mounted animal heads and fish taken, presumably, locally. Mountain sheep, moose, a variety of deer, a couple of wolves, and three big cats all greeted them with glassy stares amid a plethora of mounted trout and salmon.

Then one head sent ice through Marcus' belly.

"That can't be."

He threaded his way through the guests, across the room to where a grub's head, mouth agape, hung on a shield-shaped plaque. It wasn't until he got within a couple of yards that he realized there were things off about it. The skin looked right, but the texture wasn't.

The nose, too flat... and the head too small. He reached out and brushed his fingers over the brow. "This isn't real."

"No, not at all. The rest of these trophies are the work of a taxidermist from Char. He and his son—his apprentice—were up here on E-Day. Karim Senior created this based on a few photographs he took when he ventured home to see what had happened to his family." Karima crossed her arms. "He always claimed he'd done it to exorcise demons, and I had it put up to remind everyone how lucky we are that we don't have Locust here."

Brandon shook his head. "That's just inviting trouble."

"Or would have been, but Sergeant Fenix eliminated the problem. We were, however, mindful of the risks." Karima gestured for them to follow her through a doorway leading deeper into the building. They passed into a small hallway with dark glass walls. Lights slowly brightened, revealing a variety of guns mounted on the walls, ranging from hunting rifles on up through a half-dozen Lancers, complete with chainsaw bayonets. "This is half our armory. Our perimeter guards have the rest at their disposal."

Marcus nodded. "And the cabinets below have ammunition?"

"Of course."

"Looks like a matched pair of Snub pistols. Nice." Brandon

smiled. "Razek Industrials interested in doing some trading?"

Karima's eyebrow rose, but Marcus couldn't tell if that was from the audacity of Brandon's question, or if she was considering a counter-offer. Before she could say anything, however, a scream ripped through the night.

Marcus whirled and started toward the trophy room. A heartbeat before he cleared the corridor, a grub burst through a window. It tore an older man in half, crushed the widow's skull with her husband's arm, then leaped for Marcus, clawed hands outstretched.

ACT 3

1: HAVEN CLUB

HARKNESS GLEN, SERA

27 BOUNTY 18 A.E.

Marcus snatched a tray from a cowering server's hands and smashed the grub in the face. Its head snapped around and the Drone's leap ended awkwardly. It twisted back to the left and lunged, toe claws carving wooden curls from the floor. The sharp, pointed teeth closed on the tray, biting the silver circle and leaving a ragged crescent.

The grub spat out the metal and kept coming.

Roaring, Marcus shoved one hook of the tray's crescent into the thing's mouth, then ripped it sideways. The jagged metal sliced through the grub's cheek, spraying blood and spittle over the wall and the server.

The grub howled and backhanded the Gear. The blow caught him in the ribs, he slammed into the room's corner, then his head hit the wall behind him. Sparks flew before his eyes, then the thing was on him. It grabbed him by the throat and lifted him up, its horrid grin made worse by the gash and flapping flesh exposing the dark teeth. Its claws tightened on Marcus' throat.

This is just like the dream!

Marcus reached up, grabbing the mounted head of an antelope. He drove it down into the grub's face. One of the spiked horns pierced its left eye. Shrieking, the creature released Marcus and tore at the wooden plaque. Marcus slid to the base of the wall, gasping for breath, as the half-blind thing screamed in pain, blood spraying in a dark mist.

Then Brandon walked up coldly, leveled the Snub pistol's muzzle at the grub's good eye, and stroked the trigger. Brains spattered the wall and ceiling as the creature pitched over backward. Large chunks of its brain slid from the shattered skull, leaving a dark and slimy trail slithering across the wooden floor.

Shifting the pistol to his left hand, Brandon grabbed Marcus' hand and hauled him to his feet. More people screamed from the other side of the club.

"It isn't alone."

"I hear. Shoot that thing again." Marcus rushed past his traveling companion and returned to the armory. He grabbed a Lancer, pulled open a drawer, and stuffed spare clips in his pockets. "Karima, get the rest of the guns distributed."

"Wouldn't do any good. They don't know how to use them." She grabbed a pair of Snub pistols. "I do. Lead."

Brandon reached the doorway that led back to the foyer. Marcus advanced to follow, leaping over huddled and sobbing bodies, then sprinted through. He triggered a burst from the Lancer, nailing a grub carrying the lower half of a human torso out through a shattered window. It was dotted with sores. One shot clipped the back of its skull at an angle, skipping off but smashing the creature face-first into the window casing. A second hit it high in the back, only halfway penetrating the Locust's flesh. The third punched through a sore right over the grub's ribs, shattering bone and ricocheting through the thing's body cavity.

The grub dropped its prize and turned, coming back through the window. It snarled, blood pouring from its mouth and nostrils. Bloody froth bubbled as it roared.

Marcus shifted his aiming point to another one of the sores, this one over the thing's right hip. He pumped two shots into it, spinning the grub. Three quarters of the way through its first pirouette, it slipped on gore-streaked glass shards and dropped to a knee. Two more bullets from Marcus' Lancer snapped its head back and took off its lower jaw.

A third monster burst through the wall, coming from the front room. Brandon snapped two shots off, causing it to hesitate. Then it hunched its shoulders and bounded forward, intent on pouncing on Brandon.

Its last leap would have easily carried it to its target. Claws would have shredded Brandon and his sweater. Pieces of the young man would have painted the wall, floors, and ceiling in a heartbeat.

But Marcus intercepted the grub in mid-air, ripping the Lancer's chainsaw bayonet up through the thing's flank. That flipped it over, and the return stroke took its right leg off at the knee. The creature landed hard, bouncing once, then skidding on blood-slicked floorboards. It reached out with a slashing claw as it slid past Brandon, but missed. Brandon, in turn, pumped two bullets through its face and it thrashed its life out in a bloody puddle against the foyer's near wall.

Marcus ran to the front room, viewing the carnage and the gore-streaked survivors huddling and weeping.

"Clear."

Brandon jerked the door open. "Grounds look clear."

Marcus looked at Karima. "You said your security guys are armed. How many do you have?"

"A dozen. Four are on duty, eight are on break."

"All hands on deck right now. Get a team here to guard the club. Have the others gather everyone in here." Marcus nodded to Brandon. "Get yourself a Lancer, and as much ammo as you can carry." The man squeezed past Karima.

She stared at the Gear, his bayonet dripping blood. "What are you going to do?"

"There's got to be an E-hole around here somewhere. We have to find it."

"All the grubs are supposed to be dead."

"That's what we thought, too." Marcus scratched his head. "You and the guards are the only ones checked out on those weapons?"

"In the early years we ran drills, but…"

"Yeah, yeah, okay." Marcus accepted several clips from Brandon. "Karima, get everyone here and get them guarded. We'll be back when we can."

"And if you don't make it back?"

"Get everyone you can trained up, then head out to Ephyra and tell Anya Stroud what we ran into. She'll know what to do."

He and Brandon headed back to the Birches. Once there, Marcus exchanged the sweater for his armor. He turned the shoulder-mounted lights on, and they returned to the vicinity of the Club. Finding the grubs' trail across the lawn wasn't difficult, and that led them out toward the west, toward the Glen's Shooting Club.

That small building looked intact. Behind it, in the open-range area where members shot skeet, Brandon found some tracks on a sandy patch of ground. The trail angled south toward woods and the mountain's upslope.

Brandon glanced at Marcus. "How big an infestation you think we're looking at?"

"Not sure." Marcus checked the load on the Lancer. "The grubs we killed, they were in shit shape. The sores; their skin's normally almost as good as my armor, but those sores might as well have been gauze."

"They weren't moving that fast, either. I mean, the one that came through the wall should have gotten me, right?"

Marcus growled. "Probably."

"Thanks for the save."

"Don't mention it." Marcus gave him a half-grin. "But if you're ever of a mind to return the favor, I won't say no."

The two men continued forward, catching signs of the enemy's passage as they moved up. About a mile further on they found a vertical crack in the mountainside. Tracks led from it, and Marcus found a tiny patch of skin where it had rubbed off on a rough bit of stone.

"I think this is it."

"Not typical for an E-hole, is it, Marcus? It looks natural, not dug out."

"I think you're right on the origin, but there's no telling what's deeper in there." He shook his head. "I'd give my right arm for a Jack right now, but that ain't happening, so let's go."

Marcus had to turn sideways to enter the hole, but it broadened out quickly. He entered deep enough to give Brandon a chance to get in, and sank to one knee. The cave narrowed toward the back and didn't appear to have any other opening to the outside. When Brandon joined him they searched around for any hidden passages, but found nothing in that regard. They did, however, locate more patches of skin and enough footprints to confirm the grubs had been there.

Frustrated, they exited the cavern and circled around it, seeing if they could find any other signs of the enemy. Marcus wasn't hopeful, however, given they were in a forest at night.

"Looking for their trail is going to require more light."

"Agreed. I think we should head back, then revisit this in the morning."

"That's a plan."

"I want another look at those bodies. I didn't see any collars, but…"

"Neither did I." Marcus wiggled a piece of bone from the bayonet chain. "At least we've confirmed the rumors that there are surviving Locust, but they're not in good shape. Maybe they just didn't get a big enough dose of the Imulsion Countermeasure."

"Or, if it worked according to how much exposure they had to Imulsion, perhaps these weren't that exposed. Runts of a litter they didn't waste resources on."

"Sure, and whatever was supervising them dies with the ICM." Marcus' eyes narrowed. "They're sick, left to fend for themselves. The E-holes have got to be full of dead and dying grubs, maybe even blocked with their crystalized bodies, so these things travel overland, hiding during the day. Feral creatures eating what they can, and just happened into Harkness Glen."

"To the Haven Club." Brandon slung his Lancer over his shoulder. "Talk about a buffet. Question is now, are there more of them? Was there one big repository, and we're looking for their graduating class, or were there just tiny pockets scattered around, and we have to track them all down?"

"Either way, we're definitely going to have to track them down." Marcus shot him a sidelong glance. "But you're forgetting the other issue we got here."

"Which is?"

"Someone fitted Dodger's grub with a control collar. That means someone human is a couple steps ahead of us." Marcus shook his head. "And that someone thinks they've found a way to train grubs to do their bidding. As much as I don't like the things, I like those people even less, and when we finally meet up, I think it's going to be a nasty day of reckoning."

They returned to the Haven Club and told Karima they felt pretty certain there weren't any more Locust in the immediate area. Marcus suggested they get the bodies out of the building and dispose of them. Karima agreed, but none of the Club members seemed inclined to do that.

Marcus wanted to command them to start pulling their weight, but he held back. The vast majority of these people had been spared the trauma of E-Day and watching the Locust devastate the world. Harkness Glen—by luck or dint of the area's geological abnormalities—hadn't had to deal with the things. Those who had arrived in the Glen after fleeing the Locust didn't want to remember what had happened. They hadn't forgotten what had gone before, but their relief at having escaped it took the edge off their fear. They acknowledged the risk, but discarded the horror, so that when it came roaring back, it just obliterated them.

Many have their own dead to worry about.

So Marcus, Brandon, and some of the guards cleared the

Locust bodies. This allowed them to confirm that the Locust had been ill—malnourished and perhaps even dying. Brandon crouched and used a knife to peel back the cheek flap on the one Marcus had slashed with the tray.

"You think these could have been healed up somehow?"

"I just kill 'em, Brandon. Their biology, that was my father's domain." Marcus frowned. "Baird might know. I'll call Anya and see what she can find out."

Brandon stood. "For the sake of argument, let's say you could. Let's say you could also control them. Why would you do that?"

"For no *good* reason." Marcus' stomach folded in on itself. "Security, maybe, but Locust would make really crappy garrison troops. No, you'd use them to terrorize others. Build power."

"That's what I was thinking." Brandon reached up with both hands and massaged the back of his neck. "And if that's what someone's doing, it's a bad day for mankind, all the way around."

2: THE MINISTRY OF SANITATION

EPHYRA, SERA
28 BOUNTY 18 A.E.

"*This* is the hill they want to die on?" Anya Stroud tossed the twelve-page report onto her desk.

"It's the only hill they see, Anya." Jamila Shin opened her arms to encompass the world. "Everything lies in ruins, and some of them just want it to be known that they are the kings of this steaming pile of dung."

"If it was dung, it would be useful." Anya shook her head. The report detailed means and methods for calculating the net worth of what remained in the world, and then apportioning it to people based on their net worth before E-Day. As part of the global financial audit—an audit that would only cover the assets of Coalition of Ordered Governments citizens and territories the COG had controlled—people would be required to submit affidavits attesting to their net worth at the time, as best they could determine. They'd also have to submit the documents within three months, then a panel of auditors would total everything up, and dole it back out. If they missed the deadline, they would miss their chance to have their antebellum net worth accounted for in the system.

"There are so many things wrong here, not the least of which is that there is no mechanism to redress conflicts—and we *know* there will be conflicts." Jamila shook her head. "We have no justice system, we have no treasury department, nothing, and they know it."

"Then why push this now?"

"Ah, precisely the question that needs to be asked, Anya. I will make a politician of you yet." The smaller woman brought her hands together at her waist. "Right now, those who have resources are providing services for free or barter, which means the value assigned to those services is low, the compensation is not liquid— and yet that compensation is volatile. If, for example, you pay for your water with a basket of fresh fish, the person receiving that fish has a limited time to enjoy the benefits of the trade. Now, they could pass the fish on to someone who would preserve them, but even that has limited value."

"Right. If folks don't want dried, salted fish, your trade is worthless."

"Exactly. So the goal here is to establish twin concepts: that there *is* a finite amount of wealth in the world, and that each of us is owed a share of it. Yet if anyone does not participate in the audit, they will be punished by being excluded from the economy. Those individuals, then, will be encouraged to bend a knee and join the system, and whoever offers them the most benefits will earn their loyalty and support. Thus access to the economy is turned into political power.

"That's one aspect of their longer-term goal, Anya. Another

is that if we achieve a functioning economy, everyone who has provided services at low rates can require compensation. They might demand cash payments, or perhaps tax credits that enable them to keep more of their real wealth in the long term. And since those who have the most to gain also have the resources needed to enforce their claims, they'll benefit at the expense of the rest of society."

"Their basic argument is, 'I had the money before, so I should have it again now.'" Anya shook her head. "It suggests that what went before was based on merit, yet that's not necessarily true. For example, the people who owned Thrashball franchises had tons of money, as did the players, but Thrashball isn't necessary for survival. To award those people a significant share of the new economy makes no sense."

Jamila arched an eyebrow. "Then you're in favor of canceling all of the economic measures from before E-Day. That would include the pensions earned by workers who provided the resources needed to destroy the Locust—the people who are now rebuilding our world. How heartless and cruel."

"No, wait, that's not what I meant."

"But that's what your opponents will say, and some will come at you by suggesting that you want to apportion wealth based on contribution to the war effort. They'll say that you're doing this because you—and anyone else with a unit tattoo or history of military service—would be awarded the vast majority of wealth. They'll suggest that you want to establish a military government where you rule by decree. They'll likely point to Mr. Baird's control of the water treatment plant as evidence of your plan."

"That's *ridiculous*."

"Exactly. I deserve more than a water treatment plant."

Damon Baird appeared in the doorway to Anya's office.

"Bad time?"

Anya forced a smile. "Not if you have good news."

"I have a chunk of it. Initial testing on DeeBees is going really well." Damon pointed out the window toward a ruined Ephyra. "We can recycle a lot of the rubble as needed for shelters and, based on an initial survey, water and sewer pipes are actually in reasonable shape on the outskirts. It's here in the city center, however, we can't really do any rebuilding. I'm recording a lot of seismic activity—not Locust, just a lot of shifting and settling—so I would suggest expanding on our original testbed plans and just move everyone out toward the plant, rebuild out there. The bedrock is far more stable and we won't have buildings collapsing. Plus, if we move the people out of Ephyra, there's a lot less risk to human life as we tear things down and rebuild them."

Jamila folded her arms over her chest. "Ephyra is a symbol. We must rebuild here to signify that we were victorious."

Anya raised a hand to forestall Damon's comment. "Jamila, let me see if I've learned anything about politics from you. By establishing *New* Ephyra, we establish our will to honor the past, and build toward a new and safer future. We transplant with us the signs and symbols of old Ephyra so we can draw strength from them. And we will leave Ephyra, which has been consecrated with the blood of so many who sacrificed so much for the rest of us— for the *survival* of the rest of us—as a testament to what we have lost. In acknowledgement of how our future must recall and honor the past, but cannot be shackled to it."

Damon stared at her, jaws agape.

Jamila blinked. "Did you two collude, or was that spontaneous?"

"Spontaneous—thanks to lessons learned from a master."

"Good, very good. The passion made it convincing." Jamila raised a finger. "One thing you always have to remember: in politics, spontaneity is best when you have practice at being spontaneous. Politics has a strong element of theatre.

"You've seen it in the others, Anya. Raul Hasterwith has stung you before with his words. That was deliberate and calculated. You need to remember that, and steel yourself. That way you do not get hurt, and you can slip in the knife and twist while keeping a smile on your face and compassion in your voice."

Anya slowly nodded. Even in the military, she had always been aware of politics, and had begun to understand aspects of it—but only because they impacted how she was trying to do her job.

It's not enough to put together a solid plan. We have to battle against those who know *it's a good plan, are willing to accept it, but want their own rewards for going along with it.* The tedium pressed down on her as if a heavy cloak, but she forced herself to stand tall.

"Message received."

"Good." Jamila turned to Damon. "I hope, Mr. Baird, that you have more good news, or shall we just move to the bad?"

"More good. Yields on the algae farms are better than expected. The stuff's not all that tasty, yet, but it's a great nutritional supplement. Once we scale this up, unless we have a blight that kills off our wheat or corn, malnutrition shouldn't be an overwhelming issue. And having an ample supply of low-cost food will encourage people to come to *New* Ephyra."

Jamila smiled.

Then Damon sighed. "There is some troubling news. Someone made another run at cracking security on the MilNet last night. Not certain who, but they were trying to hook into the satellites.

They didn't get in, but I think, Anya, you were talking to Marcus at the time?"

"I was. He and Brandon made it to Harkness Falls. There's a settlement, and they were attacked by a trio of Locust. If Marcus hadn't been there, it would have been a slaughter. As it was they had a dozen killed, eight more injured. Marcus found the Locust's lair. Nothing there. He said the grubs were sick, probably dying. It looks as if they just didn't get enough of the ICM to kill them outright."

"They're going to backtrack them, make sure there aren't any more?"

"That's the plan." Anya frowned. "You think the hackers are going to get in?"

"Definitely, It's a matter of *when*, not if. I'll add some layers of encryption, but you can't count on your comms being completely secure."

"Got it, best practices. Keep the calls short, go light on details." Anya shivered. "If I had thought things through beforehand, I would have set up some code words."

Jamila clasped her hands behind her back. "You believe this is likely Seradyne's work?"

"They have the equipment, and likely the expertise." Damon shrugged. "I don't know any other major players. Who else should I be looking at?"

"Everyone?" Anya tucked blonde hair behind an ear. "Once we make things stable, people are going to be less anxious, and think more rationally. So chaos and fear are the allies of anyone seeking power. We know what they're trying to do, but we don't want them to know how much we know. We want to keep them in the dark so that they overstep."

Jamila nodded briefly. "As for this plan to assess and allocate wealth, we will protest—not on the merits of the concept, but on the minutiae of the proposal. Let them believe that we might accept it, if the details could be worked out. That will surprise them, trigger their greed, and make them sloppy. They'll fight to create a complicated system which they can game to their advantage."

Anya winced. "Won't that leave us open to the charge of fighting over crumbs, while ignoring the things vital to our survival?"

"Not entirely. We'll continue to oversee all essential rebuilding." Jamila began to pace. "At the same time, in the 'interest of working together,' we'll commit to dealing with the proposal's details, to make sure the outcome will be equitable for all. Also at the same time, we can begin negotiating with other groups to oppose the general concept, and build a majority opinion."

"There's logic in that, but it also seems a waste of time."

"True, Anya, but politics is an exercise in speeding things up, then slowing them down. The idea is to maintain momentum without having anything run out of control." Jamila brought her hands together, as if in prayer. "One other thing... we cannot let people know that Locust may still exist. With luck, Marcus has found and destroyed the last four on the planet. Were people to learn of the threat, however, the panic would destroy our efforts at stability."

"It would encourage a military state, that's for sure." Damon Baird shook his head. "I'll suit up again if we have to, but the last thing we want is for people to die because they're panicking."

"Agreed," Anya sighed. "I'll find a way to let Marcus know that this has to be kept as quiet as possible." She glanced at her old comrade in arms. "It was a lot easier when we were just shooting things, wasn't it, Damon?"

"Seems like, but then we were trying to kill things." He shrugged. "Now we're trying to keep people alive, in spite of themselves. That's never been easy, but someone has to do the heavy lifting, and just our luck it's us."

3: RAZEK INDUSTRIALS

HARKNESS GLEN, SERA
5 FROST 18 A.E.

Marcus and Brandon remained in Harkness Glen for two days following the Locust attack. The deaths burst the bubble of invincibility which had served as a dome over the entire population. Marcus organized the local security forces—some of whom had been children on E-Day—doing his best to turn them into an effective response force that could counter any other incursions. What he taught them would certainly hold off any human marauders, and likely enable them to neutralize at least a handful of Locust.

If the grubs are as bad off as the others were.

Brandon scouted for an indication of the direction from which the Locust had come. "I found some signs that something came in from Char, but nothing definitive. Another trail came from the west. Bark clawed off trees and the like, all recent."

He showed the signs to Marcus, who agreed with his assessment. "So we head west. If we're right and they were dying, maybe we'll find the remains of others that went down along the way."

"It's a plan."

Marcus put a call in to Anya to bring her up to speed, but before he could speak, she cut him off. *"We'll have to be careful. Wouldn't want any eavesdroppers to get the wrong idea."*

"Right." *So security has been compromised on the MilNet.* "I'll behave myself."

"Good. Even so, it is wonderful to hear your voice. You sound good."

"I am. We are." Marcus' mind raced as he sought a way to let her know what they'd found, without revealing anything of value to those who might be listening in. "So far we've found three graves, and marked them. That seems to be all of them." He hoped she'd connect 'graves' with 'grubs' and understand what their investigation had yielded in Harkness Glen.

"Good. That will make work easier for the repatriation teams."

"How are things at the Ministry?"

Her weariness survived the trip up to the satellite, and back down again. *"Remember how bad the red tape could get in the military? Well, the dancing we have to do now is so much worse. It's not just laying out a plan, but the need to justify things that ought to be common sense. But we're making some headway. Damon is building a settlement out near the plant and we'll be convincing people to relocate there. We're calling it New Ephyra."*

"*New* Ephyra. That sounds promising. Do the plans include a Thrashball stadium? That's the only way we'll get Cole to visit."

Anya laughed, and Marcus felt a wave of relief pour over him.

"I'll make a note to ask. And so you know, the greenhouse is fully repaired and you have tomato seedlings just beginning to peek up out of the soil."

"That's great. How about the starter?"

"Carol Hahn has it trained like a dog. Oh, and we have two of those, too. No cats yet."

"It sounds as if things are going well there, Anya."

"They'll be better when you're here. Any idea on timing?"

"At least two weeks. I'd like to be home by year's end, but we're determined to mark every grave."

"Be careful."

"I will." Marcus sighed, wishing he could see her in real time. "I love you. Always thinking of you."

"I love you, too, Marcus. Call me when you can. Be safe."

"You, too. Bye now." Marcus set the receiver down but kept his hand on it. He just wanted to maintain that connection a little bit longer. *I never want to be away from her again. Long-distance isn't enough.*

Marcus informed Karima Razek of the decision to travel west, and to his surprise, she greeted it with a smile.

"I'm hoping that you will allow Isadora and me to accompany you. She comes from Westbrook, which is a settlement to the west. It began as a small town and they've done an admirable job of consolidating it. Harkness Glen is going to need more people, and I would like to negotiate with the townsfolk to see how we might ally our communities."

Marcus recalled how she had stepped up the night of the attack. "I'm not going to say no to another gun. How good is Isadora?"

"We've made this journey before, and survived it." Karima pointed toward the setting sun. "It's about five days out, though, so we'll need to carry enough supplies for ten, in order to track the Locust."

When Marcus informed Brandon of the plan, he had no objections. "Isadora is easy on the eyes. Do you think my sister would like her?"

"Wow, I don't think I've seen that healthy an ego since I last laid eyes on Damon Baird."

"That's not an answer, Marcus."

The Gear shook his head. "I think Adira would like it if you find some Locust."

"Understood." Brandon sobered. "Focus on job one."

Marcus slipped a hand into his pocket and ran his thumb over the smooth stone Nick had given him. "And finding Sierra. That's right up there on our priority list."

They set out the morning of the third day. Each woman had two horses, plus an additional one carrying a variety of trade goods for Westbrook. They plotted a course west and stuck close to the trail left by the Locust. At first this proved to be slow going, but as they got used to spotting the signs of clawed bark, or finding small caves or hollows within the roots of trees, it became easier.

The Locust seemed to range widely to the north and south of a line that would have taken them directly west. It wasn't something Marcus had seen before, but the grubs he'd fought in the past hadn't been sick and dying. *I hope to hell they weren't following an urge to go somewhere and breed.*

The second day out, they found a body. The grub had curled up into a ball and died at the bottom of a small cliff. Marcus measured the distance with his eye.

"If it fell, that fall shouldn't have killed it."

Brandon dismounted and squatted next to the corpse.

"I'd bet the fall stunned it, and it didn't have the strength to get up. I can see what I think are sores, but nothing else that could have done it in."

After a couple more hours they camped on the trail. Everyone took turns performing chores and standing watch. Because Brandon happily helped Isadora as much as he could, Marcus and Karima shared sentry duty. The evenings had started turning cold, and halfway through the night snow began drifting down.

The next night they found a small cave and built up a big fire at the front. Marcus and Karima sat near the mouth, wrapped up in blankets, watching for anything that might challenge their right to shelter.

"I've been meaning to ask you, Marcus, what you first thought of Harkness Glen?" She watched him closely. "Brandon was not pleased with what he saw, and did nothing to hide it, but I couldn't read your reaction."

He thought for a few moments, then replied. "I didn't expect you to be as squared away as you were. The lawn bowling, that had me thinking one thing, but your industry and trading, and how your people had pulled together, revealed more there than I would have expected from folks who had mostly avoided Locust attacks."

Karima shifted around, picked up a thick stick, and laid it on the fire.

"We didn't have Locust attacks, but that doesn't mean we were without challenges. We had fended off roving bands of survivors. They acquainted us with the harsh realities outside. We set up our security force to keep them out."

"Yet you never trained anyone else with the guns in your armory."

"That is my failing." She returned to the cave mouth and huddled there. "We had some residents who didn't want to acknowledge what was going on outside, so I didn't make training mandatory. The social order harked back to the gentler days when we hired well-trained servants and left menial duties to them. Our residents frowned upon training with guns—though they approved of skeet shooting because it was a sport. And then, when we learned that the Locust menace had been eliminated, well…"

"The political battle wasn't worth the energy?"

"Again, my mistake." She exhaled a thick plume of steam. "It is one thing to understand that the world has changed fundamentally, but quite another to grasp what all the changes might be. In keeping the Glen together and trying to accommodate a level of normalcy, I was able to avoid many unpleasant realities. I made it my job to focus entirely on the Glen, in the hopes that other people might straggle in."

"But you reached out to other settlements…"

"In chasing off marauders, we encountered similar hunting parties from places like Westbrook. We established relationships, exchanged goods, exchanged people. It was from Westbrook that we learned the Locust were gone." She shook her head. "I allowed myself hope when I heard that news."

"There's still a lot of work to be done before we can relax." Marcus glanced over at Brandon's sleeping form. "His sister is the sole medical provider for a refugee camp of probably five hundred, with more people coming in all the time. One little boy lost his sister to marauders, and I'd have to guess that's not a rare occurrence."

Marcus rubbed his gloved hands together for warmth. "There's a lot of evil to undo. My better half, Anya, she's in Ephyra working to set things to rights. They'll form a government, which will help us organize, deal with man's darker side, and start us on the road to a new world."

"Is forming a new government good or bad?"

Marcus shrugged. "I have my issues with authority, but she'll make certain the government is a force for good. There are people who stand in her way, of course, but Anya wants as many people represented as possible. You representing the Glen, for example, or a union of the Glen and Westbrook and some of the other places around here. That would be a great help."

"It's been a very long time since I've been to Ephyra." Karima gave him a smile. "I'll think on that. I probably owe it to my people to ease them back into the world. Getting in at the beginning would be better than not. Thank you."

The snow made finding more Locust remains impossible, but the trail was still visible and moved down onto the remains of an old highway route. The Locust had used it, suggesting some higher brain functions before they fell too ill and just headed out cross-country. The group still found evidence in caves and abandoned buildings where the Locust had taken refuge.

The road looped south of Westbrook before turning and heading east. It appeared as if the Locust had bypassed the settlement. *And with good reason.* The citizens of Westbrook had systematically deconstructed all but the biggest buildings outside of the city center, and used the salvage to create tall siege walls with towers and what looked like searchlights mounted on them. Barbed wire rimmed the top of the walls, and sharpened iron stakes studded them, all pointed toward the ground. Each tower boasted a good field of fire and could support its nearest neighbors. Entry came through a stoutly built tunnel, and the citizens had welded together tons of scrap metal to create massive gates at each end.

Fortunately for the travelers, one of the women guarding the outside gate was Isadora's cousin. She sent word of their arrival, and members of the town council arrived quickly. They recognized Karima Razek who, in turn, introduced Marcus Fenix.

Once again, Brandon was admitted based on the company he kept.

Inside the towering walls, Westbrook appeared as it might have before E-Day, with the dusting of snow making it that much more beautiful. Marcus couldn't tell if the town had avoided damage, or had been painstakingly reconstructed. The buildings all appeared to be in perfect repair, and even the signs that hung from businesses showed not even a hint of fading or peeling paint. The stores themselves seemed to be understocked—at least with the items they'd once sold. A couple of buildings had been converted into grain and feed warehouses, and a couple more into livestock barns, but from a distance the exteriors did not betray their new uses.

Nigel Izawa, the town's mayor, welcomed the visitors to his office and dispatched a clerk who went with Isadora to inventory the load of goods the travelers had brought with them. He thanked Karima, then turned to Marcus.

"I find it hard to believe you've been reduced to guarding travelers, or that anyone in Ephyra would think they have any authority out this far. They didn't think that before the Locust, makes no sense they'd think it now."

"Brandon and I are tracking down rumors of Locust sightings."

"That's strange." Nigel frowned, got up, and walked over to

a hand-drawn map of the area. "There haven't been any around here for four or five years, best I can remember. Westbrook claims about five miles in any direction. Growing season we cultivate feed for the livestock, other crops for us. We send Karima most all of our wool, about half of our linen."

"Does everyone live in town year-round?"

"No. Folks live on the farms during the summer. Saves them the walk to work each morning." He indicated areas outside the walls. "There are a few families that live further out; at least one commune worshipping something or other. They come in a couple times a year to trade, but if we don't see them until spring it won't be a surprise."

Brandon got up and tapped the map further east.

"Anyone out here that you know of?"

"Watson homestead. Two brothers or cousins, not sure which, and their families. One was a Gear, maybe. About a dozen people altogether, couple of toddlers. I think the mother of one of the wives is out there, too." Nigel brushed a hand back over his hair. "Saw them six weeks ago. They came in to our Harvest market, sold some cheese, couple of quilts. Seemed happy. Good cheese."

"Glad to hear that, sir." Marcus stood. "Maybe Brandon and I will take a ride out that way tomorrow, just to ask if they've seen anything."

"Whatever suits you."

"One last thing. Have you seen a young woman, about this tall, dark hair. Late teens? Answers to the name Sierra."

Despite his attempt not to be specific, the mayor caught his drift.

"No, and we wouldn't." His eyes tightened. "People that trade in people—we don't allow in Westbrook. This is a good town, and we keep that kind of trouble on the other side of the wall."

4: WATSON FARM

EAST OF WESTBROOK, SERA
6 FROST 18 A.E.

Two to three inches of light, fluffy snow had drifted down during the night, blanketing the countryside with purity. The day dawned clear, dropping the temperature below freezing. Bright sunlight reflected from the drifts, and tiny breezes swirled snowflakes into sparkling tornadoes that danced through the chilly landscape.

Marcus and Brandon left Karima and Isadora in Westbrook to complete work for Harkness Glen. They traveled east along the old highway, looking for a trio of oaks on the left, atop a small hill. According to instructions, at that point they were to turn off toward the southeast. They'd pass a couple of Westbrook-allied farmsteads that had closed up for the winter and then, after crossing a small brook, they were to turn east again. A couple of miles further along the brook they'd find the Watson place. If they found a rocky outcropping that looked like a giant tombstone, they'd gone too far.

The people of Westbrook had been very accommodating of the travelers and lent the two men a pair of fresh horses for their day trip. The fact that Fred Watson was thought to have been a Gear made it easy to characterize the trip as Marcus going out to visit an old comrade. Nigel Izawa had agreed to run with that story, since he had no interest in getting people stirred up with the prospect of having the Locust threat return.

Neither man spoke much on the ride, and Marcus didn't mind that. The morning felt incredibly peaceful, and the snow hid all imperfections in the landscape. He'd spent so many years living in the rubble the Locust had made of the world, or looking at the desperate defenses men had raised against them, that he had a hard time thinking of beauty unless he added "shattered" to it.

So much of what men had wrought—and thought would last for centuries—had been churned into a crushed and crippled shadow of the world from before. Traveling through an unspoiled countryside calmed something inside Marcus, and while he accepted that it was only a calm before a storm, he clung to the exotic feeling.

I wish Anya was here. I'll have to bring her here. Marcus smiled behind the blue scarf he'd donned. *Maybe we come here with the kids. We'll visit Brandon and Isadora in Westbrook, maybe wander to Harkness Glen.* For a moment the wonderful possibilities of a future where mankind could flourish again filled him, and he exhaled slowly. Tension drained with his breath.

An hour later, as the sun moved toward its zenith, they rode up a slight incline which opened out into a plain. The stream skirted the edge, dipping to the south and working around behind a large farmhouse and barn. Some harvest stubble poked up through the snow, but the white blanket lay otherwise undisturbed, including on several banks of solar panels in the middle of the property.

"Not good." Brandon reined his horse up beside Marcus. "No smoke from the chimney. Snow's pristine in the paddocks."

Marcus shucked his Lancer from the saddle scabbard. "Barn first."

His companion nodded and likewise freed his Lancer. He led the way and dismounted when they had the barn between them and the main house. They continued forward on foot, passing through pens that stood between the barn and the stream. As the main house came back into view, Brandon dropped to a knee and raised the rifle.

The building had been expanded over the years. Where they'd entered the grounds they saw a rectangular building, with a porch across the front. It had two chimneys, one on each of the narrow ends, and looked picture perfect from that angle. Approaching it from the side, however, they spotted an extension jutting out the back. The door there had been torn away and snow had drifted inside.

Spreading out and keeping their muzzles trained on the house, the two men advanced. Marcus led up the small set of steps to the doorway and quickly ducked his head in. The snow covered a portion of the floor and some of the furnishings, but lay unmarked. He entered in a crouch, leveling his Lancer toward the house's main body.

Halfway in lay the body of an older woman. Her detached head lay a bit further on, and Marcus couldn't determine where her left arm had gotten to.

Dead a while, but in the cold, no decay yet. He beckoned Brandon to follow him, then crept forward, listening for anything at all. The woman had clearly been torn apart by a Locust. Her arm lay on the kitchen floor. The Locust may have used it to batter the second body Marcus found. That had to be one of the Watson brothers. He'd literally been torn in half, and a long carving knife had fallen not too far from where his torso lay.

The next two bodies stretched out in the parlor. The man, it appeared, had been going for a long gun that hung over the mantel. Before he reached it, however, something slammed his head into the stone fireplace, dashing his brains out. He fell into the fireplace, so the head and neck had burned to a cinder.

The other body had fallen across the man's legs. Claws had shredded her from right shoulder to ankle, and her intestines leaked out of the rents in her floral-print dress. Her left hand had been trying to gather her guts up when she finally expired.

The two men continued searching the house. They went through every room, including the upper floor, but found no one else. Then they returned outside and opened the root cellar. No one was hiding down there, either. Shelves bowed by the weight of preserved fruit and pickles, sacks of flour and wheels of aging cheese comprised most of what the Watsons had stored away for winter.

The only motion they found was the blinking light on the large storage battery for the solar array. The display indicated that it still had half a charge left. Marcus pointed to a space near the battery. "We move the flour over to the corner and we can bring the bodies down here. Give them some peace and respect."

Brandon nodded. "Barn's the only other place I can imagine someone might be hiding."

"Agreed."

Lancers at the ready, they checked the barn. Aside from some very hungry animals, they found no indication of life. Marcus climbed up into the hay loft, hoping he'd find signs someone had taken shelter there, but nothing.

"It's clear up here."

"Don't know much about farm animals, but they seem in pretty good shape."

"Maybe folks haven't been gone that long."

Marcus retraced his steps into the house with Brandon in tow, and pointed to the refrigerator. Photos and artwork by children covered it, fixed with magnets. One colorful finger painting showed the house and the sun and a legion of people, each with their name printed below in a child's hand. The photos showed other shots of the family in every season. They looked happy and seemed to be in good health.

"Fourteen people in residence, five adults, three toddlers, six kids from four to twelve?"

"Seems like. The big guy is named Fred."

"Yeah." Marcus' eyes tightened. "The four-year-old girl has a stuffed bear, and that boy has a cap. See the bear again in this picture? I don't recall seeing either thing when we looked upstairs. You?"

"I don't. What are you thinking?"

"A whole lot of things I don't want to think." Marcus mounted the stairs and checked the rooms again. He couldn't find the bear, or the cap. "Did you see any mittens or jackets, heavy sweaters?"

Brandon shook his head. "No access to crawl spaces or an attic, either, no hidden panels. The family is gone."

"Okay, we have three possibilities." Marcus walked back out to the barn. He spoke as he started filling mangers with feed. "Case one: Locust enters the house and slaughters four of the adults. The other adult gets all of the kids together, gets them dressed for winter, and evacuates them. Given the state of the animals here in the barn, they were unattended for what, two or three days?"

"Possible, but improbable." Brandon pumped water up into a storage tank which, in turn, flowed into the drinking troughs. "But the condition of the house makes that seem unlikely, right? The Locust kills the old woman, then the first man in the kitchen. It gets Fred and his wife in the parlor. That takes how long, do you think, total?"

Marcus patted a cow's head as the beast fed. "Thirty seconds, tops. We know the attack came at night, after the animals had been put up for the day. Grubs see in the dark well enough, so they'd have the advantage. The question then is why, when the attack would have made noise and would have had the kids screaming, did the grub just stop with the four adults?"

"It shouldn't have."

"Not at all." Marcus refilled a big bucket with grain from a bin, and hauled it deeper into the barn. "Case two: Before the Locust arrives, one human adult gets all the kids ready to travel, they go somewhere, and the Locust kills the only occupants left in the house."

Brandon nodded. "Maybe, but I have questions."

"Like the big one in this case: where would the last adult and the kids be going? At night. In the cold. It might have been snowing. If there's some sort of danger, wouldn't you seek the nearest safe place? That would be Westbrook, I'd think."

"We're talking six–seven miles. They would have made it by at least noon the day before we arrived." Brandon turned the valve on the storage tank, letting water flow into the troughs and refill the reservoirs. "Your case three, let me guess—it's that someone had control of the Locust. They used it to kill the adults... and then what?"

A shiver ran down Marcus' spine. "Family is upstairs, all cowering. They're waiting for the grub to come up and get them. Then they hear gunfire. A team enters the building, says they lured the Locust outside and drove it off. Everyone has to move quickly and the team says they can get them to safety. They bundle everyone up and get them away."

"You're saying they hit the farm to steal the people?"

Marcus nodded. "What's the most precious resource left in the world? People. We need them to work."

"And breed."

"Especially breed." Marcus gestured off to the west. "What Dodger was doing in that quarry, but this is more coordinated. They cull the adults who are likely to resist and harvest the rest as breeding stock or cheap labor."

"The mayor mentioned a commune of some sort around here..."

"We can check on them, but this has to be a group with the technological resources to capture and control Locust, to diagnose what's wrong with them, keep them alive, and train them." Marcus hauled the bucket to the last stall and filled the manger. "What's more, mounting this sort of raid requires a degree of coordination that isn't easy to put together."

"But, Marcus, why would they target the Watsons? I mean, they had to target them, right?"

"The *why* is exactly what we said it was: they wanted the people. But the *how*..." Marcus dropped the empty bucket. "Oh holy shit..."

He ran from the barn with Brandon on his heels, ran through the drifts in the front yard to the solar panels. Marcus dug down on the base and brushed snow away from a gray panel with numbers etched into it. "There."

"The serial number?"

Marcus nodded. "Ends in SI. This is a Seradyne product. I bet if we crack it open there's a radio unit in there that pulses out information that Seradyne techs use to measure efficiency and such things. Diagnostics for when they needed to repair units."

Brandon frowned. "That would include the daily energy load numbers."

"And they use enough for a large group of people." Marcus pointed out toward the distant woods. "Someone sitting out there recons the situation and the Watsons become a target."

"They never would have seen it coming." Brandon slowly shook his head. "And the serial number makes it Seradyne, huh?"

"Raul Hasterwith himself told me what to look for." Marcus unslung his Lancer and pointed at the serial number stamped on the receiver. "The serial number identifies the manufacturer."

Brandon dropped to his knees, rubbing a hand over his forehead. "If Seradyne... Do you know what this means? It means there's a whole mountain of shit that's going to be flowing downhill fast." He shivered. "This is big, Marcus. Incredibly big."

"Nothing bigger."

"This is a lot to take on, just the two of us."

"Yeah, it is." Marcus gave him a half-grin. "Which is why it ain't gonna be just the two of us."

5: THE MINISTRY OF SANITATION

EPHYRA, SERA

8 FROST 18 A.E.

"**A**aron Griffin, this is a pleasant surprise." Anya paused in her walk and offered her hand to the man representing Char.

Griffin looked at her hand and, after a moment's hesitation, shook it. "A surprise, anyway."

"Okay." Anya nodded. "How can I help you?"

"I want things to be straight between us. You were COG. You were a Gear. Your family has ties to Ephyra. Now *New* Ephyra. My people worry, Stroud. Worry that you and Shin are going to herd us to your new city. Tell us to forget Char. Forget who we are, who we were."

What? Anya shook her head. "I know our first meeting made an impression, and not a good one, but that's not a plan at all. No one is going to force anyone to live anywhere." She jerked a thumb back toward the Ministry building. "If you want to come up to the planning office, I can show you exactly what we've done."

"Let's walk. In the open." He looked around warily. "That a problem?"

"No, not at all." Anya pulled her long, woolen greatcoat tighter around her and buttoned it closed. Ephyra hadn't gotten the snow that had fallen in the northern uplands, but winter had brought chill weather with it. "I was under the impression the other day that you liked the plans we'd presented."

"Oh, you sold it perfect."

As if on cue, a rumbling came from deeper in the city, and five hundred yards away a building sloughed off its granite facade. They stood silently for a moment, watching as a cloud of dust rose high into the air. That sort of occurrence had become less frequent in the city, but always reminded her of how far they had yet to go in rebuilding.

Griffin's eyes tightened. "Rebuilding here in Ephyra is a non-starter. Too much damage in the bedrock layers, I get that. But how long before someone 'discovers' some seismic anomalies beneath Char. Maybe the Stranded settlements. All of a sudden we're all here. In your new city. For our '*safety*.'"

The hostility in the man's voice puzzled Anya. "What would make you think that we're planning such a thing?"

"Word is out, Stroud. That's your plan. Maybe not *your* plan, but something Jamila Shin has in mind, once she's named the first minister."

"That assumption is a bit premature, isn't it?" Anya kept her voice even and her tone innocent. While Jamila likely was the leading candidate, it was because she'd taken the steps of organizing people and launching the discussions. "We haven't even begun to establish what the first minister's powers and duties will be."

"We'll bang that out in a week." Griffin shook his head. "Dr.

Shin says she's just 'facilitating.' Is that shit *real*? Griffin pointed a finger toward the sky. "She says it's a ceremonial position, but c'mon. Power's a drug. She gets in, she tightens her grip, then builds a government around her."

Anya's eyes narrowed. "When you say you're hearing this from *everyone*, break that down, please."

He started ticking points off on his gloved fingers. "In Char it's making the rounds. Then, out to the east there's Hindon, the Dells, Occam township. Their councils approved resolutions that declare them to be sovereign states. They have to agree to join any central government. They won't accept actions or legislation that interfere with their independence. They all hit similar points. They're not copies, but it's clear that people *have* talked to each other."

They turned a corner and crossed to a park to avoid a crystal-corpse harvesting team hard at work.

"How is that possible?" Anya frowned. "We've only just started warning people about the dangers here, and telling them there would be housing available soon. For them to make the leap to a plan that would consolidate everyone in New Ephyra, that's extreme."

"The COG killed a lot of folks. We all gutted it out through the end. All in the same boat, all doing for ourselves." Griffin pounded a gloved fist into his other palm. "People don't want a ruling class grabbing them by the throat. Some of them think the first minister is just the chairman under a new name."

Anya nodded. "I can see where that would make people antsy."

"What's worse, Stroud, is that those three settlements are enlightened. Talk to Cara Lima. She'll agree. They're forward thinking. They're already tied into the Seradyne Information Services network, and are coordinating trade with each other over their radio channels." Griffin glanced at his companion, and stopped. "What? What is that look?"

"It's probably nothing." Anya hadn't shared with anyone other than Jamila and Thomas the suspicions about Seradyne trying to break the MilNet security. When Seradyne had repaired communications cables and installed radio and TV monitors throughout the Ministry offices, Anya had asked Damon to sweep for listening devices. He found none, which gave her some relief, but she still remained very disciplined about what she said and did near the devices.

Maybe they don't need to listen to the Ministry, if they're listening to everyone else. If they're talking to everyone else. Anya looked at Griffin. "Does Seradyne have a screen in your office?"

"Of course. And my home in Char. There's one in the Town Assembly Hall in Hindon, too."

"Have you listened to their information programs?"

He nodded. "I'm more interested in their trade channels, but sure. Reports about what we've been doing are barebones and simple. I guess the stories of long-lost people being reunited are popular. Most of the entertainment shit they offer should never have survived the Pendulum Wars, much less E-Day. Why?"

"Have you watched a news report in Hindon, and then here? Any programs?"

"No." The man folded his arms over his chest. "Spill it, Stroud. What am I missing?"

Anya started a long looping course around the park's central fountain. "I think our colleague, Raul Hasterwith, is very smart. He shows stories about people being reunited, and we all feel hopeful. Then there's a report about how the ministers have prioritized creating an information clearing house to reunite lost people. How do you think viewers will feel about that database?"

"Good. They'll feel good. The database benefits everyone."

"Yes, but what if he runs a story about the ministers creating that registry, with intimate data on everyone, and then runs an old *Crimecracker* show. You know, the one where the COG used their database information to track people down? How would the average viewer feel then?"

Griffin's eyes tightened. "You think Raul is playing with perceptions?"

"Maybe not Raul himself, but I think he has people who could do that sort of thing *for* him." Anya sighed. "You said it yourself—people are already suggesting Jamila is behind these things. Who benefits if she suddenly becomes unpopular? Who *else* might be in the running for first minister? Given the things he's been doing, providing free communications and information for folks, Raul Hasterwith has to look very beneficent. He'd be an obvious leadership choice."

As they completed the first circuit, Griffin again pounded a fist into his open hand. "I can see it. Raul would be happy to be first minister. But we all know Jamila would like to be, as well. First rule of business: what's in it for me? What's Shin promised you if she makes it? A new military? People all saluting you, Stroud?"

"Do you honestly think I want that?" Anya blinked. "Griffin, you and all of your people were the lucky ones. You all survived the Locust because you were quick and managed to reach safety, but you have to remember—my friends and I, we were the ones who ran *into* danger. You all lost brothers and sisters and friends. I had to scrape wet gobbets of my friends off me. I had to wash their blood away and comb their bone chips out of my hair. Sometimes I had to wait hours or days to do that, and I always had to walk back into the firefights, hoping like hell I could find someone like you, and give you a chance to get away."

Anya forced her hands open. "So I've seen more than enough combat for a lifetime. If I never hear another shot fired in anger, I'm good. Right now my agenda is to make sure everyone who needs shelter gets it. People who need clothes find them. People who need food get a belly full of it. Then maybe we get to educate children, retrain people in jobs that need doing. But to answer your question directly, no, Jamila hasn't offered me anything. She hasn't even asked if I thought she'd be a good fit for first minister. If that's what she wants, great, but so far all I've seen is her wanting the best for the survivors and I'm happy to help her achieve that goal."

Griffin nodded. "Look, Stroud, we've got some issues between us, but I didn't mean to accuse you of anything sordid. It's just—the way folks condemn Jamila, it makes me wonder if there's fire where they report smoke."

Anya raised her chin. "I see that. Tricky times for all of us. But I am glad you came to me and asked. Any other questions you have, just come to me."

"I will." He half smiled. "And I'm going to find out what folks back home are seeing through Seradyne. If Raul *is* manipulating things, I can't be blind to it."

"Yes, but promise me you won't do anything rash, like accuse him." She smiled. "It could be something else going on there, and a logical explanation might be forthcoming."

"If there isn't, it's trouble." Griffin offered Anya his hand. "I won't forget what you did in Char, Stroud, but I'm looking forward to seeing what you do here."

Anya headed back to the Ministry, but took her time because she needed to sort things out in her mind.

She had full confidence in Jamila. She'd seen nothing in her friend and political mentor to suggest that she was manipulating Anya. As nearly as Anya could tell, Jamila tried to put people into positions where they could contribute the most possible to rebuilding society. Moreover, she had not come out in favor of the economic proposals that Hasterwith and Pendergast had put forward, even though her family stood to benefit greatly.

Likewise she had no doubt that Raul Hasterwith wanted to be first minister. In his pursuit of power, he would not consider it necessary to keep all his dealings aboveboard. In fact, the issue with the world was that there wasn't really a board to be above. Ethics and honor had always been seen as lawful, while unethical and dishonorable behavior often violated the law. But without all the trappings of a justice system, who was to say what was right and what was wrong?

Winning might be used to justify almost anything.

Moreover, if Hasterwith was manipulating public opinion through the information his company disseminated, he would be in a position to establish the line separating right from wrong. The tone of a single news report could transform murder into self-defense, or make it the tale of a citizen stepping in to protect others where, in the past, a police force would have had that responsibility.

If Hasterwith shaped opinion, he shaped social reality.

That gave him an incredible amount of power.

To counter it, I need proof of what he is doing. She returned to her office, grabbed the satellite phone, and hiked up to the Ministry roof. She acquired a MilNet satellite and initiated a call to Damon Baird.

If anyone can sort this out, he can.

"You have reached the inestimable Damon Baird, genius and dashingly handsome man who lives for action. Please leave a message and I will get back to you as soon as I can."

Anya chewed her lower lip for a second. "Damon, Anya. I need to speak to you urgently. Code Red urgent. Call me immediately. Thank you."

She packed the phone back up and returned to her office. She'd just removed her coat when Jamila knocked on the doorjamb.

"Anya, do you have a moment?"

"For you, sure." Anya waved her to a chair. "What can I do for you?"

"I'll stand, this won't take a moment." Jamila slowly smiled. "I just had a meeting with Diana Egami. Hanover would like more details on the algae farming proposal. They've done projections, and want to guard against what they think might be a food resource shortfall over the next three years. Will there be a problem with that?"

Anya shook her head. "If you have their numbers, I can work up some ideas."

"I'll send Thomas around with them tomorrow morning."

"Great. When I'm done I'll send the results to your office, and you can pass them along to Diana."

The smaller woman shook her head. "No need for that. I made certain she knows that you are the architect of that project. Please let me have a copy of your proposal, but you should hand it to her directly. You don't need me as an intermediary—that will simply slow things down."

"Okay, it'll be done."

Jamila turned to leave, but paused and looked back over her

shoulder. "You know, when Colonel Hoffman recommended you to me, he did so with high praise. Now I find that he held back, because the real you, Anya Stroud, is far more than I anticipated, or would have ever believed. Thank you for reminding me that there really are people for whom public service is a true pleasure."

6: WESTBROOK TOWN HALL, CONFERENCE ROOM 1

WESTBROOK, SERA

8 FROST 18 A.E.

"**W**ell?" Marcus gave Damon Baird a hard stare.

Damon caught the jeweler's loupe deftly as it fell from his eye. "This has been burned all to hell, but I'm ninety-nine percent sure it's a Seradyne C7 processor. Local field communications, general remote functions. The C7 was a proprietary design they put together for a new generation of Jacks that never got into production. So, could it be used to control a grub? I don't know, but you sure could use it to train one the way you would a dog. Or your average Gear."

Samantha Byrne punched Damon in the arm, none too lightly. "Thanks, mate."

"Hey, we're *above*-average Gears." Damon tossed the control unit on the table. "There's no training us."

The brunette groaned. "There's no training *you*, you mean."

"One does not mess with perfection."

"If you were perfect, Marcus wouldn't have had to call *us* in." Clayton Carmine's voice echoed from within his full-face helmet.

"Alright, knock it off." Marcus tried to put a fearful growl into his voice, but his happiness at being among friends took the edge off. "So it's definitely Seradyne?"

Damon opened his hands. "It's them, or a dark research site that's gone rogue. Those chips weren't mass-produced, and this controller definitely looks like a prototype."

Sam picked the unit up. "Any way to trace where they made it?"

"I could, if, you know, sixteen years of fighting grubs hadn't destroyed most of the machines I'd use to do that. However..." Damon held up an index finger. "Do not despair. See, I have been monitoring radio traffic and triangulating the various broadcast stations out. I can't crack the encryption that Seradyne uses, but I can break it down for what has higher levels than lower. I figure they'd go with the top-level encryption—especially if they're using domesticated grubs to kill people and steal their families. And if it's a really black site..."

Marcus' eyes tightened. "Operational security would mean there's little to no traffic in or out. Short bursts, untraceable."

Damon pointed at Marcus. "You win a prize, sir. So what I've done is correlate the lowest amount of traffic at the highest level of encryption going through broadcasts. I noted the locations of the broadcast stations and repeaters, then mapped those locations against all known Seradyne facilities. That produced a list of a half-dozen candidates, three of which aren't on any list of properties the company owned. As luck would have it, one is sixty miles to the southeast of here."

"Show me." Marcus rolled out an old map of the area, and Brandon helped him pin down the corners with a couple of books.

"Should be right about here. High desert, red hills. Fairly desolate except for some riparian areas along the Red River."

Marcus looked up. "Carmine? Sam? Been there?"

Both of them shook their heads.

Brandon held his hand up. "Not me, either."

"I have." Karima Razek hung in the doorway. "Twenty years ago. I used to enjoy hiking and photography. A lot of red rocks and a few abandoned mining facilities. Back when people discovered Imulsion, they dug a lot of dry holes. I shot pictures of a lot of them. Some were displayed in the Birches."

"Those were good." Marcus gave her a nod. "I'm going to need you to brief us on all you remember."

"I can do better." She crossed to the map and tapped it with a finger. "I'll lead you in. We already know the location, you just have to get close. I can get you in."

"Okay, you lead us in on the recon run. Something goes wrong, shooting starts, I want you to get out of there." Marcus looked over at Brandon. "You're on her, keeping her alive."

"I'm her guardian angel, got it."

Marcus ran a hand over his head. "Okay, we know where. It's two days out riding, and we'll go slow when we get there, so make it three days, supplies for seven. We go in like ghosts, look around, then figure out how to hit it."

Sam leaned on the table. "And how to evac the people. The Watsons, yeah?"

"Your buddy brought us here in a King Raven." Clay jerked a thumb at Brandon. "Can we get that back for the evac?"

"Is that possible, Brandon?"

Brandon winced. "That was me burning a lot of favors with a freelance pilot. Losing a Raven for a couple hours is one thing, but for as long as we need to pull this off? Might be easier to unsink Jacinto."

"Probably just as well." Clay folded his arms over his chest. "We don't have a solid fix on where we're headed, or what we'll need to bring out. Besides, we call for transportation, there's no telling who that would alert. Karima, if these were old mining towns, they must have had roads."

"Afraid not." Karima shook her head. "Narrow-gauge rail only, electric engine, running out to a terminal near Route 87. I have photos of all that, too." She pointed south. "The road here branches into 87, but if there's a mile of it intact between here and there, I'd be surprised."

Marcus' right hand balled into a fist. "Okay, so we'll have to hit and hold, and plan accordingly."

"Hitting we can do." Samantha smiled. "Holding should work, too."

Damon's face lit up. "You can hold me, Sam."

"You really don't date much, do you?"

"Married to my work, you know that."

Marcus' sat phone buzzed and he answered. "Fenix."

"Marcus, you still having your party?"

"Cole?" Marcus had put a call in to his friend, but had begun to wonder if he'd get a call back. "Yeah, yeah, we're still having the party."

"Sorry I missed the limo, so I made other arrangements." Static rode through Cole's voice. *"See you soon, brother."*

Marcus stared at the receiver as the line went dead. "That was Cole. He says he's incoming. How does he know where we are?"

"Well…" Damon shrugged, looking sheepish. "Your message was cryptic enough that he reached out to me to find out what was going on. I gave him directions to get here, and asked for a few toys."

"And you didn't think to tell me?"

"Need to know, boss." Damon smiled. "He wanted to surprise you."

I hate surprises. Marcus couldn't decide whether to hug Baird, or to tear off a piece of his hide.

Suddenly the building's windows began to rattle.

Outside, the snow swirled into the air and something descended onto the town square. As the snow began to drift down, it revealed a King Raven helicopter. Black trimmed the cobalt aircraft's body. A snarling, leaping gray cougar decorated the tail, and a more cartoonish version of the face splashed its image over the craft's nose, turning the windscreens into the cat's eyes.

That is just so wrong!

As people came out of their shops and homes, a side panel slid open and Augustus Cole hopped out, hauling a bulging duffle in one hand and a Lancer in the other. Keeping his head low, he ran out from beneath the rotor's circle and greeted the folks who had turned out to welcome him.

Marcus hustled down the stairs and burst out into the chill air. "Aren't you a little out of bounds here, brother?"

Cole dropped his baggage and caught Marcus up in a big hug. "I missed you too, brother. You knew I was going to answer your call, didn't you?"

"Technically speaking, you didn't."

"My assistant put it low on my 'To Do' list. Technically, I'm out here scouting talent. That's why they let me use the team's helo." Cole broke the embrace and smiled wide when the others emerged from the town hall. He opened his arms. "You're a sight for sore eyes, all of you."

"Once a star..." Damon laughed and opened his arms as well.

Cole stepped past him and hugged Samantha tight. "Been too long, baby."

"I missed you, too, Cole."

He offered Clay his hand, then pulled him into a back-slapping hug. "I'd say I'd recognize that ugly mug anywhere, but..."

"Says the man who made his fortune with his head in a cage. Good to see you, Cole."

Cole shook hands with Brandon, then looked at Karima Razek. "I'm Augustus Cole."

"Karima Razek, pleased."

Damon cleared his throat. "I don't get any love?"

Cole turned back to his friend. "All of it, baby." He hugged Damon. "I brought you the stuff you asked for; and got enough ammo for us to blast a tunnel to the center of Sera."

"Good." Marcus nodded. "I think we may need all of it."

"You found your grubs?"

"Worse. We'll catch you up." Marcus couldn't help but smile. "For now, I'm just happy we've got the band back together."

Marcus stood by the window of the second-floor apartment he'd been allotted in Westbrook, drinking some tea. He watched the pilot and flight engineer tie down the King Raven's rotors, and set up the generator for recharging the ship's batteries. He still couldn't reconcile the gunship being repainted in the Cougars' colors, with the mascot's snarling face emblazoned on the nose, but having the transport available for evacuating casualties took the tension down a notch.

He plugged a switching unit into the sat phone. Damon Baird had given it to him, and it commanded the MilNet satellite to reroute the call through several other satellites, specifically to make it look as if the call originated from a location more than a hundred miles to the northeast. He keyed in Anya's number.

The line clicked several times, then she answered. Despite the distance and the switching, her voice still made his heart skip a beat.

"Anya, it's me. You sound good."

"*This is a surprise, a welcome surprise.*"

"Not a bad time, is it?"

"*No, not at all. To what do I owe the pleasure?*"

He scratched at the back of his head. "I had to hear your voice. And... we have to go dark. A week."

"*I understand.*" Her tone shifted to very matter-of-fact. "*What can I do? What do you need?*"

"Nothing. I think we're five days out and back. I'll know what we need then."

"*You'll be careful.*"

"Yes. You need to watch your six, too. This is some seriously sick shit. We'll send you everything, in case the mission is a bust."

"*Don't let that happen, Marcus Fenix.*" Anya's tone softened slightly. "*Your tomatoes aren't going to pick themselves, you know.*"

"Understood..." Marcus hesitated, his throat beginning to thicken. "Remember how we thought the fighting was done, that we'd earned *tomorrow*?"

"*Of course.*"

"Now's the time we earn tomorrow for everyone else." Marcus exhaled slowly. "I love you."

"*I love you, too, Marcus. Very much.*" The line fell silent, and he feared for a moment he'd lost her. *"Be safe, my love, and bring everybody home."*

"I will. And I will talk to you as soon as I can." Marcus returned the receiver to the set and flicked the unit off. *I wish you were here, Anya.*

Brandon knocked on the doorjamb. "Is the phone free? Cole offered me use of a suite at the arena, so I want track down my pilot and see if he's interested when the season starts... You okay, Marcus?"

"I think so." Marcus poured himself a glass of water from the tap. "Having everyone here, it feels good, the way it's supposed to—but it doesn't feel the *same* as before. The pressure, it's still there, but it's not the same as it was."

"It's not, because you're not the same." Brandon started packing the sat phone back into its case. "That settlement camp, that's been my home since forever, but every time I go back it feels different. *It* hasn't changed, not fundamentally, but I have. When you were fighting the Locust you were in a long, dark tunnel for a very long time. Now you're out of it. You've seen how people survived during the time you were fighting. You've seen their lives, and what they've made of them."

Marcus sipped his tea. "And now I get to see how some people want to use the grubs as their own personal army. Not something I'd ever thought possible, back then."

"Think about it. Those days you were fighting to stop the extermination of all human life. Now you've got a better perspective on all the different ways life gets defined." Brandon shrugged. "For some people it's shooting skeet. For Otto it's the work he loves at Harkness Glen—same for Cole's career, right? Damon's all about how he can make life better just by playing with technology."

"And Anya is doing everything she can to keep people alive, the way she used to do for me and Delta." Marcus shook his head. "As for me... I don't know."

"Sure you do." Brandon patted him on the shoulder. "It's doing the right thing so others can live their lives—*and* it's going to be kicking a sourdough starter's ass when you get back home."

Anya's words came back to him. *Your tomatoes aren't going to pick themselves.* He set his water glass down. "Go make your calls. See if you can get your guy for emergency standby. I'll set up everything else. At dawn we head out to make sure other people get to live their lives as they want. Except for those who think it's a good idea to try and stop us."

7: MINISTRY OF SANITATION

EPHYRA, SERA

9 FROST 18 A.E.

Anya entered the outer office in Jamila Shin's suite at the Ministry. Thomas wasn't at his desk, which wasn't wholly surprising. Anya walked through the chamber and paused in the doorway to Jamila's office. Thomas busied himself in the corner, moving files from a cabinet and into an old document box. Jamila sat at her desk, staring at the computer screen, but her hands remained folded in her lap.

Concern arrowed Anya's brows together. "What's wrong, Jamila? What's going on?"

Jamila glanced up, her face expressionless and her flesh sallow.

Thomas looked up from his work, then turned toward Anya. "Now is not a good time, Minister. If you wouldn't mind…"

"What's wrong? I can help."

"Please, Minister…" Thomas shook his head and positioned himself to prevent her from entering any further.

"No, Thomas, it's okay. If you can give us a moment. There

are things you can do from your desk, yes?" Resignation flooded through Jamila's words. She sounded thoroughly exhausted.

"Are you certain?"

"Yes."

"If you need anything, I can be here in a second."

"Yes, Thomas, thank you."

He gave Anya a hard stare. "Be careful. She doesn't need to be hurt anymore."

"Yes, Thomas." Anya stepped aside so he could exit the office, then crossed to the desk and sat in one of the chairs in front of it. "What's happened, Jamila?"

The older woman sat forward, resting her elbows on the desk, her hands clutched together in front of her mouth.

"I don't think you've met my son, Simon. He and Thomas have been lifelong friends, but are nothing alike. Simon, well, my husband and I indulged him, compensating for all the horror he's seen. As difficult as it may seem given the world's collapse, he grew up with more advantages than most. He's never truly suffered, never worked a day in his life, and we promised him that after the Locust were gone, things would return to the halcyon days of his childhood."

Jamila turned a small, digital frame around, showing the image of a good-looking young man sprawled across a chair, relaxing on a patio somewhere, with a half-eaten apple in his hand.

"People treated him differently because of the Shin name. They deferred to him. My husband and I thought we had shown him that this meant he had a responsibility to uphold, to make society and the world a better place. I always saw the museum, for example, as something which did that. Apparently Simon only saw it as a massive building graced with his name. As far as he was concerned he owned it."

Anya reached out and held Jamila's left hand in both of hers. "I grew up with my mother having endured those expectations turned in the opposite direction."

"So you did." Jamila massaged her forehead with her free hand. "Forgive me, I do go on, but context, you know."

"Of course. Take your time."

"Well, the Locust are gone, but the times of plenty have not returned. Apparently Simon felt this was a promise I had failed to keep. In an attempt to show him how we were working to put the world back together, I shared with him a number of the things we are doing. Some people—I don't know who—approached him with a get-rich-quick scheme where he agreed to use his influence to get them preferential treatment, once we hashed out the details for monetary reconciliation.

"As we had talked about, people with real-estate holdings in the hardest-hit areas have lost everything, and possess a skill set that isn't going to translate into something we will need for a long time. The percentage at which we compensate them is something these people want to see increased. They've provided my son with a number of perquisites, which have the appearance of bribes being funneled through him to me."

"Oh, God." Acid bubbled into Anya's throat.

Jamila slipped her hand from Anya's and sat back. "These people sent me some files. Documents my son signed, some video of meetings they had, and a particularly vile snippet of my son in a sexually compromised position."

"What do they want?"

"Not money, which shows they're much smarter than Simon." Jamila scrubbed her hands over her face. "They've said that someone who cannot take care of her own family certainly cannot take care of the rest of us."

"They want you to leave the ministry?"

"They've not said that, Anya. However, I believe they want me to remove myself from consideration to be first minister." The older woman's shoulders slumped. "I think until I figured that out, I hadn't realized how much I wanted to *be* first minister. I think I'm being honest about that. It would be such an honor to bring everyone together, to shepherd mankind through a recovery. I didn't think of it as being a position of power, as much as an acceptance of incredible responsibility. But now..."

The pain in her friend's voice pierced Anya's heart, and then began to anger her. "We have to find out who these people are. Hasterwith, it has to be. Or someone connected to Pendergast. Possibly Aaron Griffin?"

"Not Aaron." Jamila shook her head. "If he was coming for me, it would be face to face and he wouldn't be hiding it. But, Anya, the *who* doesn't matter. The sad part of this is that I should have seen it coming. The instant we agreed to call ourselves ministers and began shaping our roles, people began to angle for the top spot. We've not even formally ratified the nature of the office, and people lust after it. Everyone does."

"Not me." Anya shook her head. "This sort of thing is why I hate politics. I've been willing to play the word games for the sake of getting things done, but that's not how I want to live. Let me get things set up, and then let me go so Marcus and I can raise a family and get to spend some time being normal."

"There's the problem, Anya. Special people like you and Marcus never truly get to be normal." Jamila sighed. "There are rules in politics, and you've mastered many of them just by intuition. So here's one that you can learn, and whoever did this didn't. If you take a shot at the king, make sure you *kill* the king. As devastating as this was, this was not a killing shot."

"But you'll have to step down, won't you?"

"That's likely what they intended, but that isn't the result they will get." Jamila chewed her lower lip for a moment. "If we actually had a government, with laws and a justice system, yes, I would be gone and my political life would be over. Right now, what this requires is for me to remove myself from any committees dealing with monetary reconciliation, and recuse myself from any votes on the same.

"I can easily state that this is an issue which could materially benefit me." Jamila's expression sharpened. "I would maintain, therefore, I consider it vulgar and beneath my involvement. I will also recuse myself from consideration for the office of first minister. Finally, physically removing myself from this suite of offices will show that I'm serious.

"The plausible fiction we will put forward to explain my stepping back will be that my husband has been drinking too much, and I need to attend to my family. Simon will be put in a position where he'll have no more contact with these individuals, *and* in a place where he'll have to adapt to the harsh realities of the world in which we live. That lesson, for him, is long overdue."

Anya blinked. "That's a pretty comprehensive strategy."

"One my mother used thirty years ago, during a leadership struggle within the museum's social events committee. As much as some of our counterparts think themselves political geniuses, they're infants compared to those women."

Anya smiled. "During the time off, do you plan to eliminate your opposition? Identify the target and destroy it?"

"That I can't do, not until the information about my son has been drained of its sting. Scandals go away with time, and something like this has a shelf-life of three years or so. The best I can do during that time is to lend my support to others, but only tangentially." Jamila pressed her hands palms-down on her desktop. "So I can do nothing—but you, Anya, have no limitations."

"Me? No. I'm not interested." Anya shook her head firmly. "Diana is a much better choice, or Cara. At least they've been elected, so either has legitimacy. I'm not a politician. I just make things work, and that's all I want. You pick either one of them, and I'll back your choice."

Jamila stared down at her hands for a moment, then nodded. "I will respect your decision, Anya. Not because I think the others would be a better choice, but because you've already given more of your life than one could expect. We may be starting the world over from scratch, but there's one traditional value that really needs to be brought forward: gratitude for the sacrifices others have made."

"Thank you."

"You're welcome, but please, remember one thing." Jamila's dark eyes became slits. "Those who want to be first minister may not believe your claim that you don't want the office. They see enemies where none exist, and they move to eliminate them however they can. Be very careful, Anya. Don't let them hurt you."

8: IRON HILLS RIPARIAN PRESERVE

IRON HILLS, SERA
12 FROST 18 A.E.

Their trip in took them until dusk of the third day.

Snow began falling gently but steadily as they started south from Westbrook. While it made passage slower, it also covered their tracks, and the cloud cover would keep all but the most foolhardy pilot grounded. They calculated their chances at discovery as low, and kept cold camps at night so firelight wouldn't betray them.

Cole and Karima Razek hit it off well. The two of them spent a lot of time discussing the business of Thrashball, including the resources necessary to establish a team and projected timeline for a solid ten percent return on investment. Marcus listened to them with interest. Their conversations provided him a glimpse of something he'd never before seen in Cole. He'd never believed in the dumb jock stereotype some wanted to ascribe to his friend. He'd always known Cole was bright, but the talk of business and finance clued him in to just how bright the man really was.

Karima argued that Cole's numbers seemed optimistic, and that she'd want to see a proof of concept that a league could work in the new world.

"Baby, that's what pre-season is all about." Cole went on to outline a plan for a long pre-season, with teams barnstorming around to build excitement. "If a town has a flat expanse of open ground, we'll play. Westbrook; their town square, I put the helo down at mid-field."

That broadened the scope of the conversation, with everyone else tossing in suggestions. Things went from practical to absurd, and a generous portion of good-natured ribbing was doled out. Even with two civilians in the mix, it felt to Marcus like he had Delta back.

We lost so much, but there's still so much here. Anya would love it.

Mid-afternoon on the third day Karima led them into the preserve and along a trail that ran parallel to the river but about a mile east of it. Wide enough that horses could travel two abreast, the trail wound down into a narrow canyon with a small, steaming pool of jade-green water, and natural caves. Ancient mud-bricks and stone partially closed them to the outside, providing shelter and a place to stable their horses.

"These ruins are four hundred years old, or so I was told when I first visited." Karima led her horses to the pool to drink. "A hot spring feeds the pool. It's good for drinking and bathing, though getting out of it in this cold would not be enjoyable."

Marcus looked over at the south end of the canyon. "Where does that trail go?"

"We're roughly a mile east of the mining camp. That trail will take us to the middle of the mine complex. It goes south, then comes back up north, then down to the floor. Likely half an hour to traverse." She turned and pointed back the way they'd just come down. "Back up there was a crack in the rock. That leads directly east, and brings you out at the valley's north end, right past what was the railhead for the mining train."

"Sam, let's you, me, and Karima run a quick recon."

Clay looked up from snapping the barrel-assembly for a Longshot sniper rifle into the receiver. "Want me to head up the other way, and be ready to cover you?"

"No." Marcus pointed to another set of ruins twenty-five yards away on the other side of the pool. "You and Cole set up there. If there's trouble, we'll lead them back here. If we're chased, Brandon, you and Karima get the hell out. Karima, you find the both of you a nice place to hide, and Brandon, you call for evac. No questions."

"And me?" Damon spread his hands wide. "I'm just supposed to stand here looking pretty?"

Sam shot Damon a quick look. "Someone hasn't looked in a mirror recently…"

Marcus shouldered his Lancer. "Load up, move out. Baird, maybe you have some food ready for us when we get back?"

"You're going to love the taste of algae, and…"

Marcus ignored whatever else the man said. He fell into line with Karima in the lead and Sam bringing up the rear. They skirted the pool, then headed upward. The trail quickly narrowed—a horse could have ridden it, but slowly, and the rider's legs would be scratched all to hell. In a couple of spots he had to turn sideways to squeeze through in his armor.

As Karima had said, the way led south and a bit west, then cut back north. They did a steep up and down, then the trail leveled out and turned directly west. It began a gradual descent, and well before the narrow trail allowed him to see anything, Marcus smelled water and caught sounds that weren't natural. About a dozen yards from the end of the trail Karima stopped them with an upraised and closed fist, then moved up along a spur to a lookout point.

The river canyon proved far broader than Marcus had expected. When the miners had first arrived they had blasted out a lot of rock and used the rubble to fill the riverbed. This meant that the river, which came in from the north, became much broader and far shallower through the middle of the valley. Though only ankle-deep, the center hadn't frozen over entirely.

To the north, on the far side of the river, stood the old railhead, including a massive shed and a smaller side-building attached to it. Made out of corrugated tin, the structure seemed now to serve a single purpose, holding up a solar-panel array on its roof.

The narrow-gauge track ran south from the warehouse, paralleling the river to a point south of the mining camp, where it turned west and ran out toward the highway.

The original miners had carved a big semicircle out of the valley's western wall. It contained three mine entrances. Each rose to the height of a three-story building, and all of them had twin iron doors. The doors were closed in two—the northernmost and the central ones—and coils of barbed wire were strewn across them. The third mine also stood closed, but a smaller access door had been fitted into one of the larger ones. The snow around it had been churned into mud, indicating regular use.

A number of prefabricated buildings had been brought to the site and set up. They looked well weathered, enough to indicate that they'd been there for a long time. Four had been joined to form one building about halfway along toward the railhead. Two formed a second building between the two closed mines.

None of that looked out of the ordinary to Marcus, but a set-up toward the valley's south end didn't fit. Two dozen smaller buildings, tiny homes which maybe had a footprint of ten square yards, had been arranged in four pods of six structures. Those pods defined the four corners of an area. Down the middle were two larger buildings and the sort of open space Cole would have needed for a Thrashball field. A simple wooden rail fence surrounded the perimeter, and a row of razor wire lay about four yards further out.

A bell rang in the largest building and the doors opened. Boys and girls ranging from very young through teens, all wearing red jackets and black pants or skirts, marched out of the structure. They broke into smaller groups, each led by one of the older children. Those children led their charges to a pod, saw to it that each child went to a specific home, and finally went home themselves.

In a couple of cases Marcus saw an adult woman opening the house's door from the inside to welcome the child, but there was no affection in the greetings.

Shadows lengthened in the valley, crossing the river and rising to where Marcus and the others hid. Lights went on in the camp. A squad of six people exited the largest building on the far side, which Marcus decided was a barracks. They reported to the second building and reemerged with Lancers and sidearms. Two of them headed north, two crossed the river and patrolled the eastern shore. The final two went to the working mine, entered, and in five minutes came out again.

Oh holy shit. Marcus' eyes narrowed. *They're walking a fucking grub on a leash.*

The undersized Drone lumbered along, head up, sniffing the air. A little red pinprick blinked at its throat, which Marcus took to be the equivalent of the device he'd already recovered. The two soldiers led the creature across the river—it clearly did not like the cold water—and to the space between the fence and the barbed wire. The men began a leisurely circuit around the assembly of houses, and the residents emerged from their tiny houses to troop over to the other large building, which Marcus took to be a communal dining area.

He studied the place for another fifteen minutes, then withdrew with his companions. They traveled in silence back to their camp. Marcus cleared out a space on the floor, set up some light, and then used rocks and bits of brick to create a map of the area.

"Did I miss anything, Sam? Karima?"

"Looks good to me, Sarge." Sam squatted on the northern end of the map. "That's definitely a barracks there. Room for thirty-six, I'd say."

Marcus nodded. "Don't know if they're housing more in the mine or not, but that's where they're keeping the grubs."

"How many grubs did you see?" Clay checked the load on his Lancer.

"Just the one. Slightly undersized, but doesn't look sick, though there might have been some lesions on its neck. The ICM messed it up, but didn't kill it, clearly. These clowns found it, fitted it for that control collar, trained it."

Damon started counting on his fingers. "So thus far we have five grubs that were sick, two fitted for collars. One has been trained. But where's the E-hole?"

"They're containing them in a *mine* which, last time I looked, actually *is* a hole in the ground," Marcus said wryly. "But somewhere there was a clutch of these things, all weak from the ICM, sick and dying, and they scooped them up." He shook his head. "We spent years wiping out those things, and these guys have made them into damned *pets*."

Cole rested a hand on Marcus' shoulder. "Okay, sudden-death overtime, baby. We go in and finish them."

Sam looked up. "Not gonna be that easy. The guards had body armor, looked sharp. They've had training."

"They could even be Gears." Marcus' nostrils flared. "Raul Hasterwith, the ringmaster of this circus, offered me a job. Said he needed people with my skills."

Brandon pointed toward the cluster of smaller rocks at the south end of the map. "What's that all about?"

"I don't…" Marcus hesitated for a heartbeat, then smacked the palm of his hand against his forehead. "Cole, it's what you and Karima were talking about. It's a 'proof of concept.' They prototyped an operation at the Watson farm. A Locust attack proves a space isn't safe. To be safe, folks should gather together into settlements which, clearly, Seradyne will set up. They hire ex-Gears for security and, hey, no more attacks."

Damon frowned. "Yeah, but that wouldn't work, because they only have, what, a half-dozen grubs? That might scare folks with farmsteads and stuff, but Westbrook won't move."

Clay shrugged. "Maybe Westbrook doesn't move, but they still hire Seradyne security to keep them safe. And if Seradyne is gonna be piping news into everyplace, just the *rumor* of attacks would be enough to have folks accepting their help."

Marcus' blood ran cold. "You're missing it. They found grubs, *dying* grubs. They nursed them back to health, at least relatively speaking. They trained them. What else do they know about them? Maybe they've found a way to clone them?"

They exchanged glances in stunned silence.

Cole growled. "There are probably labs somewhere in the complex. So we get into them, get all of their info, and save all the people."

"Yeah, and deal with all the hostiles trying to stop us." Marcus shook his head. "This mission is growing with every second. How many people are we looking to move?"

Karima folded her arms over her chest. "Twenty-four houses in that 'proof of concept' village. Two kids, one adult per. That's at least seventy-two people to evacuate. If the old engine is still in the shed and charged up, we could use it to pull folks out, but that's a lot of ifs. Plus it requires that the shooting has stopped, and the little houses have survived being down-range."

"We need more people. Maybe a King Raven, kitted out with air-to-ground rockets." Marcus frowned. "But we have to cut it fine. The more assets we gather, the greater the chances of a security breach. If Seradyne even *suspects* we know what they've done, they'll destroy all the evidence."

He swept his foot through the stones pretending to be little houses.

Karima nodded. "I can get my security forces into Westbrook and up here. That's a dozen."

Damon looked up. "How about you talk to Old Man Hoffman. He's got a lot of favors to call in."

"Me? Call Hoffman?" Marcus looked at his friend. "Have you been hit in the head?"

"It was just a suggestion. You could have Anya call him."

"Carmine, hit him in the head."

Brandon bent down and picked up one of the little houses. He rolled it around in his palm. "I think you leave me and maybe Sam or Clay to keep an eye on things. We call back with any changes. Karima gets her home guards. You call in favors. You get back here in ten days, maybe two weeks, and do what has to be done."

"I hate to wait that long." Cole scratched at his jaw. "But I think that may be the game plan, brother."

Marcus looked at the others. "Thoughts?"

Sam nodded. "You'll have to leave us your rations, maybe have someone else run out some more, but more intel can't hurt."

"You'll call in nightly reports. We don't hear from you, we figure you've been compromised."

Brandon stretched. "Sun goes down, you hear from us."

Marcus shook his head. "I don't like it, but we haven't got much of a choice. We'll head back at dawn and we'll leave most of our stuff here so we can travel light and fast."

Damon gave him a thumbs-up. "It'll work."

"It better." Marcus looked at each of them. "This is a disaster just waiting to happen, and we don't need anything else to go wrong."

The sat phone began to buzz.

9: STROUD ESTATE

NEAR EPHYRA, SERA

12 FROST 18 A.E.

Anya sat back on the couch in the main house's informal parlor. It abutted the kitchen and had a large hearth built into the eastern wall. She'd built up a small fire, a bit for warmth, but mostly just to have the dancing flames inject some life into the house.

Though the Hahns had brought her some dinner and left it in the kitchen, she hadn't felt hungry. She simply opened a bottle of white wine and poured herself a glass before relaxing in front of the fire.

Jamila Shin had pulled back, and the repercussions reverberated through the ministerial world, with everyone looking for a cause, and some fearing for the future. Jamila's decision would have created more havoc, but her practice of directly connecting people, instead of having things flow through her office, enabled her to ameliorate the damage.

It still created a lot more work for Anya.

Questions that Jamila would have sorted now flowed to Anya—unfiltered and unorganized. She tried her best to direct people to the proper resources and connect them with one another, but the sheer amount of time it took to calm people down devoured chunks of her day. She was used to identifying problems and finding immediate solutions. Having to quell panic and anxiety in others before she could even *begin* to identify their problems sucked so much emotional energy out of her that she had little energy to spare and even less time to get her own work done.

Not having Marcus to talk to, to be her sanctuary, that all made it tougher to get up each day and continue working. Marcus always listened, letting her vent, frequently not offering a solution until she asked for help. He always had her back, and found ways to refocus her. He'd share his own victories—everything from reconstruction to gardening—reminding her of how important little things were. He gave her perspective, or room to find her own perspective, and she knew he'd never let anyone or anything hurt her.

"I hope I'm not interrupting."

Anya twisted around on the couch, narrowly managing to avoid sloshing her wine out of the glass. She stared at the man standing in the entryway. "Minister Hasterwith!"

He gestured vaguely back toward the door. "I would have tried your bell, but you don't seem to have one. Please, forgive me and my ill manners. I arrive unannounced and lacking a housewarming gift. The latter I shall make amends for. I accept blame for the former, but plead exigent circumstances."

Anya set her wine glass on a side table and stood. "Would you care to join me?"

"So kind, but no. No insult intended to the Stroud winery or cellar, but I eschew alcohol when dealing with sobering matters. But, please, your drinking will not be judged." The man looked around the parlor. "I see you are well on your way to returning this place to its former glory. Excellent. I mourn what we have lost, but am ambitiously hopeful for the future."

"Thank you. Please, why are you here?"

"Refreshingly direct. This is a quality I hope politics will not dull in you." He clasped his hands behind his back. "I might have spoken to you sooner, once the rumors of Jamila's withdrawal became known, but I chose to delay for a bit. I wished to see where the chips would fall, and then address the situation."

"Do you know why she pulled back?" Anya crossed to the fireplace and used an iron poker to shift the logs.

"Should I?" The man's face remained expressionless. "I took her statement at face value, that she was making time to deal with family issues. Something about her husband and drinking, I think?"

"That *is* what she said." Anya hardly expected the man to admit to having arranged for Jamila Shin's downfall, but the brazen innocence in his voice surprised her. "He has some issues."

"As does her son. Please, that look of surprise does you no credit. I could not have gotten where I am without having a plethora of sources."

"You do run Seradyne Information Services, after all."

"Indeed, but I do not employ them for brazen political gain." Hasterwith's brow wrinkled. "You don't believe that her son Simon's issues just *happened*, do you? Would it surprise you that I think he—and his mother through him—was being blackmailed?"

Anya raised an eyebrow. "You do, do you?"

"Ah, and you cling to the idea that I am the person behind

it. Understandable." The man clapped politely for a moment or two. "While, in the past, I have not been above using people's peccadilloes against them, that was before the Locust. That was back in a time when compromising someone could result in a payoff worth millions. As you have so aptly noted in our discussions, we don't have money, or much of an economy.

"Now, while Jamila and I may have had different world views, the fact is that she was the most productive piece of this proto-governmental body we seek to create. Whoever did this to her—and frankly, my money, had I any, would be on Nathan Pendergast—he is an idiot who still battles the ghost of his father to prove his worth. That said, he would ape the sort of ham-handed things his father used to do. The Pendergasts are expert at snatching defeat from the jaws of victory, and this trait has bred true in junior."

Anya turned back to the fire, crouched, and put another quarter log atop the pyre. Pendergast *could* have been the one to entrap Simon Shin. Nathan had parental issues, and using her son to discredit Jamila would appeal.

Still, someone else might have influenced Pendergast.

"Was that what you wanted to discuss, Minister Hasterwith? The need to expose Minister Pendergast's activity?"

"No, not at all." The man opened his hands. "He will have to be dealt with in a different way because, were we to do this openly, the whole sordid affair with Simon Shin would come to light, further hurting his mother. I would hate to have that happen."

"Agreed." Anya stood again, but did not return the blackened poker to the rack at the hearth's edge. "Why *did* you come?"

"It is rather simple, actually. You see, in the time since Jamila has pulled back, you have emerged as a central figure in our enterprise. You are Jamila's heir apparent."

"For?"

"Oh, playing so coy, very good." Hasterwith smiled as he shook his head. "First minister, of course—and here is where you deny having any desire for that post."

"I have none. None what so ever."

"I actually believe you. Others, however, think it is a faux denial intended to add a veneer of modesty to your image, of someone who only wishes to serve 'for the betterment of all others.'" Hasterwith clasped his hands together over his heart. "I, for one, believe your protestation. I mean, look at your history. Minor COG functionary, then coordinator for Gear operations and, finally, when there's really nothing left to coordinate, you take up arms and fight to destroy the Locust. A stirring tale, really. In fact, when we reestablish an educational system and approve curriculum, I shall insist that students are made to study your biography to make them understand what true duty and honor looks like. So, I do accept that you have no intention or ambition for high political office."

The man was baiting her, of that Anya was certain, and she might have risen to the challenge. Had Marcus been there, Hasterwith would have been pinned to the wall like a specimen in a bug collection. *But Hasterwith is right. I don't want political power, so getting riled up—when he's stating the truth—would be foolish.*

"Thank you, I guess." Anya frowned. "You still haven't answered my question."

"Yes, well, I do have a purpose. Part of it was to confirm that you have no desire to replace Jamila Shin."

"Because you do."

Hasterwith clasped his hands behind his back. "I would be

honored to accept that position. The committee report on how the office will be structured makes the office one where bold leadership will move us forward. And, truth be told, I feel that with Jamila stepping back, there is need for a strong person to fulfill her role, and to take us to the next stage in the survival of humanity."

"And what exactly do you see that next evolution to be?" Anya turned toward the fire and stabbed the poker into a log. Sparks rose in a fiery display.

"As I mentioned before, my vision and Jamila's view are different. I see the world drawn in very stark contrasts. To wit, people are 'makers' or 'takers.' The vast majority are sheep. They are the takers. They live their lives in fear. They do the minimum they must to achieve enough to keep themselves and their children alive. They have dreams—frivolous dreams—and no drive or ambition. There are times they have desires, which they mistake for ambition. Their lives are brutality punctuated by moments of pleasure, and the height of their contribution to mankind's survival is their ability to donate genetic material, nothing more."

Hasterwith began to pace.

"Makers, on the other hand, are the shepherds. We are those who set goals, who assemble the workforce, who—in the past anyway—used our material capital to create something out of nothing. Without makers mankind would still be living in caves, clad in skins, in deathly fear of their only fire going out. And, before you ask, I do consider myself a maker. I feel the same way about you, Anya, and Marcus, even your Damon Baird. We are all people who see a need and take steps to fulfill it. Many can dream, but *you* can take the practical steps to make your dreams into realities. Just as you have worked to rebuild your family's estate, you will rebuild society and, I dare say, will make it better than it was before."

Anya arched an eyebrow. "You don't see Jamila as a maker?"

"Yes, yes, she is one, but a very special one. She believes that the world should be shaped to maximize the potential of all people. This would lead to a great deal of wasted effort and squandered resources, because while most people have great potential, the vast majority of them haven't the resolve or discipline to realize that potential. Look at Nathan Junior. His father was a maker on a grand scale, and Junior thinks he's one as well because he inherited the business when a Locust bit his father's head off. The truth is, Senior saw him for the taker that he is, and never trusted him with the business. Thus Junior's drive is not to make the business thrive, but to outdo his father—this being an impossibility with the ruined world we have inherited."

Anya replaced the poker in the rack.

"What is your vision for the world?"

"We need order and organization—two things at which, by the way, you are splendid. I would expand upon your ideas, frankly. I see us building viable settlements, each surrounding resources and production facilities, in which we provide schooling, housing, and medical care—in return for labor. We create multiple styles of these settlements. As people excel, they are promoted to a new settlement which is better for them and their children— once, of course, they are licensed to have children. Unregulated reproduction will create a multitude of problems, not only with the food supply, but with everything society will provide."

"You wouldn't allow people to have their own land. Marcus and I would have to move off the estate?"

He turned toward her, his eyes bright. "No, my dear, precisely the opposite. You and Marcus, Jamila and her family, you have all earned preferential treatment. The settlements would be for the takers, and they would be well cared for. And for the makers, great privilege—perhaps a return to the glory of yore, if not something which surpasses it. Makers have to be the example, and through the settlement system, we identify the talented. We cultivate them and give them opportunities their families never could. In doing this we fast-track humanity's recovery. Children of makers can be sent to the settlements to administer them, giving them incalculable experience because, as the population grows, so will the need for more settlements. We will colonize our own world and in a century or two will have gone beyond any point we could imagine at this time."

"I see."

"I trust you see the practicality of it. It is really a military system into which everyone is drafted. The takers will forever be the enlisted people, and the makers become the officer corps. Without that sort of discipline, humanity will fracture and, if we do ever recover, it will be by dint of luck and through centuries of wasted time."

Anya frowned. "People will resist being incorporated into the system. Not everyone wants to be drafted."

"We will convince them it is for the common good, because, in the long run, it is."

"That sounds, Minister Hasterwith, perilously close to suggesting that the ends justify the means."

"Desperate times demand desperate measures." The man brought his hands together at his waist.

The cold tone of his voice sent a shiver down her spine. "I look forward to seeing a formal proposal of your plan."

"I doubt we have time to debate it, quite frankly. We *may* survive this winter, provided it is mild, but we will need to take steps to organize immediately come spring, or we may not survive until next winter."

As much as Hasterwith's plan to save humanity made Anya uneasy, his vision of a famine killing off great swaths of people made her more so. "What is it you want from me? Do you want me to tell the other ministers I have no interest in being first minister? I have told them that."

"No."

"What, then?"

"I had hoped that your refusing the position would be enough, but things are moving too swiftly. They want you, and they believe Jamila saw you as her heir apparent. We have to completely disabuse them of such notions." The man held up an index finger. "What I am going to require from you is an endorsement for my candidacy—and tomorrow won't be too soon to begin letting them know."

"That's fast." She blinked. "We're not voting for another three days."

"The groundwork must be laid, prior to your announcement—which ought to come as a formal endorsement for my candidacy in a Council meeting. Circumstances do not favor wasting time."

"You're afraid someone is going to pressure you to step aside, the way they did Jamila."

"I would be a fool to suggest otherwise."

Anya arched an eyebrow. "How many skeletons are there in your closet?"

"A very few, and the last of them will be buried very soon." Hasterwith laughed. "I am, in reality, quite untouchable. But the important thing for you to consider, Minister, is that I treat my friends and allies *very well*, and my enemies always pay dearly for disappointing me. I don't mean for that to sound like a threat. You already know I am right. The future of our species hangs in the balance."

Anya sighed. "I can't say that you're wrong."

"Very good. Before the Council of Ministers meets again, I will send over a draft of the text of your endorsement. A courtesy, you understand. Mankind has been leaderless for too long. I will guarantee our survival." Hasterwith bowed his head to her. "Thank you for your time."

He turned and departed, leaving Anya alone with the fire's angry crackling. She stared after him and found her hands balled into fists. Forcing them open, she took a deep breath and exhaled slowly. As she replayed the conversation in her mind she found the point where Hasterwith had switched strategies.

If I had been enthusiastic in agreeing with his vision of makers and takers, he would have enlisted me as a co-conspirator. When I balked, he tried to apply pressure, but not wholeheartedly. It struck her that he sounded more confident when he said he'd guarantee mankind's survival. *How does he intend to make it work?*

"Something is wrong, very wrong." Anya went to recover her glass of wine but stopped and, instead, made another decision.

"Please, by all that is just, don't let me be wrong."

10: IRON HILLS RIPARIAN PRESERVE

IRON HILLS, SERA

12 FROST 18 A.E.

"**M**arcus, just listen." Anya's voice poured into his ear with urgency, but he didn't hear fear. "*Hasterwith came to the estate. He wants my endorsement for him to become first minister. He has a crazy plan to gather people into settlements and regulate their lives. He's confident he can do all this.*"

"He can." Marcus' hand stroked his beard. "He's got it all figured out."

"*What?*"

"We know how he can get folks into settlements. People are training grubs, and he has a proof of concept for one of his villages."

"*Can you prove that? In two days?*" The line fell silent for a moment. "*He's angling for the office. He wants me to endorse him. If I do, he'll become first minister. Once he has that power, he'll put his plan into action.*"

"You need proof, we will get you proof." Acid burbled up into his throat. "First, are you okay?"

"*I'm fine, Marcus.*"

"Good. Be careful. Chances are we're going to make Hasterwith really angry." Marcus softened his voice. "We won't let you down."

"*Thank you. I love you.*"

"Me, too." Marcus set the receiver down and looked at his assembled team at the campsite. "Okay, listen up. What we saw down there, that's Hasterwith's plan for humanity—happy little Seradyne villages everywhere. It'll be the Watson farm, killing parents, and harvesting children all over again."

"We can't tip them off." Sam's eyes hardened. "The man who could approve this sort of experimenting is going to cover his tracks. He'll move his assets, and this place will vanish."

"Exactly, so we have to go *now*." Marcus nodded. "Brandon, you're getting Karima out of here."

Karima Razek shook her head. "I can read between the lines, Marcus. Three minutes ago, five Gears weren't enough for you to rescue those people. I won't speak for Brandon, but I'm willing to fight to free them."

"Count me in on that, too."

Marcus' left hand curled into a fist. "I'm not doubting your courage, and I'd welcome the extra guns, but I *need* the two of you to head north. You'll take the sat phone, and when things start blowing up, you're calling Cole's helicopter pilot to fly you to Westbrook. Brandon, you'll get your Raven pilot to get to Westbrook as fast as he can and take the two of you direct to Ephyra. Tell Anya everything you know. On his return trip, Cole's pilot will come south and look for us. He'll grab evidence, and head to Ephyra to back you up with something solid."

Brandon folded his arms over his chest. "What if there's no evidence for him to pick up?"

You mean what if we all die? "Everything we've learned on this journey should convince people that Hasterwith is corrupt. You two will have to make that clear."

Karima's eyes became slits. "If we fail, if you fail, the slaughter of innocents will be frightful."

"That's why we focus this operation." Marcus returned to the stone map. "Sam, you and Carmine are going to set up here, on the near side of the river. Anyone trying to get into the settlement will have to go through you. Any guards walking the perimeter are your responsibility—and the grub they've got with them."

"Close-up work. Got it." Clay nodded. "And we're set up to pour enfilade fire on any soldiers coming out of the barracks."

"Right." Marcus looked up at Cole and Damon. "The three of us head to the lab. We kill anyone or anything we find protecting the grubs, pull computer memory and any other hard evidence, then wire it all to blow. Alarms are going to pull people from the barracks, so we neutralize them. We hold on until morning when Cole's helo comes back for us. Clear?"

Baird grunted. "I guess I'll need to wire up more charges."

Cole laughed. "As many as you can, man. I'll carry all the ones you can't."

As the Gears set to work, Marcus walked over to where Karima and Brandon were gathering up their kit. "You have to get clear. Your testimony is what's going to stop Hasterwith."

"You do know what you're doing here, right?" Brandon tightened a strap down on his rucksack and stood. "Suicide. There's no way you will survive."

Marcus rested both hands on Brandon's shoulders. "When we were at Mercy and I saw Dom's COG tag on the Flores family tomb, I realized then, he knew he wasn't making it out. I also knew he was at peace with that decision, because others lived. I couldn't see it, back when he died, but now I can *feel* it."

Brandon met his stare. "If you give me your COG tag to carry out of here—if you even *try* to do it—I'll deck you."

I bet you would. Marcus gave the man's shoulders a firm squeeze. "Our mission is to kill the grubs, save the people, gather evidence, and eliminate anyone getting in our way. Our dying isn't on the list. We're Delta Squad. All the Locust in the world couldn't kill us; Seradyne rent-a-grunts aren't going to do it either."

Karima shook her head. "If ego was armor…"

"No dying, Marcus." Brandon poked Marcus in the chest with a finger. "You owe Nick his sister."

"Right." Marcus brandished the lucky stone Nick had given him. "I won't disappoint him. See you both on the outside." Tucking the stone back in his pocket, Marcus turned and slung his Lancer over his shoulder.

"Let's move it, Delta. Leave the stuff we won't use and hurry up. Those grubs aren't going to kill themselves."

"When they see us coming, Marcus, they'll wish they had." Cole's laughter filled their temporary home. "We'll just help them do it faster, baby."

Delta Squad moved out quickly, with Sam leading the way and Marcus bringing up the rear. They made good time through the darkness, but as they approached the mine, things weren't right.

It's too bright. Marcus squeezed past his teammates and joined Sam at the overlook.

What in the…?

The guards had cleared out a large area around the mine

entrances, and set flares at the corners of a large square. They'd also set up some spotlights and used them to illuminate the square. *That has to be an LZ for a Raven.* Other guards struggled to open one of the large doors to the third mine, and workers waited patiently, wearing mechanical loader exoskeletons. *Thank God those aren't Silverbacks.*

A skinny, balding, civilian-looking guy barked orders at the guards being pressed into duty opening the mine. Other soldiers ran around laying charges and stringing wire on the barracks and administration buildings. Two of them grabbed a heavy box and two long spools of wire, and started crossing over the river to where they could set charges on the tiny houses.

Not a grub in sight. That's good news, though all those explosives are not.

Not a single resident opened a door or peered out a window in curiosity or to protest.

Sam looked at Marcus. "They're destroying all the evidence."

"That's a plan that won't survive contact with the enemy. As we discussed, but your first shots better drop those guys carrying the explosives."

"Yes, Sergeant."

Marcus hustled six yards back down the trail. "They're sanitizing the place, so we have to move. Carmine, you're with Sam, same as before. Baird, they're setting up an LZ, so shoot out the lights. Cole, you and me, we hit the open mine. Baird, you're with us once you've taken the spotlights out. Comms on Tac-seven."

Cole peeked around him. "We're sprinting across that river in bright light when the shooting starts?"

"Is there a problem?"

"No, brother." Cole pounded a fist on Marcus' shoulder. "Just try to keep up."

"This will be nasty, people." Marcus unslung his Lancer. "We'll be nastier."

Marcus worked his way forward and felt Cole crouched behind him. Marcus keyed the comms earpiece.

"Baird, you're up now. *Hit it.*"

Time dropped to an absolute crawl as Marcus sprinted toward the river. To his left the pair of soldiers hauling explosives to level the tiny houses stopped. They released the chest, but before it could fall to the water, the man on the left jerked and his head snapped back. He got perhaps a half-step further on before his leg went boneless. His body splashed down, and the chest beside him. The second man jackknifed forward, then flew backward a half-dozen feet. As he hit the water, one spotlight went dark amid a shower of sparks.

Cole passed Marcus on the right, firing his Lancer from the hip. He blazed away, and spent, smoking cartridges hissed as they hit the water. Sparks flew from the mechanical loaders. One sagged to the side and the second just froze in place.

A couple of men working to open the mine stopped and unslung their Lancers. A line of bullets traced their way across the shoreline and then through the water in evenly spaced geysers. Then two of the bullets tagged Marcus' left flank, one just below his ribs and the other at his shoulder. He heard them more than he felt them. The armor held but the impact spun him around. His feet got all twisted up. He crashed down as bullets whizzed overhead. The freezing water splashed over his face and arms, so cold it felt like fire.

Gotta move before they track me. Marcus lunged up and dove to the left. The second spotlight exploded in a shower of sparks. Darkness descended and Marcus cut back right, splashing his way in Cole's wake.

Cole's fire swept over the trio of men at the lab door. One clutched at his thigh, bright arterial blood pulsing out between his fingers. Another mercenary tried to dive out of harm's way, but a bullet caught him in the hip. Spinning in directions he never intended, he landed hard and rolled up limp against the downed loader. The third man tried to correct his aim to hit Cole, but one of Cole's bullets hit his Lancer's receiver. The projectile fragmented. Lethal splinters ricocheted, shredding the man's face. He dropped on his back, an oozing eye dangling from the optic nerve.

Time returned to normal as Marcus hit the shore.

Dripping wet, he raced after Cole and caught him beside the mine door. Cole glanced over at Marcus, then peeled around the door and in. Marcus crossed over, advancing to Cole's right through the mine's rough-hewn entrance tunnel.

Ten yards further along the Seradyne researchers had created a lab in a truncated mine gallery. Translucent wall panels let light bleed in from the lab to the tunnel, which is why Marcus caught sight of two soldiers bolting from the lab. He snapped off a shot that blew through one guard's throat, then shattered the panel behind him. Cole's fire stitched the second soldier from navel to sternum and he crashed back through the lab doors.

The two men raced to the lab and yanked the doors open. Three researchers, all in lab coats, stared at them, ashen-faced. One, a tall woman raised her hands. The other two—older men, glanced around as if looking for weapons. Both turned their gazes to the lab's back wall.

Marcus keyed the radio. "Baird, here, now!"

The lab contrasted sharply with the tunnel. They'd built out the walls and added a ceiling, as well as a floor, creating a fairly clean enclosure. The front end of the chamber contained desks and computers, but nothing that personalized the workspace at all. Over on the far side stood a glass-walled operating theatre. In the middle lay benches with beakers, glass tubing, bubbling flasks, and long distillation coils. Marcus wasn't certain exactly what he was looking at, but it reminded him strongly of the lab his father had used to conduct his research into the Imulsion Countermeasure.

Cole shifted around to cover the researchers. "On your knees, or you won't have them for long."

"But we're non-combatants."

Marcus pointed at the rear of the lab. "That suggests otherwise."

The back wall marked a serious departure from any normal lab. Five glass tubes—easily a yard and a half each in diameter—had stainless-steel slabs in them. Grubs—including a Boomer—lay on those slabs, strapped down with IVs running into both arms and into the femoral arteries. The Locust also had control boxes mounted on both sides of their head, starting from their temple and curving back around behind where ears would have been on a human. The Locust appeared healthy to Marcus' eye, and if they weren't quite as large as some of those he'd fought, he had little doubt they'd grow to that size soon enough.

Damon came running into the lab and stopped a yard past the doorway.

"Whoa."

"Yeah, that." Marcus shifted around to cover the scientists and tossed a spare clip to Cole. "Go back to the door, buy us some time."

"You got it, Marcus."

"What is this, Baird?"

Damon approached the tubes. "Well, if I was to guess—"

The female scientist's eyes widened. "Don't touch anything."

"Looks like they are sedating the grubs to move them."
Damon picked up a notebook. "Also looks like they are using a
compound to chelate the toxins the ICM left in the grubs' system.
How many of these things did you go through before you found
the right formula?"

All three looked down and remained silent.

Marcus pressed the muzzle of his Lancer to the neck of the
nearest man. Skin sizzled. "Hasterwith isn't going to be able to
save you. I *might*. Answer the question."

The man shied away from the pressure on his neck. "In the
mine here, we found two dozen. A handful escaped, these five are
all we have left."

"So you went through thirteen, fine-tuning this."

"Chelation and then training. Some had to be destroyed.
Some escaped." The man looked up at Marcus. "That's the truth,
I swear it."

"Baird?"

"That sounds like the truth, but not all of it." Damon crossed to
the computers and began poking around. "Tons of data here, but I
can't find a sat phone or encrypted radio for sending reports out."

The woman looked over at him. "There was an air gap between
the lab and the outside world. The radio is in the office. That's
where they keep the guns and the armor, too."

"Damn it." The soldiers had been expecting physical duty in
getting the cylinders out, so they hadn't pulled on their armor. *But
all of them, coming to the fight now…*

Cole's voice crackled over comms. *"Marcus, you get your furry ass out here now."*

"Baird, any of them move, kill them."

"Got it."

Marcus ran back to the mouth of the mine, hunkering down with Cole as bullets pinged off metal and whined through the air.

"How bad?"

"Worse than bad." Cole pointed north toward the barracks. "They've brought up that truck and have it across the train tracks. It's giving them cover from Sam and Clay. Soldiers are wearing armor now, and there's a lot of them. They had to be hot bunking."

A squad of men poured out of the administration building, spreading out, covering one another. They sent a withering hail of bullets that forced Marcus and Cole to keep their heads down. Marcus keyed his radio.

"Sam, what do you see?"

"Men in black, moving through darkness. Couple dozen minimum. Muzzle flashes only." Her voice hesitated. *"If we move up, we might be able to flank them."*

"Negative. You two get into that village and get people out to the south. We'll hold them for you." Marcus checked his Lancer's load. *For a little while, anyway.*

"How long is Sam going to need?" Cole fed a new clip into his Lancer.

"Too long. Same for Baird to set charges and blow those Locust to hell."

Cole nodded. "So, nothing Delta can't handle, right?"

Sam's voice crackled into their ears. *"They're sending a squad after us, Marcus, and they've got a couple more massing in your direction. If you have a miracle, let it rip now."*

"Hear that, brother?" Marcus' hand found that lucky stone in his pocket. "Time for us to be a miracle."

Cole's reply died unvoiced, his eyes widening. He looked up, past Marcus, as the mercenaries' withering fire gnawed into the mine door. With a metallic shriek, the corrupted metal tore away from its hinges and crashed down in an avalanche of heavy rusted metal.

11: IRON HILLS RIPARIAN PRESERVE

IRON HILLS, SERA

12 FROST 18 A.E.

The corroded metal curtain peeled down from the wall, the upper edge descending like a guillotine blade. Marcus tried to leap clear, but his left foot slipped. His left arm came up in a futile attempt to ward off the mass of metal.

Oh, Anya.

Augustus Cole tackled Marcus, twisting him out of the way. Marcus jackknifed forward, his midsection wrapped around Cole's shoulder. They landed hard and bounced, with Marcus rolling through the dust. Cole skidded to a halt on his knees, then got up, but a bullet caught him square over his heart, dropping him.

Bullets spanged off the mine wall and folded metal door where it sagged at the cave's mouth. Marcus came up on one knee and triggered three short bursts, catching advancing targets as they broke from cover. One man twisted around, his Lancer lipping fire into a spiral in the sky. Another dove back and the third just wilted, straddling some rubble.

"Thanks for the save, Cole, but we ain't out of this yet."

Cole quick-crawled over to his Lancer, then sprinted back under cover. More bullets struck sparks from the mine walls and pinged off the door that was providing him cover. He popped up and sent a stream of bullets into the darkness.

"They're getting a little bold, brother."

Marcus ducked down behind the wilted door's wreckage.

"They're getting a *lot* bold." Half the Seradyne mercs laid down heavy covering fire, while more emerged from behind their cover and advanced in good order. *This is not going to end well.*

"Cole, it's been nice to know ya."

"Same, Marcus." Cole jammed a new clip home. "Might as well burn all we got. We can't take it with us."

To have it end here like this. "Here they come."

Before the mercenaries could cross that last twenty yards, something bizarre happened. A crunching clatter arose to the north. Marcus looked toward the noise and caught movement far in the darkness. Then, roaring forward and picking up speed, a compact yellow engine emerged from the darkness. Racing along on the rails, it accelerated to a solid forty miles per hour, then plowed into the truck Seradyne troops had been using for cover. The engine nailed the vehicle behind the left front wheel, bouncing it up and pushing it further along the rails. Another wheel caught. The truck tipped and rolled.

Mercenaries shifted their fire and opened up on the engine. Bullets pounded the windscreen into an opaque spiderweb of safety glass. They dented the metal and spalled paint off, stippling the machine with leopard-spots. The engine pushed past the mangled truck, but lost speed and slowed to a halt before it came to a curve in the track.

The momentary distraction bought the Gears some valuable time. Marcus darted across the opening, with only a bullet or two chasing him. He threw himself on his belly and brought the Lancer up. He aimed and fired, spinning a soldier into the dust.

The man he'd hit rolled, then got his feet under him. He got back up, his armor dented but unbreached. His rifle came up and he drew a bead on Marcus.

Before he could pull the trigger, the soldier's head exploded. The man next to him flew to the side as a second bullet struck him in the left hip and exited through the right. And then, far to Marcus' left, a merc running to commandeer one of the loaders pitched forward into a somersault. A bullet had entered high on his back, blew straight through his armor, and exited through the chest plate.

That's not Lancer fire.

From over to the right Clay and Sam opened up on the Seradyne formation. With the truck battered out of the way, the two of them had clean lines of fire into the enemy's flank. If mercs moved to use the truck as cover again, they exposed their backs to Cole and Marcus. The snipers busied themselves with dropping all those who decided to do anything but make themselves very tiny behind the least little scrap of cover they could find.

Baird's voice burst through the camp's loudspeakers. *"Now hear this. We have secured the lab. We have your attack dogs. We have their control units. We know how to use them. Are you getting paid enough to want us to run a field test on this equipment?"*

"Baird's enjoying this way too much." Marcus and Cole exchanged grins.

"True, brother, but it's good for a man to have hobbies."

One mercenary stood and pitched his Lancer aside. He raised both hands, then dropped to his knees with his hands over the back of his head. A man groaned, feebly raising one hand, but unable to sit up without help. Another soldier threw his gun down and knelt, and then two more. The sixth took off his helmet, then looked toward the mine.

"Can we get a medic here? I got two guys bleeding."

Marcus stood, his Lancer leveled. "The faster the rest of you see reason, the sooner the dying stops."

Cole emerged, moving right. "Ain't like Seradyne's gonna be paying anybody bonuses for dying here, baby."

"Hell, ain't like Seradyne is going to remember this place, *or* your sacrifice." Marcus pointed his rifle at the chest of explosives. "There's a reason you were ordered to blow it to hell. You *know* you'd have been next."

The mercenaries all knew, deep down inside, he was speaking the truth. Sam and Clay, coming across the river with Lancers at the ready, smothered all remaining resistance. The hired guns threw their weapons down and knelt with their hands behind their heads.

"Cole, get them sorted. I'll get a medic."

"You got it, boss." Cole placed fingers in his mouth and whistled loudly. "Over there, into your LZ, let's just all sit down in a big friendly circle. Shuck your helmets and your armor as you enter."

Marcus returned to the lab. He looked at the three scientists. "One of you has to be a doctor. Grab a first-aid kit, and save some lives. Outside. Move it." The woman got up, pulled a first-aid kit from a wall bracket, and ran out.

"Baird, did you mean what you said about being able to control the grubs?"

"Of course not." Damon shook his head, then indicated the two remaining prisoners. "They said they could show me how, but those things are drugged up good. But I figured the soldiers had seen the grubs in action so, one way or another, they wouldn't want them on their asses."

"It wasn't what you think." The balding scientist shuffled around on his knees.

"Really?" Marcus towered over him. "You tell me what it was, because I saw what one of your grubs did at the Watson farm. I know *exactly* how it is."

"No, listen, you have to understand. When we found them, they were dying. We wanted to know what was killing them, because it was a sure-fire way to defeat them. Once we determined the cause, we figured out how to counteract it. If we're going to create a poison, it might also kill humans, so we had to create the antidote.

"In their weakened state, we noticed a few had significant intelligence. They learned things. We created the control interface to train them and to destroy them if they rebelled—but they didn't. The soldiers referred to them as attack dogs because they were loyal, and responded to verbal commands. They didn't need the pain–pleasure stimulus from the control circuitry."

"So, what, you were going to sell them as pets?"

"No, we… we wanted to learn how they lived, how they thought, how they could be trained to undo the damage, and maybe fight their own kind. We weren't making them for any commercial applications."

The other man nodded in agreement. "When the soldiers took one out for 'training exercise' we didn't know what… we thought it was just another hunting trip. They used to take them out and let them hunt some of the big-horn sheep and antelope. They're quite fast when you…"

"I know how fucking fast they are, asswipe." Marcus grabbed the lapels of the man's lab coat in one hand and hauled him off the ground. "You want to know how many people I've seen hunted down by them? You want to know how many people I've seen your grubs tear apart? In. The. Last. *Week*?"

The researcher grabbed Marcus' wrist. "No, sir, please. We didn't mean any harm."

"He's right. When we figured out what they had done, we were horrified. We were composing a report to alert management to what was going on when the orders came in to shut things down."

Marcus released the smaller man. "A report. Well, then, you should have said that in the first place." He brought his Lancer around and used the muzzle to lever the man's chin up. "What about their wiring up the little village? Why do that except to kill everyone there—the *witnesses* there? You would have been next, or didn't you think that far?"

"No, they would never…" The man's eyes just went dead.

"Understand what was going on here. You gave grubs to people who intended to use them to create a crisis. People would be afraid that there were more out there in the wild, and that no one was safe. And the tiny villages, grouping people 'for protection.'" Marcus shook his head. "They'd be Seradyne settlements, with Seradyne mercs guarding them, while everyone watched Seradyne programming and listened to Seradyne news. You'd buy everything through the Seradyne Market Exchange, and if you got out of line, the grub infestation would claim another victim. So sorry."

"Marcus, come here." Baird hunched over a computer. "I found their report. It looks like they had their suspicions, but there's nothing here about Seradyne's final disposition for the grubs."

"They had to know what they were being used for."

"Feared, maybe, but *know*? Maybe they just didn't allow themselves to know." Baird tapped a finger against the screen. "This is important, though. The chelation process, it doesn't cure the damage the ICM did, just slows it down. If they don't have constant therapy, they'll just get sick again and die."

Marcus' eyes tightened. "Did that part of the research go out to Seradyne yet?"

"Not that I can see." Damon turned around. "How 'bout it, Curly? That info known to anyone outside of this room?"

The balding man shook his head. "We held it back because, you know, of what they did. We didn't want to tell them, so the Locust would just die."

Marcus took a deep breath and exhaled slowly. He tipped the Lancer's muzzle toward the ceiling. "Okay. I need all the data, two copies, ready for transport. Then we wire this place and those grubs with enough explosives to put them into orbit."

"On it."

Marcus looked at the two scientists. "Here's a question. Right answer, you win big. Who was giving the orders here? Did Raul Hasterwith ever visit?"

The scientists looked at each other, then at Marcus, and shook their heads. "We got our orders through the camp commandant, Eric Hernandez. No files, no paper, he'd just tell us what to do."

"You gave him reports?"

"Yes, but we don't know what he did with them."

Damon glanced back over his shoulder. "Not enough radio traffic going in and out of this place to move files this size. Likely sent them out by courier, via supply transport, and they sent them on from another location."

The smaller scientist nodded emphatically. "We got supplies monthly, and we'd be asked to write reports the week before. I never connected the dots."

"There were a lot of dots you didn't connect." Marcus jerked his thumb toward the door. "Move it. You, too. Join the others outside." He let them walk in front of him. They stepped around a pile of body armor and helmets to join the circle of soldiers. Marcus stopped outside the square.

"Hernandez, Eric, make yourself known."

The mercenaries looked around the circle, then one of them pointed toward one of the loaders.

"That's him there."

Marcus jogged over and crouched. The sniper's shot had hit the man center mass, clean entry in the back, a bit bigger and messier coming out. Somewhere in the man's body the bullet had begun to cartwheel. It blew a ragged hole out of the armored breastplate. Everything between entry and exit would have been churned into hamburger, putting the man well beyond ever being able to answer Marcus' questions.

He started toward the administration building and two people came into the light emanating from the railhead. Karima carried a Lancer as if she'd be using one as long as Marcus had. Brandon had Clay's Longshot sniper rifle cradled in his arms.

Marcus pointed. "I'm a little pissed with you."

Karima smiled. "Barracks is clear."

"That's what you were supposed to be. Clear."

"It's your fault, Marcus." Brandon gave him a lopsided grin. "You said if I was of a mind to repay your saving my life, you wouldn't say no."

"Me and my big mouth." Marcus mounted the steps to the

administration building and shrugged. "I guess I'm the last person who should complain about someone disobeying orders. I'm still pissed, though."

"Good to see you, too, Marcus." Karima slung the Lancer over her shoulder and pulled open the door. "What are we looking for?"

"Anything that ties Raul Hasterwith to this place. Orders. A signed photograph. Company directory?"

Brandon entered the main office, sat down at a workstation, and his fingers started dancing over the keyboard. Karima joined Marcus in going through Hernandez's private office, and then personal quarters. The man had been fastidious in life. Marcus couldn't find so much as a speck of dust, much less incriminating evidence linking him to the Seradyne CEO. It even appeared as if Hernandez had folded the shirt he'd removed before he pulled on his armor.

He was the sort of soldier who would have stood out on parade, and been great in meetings.

"Nothing." Karima peeked into the dead man's quarters. "Aside from a stash of pre-war whiskey, I came up empty."

"Likewise. Tell Brandon about the hooch." Marcus headed back to the office. "Brandon, anything?"

"Nothing connecting this with Hasterwith, however..." He spun in his chair and tapped the screen. "This guy kept perfect records of things. Obsessive. That whiskey, he tracked every shot he drank—and back beyond the lab he has a storage facility with tons of supplies, including medical. Best yet, he has a complete census of everyone in Happytown. That's what they called their little village. Watsons are all there, and..."

Marcus traced a finger down the list. A smile lit his face.

"Oh, very good. Maybe we get a win out of this after all."

Karima had been the one who had launched the mining rail engine, driving it into the truck. She'd jammed a length of board down on the throttle-pedal and then leaped clear as the engine smashed its way out of the engine house. The collision that had knocked the truck askew had also dislodged the plank and the engine had slowed down before it could go off the rails at the curve. The bullets hadn't penetrated the engine housing, so while the outside looked the worse for wear, the engine remained serviceable.

They returned the engine to its home and attached as many ore cars as they could find. First trip out included the entire population of Happytown and a bunch of the supplies. The second trip carried out the wounded and the prisoners, along with the liquor, other supplies, and most of the team. Sam and Clay went on back to their original camp, to pack everything up and return the horses to Westbrook.

As the engine made its final trip from Iron Hills, Marcus sat in the last car, glancing back at the mining complex. The dawning sun had finally begun to paint rusty tones into the hills that surrounded the place. He recalled how beautiful it had seemed in Karima's photographs, but what they had found there had soiled the beauty.

Damon tapped him on the shoulder and extended a remote control.

"You want to do the honors?"

He stared at the device. In the past he'd have gladly grabbed it and mashed the button down, rejoicing as red, gold, and white flames shattered the landscape. Seeing the fire shoot up through cracks, knowing that part of what fueled it was the charred remains of Locust, would have filled him with joy.

Five fewer Locust to kill people... Five fewer to haunt their dreams... They would have been added to the mental tally he kept, knowing that each death was one more step toward peace.

But do we have peace now? He frowned. Peace in the fight against the Locust, maybe, but they hadn't come to the mining complex to fight Locust. They were fighting men who sought to control their fellow humans. Some of the prisoners in the cars between him and the engine had ordered Locust to commit murder as part of a calculated scheme. *They weren't even doing it for themselves, but because someone else told them to. How is that defensible?*

Marcus shook his head.

"You do it, Damon. Down there, that was science gone bad."

"Half of it, anyway."

"Yeah, well, you make that half of it go away." Marcus sighed. "Soon enough, we'll make the rest of it go away, too."

12: STROUD ESTATE

NEAR EPHYRA, SERA

13 FROST 18 A.E.

Marcus paused in the shadow of the greenhouse and watched Anya through the window. He had missed her, but until he saw her sitting there, reading through data scrolling up on a computer screen, her face intent on what flashed before her eyes, he hadn't realized how much. He'd grown to depend upon her support and her clear judgment, and to be deprived of it had been a constant irritant.

Had she been with us, it would have all run far more smoothly.

He saw it in an instant, so very clearly. He was a shaped charge, and she was the demolitions expert who knew where to place him, how to fuse him, and when to light him up. *In a world that's just a target-rich environment, I do just fine on my own. But now…*

He walked up to the back door and gently knocked on it. He caught a "Come in," and complied. Anya, intent on her work, didn't even glance in his direction.

"I wanted to make sure I wasn't interrupting."

Anya's chair shot back and she vaulted over the couch. Two steps later she hugged him so tightly he almost wished he still had his armor on. He enfolded her in his arms and buried his face against her neck. He inhaled her scent and reveled in her hair brushing over his face.

"God, I have missed you."

"Not half as much as me." She pulled back a bit, took his face in both hands and kissed him full on the lips. "I feel like I can breathe again."

"I must not be holding you tight enough."

"Well, fix that." Anya kissed him again. "Everyone really is okay, right. I know you had to keep the call short and vague, but tell me everyone is good."

"Bumps and bruises, nothing serious." He nodded. "It was a close thing. We did get something you can use, but it's still a hard sell."

She slipped out of his arms, but took his hand in hers and led him to the couch. "Tell me everything."

"I wish you'd been there." He drew in a deep breath and started from Harkness Glen. He explained about the attack and how Karima Razek had been cool under fire. "She's in Westbrook now, making arrangements for the Watsons and the other folks we recovered. Sam and Carmine will stay there in case someone decides to mount an operation to take out witnesses."

Anya's blue eyes narrowed. "More details."

Marcus dug a memory card from a shirt pocket. "Baird's got all the storage devices, but he copied the relevant files to this for you. What we found was a science experiment that had gone out of control." He described the situation and the firefight, to her growing astonishment and revulsion. "The scientists claim they didn't see how their work could be weaponized. Maybe it's true but…"

"There comes a point where evil is self-evident." Anya took the memory card from him. "They were all Seradyne employees?"

"Yeah, but the thing of it is that there's no trail of evidence to show that Seradyne was financing the operation—we have no economy, so following the money is out. You have the reports they prepared, but no sign of their ever being communicated to someone at Seradyne. Damon thinks they were copied to cards and physically carried out, just like that one, but where they ended up, we don't know." Marcus frowned. "Even if some of the mercs said Seradyne was paying them, there's no way to link things to Hasterwith. And with him controlling the information conduits, even if we were to find evidence, he might be able to bury it."

"I never expected it to be easy, but *easier* would be nice." Anya reached over and tossed the memory card onto the table beside her computer. "I'll look at everything, and we can get Damon to take another pass with the tools he has at his disposal. Maybe there's something there for us to find. Right now, though, I care less about that than finding out how you're doing."

"Better now. Much."

"I like that answer. I also like the beard."

"Good, then it'll stay." He took her hand in his and squeezed. "I've been thinking. Back when we were fighting the Locust, they were this monolithic menace. Relentless. They would never stop coming and they could attack at any second. We had no time to think, no time to rest, and no perspective. It was us or them, and there were a ton of them."

Visions of the various people he'd seen in his travels flashed through his mind. "Now it's a lot more than just Delta Squad—there are a lot more folks we have to consider. Fighting the Locust we saw people on what was probably the worst day of their lives.

Out there now there are some who haven't recovered from that. They live like animals. They take slaves, they do horrible things to each other. I always fought to save lives, but out there I had to fight against other human beings."

"I'm sorry, Marcus."

"Me, too. But, you know, there're always going to be people like that. Always have been. It's a part of life." He exhaled heavily. "But out there I saw a lot more, too. There are people like Brandon's sister, or Karima Razek, or the people of Westbrook. People like them are why the Locust failed to destroy mankind. They kept things together, kept folks focused, and haven't let them forget who they are. When we were fighting to keep people alive, it was these people. We were giving them the room to reignite civilization."

"That's a big task." Anya sighed. "I don't know if we can do it."

"It can be done." Marcus smiled. "Anya, *you* can do it."

"Not when someone like Raul Hasterwith decides to use Locust to terrorize people into entrusting him with power. I'm pretty sure he manipulated Nathan Pendergast into blackmailing Jamila Shin, getting her to withdraw from contention to be first minister. Meanwhile, we literally have *nothing*, Marcus, other than running water in a couple of places. I understand the perception of power, and how much he wants it, but there really is none."

"He's a tick, Anya. He wants to climb to the highest point and suck everything he can out of society. Not because it's going to get him all that much, but because it's all that's there." He exhaled slowly. "There's a way to deal with him. A *terminal* solution."

"No, Marcus. We can't do that, not unless he's coming after us with one of the Lancers he's so happy to have produced." Anya shook her head slowly. "I know you know that. If we are to maintain our humanity, and rebuild a civilization worthy of the name, we have to do things in accordance with law."

"Laws we don't have yet."

"We may not have laws on the books, but we know the difference between right and wrong. We have to put things in place to foster right and civilization. I just don't know yet exactly how we can do that, especially since Hasterwith wants me to nominate him in two days."

Marcus took both of her hands in his and looked her in the eye. "Anya Stroud, I have no doubt you are going to find a way. You always have, and I know you will this time, too."

She glanced at the memory card. "There has to be something there I can use."

"I'm sure there will be." He drew her into his arms. "I'll leave you to it—Cole's helo is coming back for me inside the hour. We have a couple more errands, but we'll be back here in time for your Council session. I mean, non-voters can attend, right?"

"Yes, my love." Anya kissed him. "An informed constituency is vital for good government."

"Then I'm your guy." Marcus kissed her forehead. "I love you, Anya Stroud. Now, figure out how to save the world."

After Marcus' departure, Anya fed the memory card into her computer and began to go over the various reports. She wanted to vomit as she read the matter-of-fact recitation of events in the Watson compound. She didn't bother to open the pictures, but instead studied the hastily drawn images on the attached autopsy forms.

The idea that a group of men could control a Locust and have it murder people stunned her with its sociopathic cruelty. As if that wasn't bad enough, the "rescuers" just left the bodies where they fell, in places like the farmhouse, not even granting the dead the basic courtesy of straightening their limbs and putting them at rest.

It's one thing that they were willing to do this for money, but it wasn't just money that stopped them from seeing their victims as less than human. If those mercenaries had been Gears, they would have been tried for their war crimes. But now? *What kind of justice can we achieve when we don't even have a government? Can we afford to imprison* anyone *when there are so few of us left?* Yet her thoughts kept returning to the cruelty of it all. *They would have killed the women and children to erase all traces of their experimentation.*

The enormity of the issue brought with it other problems. Raul Hasterwith was part of the ministerial group, and might be implicated in the crimes, but Anya could find no direct connection. So how could any of the Stranded trust the ministers, if they thought Hasterwith had somehow gotten away with murder?

Hasterwith might use his communications network to suppress news of the crime, but the people of Westbrook knew what had happened. Soon the people of Harkness Glen would know, as well, and then the refugee camp. Aaron Griffin would know, which meant Char would know, likewise Hanover because of Cole. Nothing traveled faster nor resisted smothering better than good gossip.

All the places they needed to pull together would be divided on the issue of what should be done.

And if we grant the first minister the power to pardon criminals, if Hasterwith takes office, justice never will be done.

Anya rose from her chair and began to pace. Logistics boiled down to inventory and time: what do you have and how fast will it take to get it where it needs to be? Getting the things there might require someone to be clever, or to trade favors, but at the end of the day, it could all be encapsulated on a spreadsheet. Problems could be anticipated and solutions prepared.

Those were things she knew how to do, and to do very well.

But politics, that was a different beast entirely. The nearest thing she could imagine was magic. Good politicians had cards tucked up their sleeves and rabbits in their hats, all ready to be pulled out at the right time. Misdirection functioned to buy time and favors, to hide the truth until it could be revealed to the benefit of all.

Jamila had been an able teacher, fashioning lessons so Anya could understand them, yet Anya had resisted because she resented the basic need for deceit in politics. Taking an extreme position to compromise later seemed like a waste of time. Promising people something to buy the time to deliver something else reeked of dishonesty. Part of the reason she'd moved from logistics to fighting with Delta was cutting away all the layers that insulated her from reality.

And yet... People would react to the Seradyne experiment with hostility, and that would hurt the effort to have humanity recover. *It could doom it.* Without people trusting each other, without having them exchanging ideas, goods, and genes, mankind could do to itself what the Locust had failed to do.

If one home in a settlement caught fire, that wouldn't cause everyone else to move away and die off. But news of the atrocity at Iron Hills could create schisms that might never heal. We can't let that happen, and yet it would be the height of arrogance to hide the truth, just to prevent that outcome. This isn't a problem of logistics.

It's a problem of people. All people.

Anya covered her face with her hands. It had been her duty

to step into the line and destroy Locust. She performed that duty because it insulated people from the horrors of the world, the horrors of which the world was capable. It had been good work, and honest work.

And very, very messy.

She sighed and hugged her arms around her belly. *If I do what must be done, if I choose to play at politics, I'll again be in a position of insulating people from the horrors. It's not honest work, nor clean, but it* is *necessary.*

I really do not want to do this.

She returned to her computer. "But it has to be done." She opened the reports. "Make a copy, a few edits here and there and, abracadabra, we take a titanic step in saving the world."

13: RESIDENT ACCOMMODATION
CAMP #2709

JACINTO PLATEAU, SERA
14 FROST 18 A.E.

The Cougars' helicopter hit all of its lights thirty seconds before touchdown outside the camp.

It set down on the perimeter opposite the medical center, dust curling up and away from the landing zone. Cole leaped free before the aircraft touched the ground, running a few steps then somersaulting forward and rising to one knee just beyond the edge of the rotors' reach. He moved as he had in combat, with power and agility, which looked equally impressive with him wearing his cobalt Cougars' jersey.

Marcus restrained himself from leaping out with him, as he would have done when Locust roared and bullets flew. The few people who'd been awake—early risers plagued with worry about the world and their future—drifted toward the grassy field where the helicopter finally landed. As the rotors slowed he climbed out, then helped Brandon unload a couple of big boxes as the crew shifted cargo and began shutting down the engines.

People stared at Cole because, in comparison to the biggest of the refugees, Cole was a giant. A few of the older folks recognized the uniform and the name, and they just watched him, jaws agape. Little kids, still wiping sleep sand from their eyes, drifted out of tents. Far too young to remember professional Thrashball, they still knew that Cole was someone special.

Adira Turrall, twisting her long, dark hair into a coil that she pinned up at the back of her head, approached from the medical tent. She acknowledged Marcus and her brother with a nod, but made a beeline for Cole.

"I'm Adira Turrall. Welcome to Rack 2709."

"I've heard good things about you, Doctor Turrall." Cole nodded. "I'm Augustus Cole, but you can call me Cole. My friends do. Your brother, he told us that you could use some medical supplies. We liberated a bunch and flew 'em in."

Adira smiled broadly. "That's very kind of you. We're running low on everything."

"Not anymore, sis." Brandon hefted a box and started toward the medical center with it. "I'll start putting this stuff away."

"But that's not all, Doc. We've got meds for the soul." Cole ripped open a box that one of the helo crew had set down beside him, pulling out a Cougars' practice jersey and a well-worn Thrashball. "I heard you had a good field out here, and might have some recruits for the Cougars, so we brought some gear and balls and I thought I might take a look to see what you've got." Cole tossed the ball to a man who caught it awkwardly, then started handing out jerseys to adults and kids alike.

One kid ran over to Marcus.

"Did you find her, Mr. Gear?"

Marcus reached down and pulled Nick up into his arms. "Well, Nick, Brandon and I traveled a very long way. We asked a lot of people if they had seen your sister."

"Did you tell them she was funny?"

"We did. We told everyone."

"And did you tell them she had dark hair?"

"We did that, too." Marcus carried the boy toward the helicopter. "We looked high and low…"

The little boy's hopeful smile slackened. "It's okay, mister. Doctor Adira explained… At least you looked."

"Hey, Nick, I made you a promise, didn't I?"

"Yes, sir."

"I need you to do me a favor, Nick, okay?" Marcus set him on the helicopter's deck. "It will be a *big* help."

The boy nodded. "Okay."

"See that box, back there, the red one? Help that crew member get it out of there."

The boy turned and dejectedly took two steps deeper into the helicopter, and the crew member turned and pulled off her helmet. A cascade of dark hair fell over her shoulders. She went to her knees and spread her arms wide.

"Remember me?"

"*Sierra!*"

The boy shrieked and launched himself into his sister's arms, then clung to her. Tears coursed down her face and Marcus felt one leaking from the corner of his eye. Sierra slackened her grip on Nick then covered his face and head with a flurry of kisses. She pulled the flat stone Marcus had given her out of her pocket and pressed it back into her brother's hands.

Adira slapped Marcus on the back. "That was a homecoming Nick won't ever forget."

Marcus smiled and swallowed hard. "A world like this, it feels great to give someone a good memory. Both of them, really. I hope this erases some of what she endured at Iron Hills."

Sierra had been taken by one of the Locust training groups and ensconced in one of the tiny homes to take care of three children. While she hadn't suffered physical abuse, the emotional trauma of being trapped in a camp that Locust and armed soldiers patrolled still gave her night terrors. In fact, had Marcus not recognized her name on the village roster and told her that Nick had sent him, she'd never have trusted her rescuers enough to open up about what she'd endured.

Sierra slipped out of the helicopter and lifted her little brother down. "Marcus, thank you. Even when you told me he'd asked you to find me, I really didn't think I'd ever seen Dominic again."

A shiver ran through Marcus. "Dominic?"

The boy nodded. "Dominic Martin Thompson. I sometimes forget some of that."

The girl tousled his hair. "My dad vanished after Dominic was born. My mom and I kept moving. She got sick and… Then that night, I told Dominic to hide because I heard something. It was a Locust, and you know the rest. What is it, Marcus?"

Nick looked up at his face. "Did I say something wrong?"

Marcus dropped to a knee and rested his hands on the boy's shoulders. "It's just I had a friend, a good friend, named Dominic, and I miss him very much. He did me a big favor and I never got to pay him back. I'd like to think, maybe, that helping you goes a little way to make my debt right."

Nick reached up and patted Marcus on the shoulder. "It's okay to be sad. My mom said that. She said I had to be strong for Sierra, and Sierra for me, too." He looked up at his sister. "We can be strong for you, too, Marcus."

"Thank you." Marcus enfolded the boy in a hug and felt Sierra join in, taking both Marcus and Nick into her arms. The Gear hung on for a bit, and then a little bit longer. He stood, sniffed, and laughed as Nick wiped his nose on his sleeve.

Marcus patted the boy on his back. "Why don't you go join the others playing. Hey, Cole, I got a top recruit for you right here!"

"That so?" Cole snatched a Thrashball out of the air, then underhanded it to Nick.

The boy caught it and burst out laughing, then squealed as other kids started chasing him.

Adira nodded. "Feels good to hear him laugh like that."

"All of them." Marcus smiled at Adira. "A couple more boxes of supplies in the helo."

"Thanks for those. Barring any game injuries, what you've brought should keep us going for another couple weeks. After that…" She shrugged. "After that, things will get tricky."

Marcus' eyes narrowed. "You're overcrowded. Brandon and I have talked with people heading some other settlements, and they have room."

"We're not splitting families up, Marcus."

"No need. In addition to the settlements we've mentioned, Cole knows people in Hanover, and Ephyra is setting up a new neighborhood. It's not a Rack, but the first step in building a new city."

Adira nodded. "Certainly something to let the folks here consider."

"It's a chance at a new future." Marcus watched Sierra and Nick running with the other kids, trying to catch Cole. "I've spoken with Anya. You know, if Sierra and Nick wanted to come to the estate, we've got more than enough room there…"

Brandon, dodging his way around some kids, barked out a laugh. "Hey, if you're going to be adopting people, I'm in. Sis, you have to see this place."

"You're welcome at the estate, Brandon, just as long as Isadora is okay with it."

"Isadora?" Adira arched an eyebrow. "Is there something I need to know, and why don't I know it already?"

"We were far away."

"You had a sat phone."

"Operational security, right, Marcus?"

The Gear raised both hands. "I'm not getting in the middle of this."

Adira shook her head. "You get a pass this time because you found Sierra, but I'm expecting a full report, or there *will* be trouble."

"Yes, Dr. Turrall." Brandon reached out and gave his sister a quick hug. "You'll definitely want to hear about the rebuilding of Ephyra. Damon Baird has already put together a research facility, and he needs someone with your skills and experience to help recreate a medical system."

"I'm willing to listen."

"Good." Marcus gave her a nod. "We can connect you with Damon, and together you can guide us into the future. Provided, of course, that during the next Council of Ministers meeting, they give us a shot at a future worth living in."

14: HIGHWATER AUDITORIUM, MINISTRY OF SANITATION

EPHYRA, SERA

15 FROST 18 A.E.

Marcus sat in the auditorium's last row, back where the lighting remained dim. Jamila Shin, who had agreed to reduce her role to little more than a functionary, stood behind the podium at the front of the room. Arranged in a circle starting from that cardinal point, the other ministers sat at tables along with one or two staff members. From Marcus' position, Anya sat closest to Jamila, at her left hand, and Raul Hasterwith sat opposite, between Aaron Griffin and Nathan Pendergast Jr. Captain Diana Egami and Cara Lima sat facing the stage directly, with their backs to Marcus.

Cole took a seat beside him, and leaned forward. "Our girl looks sharp in her uniform. She snaps an order and I'm on it, brother."

"Me, too, though I wonder..." Marcus recalled that Anya had been rebuked in an early Council session for wearing her uniform, so it surprised him that she'd made that choice again for today.

She hadn't explained it to him that morning, simply asking him to "Trust me."

I agreed, without hesitation. Hell or high water, Anya, I have your back.

Jamila glanced at her tablet. "On our agenda, the next order of business is to discuss candidates for the position of first minister. I recognize Anya Stroud."

"Thank you, Madame Secretary." Anya stood and looked at the other ministers. "It had been my intention to rise this afternoon to place into nomination the name of Raul Hasterwith, but a very recent and important development leads me to move that we table nominations and deal with this new issue. That being the continued Locust threat."

The other ministers audibly gasped and turned to speak to their aides. There could be no mistaking the shock and surprise on their faces. Aides scrambled to sort through papers and scroll through screens on their computers.

Jamila tapped a gavel on the podium. "This meeting will come to order. Ladies and gentlemen, as your secretary, I've received copies of a confidential report concerning the continuing Locust threat. Thomas, please see that each delegation is provided a copy, but first, will anyone second the motion to table."

Aaron Griffin raised his hand. "Seconded."

The body voted unanimously to set aside choosing a first minister and to address the issue of the Locust. At Thomas' direction, clerks handed out the reports. While the ministers began to leaf through them, Jamila spoke again.

"Please, Anya, share what you've learned."

Anya lifted her chin. "We are all aware of reports that some Locust survived the Imulsion Countermeasure. To investigate such claims, Sergeant Marcus Fenix and Brandon Turrall conducted a months' long investigation, traveling from here to Hanover, Char, and beyond. They encountered a handful of Locust, which they destroyed. They also uncovered evidence that a group of people had found, nursed back to health, and domesticated some of the creatures. In at least one case, they used the Locust to murder a family and abduct the children, taking them from their homes to a compound in Iron Hills for purposes as yet unclear."

Raul Hasterwith rose. "With all due respect, Ms. Stroud, as a deliberative body we cannot accept your recitation of these allegations as *fact*."

Anya canted her head. "I am prepared to offer eyewitness testimony to the veracity of my claims, Mr. Hasterwith."

"Your paramour, Sergeant Fenix, a man once convicted of treason, perhaps? We are to accept his word?"

"No, Mr. Hasterwith." Anya looked toward Jamila. "With your permission, Madame Secretary, I should like to call Karima Razek, CEO of Razek Industrials, to attest to the facts in the report."

Jamila tapped the gavel. "With no objection…"

"Excuse me, Madame Secretary, I must object." Hasterwith shook his head adamantly. "We have no way to validate the identity of someone claiming to be Karima Razek, and even if this witness were to be Karima Razek, we have no clue as to what undue pressure she might be under to verify what could be a tissue of lies."

Nathan Pendergast stood. "While I understand what my colleague is saying, I know Karima Razek. Our families vacationed together, you know, before… I would know her anywhere, and as to her succumbing to pressure? Ha!"

Jamila again employed her gavel. "If Karima Razek is within the sound of my voice, let her come forward."

The doors in the back of the auditorium opened and Karima descended the central aisle to the floor, escorted by Brandon Turrall. Once she reached the chair that Thomas had arranged for her, Brandon peeled off and joined Pendergast at his table.

Anya addressed Karima. "Thank you for joining us and offering your account of what you saw. You witnessed an attack by Locust on Harkness Glen, a community you've been living in since the Locust emerged. Tell us about that, please."

Karima complied, matter-of-factly describing her community and the horrors of the night the Locust attacked. "Had Sergeant Fenix and Mr. Turrall not been with us, I fear the things would have killed many more people, and likely would still be at large."

Hasterwith looked at a note he'd scribbled as she spoke. "Ms. Razek, at any time did you see evidence that these Locust were controlled by anyone? That this attack was motivated by anyone?"

"No, sir." Karima's expression sharpened. "That came later."

Anya nodded. "Perhaps you'd be willing to share what you experienced at Iron Hills."

Karima quickly and succinctly laid out the entire operation, from what they'd discovered and recovered and then destroyed. Other ministers asked questions, especially about the number of people saved and the disposition of the mercenaries who had survived the firefight against Delta Squad.

Cole leaned in toward Marcus. "Isn't she leaving a couple of details out?"

"Yeah. A couple." Marcus frowned. In her testimony, Karima consistently pointed out that the Iron Hills operation had *three* Locust, not the *five* they'd destroyed when they blew the lab. *Granted she never stepped inside the lab, so it could be an honest mistake, but… Anya, what have you done?*

Captain Diana Egami rose at her place. "Thank you for your testimony, Ms. Razek. I listened closely, and have skimmed the report covering the evidence that has been offered. I see no indication of the identity of those who captured and trained the Locust. Do you know who they were?"

Karima shook her head. "I do not, but I was not part of the initial interrogations, and have not been involved in the continuing interrogation of the mercenaries and surviving scientists. I believe, however, that it is only a matter of time before all is revealed and those who put this heinous experiment together are brought to justice."

Anya looked over at Raul Hasterwith. "Do you have more questions, Minister Hasterwith?"

"I am shocked and deeply, *deeply* saddened that anyone could think it proper to employ the enemy of humanity in such a way, for personal profit." The man opened his hands and let them flutter down to his sides. "I find this all profoundly disturbing, and I would recommend that we establish units—military units—which could continue the work that uncovered these Locust, and destroy them. I don't know if such a motion would be in order at this time, Madame Secretary, but..."

"It would, Minister Hasterwith."

"So moved, then."

Pendergast seconded it and the motion passed.

Jamila smiled. "Anya, I believe you would have the expertise to handle that sort of thing, so shall we leave it to you?"

"I would suggest we bring in Colonel Hoffman to organize things." Anya managed to keep her face impassive. "He's had experience dealing with this sort of situation."

"Excellent idea. Thomas, make a note." Jamila employed her

gavel again. "I believe this would bring us back to our previous topic, choosing a first minister... Yes, Minister Hasterwith?"

Hasterwith rose to his feet, his complexion a bit ashen. "My fellow ministers, this matter has left me shaken. I realized, as I sat here, that this is momentous news and has implications which go to the larger issues we face as a body. It seems as if we must share the news of this Iron Hills situation with everyone, for only by being informed can people guard against such things. Then again, when I consider the fact that Locust may still be out there, it seems that the judicious withholding of unverified information to prevent causing a panic might be prudent.

"I am uncomfortable being in a position to pick and choose which issues are shared with people through Seradyne Information Services. While I hope you know I would make the best choices of which I am capable, I am no longer confident that I have the vision—or all of the information I would need—to make the best choices for humanity."

The man took a deep breath, then exhaled, visibly seeming to shrink. "I have decided to go forward with something I have been contemplating for a long while now. I will sever Seradyne Information Services from Seradyne Industries, and turn all of those assets over to this body."

Gasps echoed through the chamber.

Cole elbowed Marcus. "Did I hear that right?"

"I sure as hell hope so."

Hasterwith glanced down at his desk as he continued. "I would furthermore suggest that we create a Ministry of Information Services, and empower it to provide content which will unite people in the struggle we face, if humanity is to survive."

The other ministers stared at him, surprise widening their eyes.

Except for Anya. Marcus slowly smiled. *She was expecting this.*

"Marcus, what did Anya do?"

He shook his head. "I don't know, Cole, but, whatever it was, more please."

Hasterwith tapped a finger on the notepad in front of him. "Lastly, it is incumbent upon me to withdraw my name from consideration as first minister. I believe my good friend, Minister Stroud, was prepared to speak on my behalf in this regard. I have always felt that my role here was to represent the corporations that contributed so much to the world, but my good friends Ministers Pendergast and Griffin have shown me that business is well represented. I'd thought of the Seradyne family as my constituency, but this might force my employees to choose between their locality and loyalty to me. To do so would be highly unfair. Ms. Razek, who has her own community in the western region, is likely a better model for the sort of representation my constituency should have in the future."

Anya stood. "Madame Secretary, I believe this body owes Minister Hasterwith a great debt for his grand gesture. His suggestion concerning Ms. Razek is well taken, but I—for one—hope that Minister Hasterwith will remain engaged in public life. He has proven himself to be a visionary, and his help is still greatly needed in guiding us to the future."

Color rose in Hasterwith's cheeks. "Minister Stroud is too kind. I should be happy to serve humanity in any capacity the ministers see fit. To do less would be to abandon humanity in a time when we are all needed."

"Very well said, Minister Hasterwith." Jamila Shin smiled and looked out at the assembly. "And now I would entertain a motion to adjourn. We have done good work here today."

15: HIGHWATER AUDITORIUM, MINISTRY OF SANITATION

EPHYRA, SERA

15 FROST 18 A.E.

Anya began to pack up her things. Diana Egami and Aaron Griffin both approached Karima Razek to begin politicking her about becoming a minister for a district including Harkness Glen and Westbrook. Raul Hasterwith left his table and stopped by Pendergast. The two men spoke briefly, then Hasterwith departed. His aides cleaned up and chased after him.

Marcus and Cole descended to the floor and, smiling, joined Anya. Marcus hugged her tightly. "You were fantastic."

"Thank you." Anya kissed Marcus quickly but firmly, then slipped from his arms. She turned to Cole, then pulled him into a hug. "You, sir, are a very welcome sight."

"Who you calling 'Sir?' I work for a living, girl." He embraced her warmly. "And what you did there to Hasterwith, that was some of the finest knife work I've ever seen."

Anya kissed him on the cheek, then pulled herself free,

hugging her arms around herself. "It was nine-tenths bluff, but Hasterwith didn't know it."

Marcus frowned. "I noticed everyone kept referring to there being *three* Locust at Iron Hills. What happened?"

Jamila Shin approached, stroking Anya's arm with a hand. "That was the number of Locust mentioned in the report we distributed."

Anya shook her head. "You have to forgive me, Jamila. Marcus gave me the report directly from the Iron Hills computers. I doctored it, so in the copy you saw I reduced the number of Locust from five to three. I was confident that Minister Hasterwith already knew exactly how many Locust there had actually been at Iron Hills."

Jamila's expression slackened for a moment. "This means that Iron Hills was a Seradyne operation. Is that what you found, Sergeant Fenix?"

Marcus' eyes tightened. "We found a lot of things, but no smoking gun. The facility was a Seradyne unit, yes, but Hasterwith could have just declared it a rogue operation. None of the people we extracted and interrogated can tie him to it. The facility commander, who might have been able to do that, didn't make it."

"I see."

"So after I sent the report to you, Jamila, I waited several hours and then visited Hasterwith." Anya smiled slowly. "Just before dawn. I slipped past his security. It felt so good to be back in my armor for at least one final time. I was returning the favor he'd done me a couple of nights earlier, when he showed up at the estate and pressured me to endorse him as first minister. I told him that we had his staff, his mercenaries, and *all* of the Iron Hills records—including his commander's personal journals. I told him they'd stay buried if he turned Seradyne Information Services over to the Ministry. Otherwise we'd reveal everything, and he would be tried for crimes against humanity."

"That." Cole laughed. "*That* right there is my Anya."

"Uh-huh, that it is." Marcus gave her a huge smile. "I'm going to guess he didn't take the news well."

"Shock. Anger. Forced outrage. He told me I was bluffing. He said no one would believe Marcus or any of my friends, and that he'd use SIS to paint us all as a military cabal staging a takeover of the government. He spun out a great anti-Gear conspiracy fantasy that he said would cause the people to turn against us and support him as their defender.

"I told him he could believe that if it let him sleep at night, but I suggested he beef up his security, 'while you wonder where the other two Locust are, and just how well their hunter training worked.' He said, 'You wouldn't.' I told him we'd make it look like he died valiantly. 'You'll be a hero, dead, but a hero.' And then I left."

Anya glanced back over her shoulder toward where Nathan Pendergast and Brandon Turrall were talking. "Pendergast called me—I'm guessing at Brandon's urging—and suggested Karima Razek would be a wonderful witness. He sent a King Raven to collect her from Westbrook. I spoke with her briefly, clued her in on the number of Locust, and that was that. Pendergast confirmed her identity, and Hasterwith found himself trapped."

Marcus frowned. "Why didn't you let us know?"

"Plausible deniability. If Hasterwith had some other play, you had to be clear of it." Anya shrugged. "But he accepted his end of the bargain, and believes he's narrowly escaped with his life. He'll be good."

Jamila shook her head. "He'll be quiet, but not necessarily good. And he *will* make another play for power. Do not doubt that."

"I don't, but with new people such as Karima bringing in new places like Harkness Glen and Westbrook, we expand our base and dilute Hasterwith's influence." Anya sighed. "It's not as strong a position as I'd like, but we're moving in the direction we need to go."

"With you as our pathfinder, Anya, we'll get there." Marcus rested his hands on her shoulders. "Where you lead, I will follow."

Anya started to smile, then caught herself. *I have never wanted to lead, I've just wanted to keep people safe. During the war, that was easier. Keep your enemies down-range, deliver ordnance in bulk, resupply, and go again. But in peacetime there are new issues and strategies. Is this what I want?*

She focused distantly. *Maybe not* want, *but it's a job that needs doing, and I can do it well. That I do* want. *Maybe leadership is my future.*

Anya rested her hand on Marcus' shoulder. "Right now, Marcus Fenix, I want to lead you back to the estate." Anya gave him a big smile. "I understand we have some guests coming to live with us, and I want to make sure they feel they've truly found a home."

ACKNOWLEDGEMENTS

The author would like to thank the following people for their help in putting this book together. Patrick T. Stackpole for walking me through transitioning from war to peace, Chantelle Aimeé Osman and Charles Bowles for introducing me to *Gears of War*, Jerry Chu and Steve Saffel for conspiring to get me to write this novel, my agent Howard Morhaim for getting all the contract details right, Bonnie Jean Mah and Matt Searcy for welcoming me into their universe and explaining how it all works, and Kat Klaybourne for keeping me sane during the writing of this book.

ABOUT THE AUTHOR

Michael A. Stackpole is an award-winning novelist, game designer, graphic novelist, screenwriter, podcaster, computer game designer and editor. He's best known for his *New York Times* bestselling novels *I, Jedi* and *Rogue Squadron*. He's written in many franchise universes, including *Star Wars*, *Gears of War*, *Conan*, *BattleTech*, *World of Warcraft*, *Pathfinder*, and *Dark Conspiracy*. Out beyond the orbit of Mars, he has an asteroid named after him (165612). He resides in Arizona and in his spare time enjoys gaming, cooking, and dancing.

For more fantastic fiction, author events,
exclusive excerpts, competitions, limited editions and more

VISIT OUR WEBSITE
titanbooks.com

LIKE US ON FACEBOOK
facebook.com/titanbooks

FOLLOW US ON TWITTER AND INSTAGRAM
@TitanBooks

EMAIL US
readerfeedback@titanemail.com